The Lamp Post Motel

**A novel by
Joe Gold**

First Printing
October 2006
ISBN # 09773676-8-1
        978-0-9773676-8-9

Published by
Dailey Swan Publishing

Cover by G. Swanson

Dailey Swan Publishing. Inc
2644 Appian Way #101
Pinole Ca 94564

www.daileyswanpublishing.com
www.thelamppostmotel.com

For my father

The Lamp Post Motel
CHAPTER 1

She was a temptress batting her eyes painted in turquoise and coral hues that were decades out of fashion. Her come hither murmured through the palm fronds clattering in the of squat Mexican palm trees. For forty years, she kept her back to the city, her two-story arches facing the Air Force base at the butt end of Tucson, Arizona.

She was the Lamp Post Motel, so proclaimed to South Craycroft Road by a big yellow sign with only slightly less subtlety than a casino. An animated arrow of moving light wrapped around that sign, pointing to the entrance, electrically beckoning one and all for private pleasures. Every night, she offered forty-two chambers of sanctuary, forty-two locked doors, forty-two clog-prone toilets. Every night, the anonymous came to hide out, shoot up and party down.

She wore a reasonably fresh coat of turquoise paint, but on close inspection, the panels below her windows were warped and blistered. Her carpets were stained and cigarette burned, but fairly clean of the beer, booze, semen, urine and blood spilled on them regularly. Most of her easy chairs managed to hold together.

A man from New Jersey named Max Zorn built her in 1970 on a sliver of land on South Craycroft. At ground level was the institutional icon that Zorn picked up in for a few hundred. The object was eight feet tall, painted turquoise and coral to match the architectural motif, mounted on a three-foot high pedestal at the edge of the driveway. It was almost elegant, with Victorian swashes in an aluminum candelabra topped by five plastic balls filled with light: a true lamppost.

The property was surrounded by bars, pizza shops, an Italian restaurant, a convenience store, a few vacant storefronts and Phil Stein's pornographic equipment shop. Across the street, what had been built as a bowling alley was the new home of a fringe religious group. On the next block, the topless bar was conveniently located next to the pawnshop and the used car lot, with plenty of dusty parking to serve those pillars of commerce.

The neighborhood wasn't all that bad for the fringes of a military base. Kids had smashed only one window and shot b-b holes in but a few more. Mostly they tried to hustle quarters they swore they lost in the Coke machine. The customers were more of a problem, stealing anything from a one-dollar smoke alarm battery to the battered furniture, and clogging the toilets with all manner of debris.

* * * * *

Elmo Skinner started his day alone with his equipment. Video screens were his eyes around the property. His computers told him how many rooms were filled last night, counted the dollars received and spent, and how the day's business compared to last week, last month and last year. Elmo built state-of-the-art soundproofing into his underground electronic sanctuary. At the moment, the sound was blessed silence.

He sipped at a mug of half-caf coffee, and then placed it gently in its cup warmer. Twenty-eight rooms

6

rented last night. Not bad for August in Tucson, up twenty-three per cent from last year.

Gray streaks slipped into the hair framing Elmo's face, weathered well beyond its forty-three years. Today he wore the same pale blue button-down shirt he had worn years before through endless legal sessions. The shirt had grown little cloth balls around the collar and maintained a minor disagreement with equally worn tan slacks. That was how the lord of the Lamp Post emerged from the office precisely at eight to survey his empire of forty-two rooms, a dozen employees, and a perpetual stream of strangers.

The maids were pushing the cleaning cart along the concrete balcony. Armed with room deodorizer and toilet brushes, they assaulted another room. Just a few steps past the candy machine, Elmo stepped in a wad of gum, sticky now in ninety-two degrees, and bound to get worse with the heat. He might have to send the robot on these morning rounds.

Betsy was making a bed in 135 when Elmo poked his head in the door. "They had theirselves a hell of a party in 143 last night, boss."

"We lose anything?"

"Yeh, a pillow and a busted lamp, but I think I can save the bedspread. The toilet's plugged up, prob'ly needs a plumber. Must of been one rocking party." She tucked the sheets under the mattress and picked up a dust cloth. "Loretta's room ain't been touched in a couple days."

Elmo smiled only a little, but it was real. "Maybe she's up in Vegas with a client or out on a ranch for the weekend. Her Cadillac's in the back lot."

"I seen Doc Perkins' fancy Jag-u-war out there in the back."

Elmo's face narrowed to a stern point. "The doctor pays her bill and she's never any trouble. What she does in her room is her own business."

"Yeh, okay, I know." Betsy was finished with the room and headed down the balcony to 136. She pounded on the door and emitted an authoritative roar, "Housekeeping!"

Last night's thunderstorm had dumped half the neighborhood debris into the pool. Elmo fished out a palm frond, a crumpled pack of Marlboros, two Bud bottles, and a Big Gulp cup.

It was getting up into the mid-nineties. Elmo retreated to his office, but not before treading in another wad of gum. By eleven o'clock the heat would crack a hundred and "air conditioned" would start flashing on the big yellow sign out front. Somewhere around four, Tucson's vaunted dry heat would hit 105 degrees and turn brains to casserole. About 4:30, the clouds would come rolling in from the southeast, whip up some nasty gusts of wind, roll thunder through the valley and indiscriminately toss around lightning like nowhere else on Earth. By 5 p.m., half-pint raindrops lashed at the city, and for half an hour, Tucson's streets would become rivers. Homebound traffic became a snarling, confused beast. Then it would clear. The streets would drain, the arroyos would carry water off to the Pantano Wash and the Rillito River. By eight, the soaked city was mostly dry. Once the storms passed, the Lamp Post would start filling up again, and Elmo would assign rooms based on how the occupants might entertain him.

Elmo took his leave in magazines and manuals. This afternoon he was buried in the schematics for converting conventional television signals to hi-def. He loved the elegant clarity in a diagram that laid bare the strategy of the machine. Down in the circuits, the world was clean and logical and consistent. He would have worked in electronics, but these days they all wanted college degrees, and college means classrooms and crowds. Elmo couldn't stand for that. He had managed a few small night classes at Pima College. Usually he found the teachers always talking about the wrong thing. Even in Pima's smaller classes, Elmo didn't like all those people in a room.

Elmo's face was small, with little brown eyes magnified behind wire-rim glasses perched on a short nose. Traces of gray were starting to show in his brush of a mustache.

Elmo had been an odd bird through high school, keeping mostly to himself. He made little time or opportunity for romance. That carried through for the dozen years he had knocked around engineering at radio stations, repairing computers. When that ran dry, he picked up a few odd hours as a desk clerk, his first connection to the Lamp Post Motel.

* * * * *

On his front monitor, he watched the truck lumber into the parking lot, and saw the young gray-uniformed driver hop out with a clipboard and an eager-to-please earnestness in his step. Elmo opened the steel door out of his private space and was standing at the front desk by the time the scrubbed young driver's hand touched the door.

"From Tektronix?"

"I don't know, Mac. I just got two big boxes here and half a dozen little ones." His jaw pummeled a small wad of Doublemint X, the chemical-enhanced gum that got you through the day feeling keen, as the radio said so often. "Where you want it?"

"Bring it under the stairway to the next room over, room 102. I'll unlock the door."

Elmo came through the rear office to the storage room. He moved a few cartons of abandoned and confiscated belongings aside to make room for the delivery.

The delivery man bumped the first box against the door jamb before he squeezed it through. Elmo saw a new scratch appear in the paint. He also saw Tektronix emblazoned on the side.

"Sure is heavy," the boy said. "Electronics stuff?"

Elmo nodded. "Two full-sized robots and auxiliary equipment."

"Damn. What you gonna do with them?"

"There's plenty of work for a smart machine around here."

The gum-charged delivery man brought in the boxes, eight in all, got Elmo's signature, wished him a nice day, and was finally gone.

A natural smile settled on Elmo's face. He tore into the boxes like a kid at Christmas, ripping the cardboard away to expose a pair of five-foot aluminum sisters who would lead the assault on dust, dirt, and disorder. He'd spent months reviewing specifications, comparing product reviews and evaluating the performance of forty-six different models before settling on the Tektronix Homebody 781. Once he placed the order last week, he had been preparing programming to operate them. He spent a minute just admiring the brushed aluminum bodies before he stuck his head into cabinet B5 for the connecting cable that would link his Homebody 781s to download instructions from his central computer.

He heard Betsy chattering to herself as she turned the lock to 102. He glanced at his watch. She was starting her break seven minutes early. Betsy pushed the door open, looked up, and halted in mid-chortle. She stared at the two machines.

"What the hell is them?" Betsy said.

Elmo leaned on one of the brushed aluminum heads.

Betsy looked with hooded eyes at the single-lens eye on each machine.

"These are your new assistants," Elmo said with as much pride as a new car salesman. "They'll make a bed, vacuum a floor, remove garbage, clean the drapes and scour the tubs. They'll check every light bulb, snake the junkies' needles out of the toilets and eventually, they'll even be able to repair the TVs. You tell them what to do. You may have to show them how it's done the first time. You might have to explain how something needs to be done, but never why. Consider them new trainees that will do exactly what you say."

Betsy half-closed her right eye. "You said 'assistants' not 'replacements,' ain't that right boss?"

"That's what I said. This one's named Nancy. She's yours to command."

Betsy wrinkled her brow. "Sheeit, what am I gonna command?"

"Tell it to do your job, as much of it as you want. You can just stand there and supervise."

"You sure I ain't gonna teach them my job so's you can fire me? You want machines working for you instead of people? Is that what you want, Mr. Skinner?"

Elmo expected the question. "No, Betsy. You've strained your back for me for years. I thought it was time you had help. Tomorrow Nancy rolls in front of you, waiting for your orders. If I put you in charge of important equipment, you get a raise."

Betsy pondered. A noncommittal "Uh-huh," was all she said. She suspiciously inspected the machine. It was bullet shaped, more trash can than android, with four tubular stalks for arms and a rolling tripod mount. It bore a passing resemblance a famous robot in the movies, which she knew was probably what had caught Elmo's eye.

"Each of the three arms can open to three meters—about ten feet long, with two elbows. It has seven interchangeable hands for scrubbing, lifting, carrying, and snaking the toilets. I'll have to buy her another hand before she can start working on circuits."

"Can't see calling it Nancy," Betsy decided. "Sounds like something white in a titty book."

Elmo smiled a real smile this time. "She's your partner. Call her anything you like."

Betsy scratched her cheek and looked up at the ceiling. "I want to call her Tyrone, like my first husband. Always did want to tell that sombitch, 'Tyrone, scrub the floor. Tyrone, cook us up some chicken. Tyrone, clean the fuckin' toilet.'"

Elmo found a button to push somewhere on the machine's backside. A blue light came on in its head. "You are Tyrone. Say hello to your new boss, Betsy."

Metallic though it was, Tyrone's voice had the squeaky, buoyant tone of a classic blonde cheerleader. "Pleased to meet you boss Betsy." There was a hint of a squeal for punctuation.

Betsy's shoulders and breasts shook. She threw her head back and her laugh became audible, and grew to a bellow. It took her a full minute to recover enough to say, "Jesus, boss, she sounds like something white from a titty book."

"What's so damned funny?" Irene appeared in

the doorway, thin, almost gaunt, with strings of salt and pepper hair tied with a scarf at the back of her head and a cleaning rag tucked into her belt. Her voice had a singsong cadence with a natural 'who cares?' undertone.

Betsy did her best to explain their new electronic assistants.

"Well I'll . . . be damned," Irene singsonged with a faint drawl.

"I suppose you've got a name for your new partner?" Elmo said.

"Yeh," Irene said chawing on a serious wad of gum. "I got me a name. Conrad. Fucking Conrad."

CHAPTER 2

Elmo stepped around a corner to the front office. He faced his customer from behind the fortification of a rounded reception desk. He had a smile in his back pocket for just such occasions. A hospitality management magazine suggested use of such conversation-opening lines as "Good morning, I trust you're enjoying your stay."

"Good morning," Elmo said. "I hope you've been enjoying your stay."

The customer was a scrambled young man, twenty at best, who wore torn and faded jeans, sneakers, and no shirt at all, probably until well after Labor Day. "Hey, man, the air conditioning ain't working in this here Rump Roast Motel. We got pretty sweaty in there." He laughed.

"Have you turned down the thermostat?"

"Yeah, all the way down to sixty."

"And turned on the fan switch below it?"

"Is that what that thing's for?"

"You could have asked the clerk last night."

"Oh, I didn't think . . ."

"Yes," Elmo said, "I can see that." He fished around in his back pocket for that smile. It didn't fit well this morning, but he wore it anyway. "Will you be staying tonight Mr. . . .." He scanned the check-in monitor. "Mr. Stone?"

"Yeh, but I gotta get the money together, down to the Western Union, you know?"

The plastic smile melted. He knew indeed.

14

Western Union was common code for I have no money, and no way to get any. Elmo scanned the bedraggled young man, probably exhausted from a night of crack, PCP, and whatever else he might have enlisted to massacre legions of brain cells.

"Check out time is eleven a.m. If Western Union hasn't come through by then, we'll gather your belongings, and you can pick them up here at the desk."

The customer was having difficulty forming words. "Hey man, some of that's my buddy's shit. You can't take that."

"You rented a room for one person."

"He's just visiting, man. Don't you like a friend once in a while?"

Elmo cleared his throat. "You have four dollars and twenty cents in phone calls."

"Friends ain't easy to come by."

"Apparently not. It took you fourteen calls. Four-twenty, please."

"I told you man, I gotta go to the Western Union, y'know?"

"I know." Elmo tapped a few strokes on the reception terminal keyboard. In seconds, a robot was tooling down the upstairs walkway toward 126. "You can check back in when you are able to pay for rent and telephone calls. My housekeepers will make up the room immediately."

The telephone rang. The call came in on the operator line, from within the building. From 126. Before Elmo could say "front desk," he heard a man shouting into the phone.

"Hey, man, this motherfucking thing of yours just come through the door and it's taking my clothes!"

"It won't hurt you. But you must be mistaken about your room. That room is rented to Mr. Stone.

15

He's here in the office with me."

The voice trailed off, but Elmo heard, "Get your ugly goddamn claws off my stash, mother . . ." Then the line went dead.

Stone was shifting his weight from one foot to the other. "Look, man, I'll have the bread."

"Of course you will," Elmo said mildly.

The robot rolled into the office carrying a small bundle around the big curved desk and into the back office.

"Hey, that's my stuff!"

"We'll consider it . . . security," Elmo said. He found that the smile fit again. "You know?"

"Yeh, man," he grumbled, walking out the door. "I know."

* * * * *

Not until evening could Elmo again be alone with his machines. Before he reached for the keyboard, he eased himself into the chair balanced to his weight, closed his eyes and took a few deep breaths. His music was the hum of computer fans, the whir of hard drives and discrete tones through the speakers. His drug of choice was the cool logic of an elegant circuit. His sanctuary was a soundproof control room, his room-within-a-room, the electronic command center where none but he dared enter.

A small city of circuitry pulsed behind a video facade of eleven monochrome monitors, a forty-eight inch color screen, three quintessential graphics adapter computer monitors, half a dozen DVD recorders, a graphic equalizer and audio mixer, three pairs of compact high-power speakers, a bank of digital audio recorders and a superconducting computer touted to digest data faster than the speed of light.

Here Elmo commanded his empire. He put in a few hundred hours modifying a programming language, SMARTS. Everything he knew from ten years in the motel business went into his program. He backtracked from a thousand dead ends. But when he had finished, Elmo Skinner had taught his Lamp Post Motel to sit up and do tricks. He had endowed her with some degree of artificial intelligence.

The computer could dispatch a robot with a rollaway bed and extra towels for a large party. It could call a noisy room with a tape of Elmo's voice on the edge of impatience. It maintained the exact status of every room, along with its theft and repair record and a history of memorable sexual encounters cross-referenced by dates, participants, and category of the act.

The video project was two years old. Elmo started it when a customer who had run out of cash left a black-and-white industrial video camera as collateral—and of course never returned. On a lark, Elmo installed it safely out of sight in 103 and wired a monitor to the storeroom next door in 102. He polished off the better part of a quart of bourbon the first night he watched his customers perform in silent, grainy black and white. At the high point of the winter busy season, he outfitted four more rooms with color video cameras and sound pickups.

A year ago, he started his plans for 122, the Lamp Post's love nest. Elmo installed a vibrating king-sized waterbed, a big mirror on the wall over the bed, and a bigger one on the ceiling. The bathroom got golden designer faucets, a shower with two heads (high and low) on a flexible arm and a quiet-flush toilet—everything to make the customer happy. On a good night he might get double the rent. On other nights, he could be a sport and throw in the Love Room at no extra charge.

Then there was the equipment Elmo installed for his own benefit. The corners concealed two high-resolution, low-light color cameras with infrared detectors. Four high-fidelity microphones went in and over the bed. The shower was monitored too, although not with infrared, since few people showered in the dark.

Elmo watched. His computers counted the strokes, counted the lies, and counted down the minutes and seconds to orgasm.

Here was intimacy without having to participate, commit, or perform. He sampled passion in a hundred flavors. He could have several lovers a day. He was invisible and invincible. No one saw him. No one touched him. None could spurn him.

Elmo had struggled with this small obsession for a time. He knew there was something dirty about this business, so he avoided "looking in" on his customers for days at a time. But he invariably returned to his monitors when he faced the unanswerable question: Where's the harm?

Elmo blinked, realizing he had been staring at his Love Room in Room 122. It was empty. Around him other monitors kept his eye on his chosen rooms, the front desk, the rear parking lot, the driveway and pool.

Everything seemed fine. That would change when the UFO arrived a few days later.

CHAPTER 3

Elmo was too timid a man to start a business. He had been but a lonely clerk at the motel working for Max Zorn. He had come into possession of the Lamp Post Motel entirely by accident: an opportunity fell from the sky.

Just ten years before, Elmo got by working part time behind the Lamp Post desk. His technical curiosity overcame his fear of people enough that he took a few advanced electronics courses in Pima College's blessedly small classes. On an uncommon whim, for no apparent reason, Elmo took a marketing course. There he found an angel.

His eyes went straight to her on the first night of class. He was so attracted that it frightened him, but then so many things frightened Elmo. The girl wore a soft, oversized sweater that looked like a light blue blanket, as if she was ready to roll over and nod off as soon as class was over. He studied the way she pulled her hair back to a pair of clips that held the darkish blonde cascade until just before it tumbled to her shoulders. He marveled at her sweet eyes and mouth. He barely noticed his own name had been called, but Elmo absently managed to respond, "Here."

Then she spoke.

The instructor had called her name: Molly Sloan. "Here," she said. Elmo kept looking at her. There was nothing strikingly beautiful about her. That would only have frightened Elmo away. Molly was pretty in a simple sort of way. Elmo liked the upswing of her nose and the shy smile she released after responding to her name. He liked the precise straight line her hair formed where it stopped three inches above her shoulder. No one else in the class seemed to pay her any mind.

Elmo managed to look up at the instructor once in a while, but for most of the evening he kept an eye on Molly Sloan. He wondered what he would say—and whether she would answer or turn and run if he spoke to her. Molly seemed to laugh at the teacher shouting about the marketing concept. When they were dismissed, she had gathered her purse and books and was out the door. Elmo stared after her, apparently glued to the floor and shaking as he put a pen back in his pocket. He gathered his books to go, cursing himself for being too frightened, too impressed, too confused to make a move.

For most of the next week, he saw her face every time he closed his eyes. He let the name roll off his tongue, "Molly Sloan, Molly Sloan, Molly Sloan." He contemplated the amber tone of her eyes, the mild mockery on her lips, and long, pale fingers that wore no rings at all. He practiced all week.

Elmo arrived early for the next class. He chose a seat at the end of the row near the door, sat one seat in from the aisle and placed a book on the desk at the end of the row as people filed in to the classroom. Two minutes before the bell, she strolled in, arms folded in front of her holding books, wearing a creamy white turtleneck sweater that cuddled up to her neck. Elmo cleared the desk next to him and motioned for Molly Sloan to sit down. It wasn't until she did that he realized he was holding his breath.

Before the hesitation could grab him, Elmo blurted, "Your hair is pretty. I like you. Could we have coffee after class?"

She blushed, fumbling for conversation, trying not to look at him. But that gentle smile, a little shy, a little bold, jumped to her lips. "Okay." She paused. The universe held its breath. "If you make it a glass of chardonay, I'll buy."

"Yah, sure," he managed to say, and floated through the rest of the class.

In an intimidating world, Elmo and Molly found refuge in each other. She was in line for assistant manager in the beauty shop. Zorn had been talking about giving Elmo a promotion. It was just months later that Elmo felt lucky enough to marry Molly Sloan in front of a little Justice of the Peace who had set a state record marrying 15,247 couples. Now, three years later, they had Nathaniel, a fair-haired little dynamo with a ten thousand watt smile.

* * * * *

When Elmo worked the Lamp Post reception desk, he waited for the phone to ring. He waited for a customer to pull up. He waited. And he sat. He sorted paper clips into precise stacks and piled, by date, the past week's issues of the Arizona Daily Star, more useless now than the day they arrived.

Most desk clerks killed time in the thrall of TV screen. Elmo took no pleasure in funnymen who harvested laughter from a sound track. He had no fondness for forty-eight-minute detectives. Television had too many too-good-looking people, too many egos demanding too much satisfaction via crook catching, vanquishing the objections of the opposite sex, or both. Television fantasies appealed to him not at all.

A buzz rattled from the switchboard. Elmo laid

Pop Electronics on his desk and walked the four steps to ancient black switchboard where he manually plugged thick cables to answer each line. The light under room 130 lit with the repeating buzz. He pushed a cable into the line.

"Front desk," he said. He spoke in a monotone, sounding not particularly interested in what he had to say. "Can I help you?" he droned, adding silently: I doubt it.

The telephone voice sounded young and out of focus. "We're leaving today, really man."

"Um-hum," Elmo said. A glance at his monitor had 130 as empty. Elmo scanned through last night's registration. Daniel Davis had checked in last night for one night. "Are you Mr. Davis?"

"Who, man?"

"I have the room registered to a Mr. Daniel P. Davis. Is that you?"

The unfocused voice at the other end snapped to attention for a moment. Elmo heard him catching on. "Oh, yeah, that's my buddy. Like he's the reason we're still here, you know?"

"You realize that after noon you have to pay for another night, sir."

"Oh no, man we was just leaving."

"And here it is just past four o'clock." Elmo clicked through the litany. "If you stay beyond noon, it's too late for us to prepare the room for the next guest. So right now, you are entitled to spend this evening with us. We do require you pay exactly fifty-one dollars and fifty six cents with tax for the privilege."

"No man, we was leaving." The words tumbled out of his mouth, then the voice hesitated, and returned on a soft, earnest note. "My buddy's dead, man."

"Excuse me?"

"Dead, man, fucking D-E-A-D dead, can you dig it?"

Elmo took a quick breath. He hated emergencies. "Are you certain? Dead? No breathing, no pulse, checked out. Truly, literally dead?"

The blurred voice wavered. "Well no, man. Not like that dead. He like didn't get a lot of sleep, and he's like dead just for right now. Like really sleeping, dude, like he can't get up yet, y'know? But don't worry, man. We was just leaving, honest."

Elmo knew that when a customer of this ilk said "honest," it was anything but. "You are welcome to spend tonight," Elmo said through his nose, "because you will pay for tonight."

"We don't have no fucking money, man. We'll be gone in ten minutes, really man."

"Of course." Elmo called the police and asked them to look into a possible overdose as they escort the Davis party from room 130. He was having another lousy day, which was about to get worse.

* * * * *

The F-22 scratched the sky like a Mach 1.3 fingernail across a hundred mile chalkboard. Sealed away from the trembling desert below, cracking sonic booms as he went, Captain Melvin Putnam wore a big, goofy grin. The fighter jet crossed a twenty-mile mountain range in a minute. His heart hammered to match his glee. Penetrating the sky gave him the same supreme satisfaction as penetrating a woman, and he had a hell of an erection to prove it. Who wouldn't, flying $190 million dollars of the most powerful machine a man could handle, and doing it for God and country?

Putnam's career was approaching Mach 2. He was at the top of his class, a sure bet to wrangle an invitation to the Astronaut Corps next month. He was doing well with the ladies, too, often at the Lamp Post Motel.

He headed for home, a strip of concrete at Davis-Monthan Air Force Base, just settling back with the machine when he glanced at the fuel gauge. His smile crumpled. So did his erection. Too much full-throttle hot dogging out over the gunnery range had ravaged his fuel supply. But the challenge was there: he led his class in lightly touching down with next to nothing in the fuel tank. He stuck out his jaw and guessed he would taxi to the hangar and sputter out the moment he was ready to power down.

Captain Putnam guessed wrong. In ten minutes, his supersonic career crashed and burned two miles short of the runway.

* * * * *

Molly bounded around the kitchen, attacking vegetables with formidable knives, washing down the pot roast for its date with the waiting onions, carrots and potatoes. She peeked around the corner at Nat jumping up and down with Bert and Ernie on Sesame Street on one TV, while on the kitchen TV, caught Katie Couric's report on the questionable personal habits of some high government official. She sneaked a look out the window at a clear Tucson sky, untroubled tonight by the usual summer thunderstorms. She sprinkled parsley flakes on the roast and shook in a healthy dose of garlic salt, and heard about political unrest somewhere in South America. She set the microwave for thirty-two minutes on high, thirty-eight more on low, hustled the utensils and bowls to the sink, washed her hands, hung up her denim apron and dashed into the living room to plop down on the floor and smother little Nat with kisses.

Nat giggled and rolled across the carpet. His little sneakered feet flailed. In a moment, he found his ground and stood ready to attack, a big open-mouthed smile on his round little face framed with loose blond curls. He howled with glee as he attacked, squeezing out his best baby bear hug, hugging and cuddling and snuggling until a sleepy little voice smiled in satisfied conviction, "Mommy."

She hugged him, reciting the poem she used to rock him to sleep:

> *Nat, Nat will you be fat*
> *Or will you grow up thin?*
> *I don't know what you will be,*
> *Only what you've been.*

> *Nat, Nat, nothing's better than that,*
> *The ultra-super-boy.*
> *Some say you're just to good to be true,*
> *I'm just glad you're mine.*

She knew it didn't rhyme all that well, and decided she'd have to make time to work on it. She caught her watch creeping toward six.

"Nat thirsty, mommy." He wore an expectant pout.

Molly opened her eyes wide. "Big Gulp!" she said. "And then we'll go pick up daddy."

"Pick up daddy!" Nat squealed as she dashed off to the kitchen for the sixty-four ounce waxed cardboard cup filled with watered-down Coca-Cola.

Nat was bouncing and singing "Big Gulp, mommy, Big Gulp," when he heard a faraway roar. "Airplane, mommy." The sound grew, and he put on the stern face his mother had worn that morning when the jets overhead were especially loud: "Too low, mommy," he scolded. It got still louder. Molly rushed to the boy, spilling the Big Gulp on the carpet. He saw the confusion in her eyes and leaped at her again, screaming this time.

"Mom-m . . ."

In half a second, one hundred ninety million dollars of the hot F-22 reduced itself, the modest little ranch house near the park, a mother and son to flames.

Captain Melvin Putnam ejected. He landed in the Reid Park Zoo, altogether too close to the near-sighted rhinoceros, which looked confused as Putnam vaulted the fence and escaped unharmed.

CHAPTER 4

Three-and-a-half miles away, Elmo was counting the cash drawer before turning the motel over to the night clerk. He counted everything twice, totaled his take on the adding machine, confirmed, as always, that his drawer was exactly equal to the money he had taken in that day, removed any large bills in excess of a hundred and dropped it in the safe.

It was about that time that he heard that distant thud. He thought little of it. With all sorts of engines roaring and occasional sonic booms, muffled explosions were standard noises from Davis-Monthan Air Force Base. Nor did he think about the faint wail of fire trucks half a mile away on 22nd Street. There was nothing out of the ordinary in Molly being late to pick him up. He had little to say to the clerk coming on for the evening shift. He just sat there and waited. Elmo bounced up looking for Molly when a car pulled in, but it was a customer. A few minutes later, another customer rolled in, this one wanting a room with two beds for one person. The clerk handled them. Then a police car rolled under the canopy. Two cops stepped out, not the same two that had been here a few hours ago to remove the human debris from room 130. The officers looked like they had each drunk a pint of vinegar. The older one asked if Elmo was there.

The clerk's eyebrows shot together and his mouth dropped open. Elmo? The police? No way. By that time Elmo was coming out of the back office.

"Are you Elmo Skinner?"

27

He nodded.

The second officer's voice was soft. "May we speak to you . . . outside?"

Puzzled eyebrows met on Elmo's face as well. He shrugged. "Sure." Elmo shuffled a little. As he went through the glass door, 109 degrees of June in Tucson stepped up to meet him. Both the engine and the air conditioner were running. "It might be cooler in the car," the younger officer said. That may have contributed to Elmo's sense that the policeman's voice track wasn't synched with his video. Besides, the cop sounded like some TV melodrama.

"There's been an accident."

The puzzled look on Elmo's face tightened. "What accident? Why are you telling me..."

The older officer flattened his jaw. "Mr. Skinner, an Air Force jet has crashed. Your wife and son..." He finished the sentence, but Elmo never heard it. What Elmo did hear was a strange, low moan. He wondered about it briefly before he realized it was coming from himself. Elmo swayed in the back seat of the patrol car. "We'll need you to identify them," the blond young cop said.

They drove him away across the sun-softened asphalt. Elmo counted the white lines along 22nd Street, but the thought crept back to him nonetheless: what do I have without them?

Chartreuse fire trucks, blue and white police cars and black and yellow barricades surrounded the wreckage. Elmo was wobbling as he stepped out of the car. The smoky wet stink from the house jumped at him. He tripped over scattered chunks of slump block at his feet, shaking his head, muttering "No, no, no," at the charred walls and the badly bent F-22 tail a few feet from his chimney, sprouting from his roof like some alien metal tree. He tripped over the bright plastic tricycle with Big Bird's sunshine smile in front of the little handlebars. He let out another animal moan. The officers moved closer to steady him.

The first officer grasped for words. "If you'll come this way, Mr. Skinner. . . Mr. Skinner, could you . . ."

Elmo closed his eyes, took a deep breath of dank smoke, and emitted a trembling sigh. He said in a voice that sounded a hundred years old, "Yes, I must. Proper procedure."

They led him to the waiting ambulance. Its rotating red lights flashed blood reflections in Elmo's eye. He looked inside. No one could tell who these people had been. No one, that is, except someone whose meager universe was defined by those two bodies. Elmo recognized the specific curve he clung to every night. It was the curve of the shy girl who had carved out the only four good years of his life.

And that sweet, innocent boy. Those delightful little legs had churned so sweetly when Nat mastered balance and toddled off to conquer the world. Elmo could Forget school plays and camping in the Catalinas. Never mind about soccer or little leagues or . . .

Elmo clutched at his throat. First the ambulance was swaying. Then it was swirling. The ground rolled under him. He never felt the two police officers catch him before he could land on the pavement.

The second cop looked at the first. He rasped, "I guess that's them."

* * * * *

For the funeral five days later, Molly's mother had taken a bus in from Phoenix. She had once told

29

Elmo to his face that she wanted no truck with him. She certainly hadn't changed her opinion of him since he had been fool enough to place her daughter and grandson in the path of an errant fighter plane. Elmo's own parents were dead, or maybe retired military somewhere on earth, he wasn't sure which. They had treated him like unwanted baggage that they lugged around from base to base. He had long since lost contact with them. Nobody had a problem with the arrangement.

Elmo had no friends to invite. He was goggle-eyed and slack-jawed throughout the service, moaning now and during the psalms. He never said a word. He had asked for no press, and what with reporters and photographers on vacation, editors and news directors accepted it.

Elmo's insurance man Todd Vogel was there, wearing the same kind of artificial smile Elmo's mother once warned would freeze that way. For the occasion, Vogel managed to turn that smile down a notch. Or maybe just half a notch.

Two of Molly's friends from kids' swimming lessons at the YMCA showed up in low-neck black lace. Each had effectively driven off three husbands. They put on a bad act of consoling Elmo. He was too numb to respond. He ignored a subtle invitation to an intimate evening for three. When he failed to respond to their entreaties, Elmo watched them go to work on the insurance man.

Phil Stein, the owner of Stein's Beer Bar next door to the Lamp Post and of the Hard Core Store down the block, came with Max Zorn. Colonel Tork, the base commander, was there wishing he could hide in his shadow. His picture was always in the little newspaper the base put out, but few people realized there was a body attached to the photographic head-and -shoulders portrait. He treated public attention as an invasion of military privacy. He tried to make his gaze hawklike, appropriate officer's bearing, he thought. Still he kept sneaking looks at Elmo, hoping Elmo was enough of a patriot that he wouldn't cause trouble, hoping nobody would ask where Captain Putnam was today. Likely Putnam was having a party. Likely at the Lamp Post Motel.

A few other people seemed to know Elmo. He didn't feel he knew anybody. Most of him was buried that day.

* * * * *

The next day Elmo came in to work right on time. Zorn had already called in someone to cover his shift. He met Elmo at the door and put a hand on his shoulder.

"You shouldn't be here."

"I want to work, Mr. Zorn. I need something to do."

"Do, Elmo? What's to do? Sit here and be miserable? Maybe you got a cheery telephone voice today? You feel like kibitzing with the customers? Come, today you work with Zorn over a beer, yes?"

Elmo managed something like a smile, even a little laugh. Neither of them was a drinking man, but they walked two doors up Craycroft to Phil Stein's Beer Bar.

"Take the week off. I'll pay you for the time—call it an extra vacation due to circumstances beyond your control." Zorn put his hand on Elmo's forearm.

Elmo sipped at his beer and looked at his boss across the table, stared for almost a minute, not with

anger, but with empty in his eyes. His natural monotone was taut. "What would I do with a week? Take
Nat to Disneyland? No one is home. Home isn't even
home."

"Where have you been staying?"

Elmo didn't answer right away. Pool balls clattered through the bar. Ancient music croaked out of
the jukebox.

"A motel?" Zorn asked. "Oy, why I didn't ask
you before? So where?"

Elmo nodded left, north, up the street. "The
Coachlight."

"No, that goniff up the street doesn't need your
money. Take 138."

"I wanted to see what the competition was like.
Their 'suite' amounts to a wall. Same space as our
rooms, but they have a wall. And a kitchen. Two small
rooms instead of one big one. That's it."

"Elmo, are you all right?"

Elmo drew water circles in the moisture left by
the beer bottles. The dead tone came through his voice.
"I don't know. What's all right? When everything that
matters in the world is blasted out from under you.
When two beautiful innocent creatures are nothing
but filthy ashes. Would you call that all right?"

"Elmo, I. . ."

"I did nothing to deserve this. They did nothing
to deserve this." He let the tears fall easily, but he was
still venting steam with a torrent of words.

It got uncomfortable for a while, but Zorn nodded and groaned in the appropriate places. "What can
you do when life hands you injustice?" he said.

Elmo stopped to put away half a fresh beer.

"It was too soon," Zorn said. Like so many, when
faced with someone's deepest pain, Zorn fell back on

the worst clichés.

"Yeah, it was that all right." Elmo swabbed his wet face with a napkin. He let his head fall back on the red plastic upholstery, took a long breath, then another.

"I'll tell you one thing, Mr. Zorn." His eye shifted into sharp focus and his voice steadied. "I'm gonna make the bastards pay."

* * * * *

Half the lawyers in Tucson wanted the case. Elmo didn't care to deal with the army of military specialists, former prosecutors, and the local personal injury barracuda. Elmo went with the barracuda, Noah Lyons, who milked the case for all the airtime and newsprint it was worth, which was plenty. The barracuda loved the camera as much as Elmo hated it. Lyons did all the talking while Elmo squirmed at his side for every newscam in town. Lyons was quoted in the two daily newspapers. The muckraking weekly newspaper gleefully spread blame to Putnam, Davis-Monthan Air Force Base, the United States Department of Defense and a world order that still relied on high-price, high-tech hardware to intimidate small nations.

The barracuda first insisted he was going to a jury trial. Once the government got ready for a long haul, Noah Lyons blew the Air Force out of the water in pretrial conference with the judge.

"Would you like me to drag that know-it-all son of a bitch Putnam before a jury so he can tell them how Mach Two gives him a hard-on? Wouldn't you like to remind the public how you promised Congressman Udall you would—exact words now— 'sharply curtail' flights over the city? That was thirty years ago—

after you dropped a plane on the university football practice field next to Mansfeld Middle School. You want a jury to hear what you did to this man's *life*?"

It took a year. They settled for a little over twenty-one million dollars. Noah Lyons took home seven million for his trouble, leaving fourteen million dollars for Elmo's piggy bank. The barracuda was only sorry the deal didn't include Captain Putnam's balls.

For that year, Elmo spent half his time with Lyons. He wore a suit to court conferences and depositions, something gray and polyester, which was the best Lyons could get him to wear. For the time being, however, the lawyer changed Elmo's drinking habits. By the time he celebrated his victory with Zorn, he was ordering single malt scotch.

Zorn raised his glass in the Hebrew greeting that says good luck, congratulations, and more of the same. "Mazel tov." Damn good scotch, too, he thought.

Elmo's hair was brushed with a more stylish precision per Lyons insistence. He wore the gray suit. "They say I was lucky, like I won the legal lottery."

"It's a lot of money, fourteen million dollars."

"Yes." Elmo sipped the scotch. He approved of the smoothness of the brand. "But it doesn't buy a life." He said it clipped, businesslike. It was the same thing he told the newspapers and video cameras.

"No?" Zorn scratched his chin. "Not all by itself, maybe. But there's plenty people running around who think money like that could buy a lot of living. They think it could buy their dreams." He looked up. "You got a dream, Elmo?"

Elmo shook his head, just slightly. The polyester suit turned with him. "My dream was to whip the bastards." He took a swallow of beer. "We did."

Zorn shook his head sadly, as he had much of

the afternoon. "Not enough, is it?"

Elmo's small enthusiasm melted from his face. "No. It's nothing but money. How many million pay for a thousand of Nat's hugs? Is there a fair price to compensate for pulverizing the only woman who ever gave a damn about me? How much did I get for every night I sleep alone?" The words were paraphrased from the barracuda's comments in the judge's chamber.

Zorn put his hand across the table to Elmo's wrist. "You can't buy back Molly. But there are women everywhere. The whole town knows how much money you have."

"No woman ever cared for me like that. No one ever will again." He misted for a moment, then focused intently on his glass. "I won't have my heart ripped out again."

"You can't bring them back," Zorn said. But you can move on."

"What," Elmo grunted, "follow my dream?"

"So I'm still waiting. You got a dream?"

"No." Elmo sighed.

"What's the first thing you want to buy?" Zorn spread his arms up on the back of the booth. "A house in the foothills? A fancy car?"

Elmo released the threat of a smile. "Maybe a hot new computer."

"*Oy.*"

Elmo shook his stylishly cut head. "To you a computer is something that watches your cash flow and figures out payroll. But you don't know. It can do anything. Client tracking, repair records, cross-tabs to track down a regularly destructive customer. Why, I could write programs that would have the Lamp Post Motel sitting up and doing tricks."

"She's not a dog," Zorn said a little too sharply.

Then, softer, "But she is a life."

Elmo stared, his brow folding in confusion.

"Maybe you should buy the Lamp Post Motel."

His jaw dropped. "You would sell . . . ?" Elmo bought his eyebrows together. "Mr. Zorn, the Lamp Post is your whole life. You built it. You made it everything it is. You can't sell off your life." His tone turned bitter. "You can only have it taken from you."

Zorn stared past the wall. "She's been forty-five years of my life. Every time I thought about you, I thanked God I have my Sarah and the kids and their kids. I know what you lost, because I still have it. You taught me to appreciate them. So what do I do with family like this? I let them sit. We live across from each other. I should take Sarah to Israel. Instead I buy a new ice machine."

"You don't really want to sell . . ."

"Why not? All this mishugas with this AIDS and everybody's afraid to go out and screw. It's no good for business. I spent too many days fighting with the titsi dancers for money, screaming about the new taxes they keep finding for hotels. The Lamp Post is always open. All day, every day. I'm tired."

Zorn caught himself sullying his sales pitch. "It's a life, Elmo. You could be the boss. You see most of what I do. I'll teach you the rest. Do whatever you want with her." Zorn allowed a smile. "Even make her sit up and do tricks."

Zorn had him hooked. Elmo found himself staring off into nowhere.

"Mr. Zorn, I. . ."

"Call me Max. It's about time."

"Max. After all these years you could just walk away from it?"

"Why not? What do I work for? To give a dozen

people jobs with lousy pay? To make sure some junkie has a place to shoot tonight with a toilet he can plug up with his damn needle? To keep the linen service in business? No. That's not why. Elmo, I work for the day when I won't have to work anymore. And now it's time." He looked at his hands, then back up at Elmo. "You need a life, Elmo. I happen to have one I'm about through with. I need enough money to get out comfortably. You have money, no? To me it sounds like a deal where everybody gets what they want."

Elmo tried on the idea. "I could run the Lamp Post Motel?"

"Better than me," Zorn said with a wan smile. "You're young, you have ideas. You want a fancy-shmansy computer? Put it in your motel. It's deductible. You want to see who rented 118 on a Tuesday last year? Your computer could tell you in a second. You want to know which TV set breaks down the most, you ask the computer." Zorn waited.

"I could do more than that. I could do a lot more." His looked off into a nonexistent distance.

Elmo didn't need Zorn to warn him of the thousands of people coming through, the innocents, crack heads, bikers, salesmen, construction workers, con artists, snowbirds and even a few damn nice people.

"You got capital. Give her a facelift. Get her a few new carpets and beds. Make her yours, Elmo."

He narrowed his eyes. "How much?"

Zorn shrugged as casually as he could. "Two million."

Elmo's face was expressionless. "It's hardly worth a million and a half."

"A million seven-fifty. Could I get that much to sell you my life?"

"One point six five."

37

Zorn slapped his palm on the table. "Sold."

Zorn yelled across the bar. "Dan, what's the name of Elmo's fancy scotch?"

Phil Stein was there filling their glasses in seconds.

"The Glenlivet," Phil said. "This one is on the house." He took a third glass and poured himself a good splash. "*Mazel tov*," he said.

Phil was a good listener.

CHAPTER 5

Within two thousand years, the Earth falls prey to the imbalance of hot heads with nuclear testicles and a point to prove. By that day, we shall suppose that humankind has been moving out into the Sol system. Evolution can't do much with an ornery species in a mere two thousand years, so human still shoot themselves in the foot, they just do it with gravity waves instead of bullets. So of course, our insanity came with us.

–X. Arbodor, The Exodous

Saturn orbit, Year Standard 4157

Xaq Hobesian Arbidor 7906021 burps in his dormitory room. He can smell the vacuum of space reaching for him. It's pulling at the walls, almost breathing though the plastic, geodesic space. A moment later, the walls are contracting in on him, It happens ever so slowly, but relentlessly, just beyond the edge of direct perception. Xaq is aboard an artificial moon, the University of the Rings hive campus, in orbit around Saturn. Xaq suspects the weight of academe is squeezing him out like a mild—but not unexpected—case of gas. This was academe, intent on blowing him out into the galactic real world.

Sometimes he thought the only thing that really kept him from being blown out of the University of the Rings was pressure from the outside worlds to keep him in. He stared out through his coveted half-meter window, across the striped plain of orange, green and a hundred other dust colors that spread ten thousand miles to horizon's edge, still one of the greatest set of rings in the galaxy. On the right was the black inner solar system and the little world that had cradled humanity more than a thousand years before. At the center was the sun, but Sol had never been much help from a one and a half billion kilometers away. Down 45,000 kilometers below was big, gassy Saturn, where tourists from Jupiter came to gawk at real rings. But it was out there—beyond the local planets to the interstellar spaces where even light years were inadequate to measure distance—out there, no one clamored for another Ph.D. in sexual anthropology.

Xaq was a local boy, born planetside in Saturnopolis, a hundred-kilometer egg that was once the crowning glory of a terraformed city. His mother had often reminded him how lucky he was to have such a fine school as the University of the Rings in his backyard—and that would feel obliged to take him. Xaq's grades kept him out of Nucleus U or the other prized schools, so he made do with the University of the Rings and its uninspiring freeball teams. Xaq thought anthrosex could send him gallivanting around the galaxy investigating civilizations. So far he was a professional student, still hanging out in the Sol   system where little remained besides history. Xaq had been out to Jupiter a few times. He had spent a few weekends zonked out on Mars.

Through all that, he had somehow attached a string of letters to his name that concluded in Ph.D. But even in the fortieth century, the market for philosophical dissertation was marginal. Xaq was moving on to Maven with designs on getting his AE! (Acknowledged Expert!) before his first Saturnine birthday, when he would be nearly thirty by Earth reckoning. An AE! could get assignments across the stars. All a Ph.D. was good for was a little office space and a job standing in front of a few hundred students mumbling at his shoes, like the dead-ended professors all around him. These days, Ph.D. was barely a step above lab assistant. Goal-directed they called him. Maven was just a boundary line to cross on the path to AE! The walls were a more treacherous obstacle.

All he needed now to get his Maven degree was completing his Equivocation. Xaq Hobesian Arbidor 7906021 had to say something notable about human sexual anthropology. Xaq had nothing to say. Could the walls hold back thousands of years of academia?

For the past six hours he had studied thousands of magimages of Mother Earth. His dissertation had analyzed the twenty-third century Earth exodus from social, political, economic and ecological perspectives.

He kept looking. Xaq paged through history reports about that same old Earth on his screen, yawning, forcing his attention to pick up something, anything, scanning for biological quirks, generating a list of medical anomalies, until he came up with an alphabetical list, and right there at the top was one spelled in capital letters: AIDS.

There was something about that in class a month ago, something he had marked in his notes as significant. He pulled the quotation from his notes and Professor Dendiger was on the screen, talking to his shoes.

"AIDS was the last critical hurdle for medical science. Its defeat in the twenty-first century marked

41

the turning point from biological to social evolution. In that century, medicine came of age. People who should have died of illness or injury under natural evolutionary rules survived with medical help. The crippled, who would have died away under Darwin, were getting along tolerably well.

"AIDS was nothing less hideous than a sexually transmitted time-bomb that ticked until it shut down the body's defenses. Then any minor infection brought on death. The medicals were up against something new, a 'retrovirus,' what came to be called a smart virus. The standard viruses of the time attacked the immune system head-on, and usually lost. The AIDS virus went into hiding, apparently dormant from the lack of symptoms. But this virus was far from dormant. It was quite busy duplicating the body's own genetic code. Once equipped with the genetic password to get by the immune system, it could quickly convert a minor infection to terminal illness. The mortality rate was only moderate. The threat was more a cultural shock, a flashing warning in the path of less repressed sexuality brought on by contraceptive technology.

"The medical battle lasted half a century. But the sustained intensive study of the immune system yielded more than the anticipated results. It was a moment in history when medical science could finally claim to understand the human body. Breakthroughs in genetic engineering were timed just right to combat HIV, a genetic engineer of a virus itself.

"By the middle of the twenty-first century, the secrets of the human immune system were coming unraveled. By 2060, every doctor's office ran computer simulations of the inner workings of every patient. The prescription was ubiquitous: DETOX, the immune system supercharger that restored the body in days, and serious cases in a few months. And while all this was going on, a genetically engineered enzyme proved foolproof fertility control, with a simple vitamin antidote for conception.

"The potency of these emerging biosciences provided entirely new methods of repairing and restoring the body. AIDS was a bad memory. Cancers became curable. Legions of diseases dropped away. Then word got out that hard-pumping hormones could act as a catalyst spurring DETOX to greater heights of bodily self-restoration. At the end of the twentieth century, a shot of DETOX and good old-fashioned lust were the keys to health and vitality.

"Evolution was whipped."

* * * * *

Xaq squirmed like a lab worm in front of Professor Dendiger. The office had racks of meticulously organized chip files along smooth walls that absorbed excess sound. The professor gazed coolly across the expanse of desk unmarred by even a single slip of paper. Dendiger's long, narrow head was accentuated by a total absence of hair right down to the missing eyebrows.

Xaq was just another shaggy, forlorn student, lost in a sea of data, exhausted from analysis, wondering what meaning meant anymore. Dendiger let him squirm a trifle more.

"You have no major hypothesis to research, no arcane little corner of human sexuality to study, and no idea where to start looking. What could possibly give you the right to carry the title Maven after your name?"

43

"My thorough analysis of the Exodus . . ."

"Is last year's news." Dendiger waited for the lanky, disheveled fool to fall back on last week's lecture.

"I had been giving some thought to the AIDS episode, professor."

"Indeed?" The skin lifted where an eyebrow once was.

Dendiger watched Xaq's hands, his whole body, fumbling. The boy was going to make it up as he went along.

"About it being the end of Earth-based evolution and all. How sex was the healthiest sport."

"You have a personality disorder, Arbidor 7906021." Dendiger knew students hated it when he called them by their numbers. "You snigger. It is most unseemly for a serious student of sexual anthropology to approach his subject with all the galactic sophistication of a barfly. I question whether you are an adequate candidate for the degree."

Xaq pressed his lips together. "It must have affected the culture. The economic impact on the hospitality industry would be substantial. It would likely have created turmoil in the medical profession."

An adroit moment, Dendiger conceded. Maybe the kid was worth something yet. The professor tossed him a bone, an old favorite for leering students who needed only an overdose to be cured. "I authorize clearance for eight hours on the vidchron. Tomorrow. Be ready."

* * * * *

Xaq was parked at the window, asking a hundred billion stars what was there for him, when the

44

console on his white plastic demidesk blipped to life. He would have been glad to see any smiling face. But he especially welcomed grinning, round-headed Yot, a slightly out-of-whack engineering student.

"Ho, how's it spinning?"

"Ho yourself. It's spinning halfway to the floor," Xaq moaned.

Yot's voice was so low he might have had five balls. He spoke slowly, almost counting his every word. "How about we go . . . planetside . . . and look for some . . . women?"

Xaq shook his head. "I have a vidchron session tomorrow. Too much work to do."

"You got it all wrong. Some heavy . . . viewing time calls for a . . . relaxed mind. If you're going to put your head into history tomorrow, you should get loose tonight."

"I think I'd better . . ."

"Get yourself some xufa," ordered Yot's baritone.

Xaq allowed a smile. "Professor Dendiger says I snigger."

"Sure. The old bofo probably never had a good snigger in his life. His nuts are probably as . . . bald as his head." Yot stepped off-screen. Xaq's tele-receiver blurped. He typed the signal to admit the transmission.

Yot materialized in the middle of the room. His bulk shoved against the advancing walls, giving the illusion of breathing room. Or had those walls retreated a centimeter or two?

"Let's go, I've got a hardo that needs . . . immediate service." Yot spread himself out on Xaq's paltry excuse for a bed. "You won't do any entertaining in this rack."

45

Xaq sat with his back to the console and bent his thin lips to something of a smile, but said nothing.

Yot made his clown face—with his jaw jutted forward and upward, raised eyebrows and a twisted grin. It was Yot's most philosophical pose, declaring that the universe was feco, so there was no use in caring about much of anything. The voice he used with the clown face was a howling, mocking, elfin sort of thing. "How can you think . . . objectively about sexual anthropology when you haven't had any . . . xufa in two months?"

"That's six weeks," Xaq snapped.

"And five days, most likely."

"I don't have the time."

"You can't . . . put it off much longer. Neither can I," he said.

Xaq's stern determination crumbled in a chuckle. "Maybe I'll get inspired with a little free time."

"Now you're talking. Let's go."

"Have I got time for a shower?"

"Just barely," Yot shot back.

"I'm hurrying."

Within half an hour they faxed themselves down to Saturnopolis. Yot swaggered gorillalike along the tubeway, eyes out for a dark, steamy pub. Xaq had a little bounce to his gait as well, happy to navigate the now-familiar tunnels forbidden in his youth. Yot steered them to The Snarling Beja, a hangout where he said he got lucky once before with a well-trained coed from the Saturnopolis Academy of Cosmetology and Concubinity.

Tonight the Snarling Beja was inhabited by a lonely bartender. Probably just a Ph.D., Xaq thought glumly. The big room was of the same tubular construction as most of the city, dimly lit with light-stripes along the walls. Two dozen booth modules looked empty, their laser call buttons awaiting customers and orders.

"Ho, where'd everybody go?" Yot asked.

"Uranus, I think," the lanky barkeep drawled. "But classes at the school around the corner let out in a few minutes. We'll have girls. Jandow for you?"

Xaq and Yot nodded. Two ice-sheathed mugs appeared before them at the bar. They sat and drank for a moment before Xaq started his lamentations. Yot signaled for another round. Two men engaged in intense negotiations brushed in the door and drifted to a table near the back, but there was still no sign of women.

Yot finally concluded he couldn't avoid the subject. "So where you going to view on the vidchron? How far back . . . will you look?"

"That's what I've been trying to tell you, fecobrain."

"Wha?"

"I don't know." Xaq took a long drink.

CHAPTER 6

"Ho," Yot said. "You've got a problem."

"You ever been to Earth?"

"What for? It's a garbage planet. The air is still unbreatheable. There's nothing down there but tourists in sealed busses on the ruins of London, Tokyo and New York. Why would I want to go there?"

"Why?" Xaq erupted. "Why go where a day is one day long, a year one trip around the sun, a month one lunar orbit? Why go to the cradle of humanity?"

"Yeah, why? If it wasn't so damned historic, they wouldn't be pissing away government money on this 400-year planetary rehabilitation feco. The place reeks. Terraforming Earth! They're crazy."

"Nah, it's poetry. It's the irony of terraforming the original Terra. Just as historic as the twentieth century when they took their first meager steps off the planet."

"The place will be hot for another thousand years. They can't just wish away a radioactive world."

"It's cooling down, or they wouldn't be running tourists through it, sealed busses or no. It's perfectly safe at the bottom of the oceans. Oceans! Can you imagine water for thousands of miles in every direction? Where all sorts of water-breathing creatures live? Oceans are more water than you can possibly imagine, stretching across a world, interrupted by only 32 per cent of surface land."

"I don't need some dead planet."

"It wasn't always dead," Xaq said.

"It's dead now."

Neither of them had noticed the men in the back until one of them left. The one remaining behind was a short, stocky man with dark narrow eyes and a black beard. He swung up to the bar and ordered a jandow on ice.

"Slim's right, you know," the stranger said to Yot. "Used to be Earth was a hell of a place. More alive than any world you'll see in this sector of the galaxy."

"How would you know?" Yot challenged.

The stranger looked around. No one else save the tight-lipped bartender was in the Snarling Beja. His voice fell to a hoarse whisper. "I been there."

"Hot feco, riding around in a bus and a radiation suit looking at ruins," Yot said. "Not exactly what I call a good time." He was tempted to flash the clown face, but decided it could be hazardous and restrained himself.

The stranger's eyes narrowed further, and a conspiratorial smile crossed his lips. "Time," he whispered, "is what it's all about."

"Yeah, so big deal," Xaq lamented. "I get a few hours on the vidchron, look through a window on the past and. . ."

A chuckle grunted in the stranger's throat as he shook his head. "Noooo, my man, you've got it all wrong. I'm not talking windows. I'm talking doors!"

There was a rustling at the entryway. Three young women shuffled in and made their way to a booth.

"Time travel?" Xaq blurted. "That's illegal."

Yot nudged him. "A little louder, fecohole, maybe one of those little chippies over there missed it."

The stranger waited and watched through

drooping eyelids. The three of them looked at each other.

"Sorry," Xaq peeped.

The stranger gave the slightest nod, then ordered a round of drinks. He let the chair back take his weight. "You're students. History?"

"Anthropology," Xaq muttered ever so quietly.

The stranger rolled the word around on his lips a few times. He looked at Xaq sideways. "You mean bones and artifacts and that feco?"

Xaq nodded, then wagged his head toward Yot. "He's in engineering."

The stranger ran his fingers through his beard and peered out from under the heavy lids. "I do believe we can do business."

Another knot of students came through the door, more women than men. Yot nodded approvingly at a redhead with flotation perfect for an Earth ocean.

The stranger gave the slightest gesture to the bartender, and a fresh round of drinks appeared on his table in the dark corner. "You can call me Rej." He stood and stepped toward it. "Please, gentlemen, step into my office."

Both of them paused for a longing glance at the growing selection of nubility, but followed Rej to the table. Rej stopped before sitting down. "You are Xaq Hobesian Arbidor 7906021 and Yot Chulig Pehard 7821277, students down from the U of R. You, Mr. Arbidor, are needing a research subject before you blow your Maven degree. You have a viewing tomorrow morning." He eased himself down on the pseudoswank artifur upholstery and spread his arms and his smile to Xaq and Yot. "Or could I be mistaken?"

Yot snarled. "Is this supposed to be some psychic feco or . . ."

Xaq felt his feet suggesting they flee.

Rej chuckled. "You don't understand. We're old friends. Go on, Yot, let's see your clown face."

Yot actually got as far as shoving his chin forward before he shook his head and glared at this Rej, whoever he was.

"How do you know that?" Yot growled.

Rej laughed. "We're old friends, Yot my man. At least we were in my past. And in your future. Your immediate future. Like now. Now why don't you both sit down before you blow the whole sequence?"

More baffled than appeased, they plopped down on the artifur. Xaq grabbed for his jandow. Yot locked his gaze on Rej, trying to fathom the magnanimous grin across the bearded face.

"You time trip," Yot said.

"Sometimes. Mostly I'm the doorman."

"To time," Xaq said, his voice quavering, not sure whether to add a question mark to his tone.

"To time," Rej said, raising a glass. Because this is your night."

Xaq gripped the jandow mug firmly to stop his hand from shaking. "I've got a viewing in the morning. I don't have time to go traipsing off into history."

"Xaq my man, time is what you have in abundance. You have time enough to run an errand for me and still spend a week on pre-exodus Earth. You have time to return home, put your notes together, and get a few extra hours rest before that viewing tomorrow."

Yot rolled the edge of his mug on the table. "How do you. . . know us?"

Rej's benevolent smile returned. "Simple. You returned four days ago. You're both sacked out at home at this very moment. Xaq will be quite ready for the morning."

"What's this about an errand?" Yot asked.

"We have to pay for this excursion, do we not?" Xaq dropped his mug to the tabletop.

"Don't be alarmed, my man. There's plenty in it for you too. All you do is plant a financial seed two thousand years in the past. Open an account with Global Express. They were around even then. When you return we split up the interest. And we all spend the rest of our lives moderately wealthy."

Yot looked unconvinced.

"We'll do it," Xaq said, not yet believing it himself.

"I know," Rej said with that damnable grin. "You already have."

Rej led them through the tubular streets, past half a dozen more bars where music and shouts poured out at their feet. The sidewalk cruised them past the darkened front of the Saturnopolis Academy of Cosmetology and Concubinity. Xaq and Yot exchanged questioning glances, but said nothing to Rej. They nodded finally, just as Rej took them past a cluster of shops to what looked like an empty house that needed a new skin and a few repairs on the shutters.

Rej hurried them past his living room strewn with scribbled notes on orange and green paper. Some bore unintelligible diagrams. They walked single-file down a narrow flight of stairs to a room with a three-meter transit bubble and a console protruding old-fashioned wires and primitive gauges. These, too, were littered with more scribbled pieces of paper, these blue and yellow.

"Tonight you fly," Rej said. He held up a finger for a moment's pause and scurried back into a corner to emerge with two twentieth century attaché cases. "You will need these." He handed a case to each of them. Xaq took it, expecting it to explode at any moment. "Twentieth century money. Twenty thousand American dollars. Ten thousand goes into the Global Express account, with the stipulation that the account remains open for five thousand years. Don't mind if they laugh. But insist. Then you simply use the balance of the money for your expenses."

They searched for a button to open each case, touching all over them. Rej let them go on pushing here and there before he reached over and slid the catches open. He let Xaq examine the oddly printed currency, the bizarre characters depicted there, and the ancient architecture of some sort of monument.

"That," Rej said to Yot, "is what was known as a portable computer. One of the very first. It's pathetically limited, but advanced for the period you're visiting. More important, it's compatible with the machines you will encounter on Earth. The instruction manuals are on what they called a hard drive." Rej smiled at Yot. "I wouldn't want to tell the engineering student any more. I'm sure you would rather poke around with it yourself." He flipped a switch on the machine and it started whirring and flashing images on a crystal screen.

Xaq found himself absorbed caressing the fine paper that had a strangely satisfying feel. "Where did you get this stuff?"

Rej's smile was getting irritating, but there it was again. "Let's say I have some friends who like exploring outside the law. They brought back a few souvenirs. I thought they might be useful."

The bubble appeared to be nothing out of the ordinary, a three-passenger transpo globe with the normal flight controls, capable of short-range atmospheric and space flight. Rej started flipping switches and typing commands to his wire-strewn console, until the bubble seemed to melt away.

"An infrared shroud, operating just below the visible spectrum. It makes you effectively invisible when you are inside."

"Ho, Yot, are we really doing this?"

Yot was punching at the computer, which pronounced him guilty of syntax error. He never took his eyes from the screen. "You're the one that needs the damn subject. I'm along for the ride. But it sounds like Big Fun. Something to remember in our old age. You can't back out. Rej here's seen us come back. I still want to know one thing."

Xaq cocked his head.

"You're the student. When are we going to?"

This time Xaq had an answer. "The end of Earth-based evolution. The twenty-first century. Before the wars, before the planet was trashed."

"Where?"

Xaq shrugged. "How should I know?"

Once more, Rej smiled. "Gentlemen, you only just returned from a place where the post-AIDS commerce was brisk, where a student of sexual anthropology would have a perfect observation post." He reached into the paper clutter and picked up one small card printed in turquoise and coral ink. He handed it to Xaq, who read aloud: "The Lamp Post Motel, Tucson, Arizona, USA.

CHAPTER 7

The Arizona desert is one of the world's biggest beaches: all that sand, completely unfettered by any substantial body of water. From Tucson, the nearest real beach is four hours away, across the Mexican border to Puerto Peñasco, Mexico, at the top of the Gulf of California. There's a new tourist hotel in Rocky Point (as the gringos call it), but traditions die hard with Americans too cheap to go to San Diego. So east of town along the beach are strings of beach houses that families rent for the weekend. West of Puerto Peñasco is a broad, empty beach with nothing built at all, just sand dunes, tufts of desert grasses, and hundreds of Americans who pitch tents and sleep on the beach for free, entertained by the Milky Way nearly bursting out of a gloriously clear sky.

It was under the light of the galaxy that Loretta stepped out of the dome tent on to the gray sand. She listened to the night. A diesel fishing boat thrummed a mile offshore. Horny crickets chirped across the jojoba-tufted dunes. Occasionally fireworks popped from down the beach. From beyond the rise, across a quarter mile of wet sand abandoned by the tide, she heard the soft surf of the desert beach.

Her first steps across the sand were tentative. Here she was the invader. The scorpions and the snakes lived here. Still, she could do without a sting or a bite tonight, and she half-expected something slithering by at any moment. Her nose picked up the sea air, even downwind in the evening offshore breeze.

She stopped, took another breath and walked briskly to the top of the dune. From there she overlooked the body of water the sea goddess had used to intrude on the Mexican desert. She dug her sneakers into the sand and let gravity accelerate her down to the beach. Her legs and lungs pumped. Her heart picked up the pace as she ran into the night. A transparent lavender crystal jiggled from a modest gold chain. Her clients saw the elongated crystal as a phallic symbol stationed between her business assets. To Loretta, the crystal was an energy repository.

Loretta's legal name was Natalie Lipschutz. As a young girl, Natalie was bound in high-necked dresses with overstated collars and puffy sleeves. In the PS 139 Brooklyn schoolyard, Natalie Lipschutz' name was twisted around, because kids just have to do that to each other.

Natalie majored in psychology at City College of New York. Undergrads soon learned that a psych degree was worthless without going all the way for a Ph.D. Natalie responded by dropping out. She abandoned the taunting grounds, the dirty snow, the muggy summers, and the whiny singsong of the New York yenta. She fled three-quarters of the way across the country to the Arizona desert, where she became a vegetarian, a horoscope reader and a Voojoo. She made her living by going all the way—for a proper fee.

Natalie launched her career in applied psychology dancing in topless bars. The other girls at work spent their money on crack and smack. She invested hers in a marketing campaign: a slick and sleazy wardrobe and a screaming red tint to her erstwhile mousy brown hair. She socked away money. She built contacts with cab drivers, bar owners and everyone else who might be useful helping her establish herself as a self-employed applied psychologist.

Natalie adopted a professional name: Loretta Lipps.

This evening's client, Lyle, would disapprove of her wandering out of the tent. Lyle was no devotee of exploring this meeting of Mexican desert and the Sea of Cortez. He just wanted to get laid for the weekend out of harm's way and his wife's scrutiny. At the moment, he was quite asleep, and perfectly satisfied. He didn't understand Loretta's communing with the Sea Goddess.

Once clear of the tent and over the dunes, Loretta stopped in the sand, yanked the tennis shoes from her feet, tied the laces together and slung them over her shoulder. She walked out on the hard, wet, sand sculpted into long, bumpy ridges by the retreating tide. The rippled sand massaged her soles. She broke into a trot along the beach, matching her pace to the rhythm of the waves somewhere out there under the light of a low quarter moon.

Far up the beach, maybe half a mile away, she saw a campfire light. She stopped, deciding to keep to her own space. Loretta found a dry piece of beach, plopped herself down, and looked for the little breakers that she could clearly hear, but that were still two hundred yards out in the darkness. She looked up at the spangle of stars undimmed by the city lights of so-called civilization. She swore she could see millions of stars in the sinuous Milky Way, stretched across the skies much darker than in most of urbanized America.

She smelled the breeze and closed her eyes. At the top of the hill she heard a rustling. It took her a minute to make out the coyote's silhouetted head turning toward her. Loretta watched the beast take a few steps to lope away, then glance over its shoulder.

Loretta froze in her tracks. When she saw the coyote make no move toward her, she breathed. The coyote was looking past her, out to sea. After a moment she looked behind her.

No one was there.

The coyote uttered a queer little whine, then slunk away, his head low to the dune.

Even in the scant moonlight, the beach looked clearly empty. She looked at the brush-tufted dunes around her, but could feel no life present. As she looked out toward the sea, a corner of her eye caught a chunk of something that didn't look right.

The sky, or a piece of it, maybe twice the size of the moon, was...out of focus, wavy, distorted. It was low over the water, an instability just to the left of Aquarius. None of her psych training or her own studies in parapsychology had prepared her to recognize this.

It was a hole in time.

* * * * *

A setting quarter moon was exactly enough light for Lopez to clatter the battered old Chevy, headlights doused, over the washboard dirt roadway. The road jarred the body at thirty-five miles per hour, and threatened to shake the skin from his bones while he was doing sixty.

"Slow down, you crazy fuck, nobody's following us." Soto could hardly say the words without his jaw slamming up on his tongue. He was seated, if such a thing were possible when being bounced three inches off the seat several times a second.

"Got to stay ahead of them," Lopez shouted in

Spanish through the clatter of complaining metal, tortured rubber, and unrelenting roadbed.

Soto couldn't hear Lopez and couldn't reach him. He grabbed for the fifth of tequila on the floor, grateful he had saved it from being shattered. He brought it to his lips, tipped the bottle, and got at least as much on him as in him. "Slow down, chingadero!" he screamed.

Lopez looked in the mirror. He saw nothing but the plume of dust he had raised. He looked for the side mirror, but it was facing the rutted ground below. He spotted the right-hand turnoff bouncing past and slammed on the brakes. The old Chevy shuddered, sputtered, and died.

Soto held the bottle tight and jumped out. Even on solid ground, the echoes of a few thousand bone rattles ran through him. "I'll drive the rest of the way."

Lopez hurled back invective, but he'd had enough of the wheel anyway, and slid over to the passenger seat, making sure to get the tequila from Soto first.

The car started on the third try. Soto had the easy part of the drive, two miles across a cushion of sand over hard, blessedly smooth ground.

Lopez used the calm to put away an inch of tequila. "The Federales are still in Mazatlan."

"Dios, let it be so," Soto croaked.

"They won't look for us at the beach with the touristas," Lopez hoped.

Soto took his right hand off the wheel to cross himself.

Lopez snarled. "No law can stop a man when he gotta lay something."

Soto just shook his head. "For a little robbery they don't call the Federales. But rape, that pisses

59

them off. Why, because they were broke? Who's not broke? You and me ain't doing so hot."

"Aah, she needed a porking she'd remember." Lopez treated himself to a long, loud laugh.

Remember she would. So would the Policia. Federales have a special aversion to the rape of a Councilman's wife, even a poor Councilman's wife.

Soto eased the car off to the left, toward the beach, pulling as far away from the road as he could. Just far enough that the wheels spun in the sand, leaving the Chevy with nowhere to go.

"Good job," Lopez snarled.

Soto sighed. "We should get it out of this sand now. Might not have time later."

Lopez grudgingly agreed. For fifteen minutes they rocked the car in its sandy rut. No one came past. No police lights flashed in the distance. Maybe the Federales really would leave them alone at the beaches. No use riling the stinking, fat American touristas waving their money, always moaning the loudest when they had their bulging pockets picked. Lopez didn't like the way they came to brutalize his country; he wanted that job all to himself.

Both men were puffing heavily when the Chevy finally rolled free. They let themselves fall to the ground to let the sweat roll off and find some breath.

Before they stood up again they had done away with half the tequila. Soto suggested they walk up the beach, staying close enough to return to the Chevy, but far enough that they could escape if Federales closed in on the car.

Lopez grunted. Why not?

So they walked up the beach, swaying with the breeze. Soto kept the bottle cradled under his arm. Lopez stumbled along, sufficiently invigorated by the cool air to walk, if just barely.

They heard the invisible breakers and the distant chugging boat and jeered any asshole who would waste his life chasing fish in the middle of the night.

At first, Soto was sure his eyes were in league with the tequila. But he looked back at it again. When he turned his head, it was still there. "Look at that," he said. "That piece of the sky. It's—fuzzy or something."

With Soto's eyesight, everything was at least a little fuzzy. But he looked. He even looked twice, lost his balance, and tumbled to the ground.

* * * * *

Rej had poked them through a hole in time, just a minute of a ripple from the fortieth century, but lasting an hour from the twenty-first century side of the orifice. Rej told them they were dropping through time quite a distance from their target, but that they should remain invisible and they would encounter someone who would lead them to it.

Yot piloted the bubble. He was terrified and fascinated by this apparently endless liquid surface that was the Gulf of California. In the meager moonlight, he managed only a weak glimpse at this mass of water that was unheard of anywhere else in the Sol system, in any century.

"It looks so . . . heavy," he said, his eyes fixed on the hypnotic undulations. Back on Jupiter he'd seen the fluid surface, but nothing with the density, the sheer weight of a billion times more water than he had ever seen in one place.

He eased the bubble to the edge of the water. Even through the bubble wall, they could hear the primal pounding as the edge of the water broke up, collapsing on itself. It was an alien sound. They found it oddly tranquilizing.

"What do we do now?" Xaq asked.

"I want to see all this water in the daylight."

"We're not parking here all night."

"Why not?"

Xaq sputtered. "We're going to sit here for . . . for . . ."

"The sun will be up in six hours. Before we jump into your ancient civilization, I could use a little sleep."

"We're here. This is old Earth, the cradle of humanity, alive and real and all around us."

"There's nothing around us," Yot said. This feels good right here. I'm tired.

"Don't you want to see this place?"

"Isn't this the good old Earth that you said had a day that's exactly a day long?"

"Yeah, so?" Xaq hissed.

"Well, it's the middle of the night. They're probably all asleep on this side of the planet, and if you could just shut up, I will be too."

Xaq was a meager bubble pilot at best. But with Yot snoring within a minute, Xaq cautiously eased the bubble a few yards toward the beach for a closer look.

CHAPTER 8

All that afternoon Thea Nikolas had sifted sand through her fingers. She had noticed the uncommon smoothness of the grains. She had scooped up a handful and examined the sand granules in her palm. She found not silicon-loaded bits of dirt, but the tiniest shards of shell, their edges smoothed by the tides. She had looked through several handsful and couldn't find a grain of true sand. These pulverized remains of billions of shellfish made up the beach. "Nothing but a crustacean boneyard," she had said aloud to no one.

Tonight her searching eyes had been fixed on the fuzzy spot on the sky for the better part of half an hour. At times it appeared small and a few hundred yards off the beach, and at other moments seemed enormous and hundreds, thousands, maybe even millions of miles away. She wasn't sure which possibility worried her more. All four women in the camp had seen the shifty chunk of sky, although none but Thea had cared to look at it for more than a minute. She sat on the beach sifting sand through her fingers, wondering how many people were witnessing the phenomenon. Not knowing what the hell it was bothered her. That no one else gave a damn just plain pissed her off.

At the campfire a few yards away, her lover Andi was drinking Bohemia beer with Joanne and Donna.

And then it was gone. Not flicked out like a light, but fading over several seconds, more like a Cheshire cat smile, until the sky was unwarped again. "What the hell is that?"

Andi looked back an Thea. "You can come back now, your fuzzy sky is gone."

"Of course it is," Thea said, unwilling to remove her eyes from the spot. "But it left behind that little glowing red . . . I don't know what to call it a dot, a faint light . . . something."

Andi looked where the warped sky had been. "Nothing."

"Don't you see it?"

Donna stood up slowly. She staggered with her first step, but walked the twenty paces to where Thea was watching the sky. Joanne got up to join them, forcing Andi to complete the group.

Each of them gave it a game effort for half a minute. But neither Donna, Joanne, nor Andi saw a faint anything.

"How many beers have you had?" Andi smirked.

"Not half as many as you," Thea shot back.

"I don't see anything," Donna said. Joanne shook her head. They went back to the campfire and the Bohemia. Joanne spilled beer in Donna's lap and dove to lick it up. Their blood alcohol level made everything terribly funny, and they rolled, cackling, in the Mexican sand.

Thea refused to take her eyes off it. It seemed to be growing larger—or closer, she couldn't tell which. She took a dozen steps to her left, looked at it closely, and paced twenty-four steps to the right. It was definitely getting closer. It seemed to be pulsing like a lazy heartbeat.

"It's right there! How can you not see it?"

Andi looked. Joanne and Donna looked again. They looked at Thea, at each other, and again burst out laughing.

"Jesus, it's right in front of you."

"There's nothing there, Thea," Andi said as gently as she could. The other two giggled again, and spilled more beer.

Thea stomped ten paces down the beach before turning back to her friends. "Fuck you. Fuck you all."

Andi was giggling again. "That's what we're here for. C'mon, you're not going off chasing little green men, are you?"

The campfire reflected in her flashing dark eyes. "I'm going to see what's out there."

"C'mon," Andi said, "you're going diesel on us again."

Andi came to put a hand on Thea's shoulder. "Really, we've looked. There's nothing there, baby. You're drunk. Come to bed."

"I'm not that drunk. Damnit, it's right there. I can't believe you don't see it."

"Well, we're going to bed. Let me know whether little green women or marauding Mexican rapists come out, would you?" She let out a beery giggle and joined the others gamboling in the big dome tent.

"You can be a real cunt sometimes, you know that?" Thea kicked sand in Andi's direction before turning away and stomping down the beach. No one had ever pointed out to Thea that whether it was Greek genes or some other quirk of biology, she had this unusual ability to see infrared where most people could not, and what she was seeing was the infrared shroud that made the bubble invisible to almost everyone else.

She carried the anger for a few hundred yards before the breeze off the water, the brilliant stars, and that damnable red dot absorbed her thoughts. She walked south on the beach for probably half a mile when she sat in the sand to watch that faint but distinct dot. Thea felt the cool beach under her shorts, heard the tide pulling back to leave a thousand yards of puddly mud, and for half an hour, saw what no one else saw. Now it didn't seem to move at all.

Thea's eyes remained locked on it. It flickered. Who are they? What do they want? Then it moved, just as she picked her head up. The faint red dot hesitated, then moved again, not off to the left or right, not across the gulf, but directly toward her.

It moved ever closer until she could make out a bumpy sphere, glowing only around the edges and an impenetrable black at the center, slowing down as it neared. She held her breath, oblivious to the sea, the sky, and someone grunting down the beach.

Thirty yards away it stopped dead still. She hardly breathed for five minutes, but the bubble didn't so much as shiver. A thought wormed its way from way at the back of her brain. They're watching me.

She took a few cautious steps up the beach. The bubble moved with her. She walked a little farther down the beach. It matched her pace, always maintaining the same distance. Again she stopped and faced it, ready as she could be to speak for the human race.

"Show yourself! Tell me why you're here."

It didn't move. She waited, but the sea, the wind, even the stars moved more than the lumpy black bubble with the red glow. Thea was getting angry with it, thinking show yourself.

Then she heard the loud, laughing voices coming across the mud at her. Ugly, drunken, Spanish *male* voices.

Getting closer.

For the first time in an hour, she took her eyes off whatever it was and saw two thick men, stumbling along with nothing better to do than cause trouble.

Dozens of muscles tensed through her body. Men: crude creatures that preferred brutality to tenderness, so driven by their swollen egos and grotesque members that they were more animal than human.

Speaking to males was something Thea avoided, and these disheveled creatures looked worse than most. Her constricted throat emitted only a gasp. It was just as well. She had no idea what to say. She looked back to the bubble.

"Look!" she finally shouted at them, pointing at the damnably still whatever.

Lopez and Soto probably would have been too busy stumbling along the beach to notice her in the minimal moonlight if she had just quietly sat there. They fell silent for a moment, then came toward her.

"*Hablas español, chiquita Americaca?*" Lopez laughed.

"Look, it's right there!" She dug out one of a few Spanish words she knew from high school. "*Aqui!*" and again she pointed.

For a moment, Soto looked as though he saw something out of the corner of his eye. But when he looked again, he apparently saw nothing over the Sea of Cortez.

They were shouting at her in Spanish. The girls were asleep and too far up the beach to hear. She could discern few familiar Spanish words, but *chingaderas Americacas* was clear enough, along with *chingado* this and that. Gradually, Thea got the idea they were ranting about filthy American tourists.

Thea had written the book about testosterone poisoning, her theory that men didn't mean to be hopelessly animalistic, that they just had a heavy overdose of a hormone that amplified aggression and a will to dominate.

She could have predicted they would start groping for her, as though she were not a sentient human with choice, but merely someone they could dominate physically.

"Keep your stinking male hands. . ."

They grabbed her from either side. None of her kicking and flailing could stop Lopez from knocking the breath out of her. She fell to the beach. Thea's little fists only made them laugh harder, and her kicks never found any testicles. They beat her first, and the pain grew with every blow. They ripped her shorts and designer tee shirt.

Each of them raped her. The only sound she could make was a faint, terrified whine. Then, mercifully, she passed out.

"*Sí*," Soto said as they walked peacefully away, hitching up their pants. "I guess she needed it pretty bad."

* * * * *

For this event, Yot was awake, if a little bleary-eyed.

"We're talking primitive," Xaq said.

Yot nodded. "This century's going to be . . . big fun. All the xufa you can eat."

"Of course," Xaq said, "we don't know that this happens every day."

Yot seemed not to hear. "Oh feco," he whined. "They stopped."

"You think that girl's all right?"

Yot was already stretching out as best he could on the bubble floor. "She got laid tonight. Did you?"

He was asleep before Xaq could answer.

CHAPTER 9

A small part of Thea Nikolas heard the tide edging up the beach. Part of her felt the gusts. Thea was parked at the indiscernible edge of consciousness, with only impressions of senses, crammed in a shell from which she wouldn't move. The moment she considered opening her eyes, a voice within ordered: *stay down, don't wake up, DON'T look at where you are, just rest, rest. . .*

So she did.

* * * * *

Loretta poked her head out of the nylon dome well before daybreak. She finished lacing her sneakers and searched out native beasties. She was off in the mystical pre-dawn light. Lyle was good for two more hours of sleep. *Sleep on honey, the meter's running, and your aura could use the charge.*

She scampered over the dune, welcoming the salt air into her nostrils. She found a spot near the advancing water, sat, shat, and buried her mound in the sand. Her load further lightened, she jogged up the beach. She let her feet splash through advancing wavelets and concentrated on her breathing. She soaked in the muted colors of the still-shapeless beach while she waited for the sunrise and chanted a mantra given to her just last month. "Uma doo doe, uma doo doe."

She could easily have missed the dim, unmoving form lying there alone, but the shape intrigued her. A pile of seaweed, she thought, maybe a big fish washed ashore or... No, it was human, that much she could see. A woman, small. *I should just let her sleep it off.* Not until she was standing over the figure did she make up her mind. In the still-gray light, the colors were indistinct. Loretta's nose provided more information than her eyes, but she didn't want to believe either. The woman on the beach was naked, smeared with blood and sand. She was unconscious.

Loretta's first reaction came from her stomach. That lasted a few seconds. Then she unzipped her white hooded sweatshirt, swabbed blood and mud from the woman's face and body. Her hands had a nurse's sure touch given her long experience cleaning up sick drunks. This task was simpler. Loretta watched for a reaction. The woman was still breathing, but her only facial movement was an occasional twitch of the left cheek.

Loretta summoned her best coo-to-the-customer voice. "You just lie still and rest, and we'll get you all cleaned up in no time. Let's get this spot over here, love. I've got you now, honey. You're okay with Loretta, I'm gonna take good care of you."

Thea summoned up a moment's consciousness to attempt a sigh of relief, a vague thanks, something. But it came out as just a moan.

Loretta tossed aside her once-white sweatshirt, now streaked red and brown. She reached carefully under Thea and lifted what she estimated as a hundred pounds of near dead weight. It was at least a quarter mile back to the campsite. It was times like this Loretta was glad she was a professional athlete.

Her feet crunched the sand in a steady rhythm.

She felt no response from the body over her shoulder. Loretta tromped down the beach, barechested save her crystal, and hauled Thea up over the dune to the camp-site. With one hand she opened the door of the convertible Thunderbird, shoved the back rest forward and deposited her cargo as neatly as she could in the back seat.

Loretta felt the soreness down her back and shoulder. She was panting as she marched back to the green nylon dome. The sharp hum of sliding tent zippers didn't stir Lyle, nor did Loretta's first shove. "Come on, lover boy, you're off the clock," she said, and gave his hairy mass a shove.

Lyle stopped in mid-snore and let out a little grunt. He rolled on his side and made another, similarly coherent noise.

"You're gonna have to get up, sweetheart," Loretta said. "We got us an emergency."

* * * * *

While they slept, Xaq and Yot were bombarded with impressions of early twenty-first century Earth. Xaq sampled CNN interviewing the rotund, eminently confident, cigar-puffing good old President of the United States, Harlan Clayton Vomper. He took in an analysis of the global issues of the day and scanned classified ads to see what people in this period wanted. The most coveted items were Chevys, accountants, counter help and bed buddies.

For his part, Yot digested collections of Bullwinkle, Groucho, and Stupid Pet Tricks. He had some trouble swallowing early twenty-first century technology, which he found funniest of all.

Xaq watched and followed quietly, invisibly, as

Loretta removed Thea to the Thunderbird back seat. Rej had said that they would come on a woman in difficulty, and to simply follow, and follow they would.

It's easy for a child of the fortieth century to think of Sol as just another star. Xaq and Yot had never before been within a hundred million miles of the nuclear fire that was the heart of the solar system. It was a huge and terrible thing that gushed heat and light. Sunglasses were meager protection against the energy that nearly plastered them to the sides of the bubble. They were blinded, blasted, and horrified.

"Let's go home," Xaq said.

"We'll get used to it."

"Do you believe that?"

"No, not really. Not completely. But we'll learn to live with it. Besides, I can't get us back. The time hole won't be open for almost a week, local time. How do they live with this feco?"

"They must get used to it," Xaq mumbled. "Can we get going?"

"I can barely see the controls. I can't . . . think in this heat."

They cruised over the Sonoran desert toward the city. They gaped with little to say about the bizarre saguaro cacti that characterize the region, noticing that even on this small planet, signs of human habitation were sparse. The hardy shrubs and spiny succulents just spread out as if no one had planted them at all, yet there was this free-flowing air, mountains that jutted up from the desert floor, also apparently random. After the artificial atmospheres they had known all their lives, these hundreds of kilometers of open space was something of a shock.

"Life just seems to spring from the planet all by itself." Xaq said.

Yot grunted. "I could never have imagined this. Okay, you win. Old Earth is poetry. Thanks for bringing me along.

CHAPTER 10

Before she opened an eye that morning, Andrea heard the insistent buzz of one hairy horsefly on the nylon tent dome over their heads. She felt the sun on her back. Her long arms and legs splayed across the tent floor, connecting with bodies here and there. Andi decided she wouldn't be badly hung over. She opened her eyes and rolled on her back, looking up at the fashionable shade of yellow-orange tent nylon brightened by the sun. A black shadow smaller than a dime crawled across the tent roof. Then, with another buzz, the shadow was gone.

Andi stretched her willowy arms as far as they would go, all the way out to her wiggling fingertips. She pointed her toes, stretched her legs, took a deep breath, and exhaled sharply. Then she relaxed and let the filtered sunlight wash over her. She guessed it was close to nine o'clock.

Andrea rolled her head to the right. Donna was there, tall and muscled, one arm draped over smaller, darker Joanne. Andi's mouth felt like a convoy had driven through it. She turned her head to the left. Thea wasn't there. "Shit." she said aloud.

Joanne stirred. "Would 'good morning?' be too much to ask?"

"Okay, good morning," Andi obliged. "Thea's not in here. She must be off by herself in our tent. I just hope she's not going to obsess all day about her red dot."

Donna stirred lightly, but slept on.

"Why don't you fix breakfast and wake her up with food and a kiss?"

"Yeah," Andi said. "But if the great Thea Nikolas is in one of her snits, food won't be enough." She pulled herself to her feet.

"That's okay," Joanne said, "as long as you make breakfast."

"You want your morning coffee served on a silver platter?"

"Sure," Joanne smiled. "Wouldn't you?"

Andi pulled on a pale green terrycloth shift. She zipped her way out of the school-bus colored tent.

It was getting warm. The flies, gnats, and mosquitoes were already about their daily raids, but a light breeze whispered through the brush and felt good. She stretched again, swatted at a mosquito, and walked over to her own smaller blue nylon dome. Tufts of thorny grasses slapped at her feet. Andi summoned her most sympathetic tone as she played a shorter song on these zippers. She pressed an understanding smile into place, prepared to weather Thea's mood, however stormy it might be. It took two to make a fight, and Andi wouldn't let it happen. She was prepared for any reaction. She didn't expect a tent full of nobody.

"Thea?" she said, pushing around the sleeping bags on the tent floor, expecting her lover to pop out at any minute. No one popped.

Andi twisted her lips to the side. "What the . . . ?" She backed out of the tent and surveyed the dunes, the beach, but saw no sign of her girlfriend. *No bathrooms, no structures here at all. Thea probably went to to do her business in the surf. She'd be back in a minute. I'll get the coffee started for her.*

She pushed a pile of twigs over last night's campfire and used a big kitchen match to ignite the kindling. The first match snapped as she struck it. The next caught, started a heated conversation with a crumpled wad of newspaper, and had the breakfast fire underway in a few minutes. Andi half-filled a big aluminum teapot with water. She stared into the flames thinking about nothing at all, clearing every notion from her consciousness, gathering the rest she had come to Mexico for.

A niggling little thought whispered from behind her ear: *She's not back. She's not here.*

She stood and surveyed the beach again. All she saw were the little terns running stiff-legged along the water's edge.

"The-aaaaaaa!" she called. "THEA!" The sound carried across the sand made of shattered shell bodies. Nothing came back.

The zippers squeaked their tune and emitted Joanne. The sudden noise sent a dozen flies scurrying to get airborne. "Where is she?"

Andi turned up her palms and shook her head. The water on the flame started a low rumble as it eased toward boiling. Both women were looking around the beach, a little nervously now. It was too damned quiet.

"The-A!" Andi's voice was cracking. She discovered her hands were trembling.

A voice came from inside the tent. "Are you playing Tarzan out there or what?" Donna had to stoop to step out of the dome in khaki shorts and a t-shirt that said "SISTER."

"Did she come back at all last night?" Donna asked.

"I thought so. Now I don't know."

Joanne cackled. "Maybe she disappeared with her little green men."

"She prefers little green women," Andi snapped.

Donna tried to change the tone. "She must have fallen asleep on the beach. Not a bad idea, except for the bugs. Let's reload our coffee and go find her." She grabbed the coffee jar out of a cardboard box while Joanne dug out the cups.

Andi scanned the open stretch of beach. She only grunted thanks when Joanne shoved the cup of coffee at her. *Had* something been out there last night?

Fifteen minutes later, they were headed down the beach in the direction Thea seemed to have taken. Donna loped ahead, scanning as she went. But it was the sound that caught her attention, an army of flies buzzing as happily as could be with a discarded white sweatshirt streaked with red and brown. She came to a dead stop a few paces away. It wasn't Thea's, she was pretty sure of that. She picked it up by a clean corner. Donna turned to Andi and Joanne, who started running when they saw her pick up the sweatshirt. The outraged flies whirled in a cloud, anxious for their meal to settle back down.

"Blood," Donna announced. She took a long minute to pick up the sweatshirt and its streaks of color. "Something happened here." She swallowed. "Something ugly."

The three of them formed a circle around the stinking garment that dangled from Donna's outstretched arm. None wanted to be the first to voice the thought that had crossed all their minds.

"That's not her shirt." Andi's voice was shaking.

Joanne looked at each of the others. "Is it her blood?"

"The-A!" Andi wailed.

CHAPTER 11

Elmo scratched his chin. He looked at seven columns of playing cards laid out on the screen. His fingers slid along the keyboard when he laid the nine of hearts to the ten of spades. That opened up a two of diamonds that went up to the ace row.

He could have been reviewing occupancy, making phone calls, checking the bills, ordering supplies. He could have inspected a few vacant rooms to check up on the how thoroughly the robots did their jobs. He could think about dinner. He should be back in his command console upstairs. But just now he turned up the eight of clubs and placed it on the nine. He played half a dozen hands with no success. His concentration stayed with suits and sequences.

The phone rang.

That was the job: long stretches of nothing to do, with constant interruptions.

The voice was a little thin, an elderly woman, but there was a firmness to the tone. "I want to talk to the owner."

"And so you are. I am Elmo Skinner, the owner and manager. How may I help you?"

"They keep calling me. In the middle of the blessed night they're calling me. I can't stand it any longer."

"Who's calling you, madam?"

"Them. *Them!*"

"Ah, them. Now I see."

"All kinds of crazy people. It has to stop."

Elmo took the receiver from his ear and looked at it. "Perhaps it does, madam. Why are you telling me this?"

"They're calling for your motel. Asking for Ben Whatley or Alice or Lorena somebody."

"Why would they do that?"

"Three, four in the morning, when a good Christian citizen is asleep."

"I'm sorry, ma'am. I don't know there's anything I can do about it."

"Change your phone number."

"Change my . . . ?"

Elmo was usually painfully polite. He suppressed a chuckle. "Madam, if there was a way I could help you, I would. But why on earth should I change my phone number?"

"Because your number is too much like mine," she said as though nothing could be more obvious.

"Ah. That's a little clearer."

"Now don't you laugh at me young man, or I'll file a complaint . . ."

"With whom madam? I think I finally understand your problem. But it's not against the law to run a motel. I even have a license for it."

"Get another phone number!" The sternness in her voice was cracking.

"That's really not possible, madam. It's more than a call to the phone company. We've had this number since the Lamp Post opened in 1970. It's not just one number—we own a sequence of six numbers, starting with this one. Our customers know this number. It's printed on our stationery, our bills, and our checks. It's in a big ad in the Yellow Pages. It's in motel databases all over the world. I can't change all that. But madam, I believe there is something *you* can do about it. Wouldn't it be ever so much simpler for you to change your number?"

He heard her breathing for a minute before answering. "I ain't in no fancy data bases or nothing. Still, I got folks what call me."

"Well of course you do."

"There's my sister Emily and my ex and..."

"Yes, but you could change that number." He was trying to be patient.

"That costs money, young man. I don't get money from people who haven't the decency to sleep in their homes in a decent family."

From outside came the thud of distant thunder.

Elmo found himself chuckling again. She was determined. How much could it be? Thirty dollars? A hundred? "Look, I don't want my motel to cause you a problem. If the Lamp Post Motel has been that much of a nuisance to you, *I'll* pay to change your number. Would that take care of it, Mrs. . . . .?"

"Well it might." She hesitated. "My name is Beaufort, with a T, Mary Beaufort. I can't afford no charges now."

Elmo reached in the drawer for a pencil. "Where do you live, Mrs. Beaufort?"

"If I tell you you're not gonna come around and bother me, are you?"

Elmo shook his bewildered head once more. "Of course not. Why would I want to do that?"

She volunteered the address. It was two blocks from the motel. "And the telephone number in question?"

"Oh, no you don't!"

"No I don't what?"

"You'll just keep calling me and making those

nasty noises on the telephone if I give you the number."

"Excuse me?"

"I'm not giving you no number so's you can be making nasty calls."

"Why on earth would I do that?"

"Why would *anyone* do that? But they do. Kicks."

"I'm sorry." Elmo glanced out the window. The sky was clouding up for a storm. "But how can I get the phone company to change your number if you won't tell me what it is?"

They went around for ten minutes, but made no further progress. Elmo heard the front door open, said he had to go, but that he could promise nothing without the phone number, and gratefully hung up.

* * * * *

A primer-painted Firebird rumbled in the carport before the engine sputtered and died. A small girl in her twenties stepped out of the driver's side. She had freckles across her nose and hair that lacked the conviction to be either blonde or brown. She wore a white sleeveless top that revealed a small tattoo of Rocky the Flying Squirrel halfway down her right breast, which Elmo spotted as she came around the back of the car. She waited for a second girl to climb out of the passenger seat. They looked like they might be sisters. They shared a flat, freckled nose and a conspiratorial giggle. What differentiated them was that the second carried a watermelon-laden belly, ripe, low and apparently ready yield up another member of the human race, perhaps momentarily. The pregnant one signed in for the both of them as Marla Shaefer, 2713

81

S. Frick, Tucson.

"Shouldn't you be near a hospital or something?" Elmo asked.

She smiled and wrinkled her nose. "I got lots of time yet. We're still gonna drive to Phoenix today."

"That's a long stretch from here to Phoenix. You sure you want to be incommunicado that long?"

"Piece of cake," Marla Shaefer said.

"Room 131," Elmo said. He had a sunny smile for the new life about to be. This foolish young thing has no idea of the gift she was about to receive, or how it would irrevocably change her life. She would have to learn like everybody else, over time. She will resent the imposition this new life has on hers. But she will come to treasure it. The girls rumbled off to park the Firebird and clattered up the stairs.

* * * * *

"Hey Lyle, you got a cigarette?"

Lyle took his left hand from the steering wheel and reached for his shirt pocket. "You don't smoke."

"Once in a while I do. Now are you giving me that cigarette, or do I summon the goddess to deal with your impudence?"

She grabbed the pack of Winstons, shoved the Thunderbird's lighter deep into its hole and held it there. When she felt it pop out, she shoved it back in for a few more seconds. She misjudged the length of the cigarette and bent the tip, but managed to get it lit.

"Take it easy, we'll get there. We've got a couple of hours to go."

"Can't you go any faster?"

"What, on the reservation? The tribal police just

82

love nailing white speeders. I got a friend picked up three tickets in one afternoon. If I keep it at sixty-five they won't pay us no mind."

"I can't be responsible for your friend's bad karma. We're on a mercy mission." Loretta was puffing hard, but not inhaling. She looked back at her still unconscious passenger and realized the air conditioner was blowing smoke all through the car. She leaned to her window, opened it an inch, held her cigarette just inside and puffed toward the crack, letting the air stream suck out the smoke.

"Loretta?"

"What?"

"How'd we get through the border so easy?"

She blew another stream of smoke out the window before she allowed a little smile. "Good karma."

"Sure," Lyle said. "Anything else?"

"I know the guards."

"Oh."

Lyle checked the mirror, looked as far ahead as he could, and eased the accelerator down another notch. "I don't suppose you know the tribal police?"

She held a puff in her mouth, then poured it out the window. "Not all of them."

From the back seat, Thea groaned long and low, lolled her head to one side, and groaned again.

Loretta instantly flipped the cigarette out the window and scrambled over the seat back. She took Thea's head in her hands and stroked her black hair. "You'll be okay, Honey. Loretta's going to take care of you."

Thea's breathing strengthened. She lifted her head long enough to feel a sore spot at the back of her skull. She took a deeper breath, and another, and cracked her eyelids open. She flinched at the light, but Loretta's face was inches in front of her.

Loretta pressed her cheek to Thea's and whispered, "Now you take it nice and easy honey, but come on and wake up for a little while, won't you?"

Thea whimpered. The touch of the soft cheek drew her nearer.

"Nice and slow, baby, just open up those eyes a little more." She didn't have a fever, at least not much of one. "Loretta's going to get you to a hospital, and you'll be all fixed up before you know it."

Thea's whimpering increased to a plea. She managed to push out a word: "No."

"What is it, honey? Can you tell Loretta?"

The eyes didn't appear to have any focus. The whimpers became little groans as she edged toward more words.

Loretta held her lightly in her arms, waiting for the sounds to coalesce into language.

"N . . . no . . . no . . . No hos . . . no hos . . " She labored for another consonant. "No hos-p . . . hosp . . . ."

Loretta watched Thea's eyes dart like a desperate animal's. "No hospital? Baby, you're hurt. I think you'll be all right, but you need a doctor right away."

The whimpers escalated to cries. "No! No hosp . . . " She still couldn't find the end of the word.

"Honey, in your condition we haven't got much choice."

"N-no. W . . . wo . . . womon. Womon do . . . womon doc . . ."

"You want a . . . ?"

"Wo . . . wo-mon."

"Now if that doesn't beat the stars and planets."

The sound of the road and the air conditioner

drowned out the faint sounds from the back seat. Lyle looked back for a minute. "She gonna be all right?"

Thea's eyes landed on the hulking male thing peering over the seat. A low wail came from deep within her and grew to a high but still soft pitch before it faded and she went limp.

"Oh Jesus, Lyle, what'd you go and do that for?"

"Do what?"

"You scared her something awful. Did you see her face when she saw you?"

"Christ, I'm sorry," he said, and drove on.

Over and behind the Thunderbird, a bubble from two thousand years in the future floated along, invisible to the eye, although a few of the Tohono O'odham tribe looked up, feeling the presence of something damned odd.

CHAPTER 12

From the sandy ground, the tent stakes came up easier than conversation. The three women had fallen into the work of breaking camp. Andi released the fiberglass rod from its catch at the bottom of the tent and slid it out of the long nylon sleeve. With a key rod of the skeleton removed, the dome collapsed in slow motion. Andi concentrated on pulling apart the joints in the fiberglass rod, separating it into packable three-foot sections. She squinted at the sunlight through big round glasses, her pale brown hair hanging straight down to the middle of her long neck.

Joanne wrapped the food and tucked it neatly into the open spaces she created in the ice chest. There was plenty of food left. They had planned to stay another day, but after a long search that failed to turn up Thea, neither Mexico nor the beach held any further attraction for them. None of them knew the local area enough to begin to know whom to contact—other than the policia, who Thea had sternly ruled out. If they thought remaining would have done the slightest good, they would have, but they felt empty of options.

Donna worked on the other tent, striving for maximum efficiency. Quick and neat, wrapping the tent poles together, sliding them next to the aluminum stakes in their nylon carry bag, Donna was racing the clock, even if there was no clock for miles. She grabbed a sleeping bag by its foot and jammed it down into its stuff bag. Alternately tucking and rotating, she had the first sleeping bag packed in less than two minutes, the second one in a minute forty-five. She swept the bags and tent into her arms and walked with long, steady strides to the open trunk of the Volvo waiting to stow their equipment, their supplies, their abbreviated beach vacation.

The three of them formed an outward-facing triangle as they went about the chores, their backs to the soiled sweatshirt on the ground near the burntout campfire. They paid it no more attention than they did the pulse of the sea, the wavelets that rose and crashed and withdrew.

"We should look for her once more," Andi said when they were ready to leave.

"Where else can we look?" Joanne asked. It was her car, so she took the wheel. Donna took the back seat for herself where she had room to stretch out her legs. As Andi climbed into the passenger seat, she made another scan of the beach, half expecting to find Thea standing on top of a sand dune and laughing at her own marvelous joke.

"We should wait for her. She could come back to find us." Andi pulled at her fingers. One knuckle cracked. "We're not supposed to leave 'till tomorrow. We can't *leave* her here." She stopped suddenly. She didn't want to cry again.

Donna leaned in toward the front seat and looked out the windshield toward the sky. "Do you think she did see something last night?"

Joanne put the key into the ignition. "Yeah. Either that, or she had a heterobreeder moment, ran off with some *man*, and is at this moment halfway to happily ever after."

Donna rapped Joanne on the arm. "That was uncalled for. Andi's in pain here. I suppose it's pos-

87

sible Thea did see something."

"It is possible, damnit," Andi snapped.

Joanne dropped her eyes down to Andi's lap. "I'm sorry. But I find it a little hard to believe." She looked up at Andi. "And I'm scared."

"We're all scared," Donna said. "We've been avoiding it all morning. So let's say she did see something. We all saw the sky looking peculiar. But then what? You think she was abducted by aliens or something?"

"I don't know what I think," Andi said. "Maybe . . ." She looked around for an explanation and found none. "Maybe she'll be back any minute. Or in a few hours."

"Or weeks or months, for all we know," Joanne moaned.

"Jo, you could try to help," Donna snapped. She looked at Andi. "But that's possible too. Who's to say how long she could be gone?"

Joanne had another shot left. "I think there's plenty enough human nastiness out there without worrying about monsters from space."

The first tear rolled down Andi's ruddy cheek. "Yeah." She sobbed uncontrollably. "What does it mean?"

"What does *what* mean?" Donna asked. "The red whatcamacalit we didn't see?"

"No," Joanne said, taking Andi's hand. "The blood."

Andi nodded, sniffed, and fell into Joanne's arms. Joanne had spread enough bile that she now made an effort to comfort Andi.

"Great," Donna smirked from the back seat. "Thea's gone a few hours and you're already moving in on my woman."

Andi could laugh at that, momentarily halting the flow of tears.

"She could have been kidnapped," Joanne said. "I've heard it's happened down in the interior, but usually not this close to the border. Kidnappers could make a splash holding Thea Nikolas."

"They might let her go," Andi pleaded. "Maybe I should stay in town looking while you two go home to Tucson."

Donna tried to calm the situation. "How much Spanish do you speak? Ten words or so? Who could you ask? Isn't it still possible something else to her?"

"Like what?" Joanne asked. "That goddamn sweatshirt means *some*thing."

Donna wrinkled her brow in thought. "We don't know that for sure. It's possible it's got nothing to do with Thea. The tide was out way too far to drag her out. Maybe she's just lost, went the wrong direction and just can't find us. Did you see anybody else on the beach last night?"

"We weren't paying a hell of a lot of attention," Joanne admitted.

Andi was crying again, quietly. "Why didn't I stay with her?"

"We have a plastic garbage bag, don't we?" Donna asked Joanne.

"Down by your feet."

Donna fumbled for the bag before she opened the back door and stepped out. She trotted to the sweatshirt, wrapped the bag around it to pick it up, and carried it back to the car. "Maybe we ought to take a good look at this thing."

"What size is it?" Andi asked.

"The label says medium." She held the shirt in front of her. "It's too big for a woman's medium. It's

89

probably a man's shirt."

Andi's sobs grew a little louder.

"It looks reasonably new. You know, it's . . . it's a little stretched out on the chest. Whoever was wearing it carries a lot more chest than Thea."

"Does that really mean anything?" Joanne cautioned. "Are we being prejudiced thinking a woman is less dangerous than a man?"

Andi wanted to talk. "Sure we're prejudiced. But we're probably right."

"Why don't we take this to the local police and . . ."

"No!" Andi heard herself shout.

Donna gave Andi a curious look. "Well, we've got to report it."

"The hell we do," Andi said. "You know how hard the Mexican police would laugh if we told them Thea Nikolas turned up missing? I don't even want to tell American cops. They'll probably say she got what was coming to her."

"Don't you intend to tell *anybody*?" Donna said.

"No. No fucking police. Thea made that clear enough. They're all such macho bastards anyway."

"Yeah, most of them are men," Joanne injected. "But we have to report her missing to . . ."

"Why?" Andi said. "I'm the closest thing she has to next of kin. There's nobody else that needs to know right away." Her voice dropped to soft and hopeful. "Maybe she'll turn up."

"When are you two due back at Stanford?" Joanne asked.

"Not till next week," Andi said.

"Ought to be a hell of a week," Joanne said.

Donna put a hand on Andi's shoulder. "Hey, you don't want to go back to the Holiday Inn all alone.

Why don't you spend the rest of the week at our house?"

Andrea looked into Donna's motherly brown eyes. The corners of her mouth turned up ever so slightly. "I'd like that," she whispered.

Joanne took a softer tone. "Can we go home now?"

Andi nodded.

"If you're not going to report this to the police, how are you going to find her?"

Andi slouched and buckled her seat belt. "How the hell do I know?"

Neither of the other two women answered. They drove the five hours to Tucson in silence.

* * * * *

Usually Loretta smiled when she passed the Kitt Peak observatory. She liked to think about people who spent their lives studying the sky, unraveling the universe with not even a passing thought for the personal destinies tied to the rotating constellations of the zodiac. Today a scowl slashed Loretta's face. Today the big white triangular solar scope on the desert mountain only reminded her that they were still more than an hour out of Tucson.

Thea was conscious for a few minutes. Her murmurs were only a little less vague, and just as insistent that she not be taken to a hospital, something dreadful about hospitals, about people poking things at her. Loretta sat her up and got her to drink a little water, when she felt the knot on the back of Thea's head. She wondered why she hadn't noticed it before. A concussion, probably. They sat in the back seat, Thea's head lying on Loretta's breast, her eyes open.

Loretta saw a wounded puppy looking up at her, then turning away, looking off into space with the eyes of a terrified cat.

Who are you? Loretta wanted to ask. *What happened to you? What is so awful that it can terrify you so? How can I help?* But she waited. In a few minutes Thea was peacefully asleep. Loretta waited ten minutes before she climbed into the front seat.

Lyle lit a cigarette, cracked open the window, and offered Loretta a drag. "When we reach town we can take a left on Mission Road up to St. Mary's Hospital."

"No."

"That's the nearest one," he said.

"Nope."

"Should I stay on Ajo through town to Kino Hospital?"

"Lyle, she refuses to go to a hospital. She's scared to death of them."

He took his eyes off the road and looked at her over the rim of his reflective sunglasses. "She's what?"

"That's all she's been talking about back there. Nothing else. I think I've got to do what she says."

Lyle pushed the glasses up his nose and looked back at the long black roadway ahead. "So whatcha gonna do, take her back to the Lamp Post Motel and nurse her yourself?"

Loretta's eyes darted around the car. What else could she do? After a moment she looked Lyle in the eye.

"I might." She took the cigarette from his hand, took a mouthful of smoke and blew it right out. "I just might."

CHAPTER 13

No natural light ever penetrated Elmo's video fortress. He watched the storm clouds retreat on his western surveillance camera. He looked in on the new couple in 114. The man was sitting at the undersized dining table in his underwear. His pen hovered over a stack of paper. The woman was nowhere to be seen. At the bottom of the screen: Howard Robinson, Tucson, 114. 4th visit, no notables.

Elmo tapped into 127, rented to a Nigel Riverton of San Antonio. No one was in the room. He tried Julio Gomez in 136, who was asleep—alone. Robert Humphries in 138 was watching television. No one was in 140 but a TV blaring that this was the question for the big money. Elmo tuned it out. No luck in 144. Usually reliable 122 was vacant.

Elmo scratched his cheek, pulled off his glasses and polished the lenses with an optical cloth he kept neatly folded on a corner of his console. He returned the cloth, replaced the glasses, scratched his chin.

Retrieve top 5 list 8/08

In three-quarters of a second, a list of current customers and their histories at the Lamp Post splayed across the screen.

Elmo opted for a shorter session. Tucker had a history of being entertaining. Tucker had been to the Lamp Post eighteen times, recorded seven times, scored above 25 overall points six of those times. Reliable. Always scored well in intensity. Elmo called for the disk recording from 138 on 8/3/08. He bent down to a cabinet door down by his feet, extracted a bottle of Glenlivet and a small glass tumbler. He poured one finger of Scotch and set the bottle down beside the glass.

Elmo snagged the glass, stretched his shoulders, pushed back in the chair and parked his feet on the edge of the console. He took the lightest sip, letting a few drops of smoldering, smoky liquor skip across his tongue. The second sip was a little longer, and the little fire in the alcohol pleasantly burned his mouth and throat.

Jay Tucker's ass filled the screen. It was a hairy, muscular sort of ass, with a pair of thighs that suggested extended time in the Nautilus room. He was flexing with an as-yet-unseen partner.

"God, I love muscles." The voice was thin. Elmo figured it was propelled by minimal brainpower. "You in those muscle shows?"

Tucker shook what Elmo took to be his 25-year old head. "The only place I compete," he said, stepping forward and opening the screen to the room, while gesturing outward with his arms, "is the bedroom."

She was a little blonde thing, maybe all of seventeen. Maybe not, from her acne count. Otherwise, she wore a sheet over her thighs, still exposing a tuft of hair that, while light, was decidedly not blonde. She flashed an innocent smile, turned her head and nubile bosom away for a second, then turned back to stare straight at the dong that was still not visible from Elmo's camera angle. She chewed on the tip of her index finger. "Show me."

Elmo lifted the glass to his lips and shot down the rest of the Scotch. He savored that, then poured himself two fingers more.

"It's not the size of the wand that makes the

magic," Tucker snapped.

Elmo's monitor flashed: PHRASE RECUR-RENCE 315.

* * * * *

Even at midday, Phil Stein's Beer Bar is a dim island of cool with no windows to admit light or heat. At the back, just to the side of Phil's office, was Elmo's booth, isolated from the customer's view. Today Elmo and Phil shared a late lunch.

"Business looks good in here," Elmo said.

Phil was short, his head bald with a white longish fringe. He had a generous middle and a fat man's satisfied smile. "Pretty good, thanks God. Wait, this is early in the week. Friday, Saturday, it's a mess in here. They use this booth to try to sneak in a little nookie. Sometimes more than just a little."

"You ever watch them?" Elmo said. He hoped it sounded casual.

"What for? I tell them go next door and get a room. I just sell them mood. You sell the setting, and Loretta finishes the deal."

Elmo nodded. "Customers who come for sex just use sheets and towels. Junkies clog up my toilets with needles. I'll take a philanderer over some twerp who carves his name in my furniture. Then I have the bastards who say they're going to stay another day, just to squeeze a few extra hours out of my room."

Phil raised his beer glass. "So how come you're in a business with so many people if you don't like people so much?" Phil, too, hoped this sounded casual.

"They come and go. The good customers go about their business. I never see them once they check

95

in. I just deal with the leftovers who need someone to dump on."

"Two *meshugena* businesses we got here."

Elmo allowed a mild smile. "Three when you count your dirty books."

"Dirty books. *Dirty* books? What are you talking dirty? Kissing, a little bit nookie, that's dirty?" Phil was letting himself get revved up. "Killing people, dropping bombs—hell, dropping airplanes on people—that's what's dirty. Hating somebody for not being the same as you—that's filthy.

"You heard about the *meshugena* president?" Phil puffed up his chest, pushed out his lower lip as far as it would go, and mimicked Harlan Clayton Vomper. "Poornography is at the rooooot . . . of the eeevils that exist in our soooooooo-ci-e-ty. So we gonna puuuull up that eeevil . . . by the ramblin, ragin roots . . . and weeed it out of good, God-loving Amerca!" Phil dropped the mock presidential demeanor and looked Elmo in the eye. "Now that's a schmuck."

With a little assistance from the beer, Elmo was chuckling. Elmo had voted for Harlan Vomper. He probably would again.

Phil was reddening, gathering steam. "The government, they're gonna tell me what I sell is dirty? I got pictures of people doing something that makes them feel good. It's such a crime to show people feeling good? *Chob em in drerd*—to hell with them. Oh, but what if children see it, isn't that awful? So what do kids look at? They sit in front of tv, changing channels so they can watch sixteen people murdered every hour. Knives, guns, laser beams, teeth, all kinds of *chaleras*. That's what the call good clean fun— *meshugenas* killing people. Very nice. People showing how they care about each other, people making life, that's dirty. Very smart."

"Take it easy, Phil. I'm just asking how's business."

Phil laughed. "It's all right. Sex is a good business."

The subtleties of sexual commerce might have continued but for the din of somebody outside leaning on a car horn.

"Everybody's in such a hurry," Phil said.

Even from the back of the bar, they heard the door burst open. *"Elmo?"* a woman's voice blared. "Hey Elmo, you in here?" High heels came clattering up to the rear booth in seconds. Before Elmo could turn around, Loretta was standing just inches in front of him. She was pulling on her fingers. "Elmo, where the hell . . ."

Phil shushed her. "We can hear you. Sit down."

"No time," Loretta gasped.

Elmo knew Loretta could be a little excitable. For more than two years he had seen her almost every day, exhilarated, exhausted, and exasperated. But there was an urgency in her voice he'd never heard before. Words tumbled from her in a torrent until she ran out of breath, her unmistakable chest heaving right in front of Phil Stein's open mouth.

"Look at you," Phil said. "You look terrible. You're shaking all over."

Loretta brought her tone down to a loud whisper, while her panting slowed. She told them about body on the beach, a girl raped, drifting in and out of consciousness, but she won't go to a hospital and she will have only a *woman* doctor and who is she anyway?

Elmo sighed. "I sure don't know." He took her hand and pulled himself out of the booth and into the

97

late afternoon sun. "Doc Perkins should still be up in 132. Come on, we'll call her."

They trotted around sparkling puddles in the parking lot, into the motel office. Elmo stepped behind the convex curved counter and jabbed at the telephone. He tapped his foot while the phone rang repeatedly. "We might be, uh, disturbing her."

Loretta was unwrapping a stick of gum. "She'll get over it. This girl might not."

"Well, what's this stuff about not taking her to a hosp . . ." He broke off and addressed himself to the undressed doctor upstairs. "Dr. Perkins? I'm really very sorry to disturb you, but we have an emergency . . ."

"I was so *close,* damnit," she shouted into the phone.

"I am sorry."

"Okay, I heard you the first time. Can I have a few minutes to get myself together?"

"Of course, but it is urgent. A young woman was beat up and probably raped."

"And not even a full moon. All right, I'm on my way. In the office?"

"No, go down to Loretta's room, 116—end of the downstairs row nearest the street."

"About ten minutes," she said, and hung up.

CHAPTER 14

Davis-Monthan Air Force Base is America's aircraft boneyard. Thousands of warplanes that once ruled the skies were now broken hulks lounging on the desert floor, too tattered to fly, too venerable for scrap, parked in the dry desert air where they wouldn't rust. They spent a quiet retirement in Southern Arizona, row upon soldiers' row, stretching for miles along Kolb and Golf Links Roads, just around the corner from the Lamp Post Motel.

During the deepest Cold War chill from 1963 to 1986, Davis-Monthan was headquarters to a ring of eighteen Titan II missiles around Tucson. Each 103-foot missile was sheathed in its own concrete and steel silos, dug into the desert and hardened to resist anything short of a direct nuclear strike. Each Titan II carried multiple warheads. Each warhead had its own target, and each was a blast at some classified number of megatons that would obliterate a whole city.

In an unexpected flash of human wisdom, arms reductions treaties in 1972 and 1979 doomed the already-obsolete missiles, with a mere 10,000 nuclear weapons allowed to each side. The United States of America says it has 9960 warheads, 5760 of which are deployed and in position to attack someone.

Pilots still train for desert warfare over hundreds of square miles of Southern Arizona gunnery ranges in the clearest skies in America. But once Soviet Communists ceased to be the enemy, the base and its strategic mission became as irrelevant as the rows of retired and mostly rust-free warplanes.

Major Melvin Putnam felt irrelevant this afternoon. Once he had ripped through the skies at dizzying speed. Now he watched a man who watched another man watching a radar scanner. Putnam watched the clock too, but today the calendar had his eye. He hated August, not just for the damnable heat or the freak storms, but the memory of that miserable Tuesday afternoon, out of fuel and out of luck, when he tried to ditch his F-22 in Reid Park and bail out, killing a mother and child. He had bailed out into a zoo and half a dozen inquiries. They had frozen him at captain for five years before promoting him. But even now they kept him well away from the cutting edge of national security.

"Sir, there's something strange on my screen."

Putnam didn't look up from a crossword puzzle. "What's that, son?"

"Well, the radar graphic display is giving me a text message."

Putnam frowned. "The screen doesn't have text. Just circles and dots."

"Yes, sir." Big blond-brushed Sergeant Lancaster stammered. "I mean no, sir. I mean yes, I know it's just supposed to show circles and dots. But somehow random letters are popping up on the screen." He turned back to the console. "Look, sir, there's even more of them now."

Putnam took four steps to the console and looked. His head jolted back. A sentence was scrolling on the radar screen, away from everything else. A few more letters faded into place, one every second until it spelled out a message:

Scan west on infrared.

Putnam looked at the sergeant. "So why don't

you, Lancaster?"

"Yes sir." Lancaster started to turn away. He spun his head, facing his pocked young skin at Putnam. "Then you saw it." He bit his lip. "How did it get there, sir?"

"I don't know, Lancaster. Maybe it's a message from God. Or the President."

"Or some dork hacker in the computer room, sir?"

Putnam stroked his neck against the grain of the growing stubble. "Check it out when you get a chance, would you, sergeant?"

"Yessuh," Lancaster said. On the console, he flipped a red toggle switch. A status screen reported: scanning infrared. Instantly a blip appeared about forty miles away.

"Why isn't that on radar, sergeant?"

"It may be too low or too small, sir." Lancaster switched back to radar, adjusting the sensitivity to smaller objects and scanning lower along the horizon. A tiny blip appeared, heading for them at five miles a minute. "It must be pouring out hellacious infrared for the scanner to catch it."

"Get a look at it from the satellite overhead."

He looked at every foot in the target zone, which was growing uncomfortably close. "Nothing on the screen, sir. It looks to be about ten feet across, but it's invisible to the bird. Sir..." The sergeant swallowed before he finished. "I think we have us a UFO."

Putnam whistled. "Well I'll be dipped in shit."

"It's coming toward us, sir." Lancaster said.

Putnam stiffened. He snatched the red phone. "Get me Colonel Dayton. It's urgent."

Lancaster had a tremor in his voice. "Slowing down—looks like about a mile north of the base."

The colonel grunted. Putnam could picture him picking up the phone with his left eye closed. "It's been a perfectly good day so far, major. You wouldn't want to ruin it for me, would you?"

Putnam wanted to sound authoritative, but there was a quaver in his voice as well. "Sir, we've got an unidentified flying object, coming almost directly toward us."

"Then I suggest you identify it," the colonel sounded ready to chomp on a cigar. "Is there anything you can identify?"

"It's a moving spot of infrared with no visible source. It's been coming toward us at 112 miles per hour, now about stopped a mile north of the base boundary."

"Hmmmmmm," was all Dayton said.

Putnam couldn't tell if it was a skeptical or agreeable hum.

"Why don't you be a good lad and keep an eye on it for me? But do let's keep this to ourselves for now, don't you think?"

"It's gone," Lancaster announced.

"Best forgotten," Colonel Dayton said as he hung up.

* * * * *

Elmo retreated to his command center with a mug of black, sugarless coffee. He ignored the mostly blank screens of the rooms at midday, and gave scant attention to the pool and parking lot surveillance system. He spun the swivel chair to his keyboard and clicked on LP MANAGE DAILY. Numbers danced into place, summarizing yesterday's transactions. Elmo scanned the totals for room rent, sales tax (currently at eighteen per cent and threatening to climb), telephone charges, miscellaneous income and vending machines.

Elmo was something of a fanatic about vending machine income. Phil Stein once told him, "I think maybe you're the only man on Earth that reports every last nickel. That's uncounted cash in there 'till you *count* it. So you can push away a little for yourself and count the rest. If you report fifty per cent of it, the government thinks you're doing them a favor."

"But that wouldn't be an accurate count." Elmo had shivered at the thought. He did count and account for every cent—from three soda machines, a snack machine, a hot popcorn machine and, in the laundry room, a washer, dryer and an old condom vending machine that now saw little use except as a novelty item.

"No, schmuck, you got free money in your pocket," Phil said.

"It would contaminate my data. How can I assess performance without accurate data?"

"Free money, Elmo. Is that such a bad thing?"

The argument never went anywhere. Neither could see where the other's point of view had any relevance.

Twenty-two rooms rented last night, fifty-five per cent occupancy, nearly forty local and six long distance calls and a moderate take in vending. Not bad for a Monday night in the second worst month of the year, when anyone who can afford to leave Tucson's 108 degrees, does, while everybody else sits at home wishing they could. Afternoon rentals were higher than usual, but in August more people checked in early for the air conditioning.

Elmo assembled the day's take down to the last

cent, wrapped it in an electronic bundle, and transferred the funds into his account. The process took him twelve seconds. Back in his clerking days, Zorn' spent the better part of an hour with the drive to the bank.

He scanned the records of Augusts past for comparisons. But records from two years ago, before AIDS faded away, were no longer a fair basis for comparison. Still, performance was well above last year when DETOX was new and word hadn't yet gotten out about how good old-fashioned lust was an excellent booster for the biologically-engineered cure-all.

August usually meant higher electric bills for the air conditioning and lower gas bills while the pool heater was on hiatus. The linen bill was up, but that reflected the higher occupancy. At fifty-eight per cent, this August looked good for a weak month.

The rooms were still quiet. One couple was checking in, and might be worth checking out. Nothing was happening at the back of the building. The front monitor picked up a brief flash that just caught his eye. He saw the thunderheads rolling in from southeast. The massive flat-bottomed clouds towered into monstrous twenty thousand foot tufts, mocking the 8,666-foot Rincon Mountains below. Another lightning bolt flashed on the screen, this one much closer. He typed one word on the computer console: DOWN. The machine responded by immediately cutting power to the audio/video system and stepping into low-power triple-surge-protected mode before the thunderclap shuddered the Lamp Post.

Elmo shoved his chair backwards and emerged from the throne room through the rear office to the reception desk. Out the picture window, a pair of dust devils twisted around each other in a lewd dance, spewing dirt and debris. Odd, he thought, two dust devils at once. It could be a nasty storm this time.

In fact, the vortexes were caused by a sudden change in atmospheric heat from the infrared emitted by an invisible ball that settled gently on the roof of the Lamp Post Motel.

* * * * *

They sat in the bubble, speechless, frozen, and afraid to move their eyes. None of the thousands of magimages Xaq had seen of Earth quite caught the flavor of sitting atop the Lamp Post Motel.

Approaching Tucson, they had been startled by how the hundreds of miles of desert yielded first to scattered dwellings, then to clusters of box houses spread inefficiently all across the desert, and finally to the density and towers of the city. Having spent all their lives in meticulously planned artificial environments, they gaped uncomprehendingly at the lack of clear boundaries between the countryside and the Tucson metro.

From the air, the highway patterns were obvious. Ribbons of pavement, woven fabric of urban streets that were almost everywhere. Mountains jutted into the landscape with no apparent plan to where these towers of rock appeared. Over the city itself, Xaq and Yot looked but could not comprehend the function of large patches of green grass with a diamond etched in dirt. At the center of the city, clearly manmade mountains appeared, not as imposing perhaps as the natural slopes, but with touches that even Xaq and Yot would agree contained a germ of artistic talent. They passed over the sprawling University of Arizona campus that had more of the coherent construction values they understood from home, with red brick buildings jammed into a small space, broken up by an enigmatic concrete bowl around a grassy field with a grid carefully marked off in ten-meter sections. Next to that was another of those grass fields with the dirt diamond, and alongside it was a copper dome surrounded by ramps, apparently for people to come and go from whatever took place inside.

Nothing prepared them for being out with open sky over these apparently uncoordinated constructions. At the motel itself, they came in closer and sampled the trailer trash flavor known to every airman at any base: used car lots and mechanics, bars and pizza joints, a former bowling alley converted to a Voojoo temple. Cars streamed out of the base, making the midday traffic on Craycroft Road a perpetual rumble punctuated by screeching rubber. They saw people occasionally, but these sealed vehicles seemed to dominate the city, naturally adapted to the roads on which they traveled. Just a kilometer south of the Lamp Post was another sudden large expanse with long gray strips and sparse buildings, then a few enormous buildings. Aircraft of all sizes came and went here.

The neighborhood immediately surrounding the motel was a monument to cinder block and its sad sister, slump block. Half the land was asphalt ribbon for noxious chugging automobiles. A halo of black power lines encircled the motel. But the horizon was sawed with the mountains of a raw old Earth where miles-high pieces of land interrupted the desert plain. In between was a city, a squat sea of one-story flat roofs they could scan from high atop the second floor. For this, they had just crossed two thousand years and more than a billion and a half kilometers.

Viewed from the fortieth century, weather had seemed like a minor topic for study. But the curious little man-made structures were trifles compared to what unfolded across fifty miles of desert sky. Just minutes ago, the sky had been a canopy of unbroken blue. Suddenly clouds invaded from the southeast, a great puffy flotilla that blotted out the scorching sun. In the miles of sky over Tucson, the clouds massed for attack. First they dropped virga—a curtain of ethereal gray, trailing tendrils of rain that evaporated before they reached the ground. Dragging from the clouds' bellies was a darker column of opaque gray rain. Most startling was raw electricity surrounding the downpour, a dance company of lightning in virtuoso performance. Its bass line thundered through the valley as fair warning to all in its path. On the leading edge of the storm, winds slapped at the dry desert and kicked dust everywhere. One gust rocked the invisible bubble hovering over the roof of the Lamp Post Motel.

Xaq expected to find semi-civilized behavior and quaint customs. He had not expected to be awed. But he gaped at the massive sky, eyes almost bulging. "A natural, breathable atmosphere. It's fantastic."

Yot nodded and pointed to a large, menacing mass of gray clouds rolling across the Air Force base. "It's coming this way. I don't think we want to be up here in the middle of that. Can we get inside?" He didn't wait for an answer, but took the invisible bubble down between three palm trees that shielded them from the street, and the pool wall that hid them from the motel. He raised his eyebrows, hoping that after an hour in the period costume, he might feel more comfortable. Coarse leather loafers chafed his ankles. He was swimming in his tee shirt, but the shorts kept tugging against him. Yot grasped the handle of his twentieth century attaché case. "Let's check in on Mother Earth. Lead on."

Xaq took a deep breath and stepped on Earthen soil. He thought he should make some clever speech or remark, but suddenly big, wet globules were dropping from the sky. They heard it first, the splattering on the asphalt. Then little bombs of water detonated into pint-sized drops on their skin and this odd clothing. With a gust of wind, more of the fat raindrops came to join their friends. The students of the fortieth century university did what the primitives of this era would do: they ran for cover. Into the Lamp Post Motel.

CHAPTER 15

Elmo saw them approaching the door and stepped up to his concave side of the curved counter. "Good afternoon," he said through plastic lips. "It looks like you just beat the storm. Can I help you?"

Xaq had not yet spoken to one of these creatures. He fumbled for the plastic card lost somewhere in his ill-fitting shorts. Yot, left looking around the office, felt compelled to speak.

"Ho, innkeeper, can we take shelter for this week?"

Elmo couldn't begin to place the accent. "That's what we're here for."

Xaq found the plastic blue card and laid it on the counter upside down. He looked at Yot, who was looking anywhere in the office except at the innkeeper.

Elmo nodded and smiled as he slipped the card through a magstripe reader. On the screen in front of him instantly flashed:

Ring Industries
James A. Zachary
8423 Sunset Blvd.
Los Angeles, Ca 90152
Enter amount:

A cursor blinked patiently, awaiting the input. Below it from the Lamp Post databank:

No previous history.

No outstanding debt.

"Shall I authorize you for a week's stay, Mr. Zachary?" Elmo liked getting a week's rent in one fat lump. He punched the amount into the keyboard, the console asked the bank's computer, which replied with authorization BF0048 and transferred $300 into the Lamp Post account.

Rej was right on the money about the card's magical qualities in this culture. Yot tapped his foot. He examined the microwave popcorn machine.

Rain started slamming at the windows. A thunderbolt very close by rattled the building and sent Yot two inches off the asphalt tile floor.

"The storm is early today," Elmo said. "You just beat it."

"Could we have a room near the front? We'd like to see the street and the pool."

Elmo peered at both of them. He read their quirky, out-of-place appearance as gay, and he had no interest in watching them. Better to keep the camera rooms for the one-nighters. His console spit out an imprinted Global Express slip. "Sign here please," he said, holding out a cheap black pen. "Room 126, a few steps to your left at the top of the stairs right outside the door. Dial nine on the phone for a local line, eight for long distance, zero to call the office. And let us know if there's anything we can do to help you." He handed back a magnetic room card and the Global Express card.

Yot turned toward the window. The pounding had slowed.

"I suggest you get up to your room while the storm takes a break. They come and go quickly, and they can be pretty potent."

"Ho, let's go," Yot said, pushing for the door.

"Thank you," Elmo said. "I'm here should you need anything."

"We will . . . remember that," Yot said, backing toward the door.

Odd accent, Elmo thought. Then he lost the thought and burrowed back into his command center.

* * * * *

Room 126 had two double beds with faded blue bedspreads, a desk and small dresser swathed in genuine artificial wood grain formica, a phone, a sink and mirror facing into the room. The serviceable bathroom had a molded fiberglass shower and tub with brown cigarette burns etched in, matching the four cigarette holes in the heavy commercial purplish-brown carpet.

The room faced south, looking over the pool and past the palms across the Air Force base, and finally to the Santa Rita Mountains closing off the end of the valley twenty miles away.

Xaq sat on the edge of his bed, looking out the big window, watching the storm thin out, leaving thin veils of virga and dropping a shaft of lightning just to show it still meant business.

"Nobody makes that happen," he said. "A natural atmosphere, out of control." Across the base, another lightning bolt punctuated his thought. "It's enormous. How much power do you suppose is in that storm?"

Yot was too deep in his computer to hear.

"You want something to eat?"

"Why don't you go . . . get something?" Yot mumbled.

"Like what?"

"How in perzidia should I know?" Yot pulled his head away from the screen. "I've never been here before. You're the fecing cultural expert here. What are the staples of an Earth diet in the twenty-first century?"

"Hamburgers, pizza, and beer."

"Sounds like something from the . . . Horsehead Nebula."

Having soaked in contemporary American television, Xaq already wanted to try the burgers.

"Anything. Just go get it." Yot turned back to the screen, oblivious to all else.

Xaq shrugged. He snagged the room key, shuffled out the door and listened to his loafers clatter down the stairs. He looked around at the motel from ground level. The air was thick and humid after the storm, but it smelled clean.

Now what? He had no idea of distances or places. They hadn't surveyed the neighborhood. He didn't trust himself navigating the bubble. The cars whizzed past. Operating one of them might be worse yet. Yot could do it. After a few minutes Yot could be in control. Xaq had no such facility with equipment. Uncomfortable loafers or not, he walked.

He walked north on Craycroft, past Stein's Beer Bar and his Hard Core Store, across 29th Street past the tire shop that did most of its business in sexy spoke hubcaps. Xaq ogled this primitive world with its touch of the precocious. His eye caught an icon he recognized from months of scanning twenty-first century media. Four feet tall at curbside, it stood with a cameo in gleaming red and white plastic, of two bearded, bespectacled men shaking hands and the letters he found so comfortingly familiar: Kentucky Freud Chicken.

He staggered toward the sign just as a car came slashing out of the parking lot, took a bounce in a pothole that sent a wave of water into the air, a fascinating geometric pattern, Xaq observed. One second later, that wave of water crashed into Xaq. Water drenched his face, his eyes, his hair, plastered the tee shirt to his skin, and filled his shoes. Xaq sputtered. He heard the cackling laughter before the car roared away. Xaq looked over his shoulder at his fleeing tormentor. "Primitives," he mumbled. Xaq wiped his face with his hands and dragged his sore, soaked feet into the fast food stand.

Inside, chairs and tables were tranquilizing hot pink plastic, with occasional stripes of midnight blue for contrast. Above the counter the two menus glowed. On the left was listed Colonel's Pride, and the old-fashioned buckets of barbecued breasts and thighs and secret herbs and spices. To the right were Doctor's Orders, chicken toppings, thiamint potatoes, and for desert, benzedrookies, vali-yummies and DETOX ice cream.

Beneath the sign was an artificial blonde with facial eruptions. Her head tilted to the left as her jaw mashed a wad of gum. Xaq saw her breathing through her mouth, and slowed his speech accordingly.

"How much do I buy for two people?"

She never broke the rhythm of her chew to speak. "Bucket of ten. What you want on top?"

"What's your favorite?" he ventured.

She stopped chewing long enough to giggle. "I like the niacinnamon with the benzedrookies for desert."

113

Xaq tried another angle. "What do your customers like most?"

"They like the calciyummy topping, ribofries on the side. And vali-yummies for desert."

"I'll have two of each."

She smiled at him. "Coming right up!" Her voice almost squeaked.

"Hey, man." At his side was a dark young man wearing a tank top, exposing his muscled arms, illustrated with an eagle on his right shoulder and a heart with the scrolled legend Irma on his left forearm. "Hey, man, you're all wet."

"Thanks. I know."

A chuckle rumbled around the man's chest. He ordered a small bucket and two dozen vali-yummies.

"I'm sorry sir," the little blonde thing said, "no more than a dozen valiyummies to a customer."

The man nodded. At the same time his head bobbed sideways. "Okay, man."

She disappeared for a moment, and returned with a large white paper bag. "Here's your order, sir," she said to Xaq. "That's $23.19 with tax."

Xaq knew he hadn't ordered tacks, but maybe they were tasty. He reached into his pocket, pulled out the magic green card, and handed it to her with a smile.

Her eyebrows gathered for a conference. Her mouth turned down. "What's this?"

"A Global Express card, isn't it?"

Her head wagged. Her jaw went back to the gum. "We can't accept this, sir."

"What's wrong?"

She would have just kept shaking her head, but the confusion on his face of this soaking boy made her giggle.

"We only take cash here, sir. No credit cards."

"Why not? I thought these things were good for everything." Xaq shuffled his soaking feet in the puddle he had created.

A thick man with graying hair stepped in from behind the girl. "Something wrong here, fella?"

"I just wanted to pay for . . ."

"You heard the lady, Mac. No credit cards." His voice sounded like it was being dragged across gravel.

The card sat patiently in his hand. "Then what do I do with this?"

The manager crossed his arms and laughed once through his nose. "You really want me to tell you?"

"Of course."

The manager resisted his best instinct, softened by Xaq's confused innocence at being set up. "Look, Mac, we take cash."

"Why do you call me that? My name's not Mac."

"You want I should call you asshole instead?"

"I don't think so."

"Okay, here's what you do. You go out that door there, take that fancy credit card down to the bank just up at 22nd Street and you ask them for a cash advance. Then you come back here, pay us in cold cash, and we'll give you your food. You think you got that, Mac?"

"Why does it have to be cold?"

"Hey, Bud, we'll keep it warm for you, okay?"

"No, I mean the cash. Why does it have to be cold?"

"Get outta here," the manager growled.

Xaq dragged himself back down Craycroft, his feet aching from sloshing around in the wet shoes. He pulled himself up the stairs and touched his magkey to the door of 126.

115

Yot was in precisely the same position as when Xaq had left. Reluctantly, he looked up. "Where's the foo . . . Feco, what happened to you?"

"I needed cash."

"You're all wet."

"Why does everybody keep telling me that?"

"Maybe because . . . you are?"

"Thanks." Xaq pulled the soaking shoes from his feet and threw across the room. "What the hell are you doing with that computer?"

"Testing out the utilities Rej put on the hard drive. You won't believe it."

"Try me."

"I can move . . . minds."

"How's that?"

"Well, I started by tracing the circuits through the building. It's incredible! That little guy behind the desk downstairs has circuits going all over the place, audio and video hookups in eight rooms, and he watches them carning. Then he's got a central computer that must be pretty respectable for this time, and connections to web sites for messages. I left him a note and signed your name."

"Terrific," Xaq said sourly. "What's that got to do with minds?"

"I was testing out the . . . utilities. That one traced the circuit patterns. Another one's even better. I can reduce a conscious mind to its electronic patterns."

"Huh?"

"And transport it, man, transport it! Don't you see?"

"Not entirely."

"With this computer I can take somebody's mind and move it into somebody else."

116

"I heard they were messing with that on Antares," Xaq said. "It's illegal."

"So when did that ever . . . bother a guy like Rej?"

Xaq laughed. "What are you going to do with it?"

"You're the one that's got to write a fecing equivocation. You want to study this culture? Then study that little snoop downstairs when we give him the . . . ride of his life."

CHAPTER 16

Elmo was at the front desk when the shot rang out.

It came from upstairs, from inside, just a few rooms away. He started for the stairway, but before he reached it, the door to 112 came flying open. A tiny young woman with a baby in her arms rushed out screaming something in Spanish, pointing up, her eyes frozen wide.

Elmo darted from around the desk and out the glass door to meet them in the parking lot. "Are you hurt?" He hunted for a Spanish word. *"Dolor?"* No one appeared hurt, but language was useless. Elmo stepped up to them and awkwardly put his arms around them, shielding the baby with his body from the explosive terrors that had propelled them from room 112.

Elmo's eyes were wet. Some of it was perspiration.

Doors around the motel started opening as rubberneckers peeked out. Then the door opened from 134, directly above 112, and a scrawny, shirtless young man in torn jeans wobbled out on the balcony. It was Stone, the same one he had thrown out of 126 yesterday. He had the pistol in his hand.

"Hey, I'm sorry man," he slurred at the parking lot. He grabbed the rail, but continued swaying.

Elmo gestured toward the office. "Please go inside." He said, hoping his body language and tone would communicate. He opened the glass door and gestured them in, then held out a hand that said wait.

Doc Perkins stuck her head out the door to room 103, just next to the office. Elmo shouted over to her, "Would you take the woman and her child into the office where they'll be safe?"

Perkins nodded.

Elmo pulled a remote control unit out of his pocket and dispatched a robot to 134. He bounded across the parking lot to the steel stairway, took three stairs at a time and swung around to face the man down the balcony. His eyes could have burned a hole in the youth.

"Man, I was just cleaning it and it . . ." he mumbled.

It's dangerous, Elmo thought before advancing. He saw his robot roll at Stone from the opposite direction, creating just enough of a distraction. He kept his hands in the open, and moved in with quick gliding steps while Stone was still wavering. With each step he kept watching the gun barrel and the youth's unfocused eyes. The robot rolled toward Stone as well. Gently, as non-threateningly as he could, Elmo eased up to his loaded customer and slipped the gun out of his hand. With a single motion Elmo tucked this unclean weapon into his pocket.

"I was cleaning it, man. I didn't mean nothing." Stone barely kept from toppling over. His eyes never quite focused.

Elmo felt his heart pounding in his temples. "Asshole! You damn near killed a mother and her baby. What the hell are you doing anywhere near a gun in that condition?" He blew hard out his nose.

"What condition, man?" He managed to reach out for the wall and keep his feet. "Hey, ain'tcha gonna gimmee back my gun?"

119

Elmo took a deep breath. His fists tightened, but he stood his ground. "Not a chance. Now get in that room," he said through clenched teeth, "before somebody hurts you. Somebody besides yourself."

The befuddled Stone tumbled back through his doorway.

Elmo remained on the second-floor walkway, his heart hammering. He stood with his eyes closed and took three deep breaths, then looked down at where the woman and girl had been standing with him in the parking lot.

Elmo was standing in front of a vacant room, 135. He was shaking as he reached in his pocket and withdrew the master magkey, touched it to the lock, and opened the door. He called the police from the room phone and reported the incident. Elmo punched a code into the phone that reached into his computer, electronically locking the door to 134. Then he sat on the bed. For two minutes Elmo just bawled from fear, anger and relief.

A few minutes later, his eyes dry, he came slowly down the stairs. The woman looked Mexican. She was seated on the couch, the baby still snuffling on her shoulder. Elmo put a hand on her arm. "Are you all right now?" She understood his tone if not his words, and nodded. "Uno momento," he said, and signaled for a robot. The machine rolled into the office from the next-door storage room.

Doc was washing her hands at the sink at the back of the room. "They're okay, just understandably shaken up. The bullet came through the ceiling and missed the headboard. Missed them by two lousy feet." She dried her hands on some paper towels. "Now if you don't mind, Elmo, someone's waiting for me in my room."

"Thank you," Elmo said.

"That didn't look like you up there on the balcony," Doc Perkins said. "You looked like some movie tough guy."

Elmo shook his head. "Purely an illusion, I assure you."

He turned to the frightened woman and her child. "The machine will translate for us," he said.

"La maquina va a traducir para nosotros," the robot repeated.

The woman looked surprised, then impressed. She started talking quickly, and the machine flawlessly reproduced her speech to English. "Juanita has been cranky all day. Then she got overtired and couldn't fall asleep. I sang to her, I rocked her the best I could sitting on the bed, for half an hour before she finally fell asleep. I held her for another minute, then I put her down in the middle of the bed. And that is when . . ."

"She's asleep now," Elmo whispered. "Your Juanita has a sweet little face."

As much to his tone as the translation, she smiled and looked away. "She will be a beauty. No man will dare to betray her." She was slight, barely over a hundred pounds. Her skin was the characteristic Mexican brown, but high cheekbones and sharp eyes suggested Indian genes. "She comes from beauty." Elmo was surprised at his own words.

After the few seconds for the translation, she took in a sharp little breath of surprise. With her face turned down, she looked up at him and said, *"Me llamo Carmen."*

"Welcome to the Lamp Post Motel, Carmen. I am Elmo Skinner, the owner and manager here. I apologize for your difficulty. The police will be here any minute to put him in jail. But to see some damn . . . some fool endanger a mother and child . . ." His face reddened. "I can't . . ."

"*Gracias*" needed no translation, but the robot supplied it nonetheless. "Did you lose your . . . ?"

The short WHOORP of a police siren interrupted.

Juanita stirred on her mother's shoulder, but settled back to sleep.

"You'll need to tell the police what happened." He held out his hand.

Carmen smiled, took the hand, and let Elmo lift her to her feet, baby and all.

* * * * *

Elmo was grateful when the police pulled away with their suspect handcuffed in the white Dodge. The police had been reasonably prompt, always courteous, usually helpful whenever he called. But nothing, certainly not millions of dollars, could remove the bitter taste of his encounter with the police in that same parking lot six years ago. Was it already so long? It seemed at times like yesterday. And at other times like a lifetime ago.

Carmen looked up at him. "You were very brave," came the robot translation.

"He belongs in jail," Elmo said.

"I feel you had saved my life—our lives."

Elmo shook his head and started toward the office. "I didn't. I'm not really very good at saving lives."

He let Carmen and the baby and the robot follow him. He opened 103. "You won't have to stay in that room. I'd like you to use this one tonight, and tomorrow, with my compliments." This room had two beds, and, unlike 112, no bullet holes in the ceiling or bedding. Otherwise it had the same utilitarian desk and chairs and the small round table found in every other room. It offered an excellent view of the stairway. It also had the first little black and white camera Elmo had installed, which he could use to see that Carmen and Juanita were safe. "The robot will bring your possessions from the other room."

"*Gracias*," she said. She stretched up to kiss him. He leaned down and woodenly offered his cheek. "Can I thank you with a drink when your work is through?"

"Thank you, but now is not a good time. I'm terribly busy." He wasn't. In the hour since the shooting began, not a single customer had checked in at the Lamp Post Motel. "Busy place, you know."

The baby on Carmen's shoulder lifted her head and grabbed for the lock of Carmen's hair dangling in front of her face. Carmen laughed. "It looks like I have work too. I will be here."

Elmo's feet shuffled on the carpet. "Yes, you'll be all right here." He abruptly turned and walked the few steps to the office. The automatic closer paused before thumping the door shut behind him.

* * * * *

Thea Nikolas floated up toward the surface of consciousness. Once more a voice from within implored her not to go out there. But she had been shut down long enough. She wanted to step out of the haze. Her body wanted to be up and running again.

She had a fuzzy picture of being in the back of a car, but what came screeching at her memory was the crystalline image of these two brutal creatures, abusing her in every way she could imagine, and in a

123

few more she hadn't. Her mouth tasted like shit.

She forced her eyes open. The first thing she saw was a ceiling with a soft, artificial texture that would dampen noise. She was in a bed, in a room of cheap generic, formica-clad furniture. She looked at the modular sink and mirror at the other end of the room and the small bathroom space alongside it. She recognized the generic motel layout. This isn't a hospital!

She heard a slice of a whisper from behind the door. That woman—is she one of those voices? This isn't a hospital! If a woman comes through that door, she might survive this. She has been abused and humiliated. No one can know, NO ONE. They can't know. Can't, won't, mustn't. Especially her friends. They, above all, could not know the depths of her degradation.

Whatever they're saying out there, it's not Spanish, and this isn't Mexico. She sat up in the bed, slowly, feeling a little dizzy when she rose. On the desk across the room, the phone sat on a directory. The black letters along the spine said Tucson. She was back in America, or as close to America as Tucson could claim to be. There was nothing else noteworthy in her surroundings. She noted some pathetically cheap imitation of art on the wall, a Spanish galleon in fluorescent colors. A big blank television was bolted to the wall in front of her.

A lavender diaphanous fabric was fastened to the walls and ceiling around the room, giving the space a wispy look. A small bookshelf on the wall to Thea's left held volumes on numerology, pyramid power, Marilyn Monroe, palmistry, a Buckminster Fuller text that defied classification, and volumes of Freud and Jung. Next to the astrology text was a Deirdre Mardon romance, *A Touch of Madness*, and beside that a study of numerology. The dressing area was littered with jewel-faceted bottles of perfumes, creams and powders, with cubicles for cotton swabs, cotton balls, a variety of tissues, brushes, eye shadow swabs, a dozen lipsticks and a five-gallon drum of brilliant red-orange hair tint. Crystals of all shapes and sizes dangled in front of the three-sided mirror where they could catch the light of the mini-stage floodlamps. It looked to Thea like a supermarket-rack dream of a woman desperate to impress a man with artifice to compensate for a lack of character. It reminded her of *Ultrafemme*, a book she and Andi had giggled over a few months ago.

Andi! What must she be doing? What could she be thinking? Andi wouldn't call the police. Would she? No doubt Andi would be wondering what happened to her.

Well, what did happen to me? That bubble, just hanging there. What was it doing? Where the hell am I? Why?

She was feeling a little dizzy. She let her head sink back to the pillow. She felt around her body, re-alizing for the first time that she was naked. Clean, at least, of the shit and blood. Her mouth still had that remnants of that fecal flavor, but it felt like the woman had been thorough enough to clean her mouth, at least some. She looked over at the sink and wondered if she could make it. Her head ached, her legs and arms felt bruised. Her vagina, her entire bottom had a burn-ing soreness from the creatures and their loathsome battering rams.

No, she wouldn't make it to the sink, and even if she could, she wasn't sure she could negotiate her way around all those bottles and vials.

She heard someone reaching for the door, closed her eyes and braced herself.

A mask, she thought, making her face as blank as she could.

CHAPTER 17

Dr. Dolores Perkins was a fiftyish, lumpy woman with a casual thatch of grey-streaked black hair falling into her eyes, which were shielded with jet pilot frame glasses. She had just adjusted her clothing as she knocked on the door to room 116.

Loretta recognized her as a frequent flyer in the Lamp Post's waterbed and the owner of the Jaguar with the medical stickers on the window. She directed the doctor to the patient tucked neatly in bed, lifting her head at the sound of the door. Their eyes met. Doc saw a focused mind in those big brown eyes she felt scanning her less-than-professional loose shirt, blue jeans and sandals. She didn't know how to regard the decidedly casual attire.

"Who are you?" Thea asked.

"The medical help you asked for."

"You're a doctor?" the patient blurted.

"That's what they all say."

"I hope they're right," the bedridden woman said with a hint of a smile.

"Me too, honey."

"You look . . . informal."

"Oh this stuff? Well old Elmo, the manager, he sort of *interrupted* me, don't you know. I was really just minding my own business. Now how about we have a look at you?" Doc stepped to the edge of the bed and sat.

Loretta was sitting in a chair across the room, pulling at her fingers. Doc turned to her. "How about

126

you soak us a washcloth in hot water?"

The patient's voice croaked. "I don't know why she's bothering with me. But she's been doing a hell of a job."

Loretta smiled from across the room. "You're welcome, honey. The name's Loretta, and this is home, the Lamp Post Motel."

"We're not in Mexico?"

Loretta smiled. "Worse. Tucson, Arizona, home of saguaros in the sunset, rodeo riders and godawful summer heat."

Doc noted the bruises on the patient's face, the knot at the back of her skull. She pulled back the covers to examine the rest of her body. Mostly there were scratches and contusions on her arms and legs. But her entire lower abdomen was inflamed from hundreds of indelicate jabs. "That must hurt."

"Definitely."

Loretta lay the warm cloth on Thea's forehead. Thea touched her arm and smiled. "Thanks," she whispered.

Doc walked to the phone and called 132. "Be a love, and fetch my bag out of the car and bring it to 116, would you? No, don't go home, Larry. I'm just giving you a few minutes to recharge." She came back to the bedside. "You can call me Doc. And I'll bet my Uncle Arnold's suspenders you've got a name too."

"My name is . . . Terry. Terry . . . Norwood." It was better than her own name, and close enough.

Doc raised her eyebrows. "You're sure now?"

The patient smiled a little. "Pretty sure. I work in a bookstore in Palo Alto. Near Stanford."

"Well Terry Norwood," Doc said, sitting her lumpy body back on the bed, "maybe you can tell us what happened to you."

127

She told them of two drunken, slovenly beasts hooting and wailing as they battered her again and again. She told how she gagged, and for all she spit, she could not remove the sewage from her tongue and teeth, and each time she spit they slapped her and fed her more, all while they thrust up inside her, on and on, reaching to try to take part of her away.

She stopped to cry. Doc held her. "It's over now."

Loretta disappeared for a minute, and emerged from the bathroom with a red toothbrush, a tube of Crest, a chipped blue coffee cup and a towel.

The patient's eyes widened when she saw Loretta's cargo. "Please, help me to the sink." Doc steadied her as she slipped to the edge of the bed and slowly stood up. "Why won't the damned room hold steady?" She eased herself back on the bed. "This might be a little harder than I thought."

Loretta brought her dental office to the bed. She sat down and squeezed from the bottom of the tube, and the gleaming white paste oozed on to the brush.

"Terry Norwood" managed a slightly dazed smile and took the brush, thrust it into her mouth, and scrubbed her teeth, the roof of her mouth, all under her tongue, almost back to where her tonsils once were. She scrubbed in there for five minutes before Loretta suggested she rinse with the cup. She spat the residue into the towel, sipped the water and spat that back. She stretched her newly liberated mouth, opening wide, letting the air flow.

"Again, please," she said. She took the brush a little less frantically, but brushed happily, feeling the taste that had plagued her finally rid from her body.

When she was finished, she sat up against the headboard and took several deep breaths through her newly-cleansed mouth. She lolled back her head, closed her eyes, and the sound came from the back of her throat, up across her unchained tongue, across teeth that felt like they sparkled, through lips curled into a smile.

The sound was: "Aaaaaaaaaaaahh."

* * * * *

Doc Perkins wandered back past the front desk a few minutes later. She found Elmo sitting behind the big, battered oak desk, surrounded by a banker's lamp with a green glass shade, the main telephone set, a marble block with six pens in six holes, and a single pad of memo paper. He was typing instructions into the terminal beside the desk. Doc seated herself on the couch facing him, and sank in a bit too deeply.

"She's going to live?" Elmo asked without taking his eyes from the screen.

"No question about it," Doc said. "But living might not be much fun for her for a while."

"How's that?"

"Elmo, she's been raped, beaten, and humiliated. From what Loretta tells me, I'd say she's been in shock for most of the day, but she was coherent by the time I got to her. She's on edge. Lots of lacerations and contusions, her whole pubic area . . ."

"Let's skip the gore, Doc."

"Okay," she smiled. "Physically she'll be all right, although it will take her a few days. Emotional healing could take quite a bit longer. She says her name is Terry Norwood, although she didn't sound convinced. She's got this anger toward men. Doesn't like them one bit. After what happened to her last night, I can't say I blame her. But I get the feeling this isn't just an emotional reaction. Seems like she's been like this quite a while, which makes being raped all the more traumatic."

"And that's why she won't go to a hospital? Because of the men?"

"I think that's part of the reason. She also talked about being poked and prodded an awful lot. Hospitals do that all too well."

Elmo put his hands on the desktop. "So what do I have to do about her?"

"Not much." Doc struggled to pull herself to her feet. "Loretta seems to have her under control. Your best bet is to stay out of sight and help her out when she needs it."

Elmo frowned. "She's that bad about men? I should stay out of sight at my own motel? I suppose you're going to run this place?"

Doc walked to the sink, turned on the hot water and lathered her hands. "She appears to be just about that bad. You don't have to hide from her. But don't talk to her, at least until she's had some time to get over this."

"You're sounding more like a shrink than a doctor."

"That goes with the territory these days." She dried her hands on three paper towels, wadded the towels into a ball and shot it over Elmo's head toward the wastebasket.

Elmo dropped the errant wad into the basket. "Can I ask you a question?"

"That's all you've been doing so far." She walked to the sturdier sofa arm and half-leaned, half-sat on that.

"How come a doctor's got so much time to play around?"

Doc laughed. "The doctoring business ain't all

130

it used to be. What with DETOX and all, people don't turn up sick very much anymore. Of course, there's two things they still need us for."

Elmo's eyebrows raised to a question mark.

"Well, there's injury. It's kept me busy enough this afternoon. And then there's the other thing that DETOX won't fix. The mind. Every doctor who expects to survive in medicine had better become more of a counselor and psychologist. Only the most obvious of this Terry Norwood's injuries are physical. Most of the damage is up here. But that's my specialty these days."

"So that doesn't keep you busy?"

"Not in August. The heat drives people out of town. I'm on vacation myself."

Elmo leaned his head to the side. "So why aren't you in La Jolla or San Francisco?"

"I found myself a young Adonis. With Larry, the Lamp Post Motel is vacation enough for me." She stood up. "And I don't dare keep him waiting another minute. He might snort up all the coke." She giggled and was gone.

CHAPTER 18

Elmo sat alone at his desk. He listened. No phone was ringing, no customer was asking for assistance, no one checking in at the front desk. Silence was the worst sound a business can have. But after a day like this, silence suggested the Lamp Post Motel was reasonably, if only for the moment, at peace.

The peace was broken soon enough by a roaring V-8 contained in a vintage silver Corvette. Elmo estimated it was a 1965. Through the passenger window he saw a perfectly painted blonde woman who looked thoroughly delectable and completely bored. The driver popped out, a superbly coifed specimen, tall, wearing a coat and tie in 107 degree heat. He pushed the glass door aside, not letting it break his stride, wearing a salesman's smile. "How about a room today?"

"Of course. Is there a room you would prefer?" Elmo took the offered credit card and fed it to the magstripe reader.

"Oh, something away from traffic. Maybe around the back."

The screen spat out the data:

Howard K. Carpenter
9524 E. Calle Glorietta
Tucson, AZ 85753

Enter amount:

Elmo looked up at Howard K. Carpenter. "Will this be one night, or a longer stay?"

Previous history: Noted
No outstanding debt.

Elmo asked for the notes.

8 occasions, 3 observations rated 6.2, 4.6, 5.5. various partners, some vocal.

"A few hours ought to suit me fine," Carpenter said.

Elmo punched in the one-day double room rate.

"Room 144, Mr. Carpenter." Elmo handed him a magkey and donned a smile of his own. *Score me a seven today*, Carpenter. "Have a pleasant stay."

Send customer summaries to main console, he typed. It did.

Elmo was headed for his command post when he saw a telephone line light up. His own voice answered the call, heard the caller ask for the nightly rate, quoted the rate and asked for a reservation date. Elmo watched the screen as it accepted the reservation data: Anthony Scroggins, previous stays: 3, none observed.

"Good night, Elmo," he said to the computer. The machine went through its security routine, locking out Elmo's private files and updating the data accumulated during the day.

"Good night, Elmo," his recorded voice responded.

A marching band tuned up in his stomach. Eating was a chore. He didn't feel like dealing with the restaurant hubbub or sitting in his room or dirtying his console with take-out.

Carmen. She would be hungry. Maybe a nicer restaurant with some quiet. The woman didn't even speak English. He had a pocket computer that could translate, but without voice synthesis they'd be passing the stupid little machine back and forth all night. Why the hell is she even here? Why would I even want dinner with someone who stays at the Lamp Post? That's all I need is getting involved with a desperate foreigner I can't even talk to.

So he walked across the street to the pizza and ribs joint and chewed on the respectably tender pork. He sat and ate in a formica booth in the corner, as far as he could get from the stream of delivery kids shooting in and out the door, the flow of people picking up their pepperonis, and the teen-agers smoking cigarettes and cursing the video games. Howard Carpenter, who had just checked into 144, sat near the counter until his jumbo mushroom and pepperoni materialized. He waited for Carpenter to leave before he wiped the barbecue sauce from his hands and chin, dashed back across the street, briefly greeted his night clerk, and sealed himself in the command center.

The only sound in the room was the soft and steady hum of fans cooling the equipment. He sunk into the gray tufted swivel chair and listened to the whirring clear the knots in his head, pushing aside the picture of Carmen with the baby on her shoulder, the bag of bones too stoned to hold a gun without firing it, and some strange woman who was terrified of men.

He sighed before he leaned forward in the chair and rolled toward the keyboard. Occupancy was   holding at fifty-two per cent, not bad for

August, three per cent ahead of last year. Year-to-date occupancy was close to seventy per cent, but from July through November that average would drop. At least it had in past years. DETOX and passion might bring up the numbers.

The room monitors showed no carnal activity. DeGregorio in 114 was making a phone call. The passion suite, 122, was unoccupied. So was 127. Still too early in the evening for much action. Carpenter and the perfectly painted blonde were attacking their pizza. So it went, down the line.

He decided to check his online communities. His clocked on The Saddle, were he logged on as Dan and headed for the message section. One message was waiting:

> **From: Arbidor**
> **To: DAN**
> **Subject: WATCHING**
>
> ***So you like to watch. You like the safety of detachment. But there is something infinitely more satisfying than just watching, and I have the magic to make it happen. Just ask, Elmo old buddy.***

Elmo swallowed hard, while fear crept up from his gut. His privacy seemed to be ripped away. He always thought nobody on any of these sites ever knew his real name. He was almost willing to forget that first message, but damn, there it was again. Instead of replying to the message, he logged off. Elmo clocked on a site for local programmers were he was Marcus. Marcus had a message waiting:

135

FROM: *
   TO: MARCUS
   RE: REMINDER

You are supposed to leave a message for Arbidor, remember old buddy?

Elmo didn't even log off of the system, just disconnected from the Internet. He was disgusted. Biting his lip, he tried again at Naked Truth. There he found a new message to "Squire:"

Really now, Elmo, you must give this a try. It is designed just for you. Arbidor is waiting.

Again he broke the connection. This time he logged off of his Internet connection and to his Lamp Post Motel desktop. He found his eyes darting all around, until the words crawled across the screen:

You really can't avoid me forever you know.

CHAPTER 19

Thea jumped at the knock. She had been lulled by the TV, lost in the classic American mindlessness of screeching tires and thundering hooves, chasing bad guys and snatching cosmetically-enhanced women from the jaws of distress. She never watched television much. Now she knew why. Its stultifying stupidity, the manufactured distress, the boring villains and more boring cops aimed squarely at those with minimal brain function. Still, watching dulled the pain alarm clanging through her nervous system. That would be the pills kicking in, too. But the knock at the door still nearly brought her off the bed.

"Oh, relax honey, it's just the pizza guy." Loretta took three barefoot strides to the door, snagging her purse along the way, and opened it just wide enough to slip outside.

She greeted the delivery man with lots of teeth and the western twang she assumed when doing business. "Well aren't you just the sweetest thing, hauling that mess of food all the way across the street. You been busy?" She passed him a twenty.

The chunky kid with straight blond hair shrugged. "Not bad for August, I guess."

"Yeah, business slows down over here too." She took the pizza from his hands and planted a big, red smooch on his cheek. "If somebody needs a little service, you send 'em over, y'hear?"

He reached in his pocket for change.

She patted his hand, still in his pocket. "Don't

137

bother with that."

The delivery boy's toothy grin matched hers. "Sure. Sure lady, I'll send 'em over."

"The name's Loretta, honey. Loretta Lipps." She wrapped her right arm around the pizza box and brushed his pants with her left. "There's no telling what kind of tip you might get if you sent a little business my way."

If the boy smiled any wider, he might have cracked his jaw. "Sure Loretta. You bet. Hey, real nice to meet you Loretta." He took off, giggling.

"Any time, friend," she smiled after him. She opened the turquoise door, held the pizza high, and closed the door behind her with a foot. "I'm a firm believer in advertising." She swung the box down to the bed with a flourish and flipped up the lid. "Dinner, humble though it may be, is served." Pungent steam rose from the box, carrying with it the tug of a mass of garlic in tomato, set ablaze by jalapeño pepper and onion. "Interesting choice you made there, Terry."

"It's popular in San Francisco these days," Thea said.

"What isn't?" Loretta ducked back into her kitchenette for a few paper plates. "Did it increase breath mint sales too?"

"Probably." Thea chuckled, but the pain cut short any laughter.

Loretta put the biggest slice on a plate and handed it to Thea. "We'll get some real food when you're on your feet. But your body's going to need some fuel to get mending, so eat up."

Thea bit hard. She welcomed the jalapeño, garlic and onion up her nose, searing her mouth, hoping it would burn off the top, tainted layer of skin and leave virgin tissue behind.

"That's powerful stuff," Loretta muttered through her burning mouth.

Thea chewed. "The jalapeño does feel good. When we get out, I'd go for Thai food."

"Don't rush it. Doc Perkins says you stay in that bed for forty-eight hours, and forty-eight hours it'll be." Loretta realized she was lecturing a woman several years older than herself and dropped the schoolmarmish tone. "Till then I'll make you as comfortable as I can. What were you doing down there in Mexico?"

Thea relished the next mouthful before she replied. "Just taking a weekend on the beach with some friends."

"Some friends?"

Thea took another bite of pizza.

"Don't tell me. You had a fight. About some guy?"

Thea snarled. "My friends take no interest in guys."

"Well it's a cinch you don't. How about we tell these friends you're alive?"

Thea chewed and shook her head.

"You don't mean some little fight is going to . . ."

"It's not about a fight."

"What then?"

Thea was more comfortable eating. "I just don't want . . . I can't tell them . . . that I was . . ." She dropped the plate on the bed. "I'm sorry, it's just too much. They can't know."

"Not even that you're alive? Tell them you fell asleep, that you fell in love and ran off with a little green man—or a little green *woman*—from Mars."

"That's probably what they think. That's what we were fighting about. They didn't see the little red globe."

139

Around a chunk of pizza, Loretta said, "Huh?"

"Well there was this peculiar wrinkling, a warped patch of the southwestern sky that lasted close to an hour."

"I saw that." Loretta said. "Yeah, it was strange. Wiggly or something."

Thea snapped alert. "Did you see the little red ball it left behind?"

"No," Loretta said cautiously, "but I didn't watch it for more than a minute or two. Sure spooked a coyote out there."

"Something was there," Thea said. "It was faint. None of my friends saw it, but I watched it. It came toward me. And followed me I think . . ."

"You're not telling me you were raped by . . ."

"No," Thea said. "Just your basic Terrestrial low life. This was the Mexican variety. A pair of the grisliest, dirtiest bastards I ever saw, stinking of sweat, booze, blood and who knows what else. I tried to point out the red bubble. It was all I could think about. It was a bad idea." Thea looked down at the pizza that was mostly devoured.

"Oh," Loretta said in a small voice. "I'm so sorry." She put a hand on Thea's cheek.

"You have nothing to be sorry for. I'm just grateful you came around and hauled my remains out of there."

Loretta didn't bother to correct her. "They've got to be awfully worried about you."

Thea was shaking her head across a wide arc. "I can't. I just . . ." Tears filled her eyes, but now she fought them back. "You want that last slice?"

* * * * *

Elmo's eyes glazed sitting before the console. He'd been in touch with other computer freaks. But no one should be able to reach down into his operating system. He switched off the modem that connected the computer to the telephone line. The two red ready lights went out. That should break any strange connection.

But another word crept on to the screen:

Well?

It was impossible. But there it was. His mind was an electron racing through a circuit near light speed. Possibly someone had planted a virus which left these odd little messages in his system. Fairly harmless, at least so far. But damned annoying. These things aren't supposed to happen. He admired the way the messages aped real communication, as though they were genuinely prepared to handle a response. He typed: Who are you?

I am Arbidor.

Damn. It responded. Whatever an arbidor might be. Okay, but that, too, can be easily programmed. He tried a more subjective question to throw it off: What do you want from me?

I want you to take the next step.

It was sufficiently vague to be a highly programmable, if curious rejoinder. What step is that?

The next step in your hobby, Mr. Skinner.

Who are you? Where are you? How did you get in my system?

I am Arbidor. Where I come from, the commonplace is what you consider impossible.

Damned riddles. Some hacker kid and his pranks. Why do you call me by that name?

Oh, but I know so much more than your name, Elmo Skinner. I know your favorite game of observing, recording and rating acts of sex in your eight cameras. You watch and you masturbate. Then you replay your favorites.

Elmo nearly forgot to exhale. No one, not Phil or Loretta or anyone else on Earth knew that. He had built the system alone. No one, no one, had ever been in his control room. How could he know? Who the hell is this Arbidor and what will he do next, blackmail me?

Elmo reached for the power switch.

Don't bother. I have you on external power.

Elmo clenched his teeth and snapped the   computer off.

Satisfied?

You are impossible. No one can enter my system this way. You are an electronic hallucination. I refuse to acknowledge your existence.

And yet I exist. Can your personal reality be anything other than a minuscule portion of what

142

exists in the universe?

Elmo fell back in his chair and exhaled. It couldn't be real. He looked at the power switch. It was off. Maybe there was a way to bypass the switch. But the plug . . .? He rolled the chair back, ducked under the desk, reached back around the machine, grasped the plastic plug and yanked it from the wall. He saw the spark when the connection broke. He listened. Just over his head, he heard the fans still whirring inside the computer. He crawled out, grabbed the edge of the desk while still on his knees, and looked up at the screen.

I do wish you would relax. I could easily have electrocuted you. But I don't want to hurt you. Please stop trying to disconnect and talk to me.

Slowly, Elmo picked himself up. When he reached his feet, he glared at the system that hummed when it was off and kept at him. This was a real-time presence on line, not some clever program. Nobody's that ingenious. If it was an electronic hallucination, he might just have to walk away from it.

He leaned over and typed: What are you? What do you want?

I am from another time and place. I have come to study your hobby. And to assist you in taking the next step.

Elmo's eyes bulged. His head shook, almost vibrated. When he took a breath, he felt his chest shivering. He turned his back to the screen. He was a circuit man. He didn't go for any of that astrology crap and its academic sister parapsychology. UFOs were bullshit. Alien abduction stories were fools looking for attention. He never bet a longshot, though it was a longshot that had landed him in the Lamp Post Motel.

He turned and stepped to the keyboard. His hands were trembling, but he managed to type out: Where? Where are you from?

Even what little I have told you is more than you should know.

I propose a deal. If you plug the system back in, turn on the power, go back online, I will address you only there and stop tampering with your system.

Agreed?

His feet would gladly have walked out on the madness. It could not be real. It must not be real. But in his gut, something urged him on.

Agreed.

He waited for a response, but none came. It was almost a relief to crawl back under the desk and grab hold of the power cable. If the computer was plugged in and turned on, maybe he wasn't quite insane. Maybe. He pushed the plug back in its socket, wiggled out backwards, and mostly stumbled back into his command chair. He rolled up to the desk and flipped on the power switch.

The screen was back to his Lamp Post Motel desktop. He checked his file directory. No unusual files anywhere, no ethereal communiqués. It was a hallucination, must have been. He jumped back online. Nothing. No one. Yes, a hallucination. Of course. What else could it be? He was alone, in his control room, a little bleary after a strange day.

He looked around, wondering what he was waiting for, relieved he had imagined it all. His eyes fell on the modem, still switched off. He was confident now that there were no bogeymen, that he just needed some sleep, and defiantly snapped on the little chrome toggle.

Thank you.

Little beads of sweat formed on his brow. I'm not crazy, he told himself. I want to go to bed. What is this guy *doing*?

What is the next step?

He didn't believe he had typed the words. But something inside him wanted to know. He reached for the bottle and a shot glass.

Yes, do have a drink, Elmo. You look like you need it.

Then I'm going to bed.

It's early yet. Your best guests haven't even checked in. We want to choose from the best, don't we?

Just what do you imagine "we" are going to do?

I simply provide transportation. You, Mr. Skinner, are going to proceed as you normally would. Choose a room to visit.

The beads on his brow were growing. Elmo took a sip of the Scotch, then knocked the shot back. The blast at his tongue and throat seemed to coat his frazzled nerve endings.

Just what do you mean "visit"? My guests must have their privacy respected.

You speak of privacy? You violate your guests at every opportunity, and make sure you have plenty of opportunity.

Or is it perhaps your fear speaking?

More my confusion. What is this "transportation"? What the hell are you planning to do to me?

I intend to take you one step closer to that which you observe. Tonight when you scan the rooms, you may select your favorite target. But tonight you shall be the ultimate voyeur. Tonight, you will not watch from behind a screen, nor even step in for a closer view.

Tonight, you will be transported into someone's mind.

Chapter 20

Elmo felt his heart thumping. He looked at the screen. It was still there:

Tonight, you will be transported into someone's mind.

Instinct told him to run, lock the room, and stay away until this electronic intruder was gone. The circuits were protected. Well, this Arbidor seemed to make good on his promise to intrude only over the network. Certainly his apparently impossible capabilities included sending power through a back port in the computer. But moving into a mind? It can't be. Did he even *want* to go leaping into someone's head? Would it drive him insane? What about the other man, the man whose head he would enter? What would happen to him? What if he could really go and not come back? Would his body die once he left?

Elmo didn't like this. Too many loose variables. It would be completely disorienting. He should walk out of the room and go to bed. He didn't. Instead he typed.

I don't believe you exist.

I am having the same difficulty. I wonder if you are fully human.

Couldn't I have a day to think about it.

Opportunity, friend, is a point in time. It as a rare moment when one's actions truly can make a difference.

Now you sound like a salesman. How big is my hole in time?

The next thirty minutes. And that's pushing it.

Elmo looked away from he screen. He couldn't focus on anything in the room, but his glazed eyes pointed in the direction of his monitors. His hands, poised over the keyboard, trembled, rapping out **KDJANVIRVROVHE** before he realized what he was doing.

Do I take that as an expression of confusion?

Can you be more specific on just what your going to do?

I am going to take your consciousness out of your body for, shall we say ten minute? Or until you ask me to return you.

I would be in someone's body? Feeling what he feels, thinking his thoughts,
The answer came before he finished his question:

Yes.

Elmo froze, terrified. And yet tantalized. After

a pause,

That's impossible!

You know so little of what is possible.

Would i push out his mind or would it be...

This you will know when you return. You will be perfectly safe, only in danger of learning a new perspective. Now select your target, or shall I select one for you. How about a few minutes in that hot Mexican number in room 103?

On what had been his blank main screen popped a grainy black and white signal from the first camera he had installed. He saw the wide-angle view of the room, the two double beds, a generic lamp on the chipped night stand between the beds, and a table in the corner. A few stray pieces of clothing lay on a bed, but no one was in the room. The background sound was amplified. He heard Carmen's voice echoing in the bathroom, water splashing, and little Juanita's happy squeals.

"We leave them alone," Elmo said sternly. He was reaching for his keyboard to type in the message when the image shifted to 114 on the main screen. The messages shifted from the computer monitor to the big video monitor.

Elmo thought he should just get up and walk away from this insanity. He wondered why he was playing this game. But he knew why: The next step.

The Love Room, 122, was vacant. In 127, Clarissa Wright and a male companion were using a small butane torch and a glass pipe to smoke crack.

"Pass," Elmo said quickly. "Lets have a look at Carpenter in 144."

Room 144 featured a simulated painting of a Spanish Galleon on an orange sea. Across the room, at the pedestal table near the window, Howard Carpenter still had every hair in place, although his jacket was off and his tie loosened. He and the blonde were finishing off the pizza. Elmo reached for the camera controls, but the image on its own panned right and zoomed in on the blonde.

Her paint job must have taken the better part of an hour, but it succeeded in highlighting her otherwise small random eyes that kept the world a soft blur. He looked over her clothed body with the practiced eye of one who has watched women strip in front of his lenses several time a day. Long, delicate fingers held a champagne glass that she greedily sipped with glowing red lipstick. Elmo found himself wondering if kissing those lips would bring an electrical charge. He could kiss them to find out. He panned slowly down her body wrapped in a tight green dress too warm for a Tucson August afternoon. So were the shimmering hose on her long legs. They probably worked in an office that was air-conditioned down to sixty-eight degrees.

"I used to sell toothpicks," Carpenter said. "Manufacturers rep for six states west of the Mississippi."

Oooh, is Florida in there I got a sister lives in Florida."

"I don't think Florida was in my territory. It's east."

"I never could get the east-west stuff. Everytime I turn around, it's somewhere else.

Elmo recognized Carpenter's salesman's smile.

Elmo had worn a similar model. The number if visible teeth a bullshit meter, and Carpenter was giving his companion a high rating indeed. "You're a sweet little thing, Sally, you know that?"

She showed teeth too, but these high marks were for the flattery she ached to hear. She fluttered her lashes at him.

"And you've got a pair of eyes that should be in the hall of fame somewhere."

More likely a vacant hall of fame, Elmo thought. Not this room either.

He reached for his keyboard and called 140 to the screen, a little surprised the system still responded to his commands.

The only room light was by the blue corridor bulb that filtered through the too-thin drapes. Elmo turned on the infrared before he could make out two bodies curled together. It took several seconds for him to make out the little boy sleeping between them. He lingered there a moment. Before a tear could form he cut to 138.

Two men. No thanks. *I'm insane to be going along with this. Can he really do that?*

He tried 136. The TV was blaring, every light in the room was on, the air conditioning was at full blast. In the bed near the window, a man and woman were generating heat.

Elmo automatically reached to start the recorder, while keeping his eyes fixed on the screen. Muscles all along the man's body were taunt. The grunts sounded more like effort than pleasure. The woman, dark-haired but fair skinned, also seemed to be laboring at this act of love. A glint of urgency caught Elmo's eye. His monitors reported the data. **Michael H. Giordano, 4th stay, monitored twice, high intensity readings.**

Elmo's own sexual experience, all of it with Molly, was usually of the comfortable variety, with little taste for innovation or spice. For all the thousands of sex acts he had witnessed by now from his room, few were so fervent as this. What passion drives them so hard? He admired the muscled bodies pushing at each other, clutching for each other. There seemed little coordination between them, little anticipation, as if the couple were strangers before tonight. How do strangers in a bar find each other? How do they find there way to intimacy? For all he had seen, Elmo didn't know. What drives Giordano that he plunged into her mercilessly, his body conditioned for stamina in critical situations. Elmo closed his eyes trying to feel what that might be like.

Elmo felt a jolt, knew he wasn't watching a screen anymore, or seated in a chair. His head felt disconnected, swirling and losing focus, until that too melted away. He felt, saw and heard nothing, but sensed he was in a strange place. Then he felt his heart pounding. He felt his body pounding something. It was nonsensical. It felt like he had a headache and what was he...

My God, I'm here. I am Giordano! He felt power this still young toned body, hammering with his abdomen and buttocks. *I'm fucking! Sweet Jesus I'm fucking and it feels so damn good!*

He revealed in the sensation he had denied himself for six years, smiling inwardly. He decided to make this fuck a concerted effort of all three of them. He reached for Giordano's thoughts to get a taste of the man's passion. He heard these thoughts instead:

Take it slut, you deserve to have your brains fucked out. Only a stinking whore like you enjoys degrading yourself with the privacy of your body. Only

152

slime does this and likes it. You are earning your pun-
ishment, and I am here to see that your punishment is
complete, that I take you and ravage you for my plea-
sure and God's revenge.

Elmo nearly called Arbidor to bail out of this madmans's mind. Then he noticed they were slowing down, that the force driving his body was waning. The physical intensity was drifting. It took Elmo a moment more to realize that *he* was the break in concentration, that his thoughts were slowing this twisted passion drive behind the body's force. He felt as much as heard Giordano's resolve to refocus his energy. *Okay, if we're fucking, let's fuck good and hard.* He took hold of this body and took up the work of bringing himself and...Karen, yes, a clerk in the county recorder's office. Giordano picked her up at the dance hall up on Broadway. *Come on Karen, let's sprint to the finish.*

Before Giordano knew why, he said to her "You are fabulous. I will remember this night always." Before he could feel Giordano's confusion, Elmo mentally shouted "out" to Arbidor, and found himself once more--or was it still--seated in his grey chair, watching a screen where a confused Michael Giordano looked towards the camera, wondering if he had been hearing voices in the room.

Elmo watched Karen reach up and kiss him hard on the mouth. "Thank you," she smiled. "You're sweet."

Across the camera, the wires, and the video stream, Elmo replied, "You're welcome."

CHAPTER 21

Elmo crawled out of his command room at 2:37 a.m. He let himself tumble to the bed without removing his clothes. When he closed his eyes, he saw Karen taking her pleasure from—from himself? Elmo had been looking into her eyes. But the body was Giordano's. The seduction was Giordano's.

Elmo could get no picture of this unstoppable force beyond the computer, this Arbidor. Somewhere after three he undressed, pissed and brushed before falling back in bed. He had no compartment for this experience. God, he had been in another man's body! What looked like passion on the video screen was seething hatred on the inside. Elmo felt soiled. But the intensity! The break from civilized standards fed Giordano's primitive energy. It had no beautiful order, just this drive to despise and this bizarre if at least passionate connection to sex. Somewhere around four, Elmo tumbled into semi-sleep. He saw himself crawling on the floor to disconnect a renegade computer, fleeing Carmen in the parking lot, chasing armed neohippies, dancing through puddles with Loretta toward the invisible victim. He forced his eyes open at 5:19 and took hold of the Scotch. Elmo, who never drank without a glass, slugged two good swallows from the bottle. His heart thumped like a frenzied drum. Through the drape, a hint of morning. I've got to sleep. He could not. He reached for his prick, modest by the standard of the thermonuclear device Giordano lugged around. Elmo lightly stroked himself. Mentally, he had

154

been laid royally, but his body was cocked and waiting. He closed his eyes and saw Karen, who opened her legs so someone might care. He heard Karen's voice rasping urgently in his ear. Somewhere during the night he spewed seed toward no fertile ground. Around six he fell into a light sleep. He saw Carmen's grateful smile and heard her winsome-toned Spanish. He blinked that away and saw eyes, just eyes, eyes he knew, eyes both young and old; accepting, trusting eyes that crept into his heart. At the moment of recognition, the eyes melted, spattering little bits of boiling flesh, browning, crusting, burning and melting away.

* * * * *

Doc Perkins found the patient sitting up against the headboard wearing a wan smile. "How's Terry this morning?"

Doubt flickered in the patient's eyes before she responded to the name. "Feeling like I want to move a little."

"A little is the best you'll do for today." Doc examined the bruises that seemed to be healing apace. She checked Norwood's eyes, her pulse, her blood pressure, temperature and reflexes. "You're still suffering from shock, but it's only a carryover from yesterday. It should clear up. How is your thinking, Terry?"

"It's a little foggy, but as you say, seems to be clearing up." Norwood looked over to Loretta seated in the corner. "Loretta's been good to me."

Doc nodded. "She's good people."

"Do you think I could get this in writing?" Loretta chirped.

Doc Perkins kept her voice even. "Terry, is there someplace you're supposed to be today? Is anyone

155

expecting you?" She saw the patient flinch again at the name, saw her eyes fall to her lap and fill with tears.

"No." Thea looked up and sobbed. "Nobody."

"Terry, you act as if you've done something wrong. Do you need to punish yourself? Are you going to run away from your life because of some accident?"

The words came out as just a breath, but Doc and Loretta read them: "I have to." She said something else, intended for and heard by herself.

Loretta could have predicted Doc's basic clinical response: "Why do you feel you have to?"

Doc saw uncertainty cross the patient's face. She shook her head. "I just can't."

"You mean you won't." the doctor replied.

"Whatever," patient "Norwood" snapped.

"Now, honey, we're only trying to help." Loretta went for the phone. "I'll bet you could use breakfast. I'll call for bagels, cream cheese and bacon."

"Breakfast I would prescribe," Doc said. "But bagels and bacon are cultural sacrilege." She looked at Loretta, and back at Norwood. "No coffee for you just yet."

Thea nodded.

The doctor stood, feeling the soreness in her own abdomen. "You can try to move about today, but don't walk without help. Mostly I want you to rest up some more. Are you going to be here for . . . ?" Her eyes turned to Loretta.

"As long as she needs me, Doc."

Doc nodded gently and appraised Thea. "You need to heal. You need to go back to living. I hope you're ready soon."

She reached into her purse for the keys to her Jaguar and left.

* * * * *

The little two-bedroom house was a mid-century vintage in an older Tucson neighborhood, a mile east of the university. It was a flat-roof box with a good living room window facing the sunrise. An old pendulum clock ticked in the dining nook. Andi heard a jet glide overhead toward the base runway. The chewing was quiet, but there was an occasional scrape of fork on plate. Joanne and Donna looked at their food. The evaporative cooler on the roof pumped water over aspen pads blowing air through the wet pads and into the house. It worked during the dry months. In the more humid summer thunderstorm season, it cooled only a little.

Joanne had lived here for the past five years, with a mortgage payment pitifully small by Andi's San Francisco Bay standards. Donna had lived with Joanne for the past year. Andi held on to a mug with long-cold coffee. She poked around in her purse for a stray stick of gum that wasn't there. Her eyelids bounced. She found herself just looking at her fingertips.

She didn't look up until Donna slid back from the table. "I need to get to campus to make somebody a better swimmer today. Why don't you try to sleep? I'll see if I can get away to meet you for lunch."

Andi sighed. "I've been trying all damn night."

Joanne reached for Andi's cup. "Let me warm it for you."

Andi shook her head. "I can't get anything down."

Donna picked up her purse and took a step toward the door. "Lack of sleep and food don't help mind and body much."

157

"Probably not, coach," Andi said.

* * * * *

Yot had slept only a few hours before Xaq found him back at the keyboard. Yot's body was in 126, but he was connected through a screen and a keyboard to a computer world Xaq could never enter.

Xaq was across the room on the telephone, scribbling notes and moaning, tugging at his hair. Nothing budged Yot from the screen and keyboard. He had been there for hours, barely breathing at times, trancelike. Xaq pulled back the drape and looked out the window. A kid downstairs was doing his best to splash the water out of the pool. Cars straggled down Craycroft toward the base. An Air Force jet sliced an arc through the sky. Yot remained a statue in a chair.

Xaq walked across the room to his mesmerized friend. "Ho, Yot, you in there?"

You's voice came from deep within a long electronic tunnel. "What?"

"I wanted to see if you were still alive."

Yot spoke while his eyes remained on the screen. "Just a minute. I'm almost out." The minute turned to five, fifteen, finally eighteen minutes before Yot returned to the world of the living. "I called the bank."

"Wonderful," Xaq said dourly. He was pacing the scant space between the beds. "We have to go down there, fill out all these feco forms, answer a lot of questions, give them current identipapers, and probably have to face the same suspicious old lady I was just talking to."

Yot smiled. "Now you're afraid of some . . . bofo old lady?"

158

Xaq paced, hoping he could raise Yot from the chair. "We're not real people here. We weren't born anywhere or at any time these people can handle. They ask all sorts of personal questions to verify identity. We have no fecing identities."

Yot was unmoved. "Make some up. They'll be absolutely verifiable. I just look into the bank computer for what information they want. Invent your own life. Tell them you were . . . born in Moscow or Paris. When they go to verify, I look down the datapath they check and have . . . matching files waiting for them. Piece of cake."

"You're going to leave me to face them alone, aren't you?" Xaq said.

"I have been getting some work done." Yot still wasn't looking up.

Xaq's hands were flailing. "Well I would hope you got something done for all the time you've spent locked in that machine."

Yot wouldn't be drawn into a fight. "I recall that we handled Elmo Skinner just fine last night."

Xaq had to smile. "All right. But are you going to send me to that bank alone?"

Yot was contemplative. "Where at the bank? Where does that . . . account actually exist?"

Xaq contorted his face into a question mark.

Yot put on the forced grin and the jutting jaw of his clown face.

Xaq's eyes lit up his face. "In the computer? Do you think you could . . . Can you find out how to . . . ."

"Xaq."

The flat tone in Yot's voice stopped him.

Yot just sat there. "I already have."

"How's that?"

"This bank account." Yot explained slowly. "It's

done, bofo. Among the more . . . useful utilities in the machine was the one that made other systems transparent. I looked into the system, intercepted security codes, and manipulated files. I had command of . . . every system connected to a telephone. I called Arizona Bank, created a deposit in the . . . Global Express account and routed to GlobEx headquarters in New York, there is now a new account *in perpetuity* for one Xaq Hobesian Arbidor. I dumped in thirty thousand dollars, triple what Rej . . . asked for. If we could live comfortably on a ten thousand dollar deposit, thirty thousand ought to make each us downright wealthy. Hell, it was only data."

"Oh." Xaq dropped down on the bed and stared at his friend. "You mean you . . . you mean it's all . . ."

"Done."

CHAPTER 22

Andrea Norwood spent most of the morning scribbling notes on a yellow memo pad. All her facts added up to the obvious: Thea was gone, maybe floating in the Gulf of California, dead on that Mexican beach, abducted for alien anthropological analysis.

She paced around the little square house, pad and pencil in hand, but only generated more heat moving around. She tried to lie on the couch, but she couldn't rest either. She couldn't shake the picture of the night that Thea made her feel like they were an old married couple. It had been after they made love in her last apartment in Menlo Park, feeling warm and good, when Thea started weaving disaster plans, binding her with those "If I ever . . ." vows one makes to a trusted life mate.

"If I ever disappear, if something ever happens to me, no one is ever to know. They can have Thea Nikolas vanish into the mists of time."

Andi had twisted her lips sourly at the overdramatic proclamation, but that had only made Thea more insistent.

"This is serious," Thea had said with storm clouds at the edge of her voice. "If ever I am just gone, you don't do a thing. No police. No testosterone-poisoned authorities. Forget me. I'm history."

Andi had tried to lighten the tone with a joke. "Is someone planning to do you in?"

"Someone might," Thea had snapped. "Or I

could . . . walk out of this life into another."

Had Thea just walked out of her own life? No, Thea hadn't disappeared on her own. Andi would have noticed any preparation, however subtle. And then there was the shirt.

Damnit, something had happened.

The jangling phone shook her. Andi grabbed it in the middle of the second ring. Was it . . . ?

No, it was Donna, taking an early break at work, and how about a shot of whiskey and coffee on Fourth Avenue?

Andi looked around, unable to see any reason to refuse, and got the directions to Gertrude's, a les bar on the street of shops that was Tucson's lone remnant of Sixties hippiedom.

It was a dozen steps from the back door to the carport, but as the morning slid past 100 degrees, it was enough to sap Andi of any available energy. Even in the shade, she nearly burned her hands on the window handle. Holding the steering wheel was impossible. Careful to touch as little metal as possible, she finessed the key into the ignition, waited a moment for the Honda's engine to catch, and slammed the air conditioning into high gear.

After a minute, she was able to close the window and breathe. The air conditioner didn't work well at low speeds. After a mile, Andi was sweating and swearing. Andi made the right turn onto Fourth Avenue. She cruised up the block, spotted the bar and drove up another block to find a parking space. She was panting by the time she parked. Damned air conditioner. Damned *heat*. She was locking the car door when she noticed the damned parking meter. Still damning, she angrily stuffed quarters into the smug police machine.

When she looked up from the meter, she was facing a tidy little house with a neat patch of almost emerald green lawn, the only such green she had found in this dusty brown town. She wanted to be back by the bay where green was an everyday sort of thing. The patch of grass held her attention long enough for her eyes to find the black and gold stenciling on the glass front door:

Lydia A. Cosgrove
Investigations

Andi stood on the sidewalk for a long moment. Her pledge to Thea rooted her to the spot. But a bellyful of worrying and wondering, of needing to respond somehow, pushed her toward the little house. A private investigator was private enough. She pushed herself to step between a pair of parked cars and weaved through the slogging ten o'clock traffic on Fourth Avenue. Every step closer to the door, she wanted to turn back. She was commanding her legs to advance while the brain kept trying to shift direction. *Take some time to think about this*, her mind warned, but her legs continued past that patch of lush green, up the two stairs that led on to a porch until she was faced with the glass door and its gold lettering. Her hand grasped the brass doorknob even as her mind begged she reconsider. Andi needed to do something, anything, but sit around wondering if Thea was going to suddenly pop up, if she was dead, or off in some damned flying saucer.

She turned the handle and pushed. The door groaned, but opened in front of an unoccupied receptionist's desk. The office was a converted house built in the 1930s, with a waist-high wainscot and art deco carved doors, architectural flourishes nearly vanished in the monotonous efficiency of the last half of the twentieth century. It felt more like Palo Alto than anything Andi had encountered in Tucson.

For several minutes, the office was silent. "Hello?" she called. No reply until seconds later, perhaps in response, a toilet flushed. Water ran for five seconds. A tall, broad-shouldered woman clattered around the corner on the hardwood floor.

"Hello yourself," the woman said. "If you're here about the job, you should have called first."

Andi fumbled with her fingers and looked for her tongue. "No, I . . ."

Lydia Cosgrove was dressed in a man's gray pinstripe business suit, precisely tailored to flatter her form. A red-striped necktie wrapped her shirtless neck and got lost in her bosom. Cosgrove was a little overdone with mascara and purple eye shadow counterpoint.

"I . . . I was coming for a whiskey and coffee . . ." Andi started.

"The les bar's across the street and down the block."

"Am I that obvious? Do I look les?"

"Nobody looks les. Except to the trained eye."

Andi's head wagged around the room, looking in the corners for something to say. "I need help," she said lamely.

"Who doesn't?" Cosgrove said.

"I need *your* help."

"Most people do, but just don't know it. So tell me."

Andi took a breath and smiled. "I was on my way to meet a friend at Gertrude's. We could talk business there."

Cosgrove set her jaw and considered. "You're buying?"

"Sure," Andi nodded, and smiled more easily. "I'm not keeping you from anything, am I?"

"Yeah, I was all set to nuke a frozen dinner for breakfast. What's your name?"

"Andi. Andrea Norwood. I want you to find a missing person." There, she said it before she could stop herself.

"Yeah, I get a lot of that in the les trade. They come stumbling out of the bar wondering what to do about another lost lover. That's when they see my sign. I'm like the mother confessor and the problem solver. Lost lovers, lost causes. Sometimes I succeed. And my rates ain't half bad."

"You're not les?"

"No. The clothes can fool you. That's just for style."

"The style reflects the woman within."

"The style," Lydia Cosgrove said with a wicked grin, "says I'm just as good as the titless unfortunates of the species." She fetched a satchel-sized purse.

"There's a problem about finding my friend."

"Just one?"

"She doesn't want to be found." Andi waited for Cosgrove to ignite.

"So what's our missing person's name?"

Andi looked Cosgrove in the eye. "Thea Nikolas."

Cosgrove's lifted an eyebrow. "The Thea Nikolas?"

"That's her," Andi said.

Cosgrove whistled. "Thea Nikolas. The bitch queen who blames half the problems of the world on testosterone poisoning. That Thea Nikolas?"

Andi nodded. "That Thea Nikolas."

"You're a brave one to put up with the likes of her."

"She's brilliant," Andi said.

Cosgrove raised the eyebrow before she answered. "Let's get that coffee. Especially with a shot of whiskey."

CHAPTER 23

Thea had been in bed for nearly twenty-four hours. The only thing worse than television was the vacuum of sensory input in the room. Loretta was out all morning, so Thea calculated the IQ's of game show contestants and tried to guess where they came from before they said it for the folks at home.

Folks at home. Andi knew the rules. Was she on her way back to Palo Alto?

The TV was selling little pseudogold neck pendants of the chemical formula for DETOX, a vacation trip to Alaska, and some dandy used cars. Then Marge spilled her guts about a secret liaison with Don to wicked Angela, who had been seeing Don for years, unbeknownst to poor stupid Marge. Meanwhile, Richard was making illegal deals that Greta had warned she would not tolerate, while she continued her secret affair with Don. Tide, Dentucream, and Preparation H took their pricey seconds on the screen, then Nelson admitted to his wife Clair that he was gay and wanted a divorce, to which she replied, "I thought you'd never ask."

Loretta, her arms loaded with bags, was kind enough to intrude at that point. Thea could have applauded.

"Boy that air conditioning feels good. It's a hundred out there already." She dropped the bags on the vacant bed and plopped down beside them, slurping in the cool air. "You look like you're having a wonderful time."

Thea shook her head, eyes drooping. "People spend their lives watching that on television?"

"Different lives, I guess."

"Empty lives."

"I brought lunch."

"I smell Chinese."

"More hot stuff, just like you wanted. General Tso's chicken."

Thea looked sad and grateful all at once. "You don't even know me. Why are you so good to me?"

Loretta couldn't shrug lying on the bed, so she tossed her flaming red head. "Somebody brutalizes you. Somebody else has to help. It averages out. The universe says it must be so. I'm just the universe's tool that happened to be there. How are you feeling?"

"I want to get out of this bed." Thea said.

A wisp of red hair dangled between Loretta's eyes. "I'll bet you got to pee pretty bad."

Thea managed a little laugh. And a nod.

Loretta lifted Thea almost effortlessly. Thea had a vague memory of Loretta's having carried her before. Now she sank comfortably into the larger woman's arms and smiled up at her. Loretta dumped her cargo on the toilet seat, then turned to lunch.

"What's your sign?" Loretta asked while opening the cardboard food boxes.

Thea shook her head in dismay. Dear Sappho, not one of those airhead astrology types. "My sign? Yield right of way. I was born in moderate traffic."

"Great," Loretta said from the other room. "When's your birthday?"

"I think it was a Tuesday."

"You know darlin', I could leave you sitting on that toilet for a while."

"Sure. You could have left me there on the

168

beach. You helped me then. You will again."

Loretta didn't say anything. Thea heard her snatch at a plastic fork. "Good chicken."

Thea's voice softened half a notch. "Could you . . . Would you . . .?"

Loretta's footsteps came toward the bathroom. "How's about we start this conversation again?" She stood just beyond reach outside the open bathroom door, arms crossed. She took a few breaths.

Thea reached forward.

Loretta didn't move for a minute. "The stars say it's a good day for General Tso's chicken." Then she ambled away, returned with the cardboard carton of Chinese, and plunged a pair of polished wooden chopsticks into the rice noodles and chicken. "Damn good," she said.

Thea kept looking up, expectantly. Loretta took three more bites.

"Excellent, in fact." A piece of noodle stuck to her lower lip.

Thea sat on the throne, slowly shaking her head. *This is asinine superstition. I won't give in to infantile horoscopes. No matter what I say, she comes back with something like 'I knew it' or 'the stars said it must be so,' or something equally stupid. Well, it takes two to play that game, and I'm not playing.* She smelled the rich spiced chicken. "I'm a Virgo."

Loretta lifted an eyebrow. "Bullfeathers," she said. "You're a Capricorn or a Taurus, maybe a Gemini." She reached for a booksized case, which she cracked open to reveal a notebook computer. "The manager here gave me this after I'd been working here a year. He told me I could organize my business." She tapped on a few keys. "Tell me the time, date and year you were born."

"This is stupid," Thea said, still on the toilet seat.

"Where's the harm? Or do you intend to spend the day on a toilet seat?"

"You wouldn't," Thea said.

"I am." Loretta said "When were you born? Where?"

"This is stupid."

"As stupid as spending an afternoon on a toilet?"

"As stupid as superstition can be." Thea grumped.

Loretta walked over to Thea, reached down and yanked her off the toilet seat and trundled her to the bed. "You're right. I should have left you to die on the beach. But I'm one of those stupid people who thinks life is worth something. You refuse to tell anyone where you are. Or who you are. You've got this weird thing about hospitals and men. As for my horoscopes, I'm entitled to my diversions. If it makes you feel any better, I don't put all that much stock in this stuff, but it's often fun and usually a good conversation starter. It helps me find out what people think they're about. Okay, so you've had a rough time of it. I thought I could help, but you don't seem to want to do a hell of a lot of cooperating. So eat your goddamn chicken and maybe you should start thinking about who's gonna nurse your ass when I get tired of your inflexible crap."

Thea couldn't argue. "I hurt in a hundred places. I'm hungry. And you're right. Can we try it again?"

"Sure," Loretta said. "Let's start with your birthday."

She hesitated, and even when she spoke, she begrudged the words. "I was born on August 14, 1965.

"What time?"

170

"What's the difference what time?"

"I asked. Is this a national security issue or something?"

"At 2:45 in the afternoon."

"Where?" Loretta asked mildly.

"Schenectady."

Loretta typed the data into the silver notebook. "Happy birthday. You'll be, let's see, forty-one tomorrow." On August 13th your sun is in Leo. Schenectady at, let's say 9:30 at night . . .hang on while the computer checks the latitude and longitude coordinates for Schenectady. You've got Pisces rising. Sensitive, idealistic, in danger of being overly empathetic. Sounds just like you, don't it?"

"Well, I'm not sure about the time. And beside, this is a load of. . ."

"Watch it, sister," Loretta snarled. "Now where were you born?"

"Europe."

"What's it, are you CIA or something?"

"No," Thea said.

"Where?"

"Greece."

"Greece?"

"On the Isle of Lesbos," Thea said.

"You don't say."

"I tried not to."

"What time?" Loretta persisted.

"At 2:04 in the morning."

"You wouldn't happen to know the latitude and longitude of your corner of Greece?"

Thea shook her head. But she smiled, too.

"That's okay. The computer is checking online systems for the information." Loretta looked at the screen and didn't allow her eyes to flicker up. "That's a long way from Schenectady."

"In more ways than you know," Thea agreed.

Loretta was looking at the little computer's screen. "You're spirited and strong willed, always have to be the center of attention, always have to get your own way." She looked up. "Ring any familiar notes thus far?"

Thea huffed through her nostrils, but said nothing.

"That's your sun sign, Leo. The bad news is you've got Gemini rising over that Isle of Lesbos at uh..." She took another glance at the screen. "At twenty-seven degrees east of Greenwich. And that, Terry Norwood, could lean you just a little on the schizophrenic side."

"Um," Thea said. For a while, they just ate. Thea seethed at being forced to swallow this claptrap about moons rising in Jupiter and whatnot, but she swallowed the free General Tso's chicken just fine.

"I guess you have things you need to do," Thea volunteered.

Loretta nodded. "Don't you?" Her eyes remained locked, in wait.

"I mean, you have a job or something, don't you?"

"Yeah," she laughed. "Or something. A counselor, a priestess, a release valve." She had let her gaze wander.

"You're not another doctor . . ."

Loretta laughed a little. "No, we compete only indirectly. I work out of the motel here. I'm a professional woman."

Thea tilted her head like a questioning puppy. "You're a hooker?"

Loretta stuck out her jaw in pride. "Why not?"

Thea erupted into a laugh that escalated to a hoot, and continued when the pain ran through her. "I've always thought it would be a good business proposition. No more insatiable need in this world than a man's single-minded devotion to pleasing his prick. You make him pay for his weakness."

"You got it pretty bad, don't you?" Loretta raised an eyebrow.

"Feminism? I've always felt that the oppressors . . ."

"Whoa, girl. Feminism is one thing. I can see why lesbians gravitate to it. But what is this thing you have about men?"

"Well, I don't much like them." Thea said.

"It's hard not to notice. Those two assholes on the beach . . ."

"Were just doing what every man does, in some way or another."

"How long have you been like this?"

"All my life."

Loretta shook her head. "You discriminate against half the human race. Don't you think that might be a little extreme?"

"Look, if they don't want to screw you physically, they want to some other way. Conquest. Domination. I hate it. You think there's something wrong with lesbians?"

"Sure. As much wrong as there is with everybody. I haven't met any perfect people, les, gay, kinky, straight, male or otherwise. I don't see a thing wrong with being left-handed, lesbian, or having painted red hair. The problem with being gay is that there's always assholes who'll hate you for it. They can't tolerate any variation in life, especially when you're varying from something as sacred or frightening as sex.

That's pretty important to you, being les, huh?"

"It defines my life."

"Some lesbians define themselves as teachers or opera fans or mothers."

"I'm les first. I write les books. I raise les consciousness. I practice les every day."

Loretta looked at her for a long moment. "So why are you so afraid to go back to it?"

Thea took a deep breath. A sob shook her quietly. She opened dampening eyes wide and finally looked straight at Loretta.

"Because nobody can know this happened to a les—especially not this *les*."

CHAPTER 24

Observation notes: Xaq Hobesian Arbidor 7906021

Sex is something twentieth century people still consider shameful. They are as unsure and uncomfortable about it as anything in their culture. They ignore the biological imperative of species survival that creates the human emotional need for coitus, and the addictive nature of intense physical pleasure. Despite their need, they find sexual congress dirty and distasteful at worst, naughty at best.

Their use of the phrase "fuck you" as an epithet is well documented. Reference to one of the most satisfying acts a human can perform is applied as condemnation. I suggest while they discuss sex so frequently and with such discomfort—as indicated by the heavy sexual bent in their humor—they find the matter fraught with danger. The residual pre-DETOX fear of AIDS and other STDs is observed to have left a legacy of fear. Much of that fear is a dread of the potential for emotional hurt that intimacy provides.

Their equating of sex and love is manifestly immature for a culture this far advanced. There is an ambivalence in whether they truly want intimacy or hurt, for they fear both as often as they desire them.

They are at a stage where there remains confusion between whether sex is for pain or pleasure. Their emotional requirement of security keeps them in monogamous relationships—at least part of the people part of the time. But they hold this monogamy as some sort of

175

virtue. And as much as the culture worships sex, the virgin is an honored creature. Abstinence is considered some sort of noble act, as though self-depravation somehow embodied goodness, and yielding to biological mandate is weakness.

* * * * *

On a typical morning, after an ordinarily placid sleep, Elmo was out of bed at 6:24, showered, shaved, brushed and in the office at 6:56, a cup of hot coffee ready.

Today the sound of his own animal wail woke him at 10:51.

Fragments of a dream scurried off to his subconscious, leaving the faint image of popping like frying eggs. His body ached from insufficient rest. His eyes drooped. His head felt out of focus. He shuffled across the only plush carpet at the Lamp Post Motel. Concentrate on the routine, on the motel stuck on autopilot all morning. He twisted the shower knobs, waiting for the water to warm.

And waiting.

My hot water is out. I've got to get downstairs. He hurried through the lukewarm shower, for once grateful to the August heat for keeping him from freezing under the wet stream. His morning coffee, fresh from five hours on the warming plate, had cooked into a thick, evil concoction. Elmo nevertheless welcomed the jolt necessary to reboot his nervous system.

He sat at the little round pedestal table, opening and closing his eyes. A tidy oak dresser held such stuff as socks and underwear. The room was precisely picked up and put away, except for the rumpled bed, a gaping wound from the pain of his night.

176

"It was all some crazyassed dream," he said aloud, hoping that hearing his voice might convince himself. He sipped at the caffeine syrup, and felt a stirring of life in his body. He found a lightweight white shirt and pulled himself into clothes. He might survive for a few hours. He took his mug to the tap and watered down the sludge. *No damned hot water.*

On a small typing table, a terminal waited. Elmo turned it on and entered the password SQUIRE to get into the main computer downstairs.

GOOD MORNING spread across the screen.

It is 11:11 a.m., Wednesday, August 13, the 225th day of 2008.

On this day in 1985, a Japanese jumbo jet crashed, killing 520 people. This was the worst single plane disaster in aviation history.

On this day in 1977, shuttle Enterprise made its first solo flight.

Today will be hot, high of 107, with a 40% chance of afternoon and evening thundershowers.

You have 27 messages waiting. 3 are marked URGENT. Display messages now?

He clicked Yes.

From Norman Abernathy, 117 8:55 am 8/13/98
URGENT
I smell gas. It's fairly strong. Since you are unavailable I will notify the gas company.

From Clete Williamson, Southwest Gas 9:14 am
We have a report of a gas leak on your property. A crew will shut off the gas and find the leak. A city inspector out to see you.

From Howard Carpenter #144 9:47 am 8/13/98

URGENT
Where's the damned hot water in this place?

The less-than-urgent messages were complaints and harangues about hot water. People calling for rates were directed to the computer voice that responded to most questions. Clete Williamson left two more messages asking a lot of questions, for which Elmo had no answer at all. There were two messages from Carmen, *buenos días at 9:15 and an adiós at 10:53.*

Just as well, he thought. He took another slug of the coffee and clambered down the stairs, out through the office, around the arced front desk, down the corridor and around the back to the boiler room, which he found swarming with gas company men in blue jumpsuits. Three may not constitute a true swarm, but with Elmo not at his best, with the ache in more places than he cared to count, three was swarm enough.

"You the boss around here?"

The raspy voice came from behind him. Elmo turned to face a round-shouldered little man who kept his neck crooked to try to look Elmo in the eye. Elmo recoiled at the man who seemed in such pain. "I'm Elmo Skinner. I am the owner here. And you are?"

"Archibald Haskell-Smythe, chief of City of Tucson building inspectors." He produced a badge from a back pocket. "We got a problem here Skinner?"

"It seems we do. Why don't we both find out about it?" He started to turn, waiting for the bent inspector, and stepped toward the blue swarm that was stowing equipment. "Excuse me. Could I speak to one of you for a moment?"

178

"Yeah, Mac," said a voice from under a blue baseball cap, "and who the hell . . ." When his eyes emerged from under the brim, he saw past Elmo to the little man bringing up the rear. "G-good"—he glanced furtively at his watch—"good morning Inspector Haskell-Smythe."

"Good morning yourself," Haskell-Smythe rumbled. "What the hell happened here?"

"Single leak, sir. At the meter. We been all over the place this morning, every inch of the line, sir. Th-there's no other leak."

The rumble rolled around in Haskell-Smythe's throat for a moment. "What's the flow rate?"

Elmo couldn't understand the numbers, but he read the relief on the inspector's face. He understood well enough the gas man's last remark: "It could of been a lot worse. I opened the valve without a wrench, just my bare hand." It was a strong-looking hand, but Elmo cringed with the inspector. "I think somebody opened the valve and didn't finish closing it off. It shoulda been tight, even with a strong arm with a good wrench. He should of tested it with soap and water for bubbles." The gas man looked at Elmo. "Was you the one messing with the meter?"

"No," Elmo said, not sure what to say now that he had joined the conversation. "I'm the owner here. I can't imagine that anyone would have a reason to . . ."

Despite the cap, a long lock of hair fell in the gas man's eyes. "You got anybody, like, *mad* at you or something mister?"

"I don't think so."

"Maybe a problem with the neighborhood kids?"

"Not lately."

The inspector turned to the gas man. "Are you suggesting sabotage, young man?"

"It's possible, sir. Or just plain vandalism. Specially in this neighborhood."

"Many things are possible young fella," the inspector rumbled. "More than you know, I assure you."

"Amen," Elmo muttered.

The thermometer had long since blown past a hundred degrees as Haskell-Smythe and Elmo trudged up toward the office and air conditioning. The inspector took a seat on the battered couch. Elmo sat down at a desk that was clean except for a single sheet of paper, A Notice of Interruption of Service.

"I've shut you down, Skinner. You have no hot water here until the damage has been repaired by a competent plumber, and I *personally* approve turning it back on. What is that third four-inch joint off the main line?"

"It was to the old boiler. I replaced it with a new system a few years back."

Haskell-Smythe twisted toward Elmo. "Then saw off the pipe. Random connections make a dirty system, Skinner, and a dirty system is a dangerous system. Isn't there another open connection at the pool heater?"

"Well, yes, it's . . ."

"Fix it," he barked.

"I'll have someone out here this afternoon."

Haskell-Smythe's sour face softened a bit. He may even have smiled. His watch beeped three times. "It's noon, Skinner. I will be back here in exactly twenty-four hours to inspect the repairs." The near-smile took a cruel twist. "If I'm not satisfied, I have the power to close your business entirely as a public safety hazard."

"I'm sure that won't be necessary. Would you like a cup of coffee?"

Haskell-Smythe's cocked head managed a nod. Elmo gratefully headed for the sludge pot. "Something for your coffee, sir?"

"Three sugars, no cream."

Elmo hoped all that sugar might sweeten the old man—and the dense brew. He handed the inspector a blue stoneware cup and tried not to watch the inspector bending his head to sip the coffee and the drops dribbling down his awkwardly-angled chin.

"You trying to kill me with this stuff, Skinner?"

"Farthest thing from my mind."

"Don't you have a maintenance man around here?"

"Yes, of course, but he doesn't work full time."

"Where the hell is he when you've got an emergency?"

Elmo nodded. "That's a good question. Let's ask him." He punched a two-digit code into the phone and came up with Wendell Rodgers, amplified on speakerphone room for the inspector's benefit.

"Yeh, hullo." Wendell sounded decidedly sleepy.

Elmo wondered if the whole damn world was sleepy. "Hello, Wendell. Weren't you due at work today?"

"That you Mr. Skinner?"

"Yes, Wendell. I hope I'm not disturbing you." He tried to keep the bite out his voice.

"Well, the air conditioning broke at the wife's work." The words were coming slowly, through a groggy haze.

Haskell-Smythe squirmed on the couch, twisting his neck to what looked like a less comfortable angle.

"And you went and fixed it for them," Elmo said quickly, trying to move the story along.

"Naw, nothing like that. The air conditioner was broke, so they sent everybody home, and she was feeling romantic, you know what I mean?"

"I think I know what you mean," Elmo sighed. "Listen, Wendell, we've got this problem with the gas meter . . ."

"No, that can't be," Wendell said. "I just checked out the meter day before yesterday, doing a little preventative maintenance, you know what . . ."

"Oh? Tell me what you did."

"Well, you know, ain't nobody so much as looked at that meter in years, 'cept maybe the meter readers, and I was looking out for you, Elmo, thought I ought to look it over."

"What did you do, Wendell?"

"I checked it out. Opened up the valve to make sure it still operated. It was a tight mother, too, you know what I mean? Lucky I had my biggest wrench, finally got it open. Closed up nice and easy after that. I won't have to worry about that next time, you . . ."

"Yes, Wendell, I think I know exactly what you mean. You're sure you closed it tightly enough?"

"Yeh, I gave it a few good turns. I didn't smell nothing, and it was getting late and the missus was due home, you know . . ."

"Wendell?"

Wendell paused for a moment. "Yeah boss?"

"The meter was leaking this morning."

"Im-fucking-possible. I checked."

"The chief city building inspector just shut down our gas while the whole system is reinspected and recertified in exactly twenty-four hours." The bile crept into his tone. "You know what I mean?"

"I'll be down to fix it. I mean, I'll . . ." Another long pause. "Sheeeit."

Elmo stiffened his back. "No, you take the day off. I'll take care of this one. Say hello to the missus for me," he said, and disconnected the call with the push of a button. He sat in the chair, slowly shaking his head.

Haskell-Smythe's rumbled, "I could arrest the bugger for criminal endangerment."

"You see what I have to live with?" Elmo sighed.

The inspector turned his head to an almost upright position. "You don't have to live with anything." The twisted smile returned briefly. "Except me."

Two hours later, another swarm of men in coveralls were refitting the plumbing system while Elmo called every tenant with his apologies for the lack of hot water, promising it would be on tomorrow. He knocked five dollars off his price to lure customers. When the night man came on at five, Elmo was back in his corner of Phil Stein's Beer Bar ordering Glenlivet.

CHAPTER 25

The cab driver hadn't seen such a gaggle-eyed pair of tourists in five years. Each of them pressed up against the window, jabbering questions, their eyes darting furiously at such notable landmarks as fire hydrants, phone booths and gas stations. They were odd birds, constantly gawking at the sky as though it were something they hadn't seen before. His instructions were to take them somewhere they could buy stuff. Maybe they were from New York.

They were gawking indeed, at an alien landscape from ground level, at the cactus they had flown over, now herded into little spots, making way for vast strips of a mostly smooth black surface that apparently carried these twentieth centurians everywhere they went. They puzzled at the boxlike structures that were offices and homes and stores.

They were at Park Mall in five minutes.

"Seeing as how you liked the ride so much, and how you ask so many questions, I figure I should tell you the custom is to leave the driver a tip."

Xaq had a fifty dollar bill. "Will this be appropriate?" He expected the broad grin that appeared on the driver's face. To Xaq it was hardly real money.

It was real enough to the driver. He sped off to find a bar.

"High retail, twenty-first century style," Xaq said.

"Feco," Yot replied. "This place is crazy hot."

They passed through the glass doors, leaving

184

the 107-degree reality behind. And apparently the century as well. What they found felt like a piece of home, the broad corridors and infinite nooks off every one, blaring in bright neon, plastic and glass. Even the kiosks with a map of the mall felt more like real life in the fortieth century.

A tone of reverence crept into Xaq's voice. "We could be at the beginning of true civilization. The beginning of the hive."

"They got food in this hive?"

Xaq responded with the clown face and a little wail. He was the cultural expert. He steered them to a soft pretzel nook labeled Twisted Delights. For all his study in the past, he had tasted this age only in the past twenty-four hours, but he ordered a garlic pretzel and got onion for Yot. He made a ceremony of presenting the paper-wrapped pretzel to Yot, who shoved a quarter of it into his face and chewed mightily.

Xaq waited to see Yot nod in satisfaction before he took a bite and let the garlic bite back. He let the pungency run through his mouth, and looked up, pleased at his find, when he saw the display just a few yards away. He turned his head to another corner, and there were more of them. Across the mall were more. They looked soft, cushiony, gentle leathers for Xaq's miserable feet.

"C'mon, Yot, we're buying shoes."

"In a museum?" Yot muttered through the mouthful.

"The whole damn century is a museum. Let's take a bite of Mother Earth."

The evening news came on at five-thirty. Elmo was at his booth, the TV positioned where he could see it, and Phil steps up with a pair of big frosted mugs.

Neither of them said a word through stories about a railroad accident in Baltimore, an earthquake in central California, and President Vomper tromping around the tobacco fields with company bigwigs.

"Not much news in August," Phil said when the commercial broke in.

"August is crazy," Elmo said.

Phil raised an eyebrow. "What's the matter?"

Elmo sighed. "I could use some sleep for one thing."

"What else?" Phil prodded.

"I spent the day chasing a gas leak. Now we have no hot water."

"Wendell?"

Elmo nodded. "You know him, huh?"

"Like a wart."

"It's not just that." Elmo waved his hands hoping to find words. "It's like . . . I don't know, like everything's out of control."

"I'm supposed to know what that means?"

"You saw Loretta haul me out of here yesterday for this emergency? I've never seen this emergency. Doc tells me stay away from her. I've got an asshole shooting a gun into the floor, almost kills a Mexican woman who comes on to me, my computer's gone crazy . . ."

He stopped abruptly. He wasn't sure how much about this mind-transfer insanity he wanted to tell Phil. He could probably be committed. But who else could he talk to?

"The heat makes people a little crazy."

"I suppose."

"Elmo, you're tired. You'll eat dinner, you'll go to bed, tomorrow you'll have hot water, and September's getting close."

186

Elmo snorted. "September's my worst month."

"Good," Phil said. "You'll get some peace. You could use it."

"Yeh," Elmo said. "Yeh, I could at that."

* * * * *

The telephone startled him. Elmo jumped in his seat before he answered.

It was Betsy. "Boss, you better come look at 138."

He didn't like her tone. "On my way."

Anything could be behind those doors, a drunk who pissed through the mattress. Somebody sick, injured or overdosed, another STP sniffer. He climbed the stairs in front of 116. Loretta's drapes were closed. When he touched the door handle to 138 directly above it, he half expected to see a bloody mess.

Actually, there was only a little blood, and that was confined to the sink. When he opened the door, Betsy was standing next to Tyrone, who held out a claw clamped on a pair of small plastic objects.

"What was in the needle?" he sighed.

"Heroin," said Tyrone's electric voice.

Last night 138 was rented to that very pregnant Marla Shaefer. She was young, literally bursting with life, and giving her baby an addiction for its birth day. Elmo would have preferred finding a dead body.

"You want I do something with the needles, boss?"

He took a long breath. "Throw them away," he said dourly. "They're just garbage."

He returned to the office hearing echoes of another man's skin and another man's mind.

A chime sounded when the front door opened.

187

"Don't get up, it's only me." Loretta's splash of red hair was sculpted into a teardrop pulling back from her face, wearing a slightly transparent black blouse over a zebra-striped skirt. "So what's with the hot water? My clientele isn't into cold showers."

Elmo sighed. "It's fixed. It's been fixed since the swarm of gas men closed off the meter this morning. But the inspector . . ."

"You mean Haskell-Smythe, the hunchback city inspector?"

Elmo nodded, "That's him."

"He's a son of a bitch."

"He was a little strict, but he's got regulations to enforce. How's this invisible patient of yours?"

Loretta tapped a finger on her chin, moved her head around looking for an answer. The point at the back of her hair bobbed around with her. "She's um . . . unusual."

"How about crazy?" Elmo offered.

Loretta dipped her head in a nod. Her point aimed up the wall. "Maybe she's crazy. Maybe just a little weird. Who's not? Am I sane, being in this business? Can a sane man run a nuthouse like this?"

"Of course I can," Elmo huffed. He wanted to ask her what she knew about mind transfer. Was that the question of a sane man? "I'm sorry. I'm tired. And you're right. We're all a little crazy. But this thing about men?"

"No law says you have to like everybody. But she's as private as a scorpion with an attitude."

"Well why doesn't she go home or something?"

"That's the goofy part. She refuses to call anybody to even say she's alive."

"But that's paranoid."

Loretta shook her head and with it her red

sculpture. "Don't tell a psychologist about paranoid. Reality is subjective as hell."

"Reality?" Elmo snorted. "I don't know what it is."

"You know you look like hell. Is something wrong, Elmo?"

"A lousy night and a crummy day. I'll get to bed early." Or, he thought, get back to the command console. "I've been meaning to ask you something."

"Does this have anything to do with a little Mexican lady?" she smiled.

"No. I let that go."

"Well are you going to live the rest of your life married to a motel?"

It felt like a slap. His eyes darted at corners of the room to avoid looking at her. "A friend told me something strange. I wanted to ask you about it."

A smile captured one corner of her mouth. "So now I'm your resident expert on strange?"

"Can you think of anyone better?" he said.

"Not at the moment."

"You're a psychologist and a hooker and a Voojoo. That's credentials enough. But this guy—he told me he experienced a mind transfer."

Loretta blinked. "A what?"

Elmo's hands were touching the desktop. "A mind transfer. Totally experiencing what another guy felt. Ever heard of anything like it?"

"Just on *Star Trek*."

"You don't think it's possible."

"Who knows what's possible?" Loretta laughed.

"I've been hearing that all day," Elmo sighed.

Loretta crossed her legs. "Mind transfer," she mused. "How does it happen?"

Elmo bit his lip. "The guy said someone contacted him . . . on the phone. Made this offer to move his mind. The guy figures this caller's crazy and says, yeah, sure. Bingo, he pops up in a man's mind while he's humping his wife. And he swore he was there. After maybe ten minutes, he was home and back to normal. Except he was pretty freaked out."

"Sounds like old-fashioned LSD."

"The guy's never done drugs in his life."

Loretta laughed. "Then I'd say he just started." She noted Elmo's lack of amusement. "Okay, maybe some sadistic kid slipped acid to him somehow. Who knows what might go on in this place?"

"I try not to think about it," Elmo sighed. "But LSD would seem to come from your Voojoo temple across the street."

She smiled away the accusation. "Nah. Voojoos are lightweights—strictly potheads. The serious druggies are on the street and up in the rooms." Loretta chuckled and shook her head. "Go to bed, Elmo. One of us has to work for a living tonight."

His head felt like a boulder, but he managed to nod. "Bed," he said, and with lead feet clunking up his personal interior stairway, he went.

CHAPTER 26

`Xaq laughed. "They look a lot like people, and they act a lot like people. But they're only halfway to civilization."

Yot had his back to the computer, but he felt it standing there behind him. "Four thousand years from here they'll . . . say the same about you. I want to taste some primitive xufa."

Xaq nodded. "I was wondering how long you were going to keep your ruxrol penned up. We got him laid. We should do at least as much for ourselves."

Yot replied with a clown face.

Schooled as they were by endless movies and television commercials from the twenty-first century, they reckoned they knew how to use a contemporary bathroom. Xaq had several red misfortunes shaving with an exposed blade. They tore into their purchases, baffled briefly by shirt pins, tissue paper and cardboard backs. Neither was familiar with the buttons and zippers of these primitive garments, but they managed to dress themselves.

Xaq admired his effect in the mirror. His straight black hair swept back across the left side of his head. He enjoyed the splashes of native color, the bright orange jacket, pink shirt, and glowing yellow pants. He liked the way the shirt and shoes matched.

"I don't think you'll have to . . . worry about being noticed," Yot said. He had settled for jeans and a blue oxford shirt.

Xaq moved closer to the mirror. "No woman can

resist this face, in any century."

Yot huffed. "Too bad you were never as good looking as you thought you were." He looked around the room, at the worn drapes and the TV dominating a wall, the cigarette burns in the carpet and the dent in the wall over the sink. He walked to the door. "Let's be somewhere."

Xaq managed to not flatten his nose against the cab window. He was disappointed too, being on the same street he had seen a few hours earlier.

The nightclub was another unexpected touch of home. It was one huge room with a thirty-foot ceiling, and suspended from it a black steel gridwork hanging down to support the legion of spotlights, strobes and soft yellow floods. Three islands in the cavern were the bars. Yot stepped up to the bar, smiling to himself about the hundreds of Earth scenes he had watched in ancient films where someone did exactly this. "Two beers," he said.

Yot looked across the wood floor. A few people were spread out at the far end of the room. Another knot gathered off to the left. But mostly the big room was empty.

"You won't believe how crowded it gets in here for happy hour," the bartender said. He placed two napkins on the bar and set down the mugs. "But when this place is empty, it really looks empty."

"What is a happy hour?" Xaq asked.

"It starts in a few minutes, from four to seven."

Xaq brought his eyebrows together. "Isn't that three hours?"

"Yeah. So?"

"Well why would you call it a happy hour?"

"That's what it is."

Yot turned to Xaq. "I could do with . . . some

xufa," he said. "That, you recall, is what we started out doing when we came here."

Xaq nodded. "I remember as if it were two thousand years from now." He sipped at the beer, and recoiled at this first taste. This was much coarser than the brew at home.

Yot nudged him. "Suppose all the women look like gorillas?"

"Then you won't need a blanket to bed her, the fur will keep you warm."

"What do I say to a . . . twentieth century girl?"

Xaq took a longer sip of his beer and decided he could drink it. "Same thing you say to a fortieth century girl. But slower."

They warmed to the beer, having a second and a third and hardly noticing them. Nor did they much see the people drifting in. They shifted in their seats as natives accumulated around them. The beer seemed to ease their discomfort. It also emboldened them when a throaty woman stepped up to the bar next to him. She had big brown eyes, considerable mascara and a clinging emerald green dress.

She looked Xaq up and down, at the orange jacket, yellow pants, pink shirt and shoes. "You must like color." She rattled off an order for a tequila sunrise to the bartender. "Which one's your favorite?"

"Green," Xaq said without hesitation.

She licked her fingertip and drew a line in the air. "Score one for Neon Man." She looked straight into Xaq's eyes. After a moment she slid her round bottom on to a stool. "Capricorn, right?"

"No, I'm strictly a local boy. Saturnopolis."

Yot kicked him.

"Oh, that's like around Oregon, right?" she asked. Her voice was soft and breathy.

193

Xaq took a quick pull on his beer.

She didn't wait for an answer. "I was sure you were from L.A. I'm from Ohio."

"Is that in the Coal Sack sector?" Xaq felt an elbow. He glared at Yot.

Yot clenched his teeth and whispered "Shut up."

The girl didn't seem to notice. "No, the coal mining is over in West Virginia. You sure you're not a Capricorn?"

"No," Xaq said a little more carefully. His eyes sojourned down her body and back again. It had been a worthwhile trip, with all the right curves in all the right places. Close enough to human.

"I'm a Leo," she declared.

Yot grabbed Xaq by the arm. "Excuse me," he said over his shoulder. He dragged Xaq a few feet away. He could see the dull look in Xaq's eyes. "This feco beer is making you crazy. Try to remember you're a salesman from Los Angeles, okay?"

Xaq twisted up his mouth. He wavered a bit on his feet. He nodded, if only slightly, and turned back to the girl in the green dress.

She was gone.

CHAPTER 27

Lydia Cosgrove didn't much mind that Iggy, her slope-trunked Peugeot, had been belching diesel fumes for ten years. She was perfectly satisfied that it was painted a nondescript white that at least gave the air conditioner half a chance in the marathon summer heat. The slightly battered car allowed her to come and go unnoticed. More important, Iggy's onboard computer Lydia gave access to her files back at the office. In many ways, the old Peugeot was her office. Certainly she spent more time in it than she did in her Fourth Avenue digs.

Yesterday, Iggy had hauled her down into Mexico to sniff out a trail now several days old in amorphous beach sands. Cosgrove was there to look for a struggle, to explain a stained sweatshirt and investigate signs of a UFO. She found none of either. As she expected, the tides had scoured the beach. Hundreds of tire tracks in the dunes beyond the beach told her nothing. The Americanos were all over this beach in summer. She failed to locate any campers who may have been at the beach over the weekend. The beach was a dead end.

She showed a photo of Thea Nikolas around town in Puerto Peñasco. She checked the restaurants, bars and hotels. A few people thought the face was familiar, but no one could recall actually encountering her, though some thought they might have seen her on television. Cosgrove assured them that that was entirely possible. On the perpetually reeking docks, vendors lined up in booths peddling shrimp that had only just stopped wiggling. No one there had seen that face.

At least Puerto Peñasco was a little cooler than Tucson in the blaze of August. Cosgrove asked people she knew who made it their business to watch the *gringos*. She asked the policia, she asked people in the shack homes along the dirt road leading to the beach. By midafternoon she had asked nearly a hundred people. It was easy enough to take the turnoff to the beach and never even get into town. Cosgrove checked into La Concha. As daylight faded, the waves lulled her to sleep.

So this morning she, too, awakened before the dawn. She started the day with coffee and computer.

Cosgrove's files contained every scrap of mediaspeak on Thea Nikolas, the newswire and magazine articles, transcripts of television interviews, and both her books, abstracted and full text. Nikolas' pathological dislike of men made her an obvious target of homophobic columnists, yet she remained the cool intellectual defending her radical stand for les patriation to the Isle of Lesbos. The irony was that those who despised any les in general and Nikolas in particular were the ones who agreed with her most: "*Let 'em* leave."

Cosgrove found that after days of sorting information and a good night's sleep to let the back of her brain do the work, an answer came to her almost automatically. The telling facts lined up for her. But no ducks fell in line today. What might have happened to Thea Nikolas was still anybody's guess. Even the UFO theory was possible. Why would somebody in a flying saucer choose her? Depends on who the somebody is. Maybe they were lesbians from outer space, coming to offer their world as a homeland for Nikolas' band of les expatriates.

Lesies from outer space? I need more damn coffee.

Cosgrove closed her files on Thea Nikolas. She reached for her stainless steel Thermos and dribbled out the last of the coffee, almost half a cup.

She turned her attention to Brad Keller, a wandering husband who disappeared from home for days at a time with no explanation. It was common enough these days. Once the AIDS-induced fear of sex was gone, millions of repressed libidos gushed through the floodgates to marital infidelity. Keller was just part of the tide of men letting his little head think for the big one.

He was a fat man, with dark hair and eyes. He bulged in his clothes, apparently unwilling to concede to a larger size. His wife Sheila described Keller as a real estate broker with a penchant for gambling, petty drugs and trashy women. Cosgrove's advice would have been the same as that given Little Bo Peep, although Brad Keller might not return wagging his tail behind him. But getting two thousand dollars cash from Mrs. Keller on the spot was reason enough for Cosgrove to be out looking.

The hotel restaurant was still closed at 5:30 a.m., but once Cosgrove hit the narrow streets of Puerto Peñasco, she found a fleet of battered old cars that made Iggy look good by comparison. She rolled down to the docks to the sea.

She finally edged out of town, but even along the highway she competed with trucks headed north with shrimp and produce for the Americanos. It took her two hours to reach the border. She found herself behind a line of some forty trucks. Iggy's diesel grumbled in idle. She waited. She fiddled with the radio, but nothing in English was coming in above the static.

She looked around the car, noting the progress of the rips in the headliner, observing the dashboard cracks that were threatening to become canyons, and listening to Iggy's sputtering diesel idle. Her briefcase had an open clasp. As she reached out to close it, her hand stopped. She grasped the handle instead and plopped the gray attaché on the passenger seat.

I'm getting out of this line.

She turned the wheel hard to the right to avoid the bumper in front of her, eased into gear and pulled out of the line of diesels grumbling with Iggy. She parked off to the side and removed Thea's photograph from the case.

She dodged between the belching trucks and stepped up to the first Border Patrol officer she saw. "Has this woman come through here this week?"

This officer was pot bellied and gray. "Lady, you know how many people come through here? I couldn't tell you if she come through in the past hour, let alone the past week."

Cosgrove thanked him and moved on to a second guard. "Ain't I seen her in the paper or someplace? But I don't think I seen her here." A third didn't recognize the face, nor did the fourth, who said that didn't mean she hadn't been through.

It was the fifth and last Border Patrolman, who insisted on speaking Spanish despite strict orders from his superiors in the United States government, who had an answer.

"*Sí, estaba durmiendo.*"

"Sleeping? You mean you saw her here? Are you sure?"

He nodded. "Sí, *fué ella. El lunes, por la mañana.*"

Monday morning. Cosgrove smiled, kissed the guard on the cheek, and stuffed two twenties in his pocket. "*Mil gracias,*" she said.

Thea Nikolas was alive. And in America, probably not yet aboard some hunk of metal streaking toward the uncharted wilds of the galaxy.

CHAPTER 28

The Lamp Post's blue corridor lights were still on when Elmo pulled his eyes open at 4:35 a.m. Some idiot down in the parking lot was revving an engine with a sore throat. Despite the racket that forced his attention, Elmo awoke slowly. He tried to lift his head to listen for voices. His skull felt like an overworked bowling ball. He felt it clatter when he dropped back on the pillow. The robot would take care of it.

Nine hours of sleep. Elmo found it hard to bring himself awake. His mind wanted to keep hold of a scene from a dream. He had been floating with . . . whom? Already the picture was fading. Elmo remembered that he hadn't been wearing his glasses. The gravel-voiced car roared once more, this time screeching on the pavement before hurtling down the street. Damn that racket!

He pushed himself out of the bed, put the glasses on and reprogrammed the coffee start time. An hour and twenty-five minutes before he should be in the office. He could sneak into the command room. Better wake up first. He could get back in touch with Arbidor. His heart quickened. Elmo dried himself quickly and tossed on some clothes. He poured a mug full of coffee, stepped inside his electronic haven and turned on the power.

GOOD MORNING spread across the screen.

It is 4:46 a.m., Thurday, August 13, the 226th

day of 2008. On this day in 1963.

Today's forecast is hot, high of 108, with a 40 per cent chance of afternoon and evening thundershowers.

You have 4 messages waiting. 1 marked URGENT. Display messages now?

The urgent message was another complaint about the lack of hot water. Another was verification of his appointment with Inspector Haskell-Smythe. Nothing from Arbidor.

The morning software routine reported twenty-seven rooms rented last night. Fair for August, 17.3 per cent better than 1997.

Elmo chewed the inside of his cheek. He took a long sip of coffee. He could try local Web sites. Arbidor may have left a message there.

Odd hours for such a patterned man, Elmo.

He shivered. As much as he was looking for this, he had no idea what he wanted to say. Twice he reached for his keyboard. Twice he pulled back his hands. Finally, he dropped his fingertips to the keys, but still he typed nothing.

Could you be looking for a travel opportunity?

Just as he was afraid of the answer, so was he certain of it.

Yes.

Courage becomes you. Or is it insatiable curiosity?

Call it whatever you want. But get on with it.

You're snappy in the morning. We have little to choose from at this hour. Would you prefer to check your screens, or shall I take you to the one couple beginning the mating ritual in 122?

Elmo powered up the viewer and took the input from the Love Room. Calvin Dagget, San Antonio, TX. First stay, no records.

The lights were out. Elmo activated the infrared camera, skewing the colors, but otherwise displaying the couple clearly. She was spread across the bed, her straight black hair framing a round, vaguely oriental face. He was reaching over her with a bottle of oil. He looked to be in his early or mid-thirties, reasonably trim if not athletic. Elmo wondered why they were awake at this hour. Then he saw the little square reflection on the nightstand and two lines of white powder. Yes, that was what usually had people up at this hour. Did he want to jump into someone's head buzzed on cocaine?

Why not? It's not my body.

Elmo tried not to let Arbidor's anticipating his every thought unnerve him. He flipped through his other cameras. Nothing happening anywhere. Still he hesitated. What havoc does this transfer wreak on his body? Or on his mind? His exhaustion yesterday might have been a warning that he was depleting some bodily essential. Danger flags or not, he wanted to go on.

Let's g

He had almost typed the "o" when he felt the swirling disorientation of his body falling away, then new flesh. He was there.

He felt this body jolted as it moved, almost too

202

much energy, but he felt a carefree grin on this face. He looked down on the rounded form even as these hands were pushing oil into her skin. Her name was Christina, a young radio account executive Dagget had met at a station party somewhere around nine last night.

Elmo found blurred memories of the party, but he could see Dagget mentioning nose candy, and her becoming a puppy dog, sniffing and following him around until he suggested the Lamp Post Motel. For a moment Elmo's business instinct took over and he asked this self why he had chosen this motel.

It's just clean enough to tolerate, where nobody I know would ever go, and it's cheap so I can walk up and ask for the best room in the place. After all, that was the way to be a rich man. Spend like a poor man. Leaves money for the important things in life. Like coke.

Elmo didn't ask any more.

He wanted to know who this man was. He felt around Dagget's mind and saw the pillared house outside San Antonio inherited from four generations of Daggets, from his ranching great-granddad to his daddy establishing the fourth biggest slaughterhouse in South Texas.

Elmo turned away from the butchering and found Dagget had a wife, Betty Jo, whose taste ran toward pure drugs and impure men. Dagget meant to match Betty Jo cheat for cheat, and raise her a few to boot. He'd had fourteen women so far this year, and only paid for three of them. Even screwed himself a nigger back in February.

Elmo saw he was breaking Dagget's concentration. He found no joy in Dagget's poor little rich boy life. He focused on the task at hand, on feeling the sparks running through his veins. Dagget was entirely comfortable with the sensation. Elmo liked the way it let him race around this man's thoughts. He felt these hands with long fingers, delicate for a butcher, sliding over Christina's skin. The electricity in his hands spread over her back, reached for her shoulders. Elmo was pleased by how well these hands could massage shoulders. He fell into a comfortable rhythm, working the muscles in her neck. Then he felt Dagget look down at his flaccid cock laying there like a dead fish. *Co-fucking-caine*, he heard Dagget think. *No fucking on co-fucking-caine*.

"Ow," Christina yelped. "Not so hard."

No it's not, Dagget thought. "Sorry, darlin', I guess I get carried away when I touch you."

She rolled over and smiled, giving Elmo his first real look at her. She looked to be in her twenties, auburn hair and freckles, and dark eyes that flashed with her thin-lipped smile. She pointed her head toward the little mirror on the nightstand. "Another line?"

"Why sure, darlin, it's there to make you happy." Dagget reached back, made sure the mirror was balanced on his palm, tightened the roll on the hundred dollar bill that served as their sniffing tube and presented it to her.

"*Muchas gracias*," she said, still smiling.

"Jeez," Dagget said, "Now you're part Mexican too?"

She ignored him, but Elmo watched how expertly she prepared, tightening the hundred a little further, taking a short breath, then exhaling slowly, completely. In a smooth, clearly practiced motion, she pushed the tube in her left nostril, hovered over the glass to move her body into position, and steadily snorted the three-inch line of powder.

"Aren't you going to lay out another line for yourself?"

"No, I'm still trying to get my motor running here." Dagget looked around sharply, feeling that someone was in the room watching him. Elmo had heard about cocaine paranoia. Now he felt it. Worse, Elmo found Dagget looking up to the panel where his camera was installed, and for a reason he never understood, Dagget knew what was there.

Christina paid it no mind. She curled down the bed to Dagget's dozing dong and took hold of it. "Gentlemen," she said, her lips drawing ever closer, "start your engines."

Dagget was surprised. Elmo was flabbergasted. The feeling of this warm mouth, caressing tongue, lips—all magnified by the chemical stimulant running through this bloodstream, a river of warm light coursing through him. He heard Dagget say, "Jesus, oh Jesus, oh sweet baby Jesus." He could feel Dagget in touch with the deity. Elmo thought it was probably more to do with alkaline. Together, they took long, luxurious breaths as his slowly swelling member lolled about her mouth. Elmo had never experienced anything like it.

It was a wet caress that sent signals through his body so exquisitely good it was almost painful, and it went on until Elmo's mind cried out with joy.

"Christ, there's somebody fucking watching us," Dagget yelled. He pulled back, his flag popping from her mouth at half-mast, and twisted around. "I feel it, damnit. There's somebody in here!" The flag drooped once more.

Out! Elmo shrieked mentally to Arbidor.

After a tumbling moment, Elmo was at his keyboard. On the screen, Dagget was looking in corners, trying to look under the bed, in the bathroom, and straight into the lens at Elmo. The bottom corner of his screen read Elapsed time 11:24.

"There's something in there, and I know that's got something to do with it. Somebody's watching, damnit."

"Forget the paranoid bullshit, baby, and come to bed. I still gotta get laid tonight, and you were starting to come along there."

Elmo sighed and took a swig of coffee. It was cold.

CHAPTER 29

"Doc says you can walk today. So walk."

Thea walked. Naked. Loretta saw freshly purpled bruises, the remnants of welts on Thea's small, taut frame. She took a quick step closer when Thea wobbled.

Thea held out a hand to stop her. "I can do it. It takes concentration, that's all."

"Still pretty sore?"

Thea nodded to conserve energy. She walked around the room slowly and stiffly for a few minutes. Part of the ache, she knew, was using muscles that lay unused for days. She stopped to take a few deep breaths, but would not sit.

"You're allowed to give yourself a rest," Loretta suggested.

A wan smile crossed Thea's face. Loretta never called her Terry, as if she knew the name was tainted merchandise. But neither did Loretta push the issue. She's patient, Thea thought. Fine. She took a few steps to the bed and let herself drop. She sat for a few minutes, watching Loretta watch her, and panting slightly. *Damn,* she thought, this is simple, *but it's exhausting. I don't want to be this tired.* Her body, however, had its own priorities, and pushing around bruised muscles was serious work.

"What do you say we get out of this room today?" Loretta tried to make the question sound casual, but Thea heard the urgent undertone in her voice.

The slight pained smile returned to Thea's face.

"I don't think I can go very far," she said. "And I don't want to be seen."

"Of course not, honey. I thought we'd just go across the street. Think you can handle that?"

Thea bit her lip. She didn't want to object to everything, but she was wary. "What's there?"

Loretta let out a little laugh. "The Voojoo temple." She watched Thea's eyes, and saw the guarded panic before Thea was ready to comment.

"That's a lot of people," she said.

Loretta didn't see why that should make any difference, but she saw her patient holding back. She might be able to understand the concern if she knew where it came from. This privacy thing was as obtuse as the obsession with men. Or was it all the same thing?

"Look, I'll stay between you and the men. It keeps business flowing. They'll never get near you."

Thea's face drooped, but she did not reply.

"They're very private about it," Loretta offered.

Thea's raised eyebrow suggested she was unconvinced.

"Look, they don't want the cops and all looking into their game. They know the police see Voojoo as a bogus religion. They're private people. They have to be. There's nowhere less likely for anybody to notice you."

"I don't want to go out."

Loretta thought she sounded like a child. Her voice remained soft, but she fired the question point blank: "What have you got to hide?"

Thea bit her lip. She shook her head and backed away. "I don't even have any clothes."

Loretta's smile was triumphant. "Like hell you don't. I got a friend your size. She's out of town. I brought her clothes for you. Put on these jeans. It's practically a Voojoo uniform. You'll blend right in. Besides, with those bruises, the marijuana at the service should ease the pain."

Thea knew she was fresh out of excuses. Nor did she want to start answering questions. The black Voojoo prayer shawl would hide her. From what she knew of the Voojoos, Loretta was probably right. They were a sect of convenience, assembled from the disenchanted of several faiths who liked the idea of smoking ganja to get close to God, or at least cop a buzz at the lunch hour service. Their doctrine had little to do with Voodoo or Judaism. But the Voojoo founders, having encounted a few too many pompous rabbis, had decided the name was an appropriate slap at the smug side of the religion they had abandoned. Thea knew the police like to keep their eye on the Voojoos. Were the police looking for her? There had been nothing of it on the television news.

She had been in this room for three days now. Life came only through the television. She had taken up Loretta's life, probably cutting into her business. She couldn't remain at the Lamp Post Motel and sponge off Loretta indefinitely. Still, she found it impossible to step from this inelegantly appointed room into the world.

She sat on the bed, hanging her head, but saying nothing.

Loretta stood, waiting. She crossed her arms, tapped her foot, and let two silent minutes pass before she walked out of the room, across the baked parking lot to buy herself a Coke from the vending machine in front of the office.

She looked through the plate glass window into the office, but didn't see Elmo. She went through the swinging glass door, grateful to be back in air conditioning, and poked her head around the doorway to the rear office. She caught a glimpse of Elmo seated at his desk. She brushed past the curved reception console into the main office.

Elmo was at his desk, all right. He sat. Just sat, giving no sign he had even seen Loretta bluster in, staring at an empty spot on the wall.

"So what the hell's the matter with you?" Loretta asked.

"People are strange," Elmo whispered hoarsely. His eyes remained fixed on the wall.

"No shit. Elmo, are you all right?"

His voice was toneless, his blank gaze unwavering. "I'm waiting for Inspector Haskell-Smythe."

"I can see you're going to be a lot of help. What happened to you? Elmo? Elmo! Anybody home?"

"Sort of, at the moment."

There was something dreamy in his voice. Elmo? Dreamy? They didn't much go together. She took a few quick steps around the desk, turned him in the swivel chair and took his face in her hands. His eyes refused to focus on her, but he didn't look entirely uncomfortable. "Elmo, where would you get LSD?"

He looked in her eyes, just inches from his face and not entirely in focus. A trace of a smile flickered at the corners of his mouth. He whispered, "I did co-fucking-caine." For just a moment she looked back at him in bewilderment. Then she let go of his face, threw back her head and erupted in a cackling laugh. Loretta let herself fall to the familiar couch across from Elmo. She gathered her breath to speak, but the sight of a glazed Elmo with this whacked-out Mona Lisa look overpowered her. She was laughing again. "You don't exactly look coked up, sitting there like a lump of Silly

Putty." She caught a glimpse of the white-on-red Coke can in her hand, the product of more than a century of marketing. Another wave of laughter shook her.

Elmo sat placidly, taking mild pleasure in Loretta's glee.

Loretta was able to get somewhat serious. "You look stoned to me." She knit her brow. "Elmo, this isn't you."

"Well, yes and no," he breathed.

"You don't talk like that and you don't look like that." She shook her head with the attached red mane. "What the hell's going on?"

Elmo took the question under advisement. He leaned his head to the left, then rolled it around to his right.

"And what's 'co-fucking-caine' got to do with it?"

Elmo took a breath to frame a reply, but the words eluded him, so he rolled his head right to left.

"Great. Same shit, different room. Elmo, do you suppose we could talk about this someti . . ." Suddenly, her brain latched on to yesterday's conversation about body-tripping, the questions about moving consciousness. Today, the questions seemed far less rhetorical. "Oh my God."

"Yes," he said with that maddeningly pleasant tone, "we'll talk about it sometime. I'm waiting for the inspector."

Loretta snapped off the couch. "I think this is the part where I came in." She turned to leave, then looked back at him. "Are you going to be all right?"

He gave that question, too, due consideration before he nodded. "Thanks," he rasped.

Loretta and her Coke burst back into 105 degrees and across the parking lot past the pool. No one was there. The water sparkled, reflecting the relentless sun and promising cool beneath the surface. Excellent therapy for a bruised body. Okay, maybe the Voojoo temple another time, let's get her out to the pool and let her work out the kinks slowly. She nodded, satisfied that justice would be done, and she—Terry or whatever her damn name is—would be working toward recovery. She walked a little faster, ducked around the stairway in front of 116, and slid her key in the lock.

Thea was standing in front of the mirror. She turned to the doorway when Loretta came through. She was dressed in blue jeans, a plaid shirt, and loafers. Her head was bowed. "You've been too good to me. If you want me to, I'll go."

Loretta shut the door behind the heat. "Great. After a morning like this I could use a buzz."

CHAPTER 30

Lydia Cosgrove rolled through Organ Pipe National Monument and stopped at Why for gas, as nearly every passing car did. The town consisted mostly of a pair of gas stations with a thriving trade in ice cold Dr Pepper.

She spent the hours rolling to Tucson reviewing the case of Brad Keller, a typical scoundrel inhabiting the underbelly of southeast Tucson, trying to hustle poker or pool, hanging out in alleyways to pop a pill or smoke a joint. In going through his possessions in the Keller bedroom, Cosgrove had come on a deep corner of his closet, behind the suits, where she extracted a ball of clothing—if you could call it that. Everything was old, stained in a variety of flavors, and tattered, more befitting a man who had just hopped off a Southern Pacific freight than a mildly successful real estate broker. Keller liked slumming. Mrs. Keller said he probably patronized hookers when he couldn't score a freebie.

Cosgrove preferred driving with the windows wide open through this stretch of Tohono O'odham reservation. The gentle fragrance of the desert through car windows was as close as she got to nature, but she liked it when she was there. By ten o'clock, there was no avoiding sealing off the car from the atmosphere into air-conditioned isolation. By eleven, she was approaching Tucson from the southwest on Ajo Way. She took it across the south side of town to the base, curled around the air force base on Golf Links Road and hung a left at Craycroft.

She thought she might spot Keller in the Voojoo temple for the noon assemblage. The amateurs always went there hoping to buy drugs. They were always disappointed.

She was half an hour early. She pulled into the Driftwood Lounge next door with Iggy's tail pointed at the Lamp Post Motel. She grabbed a beer, a burger and an inning of the Phillies and Diamondbacks. At ten till noon, she was in place in a back row of the temple, a discreet distance from the door, but close enough to see faces clearly. Keller's rounded face was etched in her mind, those eyes that seemed to squint in virtually every photograph, the pug nose and double chin. She waited.

The ceiling rose behind her into an arch all the way across the building, standard form for a 1950s-era bowling alley. Cosgrove remembered the Copa Bowl here years ago, how that arched ceiling drew the eye to the pins at the end of the lanes. The Voojoo who bought the building had wanted a dome, but thought the big hump-roof was a good compromise. Voojoo scholars (such as they were) postulated endlessly on the metaphor of the arched sky. The ceiling was painted black, dotted with thousands of points set aglow with blacklight. The room was dimmed to electric dusk. At precisely noon, it would go almost black for three minutes. The only lights then would be the flicker of a match or a lighter every few seconds, people starting early. If Keller came in early, that's when she would likely miss him. But if he did, she could spot him once the pulpit lights faded up.

The congregants trickled in slowly. In the foyer, each donned a thin black veil with flickers from iridescent threads, the Voojoo variant on the Hebrew

214

prayer shawl. Cosgrove cursed herself for not anticipating the detail that would obscure a side view of the
face. She thought she knew these Voojoos, but hadn't
considered the necessary privacy factor within the sect
in which membership was mildly scandalous.

All she really needed to see was that stocky form
with the slumped shoulders. Two such men passed
by. It took only a moment to see neither was Brad
Keller. They, at least, had not yet put the prayer shawls
up over their heads.

When the noon darkness came, Cosgrove was
ready. She stared into the darkest corner of the sanctuary to get her eyes fully accustomed to the light. She
darted her eyes back at the entrance, but no one
seemed to be coming in. Why was she so sure he would
be here? If Keller spent so much of his time slumming, he might know better than to show up here.
The sudden flames popping up around the room made
it hard to make out the shadows drifting through the
doorway. But there was no fat man.

She gnawed on her lower lip. Wasn't it three
minutes yet? Two more shadows, these wearing the
shawls over their heads, came through the doorway.
Women. One of them, the smaller one, was walking
uncomfortably, leaning on her companion. They came
slowly up the center isle and took seats four rows in
front of Cosgrove.

Still no fat man.

Still no lights. But the constant little flames
popping up all over the room were making it hard to
see the darkness.

A big man entered. Much too tall.

Then she saw three lanky cowboys, their boots
dragging across the floor. A mother and son were
stopped at the door. No children allowed; it would gen-

erate too much public relations heat. A few couples arrived, none of them shaped like Keller, and a lawyer she knew who looked around furtively as he entered.

The light was faint at first, a simulated dawn on the pulpit where the pins used to fall. Faintly, the sounds of insects, birds and little gusts of wind blew through. Then a voice, a chant, possibly in Arabic, wafted through the chamber.

The congregation responded, "Ah-ooohm."

To the same tune, the voice chanted a line of Hebrew. The congregation gave the same response. Same voice, in an attempt at an Oriental tone sounded more like a meowling cat. Chinese? Again the rejoinder, "Ah-ooohm." It was repeated in Greek, Latin, and finally English: "May the power of the universe be laid upon your head."

To which the congregation responded an especially emphatic, "AAAH-OOOOOHM."

Cosgrove was keeping an eye on that door. The temple fell silent, save the continuing chirping. The artificial dawn faded, and just as the darkness became complete, a spotlight pierced the room and illuminated a glittering gold marijuana leaf. On the leaf tips a Star of David, a Moslem moon, a crucifix, a dollar sign and an atom lit up in succession.

An electric bass laid down a reggae rhythm. In a puff of smoke on stage, a black man with Rastafarian dreadlocks appeared with a guitar.

May the power of the universe be laid upon your head.

May the force of life continue past the time when we are dead.

May we live in peace and harmony, may we make a decent buck.

216

When the world around comes crumbling down
May we just not give a fuck.

Again the audience chanted, then sang a second chorus with the cantor. Even with the stage lights, Cosgrove couldn't see any faces from the back of the congregation. She eyed a seat at the end of the front row, a much better vantage point. Still, she watched the entrance for the steady stream of latecomers. After the song, the cantor backed to a corner of the stage, but kept the beat going.

A sudden pop accompanied a puff of smoke on stage, but this time no one emerged from the smoke. The wisps dissipated and there was another burst of smoke, and seconds later, another. It was in the fourth burst of smoke and noise that Rev Tobias finally appeared, clad in a satin white bodysuit, trailing a black velvet, star-studded, high collared cape, a tribute to the last days of Elvis.

Cosgrove smirked. The rev looked to be all of twenty-five.

She glanced back at the door and caught the back of a man, a fat man, maybe just the right size, walking up the center aisle and stopping about halfway to the pulpit. Was that the slope to Keller's shoulders? Maybe. Now she coveted that front-row seat, but she waited for First Fire when everyone stood to light up. She watched the fat man, glanced back at the door every few seconds, and scanned the congregation as best she could. The ten minutes to First Fire felt like an hour, but she was ready when the crowd stood. She eased down the row to the far aisle, walked quickly through the smoke and took a deft sidestep to claim the prized seat. She took a deep breath and allowed herself a nod of satisfaction.

She didn't want to turn around too soon or too obviously. The congregation was preoccupied watching Rev Tobias toke on a joint and dance to the beat, and doing much of the same themselves. She turned slightly to her left, then a little more until she could see the front half of the congregation before turning her head. Her eyeballs straining left, she turned her head slowly and drew the fat man in her sights.

At first she thought it wasn't Keller, just a vague likeness. This face wasn't as piggish as the photos, but the more she looked, the more she thought this might be him. But no, maybe not. Was he too different from the photos? Impossible to tell. She might have to approach him when he left the temple and ask.

Cosgrove made another small turn, looking back toward the door. This time she caught a pair of eyes looking back at her, frightened, animal eyes. She started a thought. *What must this poor thing be so afraid . . .*

Their eyes met over the congregation. Cosgrove's opened wide in surprise. The other eyes opened wide too, the wary animal fear turning to the look of a cornered beast. "Thea Nikolas." Cosgrove said it in a breath. Even as she did, she saw the woman read her lips confirming her fears.

Cosgrove turned back to the pulpit. Nikolas certainly didn't look like she wanted to be seen. She turned around once more to see how Nikolas was reacting, but now her eye caught movement at the door. She glanced that way, blinked, and said, "Oh, Jesus."

It wasn't Jesus, of course. It was Brad Keller.

CHAPTER 31

Hey, God, whoever you are,
In another dimension or on a distant star,
We folks down here are calling on you please
Because there are so many, many, many things
we need.

We need water in the desert
We need to feel secure
We need to love each other
But we're so painfully unsure.
Oh, God please can't you help us know
What's wrong and what is right?
And tell us how to get laid
On Saturday night.

Hey, God, whoever you are,
In another dimension or by a distant star,
We folks down here are calling on you please
Oh God there are so many, many, many things
we need.

We need some politicians
With something more than greed,
We need to have a steady supply
Of omnipotent weed,
You're the ultimate connection
The universal boss
You've got to help us God,
We're being thrown for a loss.

Hey, God, whoever you are,
In another dimension or by a distant star,
We folks down here are calling on you please
You won't believe how many, many, many things
we need.

Thea found something soothing about the reggae beat, the skyvault ceiling, and the production values of a second-rate Vegas lounge act. She could feel the muscles unclench in her arms and especially her legs. She took a few easy breaths and wondered why she had resisted coming. She had heard about these Voojoos, but now she found herself getting into the funky rhythm of the service.

She still used the prayer shawl as a bunker, fending off stray eyes that might recognize her. No one seemed to pay her any attention. Well, why should they? Who would expect Thea Nikolas to pop up in Tucson, Arizona?

That one woman up front seemed more interested in the congregation than she was in the service. She was watching the heavy-set man a few rows in front. Thea tried not to look her way, but caught herself stealing glances to make sure the woman was interested in the filthy man-thing instead of her.

It was during one such glance that she found the woman looking directly at her. At first the woman's expression had been sympathetic. Thea saw her mouth go agape, saw her tongue touching her front teeth making the "th." Thea knew what her name looked like on someone else's lips.

She gasped. Her muscles went taut again. She clawed at Loretta's hand. Her voice squeaked. "We've got to get out of here." Loretta started to protest, but Thea was having none of that. She started shuffling toward the aisle. "I'm getting out of here," she said from behind clenched teeth. Her legs were already complaining from all this sudden use, but she pulled herself to the end of the pew and hobbled up the aisle to the entrance before Loretta caught up with her.

"That woman recognized me," she gasped at Loretta.

Loretta nodded. They could argue later. Now she had to calm her down. "The one up front on the end?"

Thea nodded and pulled Loretta through the doorway. "Keep her away from me."

Loretta didn't like the panic. "Okay, look, I'll have an usher see that she doesn't follow us. You wait here, I'll be back in a minute." She took a long step back inside.

Thea clung to the shawl, staring at the wooden box where she was supposed to replace it as she left. She would return this one another time. She was taking short breaths, almost panting. There was a triumph in that face as she said Thea's name. Was she going to follow them? She felt her thighs aching. Come on, Loretta, let's go.

Loretta was back in forty seconds, but Thea was sure it was ten times that. She pushed against the big carved wooden door to the street. She felt her legs push back. She wouldn't let the weight deter her.

She was out, walloped in the face with a blast of hot wind. She staggered down the handful of stairs. Her legs protested by increasing the pain.

Loretta's long strides still took a moment to catch up again. "Come on, it's going to be all right." Loretta was still not sure if anything was truly wrong. Elmo might be right: paranoid. She was stumbling and could fall on her face at any moment. Loretta slipped her head under Thea's right arm and slipped her left arm across Thea's back, careful to avoid the bruised spots. She took Thea's weight on her shoulders, and hauled her through the parking lot.

They dashed across Craycroft between lunch hour cars zipping to and from the base. Thea's thighs maintained their protest, but if she had to, she would walk back to the room on broken legs.

They paused at the curb. Thea was sucking in quick breaths, fighting the continuing objections from her body. After a minute she slowed her breaths, tilted her head back, and caught her first good look at the Lamp Post Motel.

The Lamp Post was at her most impressive from that front view, her big tan arches soaring, her trim wearing that peculiar mix of salmon pink and turquoise so popular all those years ago. Thea could almost smile at the five-ball lamppost at the edge of the driveway painted in those same exotic colors.

Then something caught her infrared-sensitive eye.

At first it was just a faint glimpse of something round and faintly red, up there on the roof. She took a closer look. Something was dreadfully familiar about it.

And then she knew.

The bubble.

The bubble no one else on the beach could see. The bubble that watched her watching back. The bubble that stayed with her, never approaching, never receding, even while she was being abused by two men even more repulsive than most of their male sub-species.

She opened her mouth to speak, but all that came out was an animal grunt. Her tongue seemed unwilling to make words, but she pointed. When she found a voice, it was a hoarse whisper. She pointed. "There it is."

Loretta looked. "There what is?"

It felt almost like dejá vu, but she had been there before. She closed her eyes, trying to draw strength from a body that had none in reserve.

"The bubble. That red sphere. The one I saw but my friends didn't. I followed it on the beach that night. It's about ten feet in diameter. And there the damn thing is again, on the motel roof."

Loretta looked where Thea pointed. A ten-foot sphere? Where? Was "Terry Norwood" having delusions? She looked hard, squinted her eyes.

"It's the same one," Thea said. "I can feel it."

"I don't see anything. Are you sure you're not just stoned?"

"Don't say that damnit, it's right *there*!"

Loretta was looking, eyes wide open, then squinting, looking from the corners of her eyes, and finally wondering what the hell she was doing. But somehow she caught a feeling of red, just a touch of a ruby glow to the air. Was it just the heat? Was something there?

Loretta pushed Thea along. "If you want to keep from being seen, they'll only hold her back for a minute or two. Come on."

Thea looked at it again. "It doesn't seem to be going anywhere. It's just sitting there on the roof."

"How about we talk about it in air conditioning behind a closed door?" Loretta wasn't sure whether she was humoring or believing "Terry."

"But . . ."

"Don't 'but' me, we don't have much of a head start here."

Thea took a last look and hobbled across the parking lot, behind the steel and concrete stairway and into 116.

The Voojoos treasured their privacy, explained the usher, a brunette with hesitant dimples and only a little acne. She told Cosgrove at some length about the unfortunate persecution of the faithful, when freedom of religion was granted by both God and the Constitution, and how sometimes guests in the temple had to be sternly reminded about the absolute need for the congregants' privacy. While she explained, she was blocking the doorway.

Cosgrove was prone to disagree, until another usher, male and barrel-chested, stepped up behind the first. Cosgrove waited, checking her watch, looking back at Keller, figuring she had been too damned lucky with this one anyway.

After three minutes, they allowed her to pass.

Nikolas and the redhead were gone, as she expected. Twenty-six seconds before, Thea and Loretta ducked behind a stairway into the end room of the motel across the street.

She walked over to Iggy, plunked down in the driver's seat, started the engine and the air conditioning. Iggy's clock may have long since given out. His heating was inconsistent, but the air conditioning and driver-controlled electric windows and door locks were in excellent working order. So was the cell phone. She dialed Andi Norwood and got an answering machine.

"I'm calling at 12:23. Thea Nikolas is alive and in Tucson. I'll get back in touch with you later this afternoon."

Back when she did such things to herself, she would have sat back with a cigarette. Now she just propped her feet up on the passenger seat, smoked the joint she picked up in the temple, and filled the air inside Iggy with a smoke that was sure-fire Keller-bait. She waited for him to come out of the service, pulled up in front of him the moment she rolled down the window, gave him time to take a breath, and asked him if he was interested in making a purchase. From there she suggested they take a little ride to negotiate, and from there she drove him straight home. It was easy, and routine.

As for stumbling across Thea Nikolas, Cosgrove figured she worked hard enough to earn an occasional stroke of blind luck.

CHAPTER 32

At fifteen seconds before noon, Inspector Haskell-Smythe was at the front desk, a snarl spread sideways across his face. Elmo drifted out with a wan smile of his own, finally composed after his morning voyage. "Good noon to you inspector. Are you ready to look her over?"

Haskell-Smythe knit his brow. "Her? Who's that?"

"Why, the Lamp Post. Would you like me along to guide your tour, or would you prefer to check her out on your own?"

"For your information, Skinner, I've already been up 'her' ass with a microscope this morning."

"Then I trust you found everything in order."

Haskell-Smythe didn't care for the reverie that told him Skinner's mind was somewhere else. Neither did he like giving so clean a bill of health.

"Everything," he said almost bitterly. "I checked more than the gas connections in the building. I looked at the plumbing, the ventilation, and the electrical."

Elmo smiled that obsequious smile.

"You got a lot of electrical, Skinner."

Elmo's eyes snapped into sharp focus. "I like to keep an eye on my property."

"All connected to a central computer, is it? Right up—oh, about . . ." he pointed precisely in the direction of the command room, "there." He eyed Elmo for a long moment. "Couldn't find a way in."

"It's private," Elmo said evenly. His heart was

pounding.

"Is that what it is? Why don't you ask your computer to call up the section of the city code that empowers the Chief Inspector to inspect any premises on which there has been a violation?"

"It's not really necessary. My circuits are clean and well above legal standards. That's my personal control center. No one goes in there but me. I'm sure you understand."

The inspector hadn't been anxious to see the room, but now it was a matter of principle. "I will decide what is necessary."

"I've been as open with you as I know how, inspector. I've made the repairs you ordered and several more. I've let you poke your nose anywhere you cared to. Can't you do one thing for me and just let my private room be? I assure you, it's all in order."

The gnarled old man cocked his head to one side, then the other. "I like you, Skinner. You run a clean operation."

Elmo gave the slightest nod. "Can I get you a cold drink?"

"If there is anything wrong with the infrastructure of the Lamp Post Motel, it would likely be at the head end of the system. Now let's see it."

Elmo sighed. He took off his glasses, looked at the dust accumulated on the lenses and wiped them lightly with a cloth from his pocket. "This way," he said, putting the glasses back on.

His feet plodded down the private stairway, with footsteps behind his for the first time—and a cane. He took the few steps through his room as quickly as he could. Nothing there was worth hiding, but the prying eyes gave him the willies.

Elmo opened the door and stepped into his

sanctuary, turned around and blocked the doorway. "No one has ever been in this room, inspector. I don't believe you said please."

Haskell-Smythe squinted at Elmo, rolling his head for fifteen seconds. He swooped his cane toward Elmo's legs. "I don't believe I have to."

He stepped inside, and let his eyes move across the rows of blank video monitors, the recorders, mixers and editors. He rolled his head around, his mouth open, tongue running across his teeth. He ran his hand across the keyboard and command console.

Elmo couldn't have felt more violated if the inspector had reached into his pants. He was grateful that he wasn't asked to give a demonstration. He simply stood behind the inspector as he bent down to check the wiring underneath the console. For a long moment, his foot begged for the opportunity to land one swift, lovely kick to toss Chief Inspector Haskell-Smythe sprawling in the cables and dust.

He didn't. He simply stood, arms folded across his chest, his right foot tapping. The inspector was sitting on the floor, his head lost in the spaghetti connections. After a minute, his head reemerged.

"You make clean connections, Skinner." He reached out a hand for Elmo to help him to his feet.

Elmo's arms remained folded across his chest. His foot was still tapping.

"Please," Haskell-Smythe said, almost as if he meant it.

Elmo took his time unfolding his arms. But he took the inspector's hand and pulled him off the floor.

"Thank you."

Elmo nodded.

The inspector settled into the gray-tufted executive chair and looked over the keyboard hungrily.

He typed "STATUS" and was treated to the present occupancy rate of twenty-two per cent. He typed "RE-VIEW 114" and got a screenful. Norman Abernathy of Tombstone, masturbating with shaving cream. The inspected hooted. More information on Giordano the night before and Howard Robinson before that. From one day the week before, he encountered stars and an 8.6 rating and the screen query Show video? He typed yes, cackling now.

Elmo had never bothered using any of the elaborate passwording or other security measures he had studied. He hadn't seen the need for them. Until now.

"Inspector, these are private records. They're for my use only. You're violating the privacy of my guests. Please, if you would . . ."

His pleas were drowned out by the speakers. This performance achieved its rating through the woman's vocal responses, not mere grunts or "oh baby"s, but squeals and moans that appeared to spur the man on top, identified as Chester Hawkins. Elmo squeezed his eyes shut. His fists and jaw were clenched. This was rape.

The inspector was almost bouncing in the chair, cackling and yowling.

"Enough!" Elmo shouted. He grabbed both sides of the chair, spun the inspector around and rolled him into a corner away from the console. "You know, I think there's a storm coming this afternoon." Elmo bent over the keyboard and jabbed at the keys. Down.

The computer shut down all but necessary equipment and locked into triple surge protection mode.

The inspector reached for his cane and stepped out of the room. His eyes scanned the bedroom before he attempted the difficult stairway descent. "Could you go out first?"

Elmo was thrilled to lead the inspector out.

Haskell-Smythe was wheezing when he reached the top of the stairs. "I thought you were going to kick my ass there for a minute."

Elmo looked him in the eye. "I thought about it."

"I might even deserve it," the inspector said. He straightened up as best he could. "That's a hell of a security system you got there Mr. Skinner."

Elmo breathed a little easier. Haskell-Smythe could have him up on several charges. "A good manager keeps his eye on the property." He gratefully followed the inspector to the door, contemplating his final chance for a good, swift kick. He settled for a thought. Twice, in that room, something happened to me, something more extraordinary than you, you pathetic little bastard, could ever imagine. Pry as you will, that you will never know.

He extended his hand. The inspector looked at the hand and grunted something inaudible. Elmo stood firm, his hand waiting for Haskell-Smythe to acknowledge ancient rules of civilized behavior.

The inspector let him squirm for a long moment before he offered his twisted paw.

Behind him, Elmo saw Loretta emerge from 116 and walk toward them. She looked much too serious, he thought. As she approached them, she hesitated for a beat, took a bright red-orange dab at her lips, which curled into a professional smile. She walked up on Haskell-Smythe's blind side and applied a big sloppy kiss on his cheek.

"Why inspector, what a wonderful surprise seeing you here—in the daylight! And don't you look ever so adorable with your clothes on." She grabbed the twisted little man and smothered him in her bosom. "Don't you think it's a little early for business?"

He pulled himself away, turned without looking at either of them, and hobbled off as fast as his cane would allow. He got in a white Ford with a City of Tucson logo on the door and a painted inscription underneath: PENALTY FOR PRIVATE USE.

CHAPTER 33

Observation notes: Xaq Hobesian Arbidor 7906021

The literature of the period inextricably intertwine sex and love. On preliminary investigation, lust and abiding affection are shown to have only occasional linkage. A hero of celluloid popular fiction is rewarded with outstanding specimens with whom he may mingle his genes. The primal urge for genetic coding, however, leads twenty-first century man to hold paramount the need to acquire an attractive mating partner with genetic excellence, which is a highly subjective matter relating to a precarious balance of similarities and dissimilarities.

Love is but a cloak for true sexual attractant, the pretext for the force that truly drives the species at this stage of development. The magnet that brings out sexual desire and attractiveness both can be composed of a matrix of factors, in which beauty, a well-proportioned body, wealth, access to illicit substances and status are weighed along with the subjective judgments of the individual.

The common bond with such causalities has been seen to be raw personal power. A noted diplomat of the period, himself not particularly physically appealing but renowned in his time throughout his world, stated that power is the ultimate aphrodisiac. He is observed here to be correct.

The examination of literature is suggestive of lust, love and marriage being a natural progression. Mar-

riage is twenty-first century primary pair bonding for genetic expansion, as evidenced by its prohibition among homosexuals who do not among themselves generate progeny. The reality within this society is revealed in a typical marriage in which the bond is of mutual resentment. The couple under investigation becomes tied more closely by their animosity and need to surpass each other's violation of the vow they took when forming the marital community. Yet because contradiction of the marital contract remains at the core of their relationship, the union is more sound in its perverse way than the more prevalent marginal-love, minor-resentment long-term pairing.

Here at a millennium of human development, a commitment is displayed by these societies to primary-bonding as an exclusive arrangement, although in practice this is widely violated. At this stage, the pretext is for a series of primary pairings through the life period. Several more centuries will pass before the strictures of interrelated primary, secondary and tertiary sexual bonding and the mobility of these statuses to individuals as momentary needs demand, form a safer base from which more of the species can claim a degree of relatedness.

* * * * *

Andi had no idea how people lived through this heat. Unless all these houses and cars and people were put here as some stupendous joke, people really lived here. She didn't like the thought of Womonbooks running without her. She was more than ready to go back to Palo Alto. Maybe tonight, tomorrow for sure.

It was only twenty steps from the car to the front door of Joanne and Donna's little ranch house on the cul de sac, but it was enough. No, she had to admit she didn't sweat much in this dry but withering heat. Andi stumbled through the doorway, braced by the electric cool. She headed for the kitchen for heavily iced tea, which she gulped down and refilled. She started looking around the telephone for the number of the les travel agent.

Next to the phone, a small red light blinked once. Andi punched the button to retrieve the message and took a swallow of tea.

"I'm calling a few minutes after noon. Thea Nikolas is in Tucson."

She spilled tea down her neck and on her shirt. She didn't care. Thea was alive!

Andi dug Cosgrove's business card out of her purse and dialed the number. The questions were stacking up at the end of her tongue.

"Hi, this is the voice of Lydia Cosgrove. I'm here to tell you that the body of Lydia Cosgrove is engaged elsewhere, doing God knows what by this time. If you want to leave a message, touch eight on your telephone keypad. If you want to try your luck with the mobile phone, touch nine. If you don't want to do either, call back later."

Andi opted for the cell phone. Cosgrove answered after one quick ring.

"Cosgrove. State your business."

"It's Andi Norwood. You've found Thea? Can we see her? What's she doing there? Where's this..."

"Whoa, girl. Just grab hold of yourself. I'm on my way back to my office. Do you know where the Sacred Cow is?"

"Huh?"

"It's a bar on Fourth Avenue. It's dark and cool. Meet me there in exactly an hour.

234

Refrigerated air awaited Andi inside the glass door. She gulped it. The Sacred Cow was quiet this Thursday afternoon. The dance floor was dark and empty. From upstairs came silence. Down half a dozen stairs to the left was a door that might have been to a janitor's closet. From behind that door came the rattling bell of a pinball machine, dinging out the points. Being the only sound in the place, she followed it.

Cosgrove was going to meet her here. Four o'clock, she said. Well, it was quarter after with no Cosgrove to be seen. Most of the light came from the pinball machine that jangled up the score as it flashed on the guy riding the flippers, a guy dressed in a black leather jacket and sunglasses.

The barstools looked safe enough. Andi sat. She tried to look around, but her eyes were still unaccustomed to the light. Behind the bar, a mirror echoed the darkness. Where was that bartender? Where the hell is Cosgrove?

"Are you drinking, or have you simply crawled into our cool dark hole?" A dark woman, Indian perhaps, slowly took shape behind the bar. A shiver bolted up Andi's spine.

"I . . . I'm looking for Lydia Cosgrove."

"Many people do."

Andi raised an eyebrow. "Is she here?"

The bartender held her hands out at the room, which Andi could see a little by now. "Do you see her?"

"No," Andi snapped, "or I wouldn't ask."

"Then she is not here." The Indian woman blinked twice. "Can I get you a drink?"

Andi leaned on the bar and crossed her legs under it. "Burgundy."

"Instantly." The bartender gave a little nod. She disappeared back into the gloom and materialized seconds later with a tall glass.

Andi saw a hand on a black leather arm slap a five dollar bill on the bar. "I'm buying the lady a drink. And I'm having another beer." The guy from the pinball machine. The leather in his jacket groaned when he moved. "You wanna dance or something, tootse?"

"Excuse me?" Andi wanted to brush this oddball aside. What was he doing in a les bar anyway? And why would he come on to a woman in a place like this?

"Oh, don't they have nothing like dancing where you come from?"

"Well of course we do. But there's no music."

"Now you're making excuses. You mean you'd dance with me if there was music?"

"Look, I'm not your 'tootse,' okay? Now what is it you want?"

"I wanted to buy you a drink. I guess there's a little music in Palo Alto, isn't there?"

Andi whirled. "How do you . . ."

"You wanna find your girlfriend or not?"

"Did Lydia send you?"

"She sends me everywhere I go." A hand reached up and removed the sunglasses. "A little bright in here, don't you think?"

Andi looked at him. Something about those eyes.

"Burgundy, huh? A good les drink. You a good les?"

"Who's asking?" Andi snapped.

A pause. A smile. "Cosgrove."

Andi blinked. She giggled. She hiccupped. Shaking her head, she could finally see Lydia there inside the costume. "Without your makeup and the man's suit, I wouldn't have . . ."

236

"That's a costume. So is this. It lets me fade into the background and overhear a snatch of conversation—maybe even a useful one."

"Where's Thea?"

"She's here in Tucson. At least she was about noon. I saw her at the Voojoo temple."

Andi tilted her head back. "You're making this up, right?"

"I saw her there."

"How is she?" Andi's voice was ready to crack.

"She was limping," Cosgrove said.

"God, I should have stayed with her. What happened to her?"

"She didn't give me the chance to ask."

"Well, where did she go?"

"I didn't see."

"What *did* you see?"

"I saw your Thea standing next to a tall, red-headed woman. A prostitute, I think. They were in the Voojoo temple. She was looking scared. When she caught me looking at her, she ran like hell, despite the limp. The ushers kept me from following. Those Voojoos have a thing about privacy. When I got outside, they were gone."

"Do you think she's still around there?" Andi had a tremor in her voice.

"I don't think there's any way of knowing. But people usually go somewhere more than once. Whatever she's doing with a professional girl in a Voojoo temple, chances are she's around there somewhere. I think we ought to get a good vantage point on the neighborhood."

Andi tilted her head. "Vantage point?"

"Yeah," Cosgrove said. "The Lamp Post Motel."

Andi glanced at her watch. Four-thirty. Thea

was last spotted hours ago. She barely noticed the heat until she grabbed Iggy's chrome door handle.

Cosgrove opened the door from the inside. "Only mad dogs and outlanders touch a chrome door handle in the midday sun. Get in, the air is leaking."

Andi settled in the well-worn leather seat and put her purse on the floor. Cosgrove pulled around the corner before Andi erupted into questions. "What was she doing there? How did you find her? What was she doing? What is this Lamp Post Motel?"

"You're going to have to take it easy," Cosgrove said. "Take a look around. This neighborhood was built in the late forties and early fifties. As we drive east through Tucson, you move through decades of development. The next two miles were built in the fifties, then the sixties growth out to past Wilmot. Sort of like reading rings in a tree trunk."

"It's an ugly little city," Andi huffed.

"Yes, but in a beautiful place. The desert in springtime is…"

"All right, if you're going to tell me to relax, could you at least answer my questions?"

"I spotted her in the Voojoo temple. She was with a tall redheaded woman. The Lamp Post is directly across the street from the temple, down by the Air Force base. It falls a mite shy of your four-star resorts. You see, when they opened the base, it was way outside the city. But Tucson just grew up around it and…"

"Have you got this secret desire to be a tour guide or something?"

"I'm trying to take your mind off Thea. We might have already missed her," Cosgrove said.

"Well, it's not working. Is she all right?"

"You can ask her when you see her. If we see

her." Cosgrove made a right turn off Fifth Street onto Craycroft. Two miles due south, they pulled into the parking lot of the Lamp Post Motel.

Elmo took a couple of vacancy inquiries on the phone before the white Peugeot dieseled to a stop in front of the office. He thought diesel described the driver as well, a mannish woman if ever there was one, with a tall, stringy blonde. Awful lot of women checking in tonight, he thought. Must be a les convention in town. He pulled out the key to a double room in the far corner of the building.

He lifted an eyebrow at the customer's registration card. Andrea Norwood, Palo Alto, California. Familiar sounding name, that. His lips were ready to pose a question. But he thought of Terri Norwood's paranoid fear, and how there might be at least some legitimate foundation to it. Privacy was what his guests paid for.

"I'm looking for someone," Norwood said. "Thea Nikolas. Have you seen her?"

Elmo's eyebrows converged. "Thea Nikolas? You mean radical feminist separatist Thea Nikolas? The man-hating bitch-queen testosterone-poisoning theorist, Lesbos-for-lesbians writer Thea Nikolas?" He turned his bullshit indicator on high, showing practically all his teeth. "Why sure. She was here last week with President Vomper."

Despite the heat outside, the blonde's voice was ice. "I hardly think so. Not with that slob, or anyone else from the male subspecies."

He handed her the keycard. "Room 144, ma'am. Upstairs, around the back."

Thea Nikolas, he mused. Could be.

CHAPTER 34

Mort Phipps took off his glasses to find the smudge that had been floating in front of him for an hour. He looked at his watch, disappointed that digital time didn't move any faster. Afternoons were becoming interminable, nursing a few computer banks, waiting for anything that required human presence. It was a good system, so it rarely did. But he was there. In case.

He was free to think of anything at all. He was thinking about Tilly and tonight. It was only their second date. She was small, chubby and encouraging. Even when Mort was boring himself, Tilly seemed enthralled by the tedium of working in Member Security for the Phoenix regional office of Global Express. She looked at him with a warm combination of admiration and desperation.

He was going to have to bring crossword puzzles to work. Or he might get a good bit of reading done. He had a stack of books waiting until he found the time.

The computer console beeped. It was an odd sort of beep, nothing he had heard for these two months in the technical dungeon. Mort rolled his head toward the screen.

He blinked.

It was a blue monitor. Everything on it every day had been blue. Always. It was incapable of anything but blue. But one line, all by itself, was a queer yellow-green.

Run a check on James A. Zachary 3745 458 459214.

There was no transmission time, place or code. Nothing whatsoever identified or authenticated the request. Had some hacker kid managed to get through the multiple levels of GlobEx computer security to leave this bogus message? It was too informal for normal in-house communication.

He wrote down the name and number. This might be a practical joke, but he had nothing better to do.

He knew he was on to something when the social security number came up bogus. He cross-checked the Los Angeles address. The suite number was a private box at a postal service established to provide a Sunset Boulevard address for its clientele. The telephone number turned out to belong to a Santa Monica chiropractor.

Mort jumped into the account records. The information said the account listing was five months old, but the account number was not listed on the databanks until two days ago. Had a hacker penetrated the smothering layers of file security? Unlikely, but nonetheless possible. Charges were all within that two-day period, all in Tucson, Arizona, including a three hundred dollar credit authorization from the Lamp Post Motel.

* * * * *

Elmo started to pull himself out of the chair.

"Don't get up on my account." In rhythm with another thud from the horizon, Loretta in a simple pale blue dress, breezed past the front desk. She took up her position on the couch.

"My patient's taking a nap. Can I buy you dinner?"

Elmo looked at her.

"Is that too tough a question? Do you remember your name?"

"Vaguely." His voice was barely loud enough to be heard. "I'm Calvin Dagget, a cokehead from San Antonio. I'm Michael H. Giordano, with a heart full of hate."

Loretta leaned forward and narrowed her eyes. "Are you okay, Elmo?"

Elmo gave a little shrug. "What's okay?"

"Let's get you some food. Or would you prefer cocaine?"

"No," Elmo managed to mumble. "Dinner sounds like a good idea. I don't think I've eaten today."

Loretta fished a set of keys from her armored purse. "Spoken like a true cokehead. Elmo, I've never seen you like this. I'll drive, okay?" She took him by the arm. Lamely, he went along. A thunderclap, just a few miles away, met them as they came out the glass door.

Loretta unlocked the passenger door of her white Cadillac. The storm was moving southeast to northwest. If they headed for the northeast corner of the valley, they might steer away from it.

The wind tousled the palms over the pool. A few dead fronds fell after one sustained gust. Overhead, a flotilla of clouds, great flat-bottomed battleships with puffy fortifications, sailed through the gap between the Rincon and Santa Rita mountains. They were mountains of tumultuous vapor, soaring above the granite hills whose shape they mimicked. Lightning was their herald.

A scattering of heavy raindrops blew across the parking lot. Loretta backed out of the slot, turned on her lights and edged warily toward the street. She held back until she found a clear opening, then roared left onto Craycroft. The rain was still sparse, but the big drops burst like small bombs on an armored tank.

Just past Twenty-Second Street, a bolt of lightning sizzled in an eerie dance with a palm tree not a hundred yards ahead of them. An enormous crack of thunder rattled the sky. The palm burst into flames. They rolled on, safe but dazed.

Traffic was still light enough to maneuver. Even under normal circumstances, Loretta pegged every driver for a drunk hell-bent on wrinkling her fenders and injuring her product. In the rain, Tucson drivers were hopelessly out of their element. She held steadfastly to the speed limits seven miles up Craycroft. The rain intensified briefly, but they seemed to be driving out of it.

The rain had one salutary effect. It had dropped the temperature thirty degrees. Loretta rolled down the electric windows.

"So you want to talk about it?"

"What? Lightning? The inspector?"

Her eyes were too fixed on the road to shoot him a dirty look.

"Body tripping, Elmo. We were going to talk about it. Sometime. Do you think maybe we could talk about it now?" She didn't like this new, spaced-out Elmo. He was in command of nothing.

"Oh, that." He said it so softly it was nearly lost in the noise of the car and the wind. "What is there to say?"

Loretta rolled her eyes. She turned right on Sunrise Drive then left on Kolb Road toward the en-

243

trance to Ventana Canyon Resort. The sky in this corner of the Tucson valley was but a thin gray sunscreen. The battle fleet was off bombarding the center of the valley.

The hotelier in Elmo sat up and took notice. Ventana Canyon was Tucson's first of half a dozen major resorts, built on what was once the Flying V Ranch. Miles up the canyon at the top of the ridge was a smooth fin of rock, perhaps a hundred feet long and twenty feet high, and in it was a hole, fifteen feet across and ten feet high. From Tucson, the morning sky was visible through the window—la ventana.

For all Elmo had heard of Ventana Canyon resort, this was his first visit. A stroll through the hotel chastened his pride in the Lamp Post. The design concept was unobtrusive luxury. The structures were made of a brown rock to almost blend into the canyon. A stream, fed by hotel pumps, started in a strategically placed waterfall and flowed directly underneath the marble-clad lobby. The deep fibers beneath his feet sucked up every sound.

"More than a few million sunk in this place," Elmo said.

Two restaurants were in the main building. This time of year, they might even get in without reservations. Instead, Loretta chose the Flying V Grille, in a separate building a little downslope from the hotel with glass walls overlooking the storm's assault on the valley.

They sat outside under the ramada, sheltered from the few raindrops that reached this far. Loretta ordered Irish coffees. "You need the caffeine and you need the booze."

Elmo nodded. "Amen."

They watched gray bristles of rain sweep the

valley floor. From the belly of one vaporous tower was an opaque column, a lighter gray, almost white, dropping a torrent on midtown to the accompaniment of frantic lightning.

"Nature cleans up after us," Loretta said.

He pursed his lips. "She turns our bones to dust."

Loretta smiled. "Not right away, at least."

The drinks arrived. The first lights popped on in the valley while they worked halfway through the round. The coffee was working. Elmo's eyes opened a little wider. His input overload agitation subsided, tranquilized by tracking a storm through the valley and a liberal shot of Irish whiskey.

Loretta ordered for both of them, swordfish steaks and rosé wine. She took his hand across the table. "This has been hard on you."

Elmo clenched his jaw and nodded.

"Tell me what happened."

He told. He gushed like the torrent that was buffeting Reid Park, about the computer and Arbidor, crawling on the floor to unplug the equipment, the bolts of fear as he realized he was likely dealing with an unexplainable power. He gushed about Giordano's marvelous body and poisoned mind.

"I've seen a few of those," she said. "Strange people."

"I know. I *was* him." He tiptoed around his observational hobby; beyond that Elmo told all of it, barely pausing while the waitress served them, talking still between bites of swordfish and sips of wine. He told her about this morning's trip to Calvin Dagget and cocaine. He brought her right up to this afternoon when she had met him and the Inspector in the parking lot, and thanked her for shrinking

Haskell-Smythe down to size.

"That was my genuine pleasure, I promise."

Outside, the storm was tossing its final lightning bolts across the darkening sky. City lights spread across the Tucson basin, shining like jewels through the freshly cleaned, ozone-charged air.

Elmo, fed, unburdened, a tad drunk and breathing ozone, felt a damned sight better.

Loretta balanced the wine glass between her fingers. "How much control do you have over these trips?"

"That's hard to say. Arbidor seems to abide by my thoughts almost before I think them. He responds instantly when I want out."

"So he's monitoring you through it. How can he do that?"

"How can he—if Arbidor even is a he—how can he do any of it? Where does such a capability come from?"

Loretta shrugged and looked up at the sky, but nowhere near the direction of Saturn.

"Not this world. This afternoon my patient—or whatever she is—said she saw a glowing red bubble on the motel roof. I didn't see it, but she swore it was there. What freaked her out was that she said she saw this same red bubble floating in the sky just before she was raped in Mexico last Sunday night. Have you seen anything weird up there on the roof, Elmo?"

Elmo shook his head. "You mean to tell me I've got aliens in my motel?" It was at that moment that he made the connection.

Loretta looked at him blankly. She added upturned palms to this shrug. "Maybe."

"And they're fucking with my mind."

"Apparently."

"Why?"

Loretta took a sip of wine. "Why does anybody do anything?"

"Because their phone numbers are alike," Elmo quipped.

Loretta wore a question mark on her brow.

"You had to be there."

Through the chocolate cheesecake dessert, they watched the storm retreat to behind the Catalina Mountains at their backs. Across the horizon, lightning flashes silhouetted the Tucson Mountains on the western end of the valley, with distant grumbles to remind the city dwellers of the fury that had passed.

"Are you going to do it again?"

"Yes." He said it without hesitation.

She took hold of his hand again. "Elmo, something could go wrong. Are you sure this Arbidor isn't setting you up for something awful?"

"No, I'm not sure of anything. He seems completely in control of what he says he is—or she, if that's what Arbidor is."

"Or what," Loretta said. "Elmo, I don't like it. What if you're stuck in somebody and can't get out?"

"Isn't everyone?"

Loretta was undeterred. "This could be dangerous."

He dropped his head and found himself looking into an empty ice cream dish. "I hadn't given it any thought. I suppose there is some risk involved but..." He looked back at her, into her. "Could you pass up an opportunity like that—to be in another man's skin?"

Loretta laughed. "You're asking the wrong girl. I got another man's skin in me most of my working day."

A smile came upon Elmo from behind and

spread through him.

"I can see the attraction," she said. "You've locked yourself away in the Lamp Post, and it's got to be a kick to be able to step out of being you for a while. What happens if you stay longer than a few minutes?"

He shrugged. "I stayed maybe fifteen minutes in Dagget, and he started becoming aware of my presence. Thought someone was watching him. Beyond that, I don't know."

"It scares me, Elmo."

"And it's scaring the piss out of me. But I'll do it again."

"It could have permanent side effects."

"So could the mercury in the swordfish or a beer truck running a red light. Life's full of chances."

Loretta chuckled. "I think it's affecting you already, but so far I like it. That's not my old friend Elmo talking." The waitress returned with her credit card. "How about if we continue this over a bottle of wine back at the Lamp Post?"

At the mention of the Lamp Post the waitress took a quick step back. Her face registered sour disapproval.

Elmo was feeling expansive. "Let's. Come on up to my room."

The waitress gasped in horror.

Elmo was surprised at his offer. In the two years Loretta had run her business from the Lamp Post, they had almost daily conversations, usually in the office or Phil's bar. He had never so much as mentioned he even *had* a room. "And a bottle of rosé."

The waitress, older and thin with sharp features, retraced her tart condemnation. She drew up to her full sixty-five inches. "I am not a bartender."

Loretta looked up at her. "You have a customer who has ordered a bottle of wine. I suggest you see to it with dispatch." She punctuated her request with a pat on the waitress' rump, which successfully launched her on her way.

They drove back to the city through dark, cool desert that thirsted no more. In the city, the Cadillac rolled through flooded streets slowly, inexorably south to the Lamp Post Motel.

Elmo brought out wine glasses he couldn't remember ever using. For the six years he had lived in this room, neither had there been occasion to use the second chair.

Loretta stared at him. "You look like a little boy whose balloon just popped. Has anybody else been up here?"

"Only one, and that was today." Elmo attempted at a British accent: "The esteemed Inspector Haskell-Smythe thought it officially important to inspect all the way up my arse with a microscope."

"The official city tapeworm," she sniggered.

"He's that." Elmo sipped at the wine. "How's your patient?"

Loretta sighed. "Not good. Sleeping the last I know."

"All this from a rape?"

"That and a lot of things it did to her head. Seeing this bubble didn't do much for her either. Doc's probably with her now."

"What's wrong with her?"

"Well, she's a little high-strung. Maybe even paranoid, like you said. But right now she's a basket case," Loretta added.

"She didn't want anybody to know."

"Elmo, she's collapsed completely. She was

249

unconscious, for no apparent physical reason. Doc says it could be dangerous, maybe a blood clot or something. She needs to go to a hospital. But she has this thing about hospitals, this thing about men, this thing about doctors. In her emotional state, if she wakes up there..." Loretta's hands jangled through the air.

This time it was Elmo who reached across the table, took her hands and found her eyes. He looked for words, but found none. None were needed. Her eyes moistened, but she forced a smile to shut off the tears.

Their hands were clinging to one another. Their eyes leveled and locked. Each gazed on the lonely places of another who had seen so many come and go. Hands gripped ever tighter, drawing strength from each other. Wistful little smiles said yes, I know that lonely place where no one ever comes. That's just what it's like in here.

"Make love to me Elmo," she whispered.

Elmo blinked. He opened his mouth, but unsure how he wanted to respond, no words fell out. "I ... I..." His eyes ran around the room. Sex? Not behind the safety of a monitor, even the thinner shield of another's consciousness, but real one-on-one, making it happen, having it happen? We have a business relationship. Sex shouldn't intrude. Sex! Nothing to be afraid of, it's the product both of us sell every day. I'm in professional hands. SEX? Me? For the first time in six years? Now? It's never free. There's *always* a price.

She leaned toward him and waved her hand in front of him. "Elmo? You still in there? I didn't mean to scare you."

He didn't want to say no. He hadn't the courage to say yes.

Loretta took his hand. "Hey, it's all right." She resisted adding 'baby' as she did with a client. "Forget I ever said it." She refilled the wine glasses.

"It's just that..."

"Forget it, Elmo. Please."

His tone turned snide. "Is this what's called manager's prerogative in your business? Fuck the manager to keep business on an even keel?"

She turned her face as if smacked. "Not fucking. I fuck twenty times a week. I meant making love. I know it's been a long time for you." She hesitated. "It's been a while for me too."

His eye blazed. "I don't need your damn pity. Save it for your patient."

"I'm sorry, Elmo. I thought we had a moment. I thought we could make it last a while." She searched for a new subject.

His head drooped. "I didn't mean that. That's not me talking."

"Forget it." She tried to lighten her tone. "What did Inspector Tapeworm need to see?"

"My computer." The wine made him bolder than he had intended. "In my basement." This might be worse than talking about sex. He knew her next question:

"Can I see it?"

He sighed. He might have had an easier time of it in bed. "That room is my most private place. The inspector invaded that space today. I felt like I was being raped."

"Never mind, I didn't mean to..."

"No," Elmo said softly, leaning closer. "I think I'd like to show you.

251

CHAPTER 35

Elmo went from disorientation to chaos.

His first sensation was a burglar alarm clamoring in an empty warehouse. The alarm rang on and on, but no one appeared to be home in this body. Elmo was continuously bombarded by the sensory static of a nervous system gone haywire. He looked for ways to take the controls of this body, but everything seemed overloaded, shut down, or both.

Damn. He didn't want to be here in the first place. She was probably certifiable. If exposure to Giordano and Dagget had affected him, how would this man-hating maniac warp him?

He was preparing to call "out" to Arbidor when it occurred to him that, for the first time, he was occupying a female body. A frazzled female body to be sure, but a female nonetheless. He tried to figure out what a vagina felt like. Sore is how it felt. The bottom of this body ached. He could feel the swelling in her thighs. Could he move an arm to reach down and touch it? It took all his concentration to get past the body alarm, but he reached down and felt the soft folds of skin. They were painful to the touch, and he withdrew the hand. He reached for the breasts on this body. They too, were aching from abuse, but he could feel the tenderness that he had only sampled from the outside, and most of that long ago. He marveled at these organs that held such awe and mystery for the male of the species. Good thing she wasn't conscious. It gave him a chance to feel his way around.

252

But this person despised men. She didn't seem to be anywhere around. If going to a hospital was enough to traumatize her, how would she respond to knowing a man's mind had invaded her body? Where was she anyway?

He was able to tune out some of the clamor. He tried to feel his way around. For the first time, he got a sense of the spaciousness of this mind. It was a mansion compared to the condos he had visited in Giordano and Dagget. There were whole rooms of thought unlike anything he had considered in his own mind.

A peek at one recollection had her sifting the beach sand and finding it composed entirely of the pulverized remains of shellfish. In the same room, a look up into the rich blackness of the Mexican sky, yielded up a sea of stars like none that could be seen from any American city. The Milky Way was a river of a hundred billion suns spinning through the universe; the individual stars she could pick out in the immediate stellar neighborhood were mere droplets in that mighty stream. How small is our corner of the universe. How ever more precious is that rare world where life gushes forth in millions of species in almost endless variety.

Elmo was annoyed by the contradiction in one who holds human life in such high esteem, yet would personally excommunicate the male of the species. In this big, open mind, he could feel the drain of that hatred slithering beneath the surface. Well, Loretta wanted him to go in and explore; here he was. He could spend a few minutes examining the interior of this whacked-out woman.

He moved in what felt like the direction of that slither, and found himself in a room of Womon, with

253

its uncommon spelling conceived to avoid including "man" within the word. He felt the reverence she held for the female form, the longing that arose from this womb and spread through this body, taking hold of her. Sweet, silky, sensuous woman, the feel of pliant skin, the delicate deliciousness of womon down to her musky depths.

The sensation was, Elmo noted, not all that different from the feeling man holds for woman. But occurring in a female, that feeling ignored the biological imperative of reproduction. No sooner had he thought the thought than he felt her subconscious reply. *The population needs no further urging to reproduce. Seven billion people in the world are hardly stuck for company.*

Was someone home after all? He felt not only her les inclinations, but a more potent and abiding love for lesbianism and its freedom from men. He swam in the thoughts assembled into Sisters, her first book, a political manifesto for the unity of les women as almost a race apart from straights. The book was popular in the les bookstores, but mostly escaped notice. It was hardly the bombshell *Return to Lesbos*, where her convictions bloomed into full incitement for les repatriation of her native Isle. This was the work that had made hers a household name. Many said her strident tone set back the les cause twenty years.

Only then did Elmo realize that this was indeed the man-hating, press-baiting, lesbian from Lesbos, Thea Nikolas, the world's most famous dyke who blamed the ills of the human race on "testosterone poisoning." Thea Nikolas, who infuriated half the country every time she was on television, whose broadcast appearance set off picketing at network studios. Thea Nikolas, the one who was calling for a Lesbian homeland.

Elmo felt the sibilant undercurrent, that hissing hatred of the testosterone that drove men to want to dominate womon. He moved toward the source.

She was born Thea Hera Nikolas on the Greek Isle of Lesbos. Even though she grew up thoroughly American, that birthplace gave Thea a special heritage. Aristotle and Aphrodite Nikolas were only waiting for the baby to be born and grow to six months before metal wings took them to Ithaca, New York. The head of the Cornell University philosophy department fancied hiring a Greek philosophy professor named Aristotle. Thea came to know the shaded walks of Ithaca that were touched with magic every October. But her parents reminded her constantly that she was blessed with a special heritage.

Her playmates were always girls. Once the boys noticed she never spoke to any of them, they resented it. A few boys would throw dirt at her to get her attention. Most of them took to calling her Thea Turtle for the way she pulled her head in when a boy approached. Others pulled her hair.

Steve Packer pulled her hair on the playground. Larry Baumgarten sat behind her and pulled her hair once a day during social studies. One day in the lunchroom, Billy Heintz crept up behind her and gave a good, long tug. Before the laugh was out of his mouth, Thea had whirled and slapped him upside the head. Billy's glasses went flying. Billy himself plopped down on the concrete floor on his butt, looking up in awe, confusion, and pain. The clatter of trays and silverware, of books slapping tabletops and the buzz of a few hundred voices stopped. Every head turned to the dark Greek girl, as surprised as everyone else. No one moved.

"What happened?" a dozen voices whispered.

"The smart girl just whacked Billy Heintz."

Finally, Mrs. Rafferty stepped in, fighting her tight skirt every step of the way. Kneeling was almost impossible, so she pulled up Billy by the hand, asked if he was all right, didn't wait for an answer, and hustled the both of them down the halls to the dreaded principal's office. Once out of the lunchroom, Thea protested all the way, demanding that he had hurt her, that all the boys were constantly picking on her, that she had to do something. Billy didn't say anything at all. Mrs. Rafferty brushed past the front desk and ushered them in to Mr. Quinn's office.

Quinn was tidying papers when the storm rushed in. "We have a problem here, do we?" He saw the left side of Billy Heintz' face bright red, and the defiant glare in Thea's dark eyes.

Thea said not a word.

"Perhaps you should begin, young lady."

She said nothing.

"Thea, the principal is *talking* to you," Mrs. Rafferty snapped.

Thea looked at the crook in Mrs. Rafferty's nose. Thea didn't know the word condescending, but that's what she saw in Mrs. Rafferty.

"You were outspoken enough in the hallway," Mrs. Rafferty rumbled.

Thea never did utter a word. She and Billy were suspended from school for three days. When she returned to school the next Monday, she sported a new short haircut. She completed fourth grade social studies without further incident.

* * * * *

It was warm in the bowling alley on a soggy

October night. The girls were twelve, out on a Friday night testing their parents while the clock edged down toward 10:30. They had rolled heavy balls at the pins more than a few times. Mostly Penny, Ruth and Thea giggled.

They giggled about Mr. Nolan, the science teacher, who scratched his nose and sniffed a lot. The English teacher, Ms. Banfield, had this awful Southern drawl that put a whole new twist on "Weil-yaam Shaykespeayah."

Penny's big blue eyes were dancing. "Ms. Banfield. I never saw a teacher that spends so much time talking about women being exploited."

Thea nudged her. "Don't you expect to be a woman someday?"

That they found wonderfully funny, maybe because it was good to laugh with the girls on a Friday night. Maybe because they knew their bodies were already beginning the radical changes into baby factories.

"I wonder what kind of guy she goes out with."

That was enough to feed another wave of giggles.

Penny flipped her long black hair and gave a conspiratorial glance at Ruth and Thea. "You know what I think? I think Banfield's queer."

Ruth froze. She tried not to look at Thea, who was trying not to look at anyone. Instead she chewed on her lip.

Penny clenched her jaw, biting the toenails on the foot she had so deftly inserted in her mouth. Both knew well enough Thea's total aversion to boys. Now they were old enough to have a word for it.

"So what?" Ruth finally said with just a slight note of defiance.

"She's probably better off if she is," Thea muttered.

"Hey, I'm sorry, I didn't mean..." Penny knew she was sputtering.

"It's okay," Thea said. "Forget it."

Ruth knew it wasn't okay. "Thea, do you think you . . . I mean you might be a . . . you know, a, um . . ."

"The word is lesbian, Ruthie. It's a perfectly good word, especially since I was born on Lesbos. In Greece. That gives me a special heritage. But yeah, I guess I'm probably the other kind of lesbian too, short hair, wears pants a lot, and doesn't dig guys. Okay? You satisfied?" Thea got up, grabbed a bowling ball and flung it at the pins. It bounced twice and hit the gutter hard about halfway down the lane.

"It's okay, Thea. It doesn't matter," Penny said.

"It damn well matters to me. I'm going home." She grabbed her coat off the molded fiberglass bench, huffed up the two stairs and turned toward the side exit. She was about to reach for the door when she looked down at her feet and noticed the bowling shoes still on her feet. She didn't want to go back for her shoes but . . .

The door opened in front of her and something in a tattered denim jacket tumbled through, something seven years below the legal drinking age who had spent the past hour in a battered Chevy in the parking lot swilling forbidden brew with his buddies. This one had stringy, dirty hair and a stench that only needed a Budweiser label to be mistaken for the real thing. Thea took a step back.

It managed to right itself after a few seconds, then spoke, almost. Mostly it slurred. "Hey, girl you got a nice ass."

Thea wanted to back away, but when she thought of moving her feet, she remembered the shoes.

Thickly, he plunged ahead. "I said 'Hey, girl, I said you got a cute ass.' Now you're supposed to say 'Thank you, how bout a ride?'"

If she carried a purse she might have hauled off and belted him with it. But she didn't. Before she could turn away, he reached toward where her breasts would be in a year. She took half a second to gasp, and used the lungful of air to emit a single scream:

"RAAAAAAAAAPE!"

Silence, almost. A few already released balls punched at the pins. The ocean of hubbub across thirty-two lanes fell abruptly still. The boy backed toward the door, but a burly Polish man darted up from the nearest alley and was upon him before he could escape. He pinned the boy's arms. The bowlers were craning their necks to see what the ruckus was about. A red-faced man with a matching tie and a too-small suit, the manager, tottered toward them at a forced pace.

Penny and Ruth passed him running toward Thea. Together, the three of them fell into one large hug and a flood of tears. The manager stood with his arms crossed against his chest, waiting for an explanation.

"I ain't done nothin', I swear the God."

"What did you say to her?" The manager's buttons were straining.

It was having trouble supporting its head. "I didn't say nothing, swear the God."

The girls, three feet away, were still crying.

"I said she was cute or something, you know?"

The manager was hardly listening. He heard something else, the sound no businessman wants to hear. From behind him, his thirty-two lanes were silent. He turned around. A hundred people were looking back at him.

He cleared his throat. "It's all right. Everything is all right. You can go back to your bowling."

He drove all three girls home. Thea never said a word to him, not in the car, not when he brought her in to her parents, who were quick to apologize for her overreacting. Her father said it was difficult to protect a girl with a special heritage. The manager left, nodding and not quite sure why.

Thea watched him waddle out toward his blue Mercury. A stupid man, she thought.

Two days later, he dropped off Thea's shoes on the front doorstep.

CHAPTER 36

Elmo heard Larry Baumgarten's chortle when he pulled her hair in fourth grade. He felt the swell of satisfied pride when she hauled off and belted Billy Heintz. He tasted the cold determination when she turned her back on every boy who spoke to her.

The slithering had grown to a steady rumble. He was getting close to something. How long had he been in her mind? Fifteen, twenty minutes? Maybe a little less. This mind works fast. What the hell am I doing to myself? What am I looking for? Why the hell am I looking at all?

He moved closer to the sound, half-expecting to find himself being raped at any second. Nor was he disappointed. He sat around the fire with Andi and Joanne and Donna, saw the warped sky, saw the bubble in an infrared that no one else could. He felt the agony attached to the memory, and knew what was coming as he followed the bubble down the beach, followed her speculation on the meaning of true extraterrestrial intelligence and what sort of physical form it might take. She thought some people would be frightened and appalled, others would expect all the world's problems to be miraculously solved, and the rest might reserve judgment. She was feeling expansive about humankind when she heard other men coming up the beach. She wanted to share this discovery, wanted someone else to acknowledge seeing it. She let down her defenses long enough to shout "Look!"

Elmo backed out of the room, but even moving

away, he felt them shove her to the ground and beat her into submission. Even in retreat, he felt her self-reproach for choosing the worst time to start speaking to men. He felt her monstrous dread of those two that poked at her unrelentingly.

Was this what truly happened? Or is this what her mind wants to recall of what happened? Was there any way to know the difference? The roar of her pain drew nearer. Now Elmo felt it pulsate, matching the rhythm of the still wailing alarm.

* * * * *

It had been Thanksgiving weekend, with only a light snow falling. This was merciful weather for up-state New York. Mother was downstairs wrapping left-overs. In the master bedroom, a football game was on television.

"Touch it."

She saw the ugly lump of wrinkled flesh in the flickering light from the TV. She was nine. Aristotle Nikolas was thirty years older. He smelled of Borkum Riff tobacco.

She didn't move her hands. She looked away.

"Go ahead, it won't bite you."

She let out a little whimper.

"I love you, Thee. I want you to learn something. Something important. Something big girls learn when they grow up." His professorial voice was Nat King Cole colored with a Greek accent.

Thea rolled back on the big master bed. Her eyes were narrowed, but she was listening.

"It is a very gifted young lady who knows how to properly handle a man. Some women never learn it. Both they and their men suffer for it." The earnest-

262

ness left his eyes. For a few seconds he looked away.

"You are part of a select group. You are from Lesbos. Such women have a special heritage, Thee. They are instructed by their fathers to be prepared for the commencement of womanhood."

Thea's suspicious look drifted into puzzlement. She knew what sex was, and that grown-ups thought about it a lot.

"First down, Tigers!" the TV announcer chortled. "They may make a game of this yet."

"It is your special heritage. And in its own way, it is a means of saving the world."

Thea wasn't buying it entirely, but neither did she back away.

"Look at our own ancestors. Would they have gone off to fight their wars had they satisfied their libidos at home?"

She hooded her eyes in suspicion again. "What's libido, Daddy?"

Aristotle Nikolas thought for a moment. "It is something nature gives us all. It is the urge that makes adults want and enjoy sex. It keeps the human race alive."

She didn't think she should believe him. But most of what he said matched with what she already knew about this sex thing. It was important to grown-ups.

"When this urge goes unsatisfied, men become more aggressive and hostile. They seek conquest. They make wars. They are reduced to animals."

From the television: "A wicked hit behind the line of scrimmage . . ."

As much as she was in unfamiliar territory, there was something that rang true about what he said. She closed one eye when she looked at him. "What does that have to do with special heritage?"

"Ah, it has everything do with it, don't you see? Among Greeks, and especially among select Greek men of Lesbos, there is a great and secret tradition—the Brotherhood of Eros. We are dedicated to training our daughters in sexual performance and appreciation. The training begins early, so that when other young women are getting down the basics, you are into the advanced stages of bringing your man to ecstasy, exploring the depths of your own pleasure, and saving the world through Eros."

Thea rolled off the bed and backed to the door. "It sounds icky."

"In time you will know differently. Your body is only now beginning to become a woman. You do not yet feel what a woman feels. But you can learn, Thee. You're a gifted child. The Brotherhood commands that the training begin early, lest the advantage be lost.

"What harm can learning do, Thee? Learn the secrets that will make men treasure you and protect you."

She was afraid to run. He beckoned with his hand. She stood her ground. He leaned toward her and grabbed at her arm. His hand closed on her arm like a claw. He more gently pulled her forward. "What harm can it do? Touch it."

It wasn't curiosity so much as an urge to be done with it that moved her hand toward him. Her first contact with the soft, spongy lump lasted half a second. A shudder shot down her spine.

Aristotle Nikolas had her by the wrist. "It won't hurt you. Go ahead."

Even more slowly than the first time, she reached forward and deliberately placed her hand on his thing, and held it there for several seconds. Her stomach sent up a distress signal.

It moved! Right there in her hand! This sick-looking thing started to inflate, growing longer, larger, more gruesome and with a single, wicked eye. Her first reaction was to let go, but just as her hands started to withdraw, another panicked order came from head-quarters.

Her right hand clawed, hard, low and long.

The howl was immediate.

Her feet churned across the cold hardwood hall-way floors. Thea dashed out to her own room, slammed and locked the door, and cried herself to sleep.

* * * * *

She remembered the windshield wipers the next afternoon, slapping back and forth with a rhythm at odds with the beat on the radio and the black seams in the concrete highway. The damp and gloomy sky couldn't dim the annual farewell performance of blaz-ing elm and maple leaves, the seasonal signature of upstate New York. The heater in the Oldsmobile made her sleepy. So did the slapping wipers, the thunk-whir of the road, and the radio whump-whump-whump.

It was a light, uncomfortable sleep. She contin-ued feeling the rocking highway and vaguely heard the music. What she found a little strange was how she felt the car stop and she didn't wake up. She was awake enough to know it was happening, but not nearly awake enough to participate. Either that, or this was all a dream. But she knew it wasn't. It all felt like a dream, especially the way at one moment she felt claustrophobic, and the next the room seemed cavernous.

Room? How did I get in here? Where is here?

Why is it so dark? What am I doing on my back?

I have no clothes on.

She was awake now. Or she dreamed waking up. It was getting harder to tell the difference. Nothing felt right. Sounds had an echoey hollowness. It sounded like gibberish to her at first, but it didn't take her long to recognize her father's fluid voice. He was chanting something in Greek, just what she wasn't sure, but that word eros came up a lot. She hadn't realized how dark the room was until the flame of a match and a candle pierced the gloom. Another candle popped up, and a third.

This part must be a dream. Around her she saw animals carrying the candles, standing as tall as a man. No animal sounds, just Daddy chanting, and now the voices of other men, a few of them, maybe four or five. Her ears seemed to magnify every sound, and next to the chanting she heard clumps of whispers:

"The wrong beer . . ."

" . . . His own daughter . . . "

". . . Twelve-year old smartass . . ."

". . . Gettin' kinda warm in here."

". . . Not much in the titty department . . ."

". . . Cock 'n bull story 'bout some special heritage . . ."

" . . . Some ancient Greek ritual . . . like two months ago ancient . . ."

". . . Yeh, slipped her some PCP in her Pepsi . . ."

"Angel dust . . . animal tranquilizer."

She wasn't coherent enough to put that together, but Thea remembered the pieces and assembled them months later. Animal faces. Male voices. A wave of nervous discharge rippled through her body, firing neurons with incomprehensible messages. She'd heard a little about angel dust. If that's what this was, she was glad she hadn't wanted to try it before.

Men were inside the animals or . . .. She blinked once, and the illusion was gone. The animals separated from the men in a moment of clarity. She was relieved to recognize what she was seeing were these old men wrapped in a goat's skin and head and horns, and wearing nothing else.

She felt the room zooming in and out on her, tilting and dizzying out of control.

Then there was a sound. A note. A flute, in some dark corner, with a few long, breathy notes. She clung to that sound of gods playing on Greek hillsides. She squeezed her eyes shut and let the sound pass through her bones until the dizziness subsided.

She held on to the music to steady herself a moment more. Something about a drug. This part is dreaming, isn't it? She opened her eyes to find a circle of men standing around her, each stroking himself and pointing his prong at her. She looked all around, but in every direction the sight was the same. Manimal in loveless heat, pumping palm on prick to the flautist's beat. A flutter of flute, a leap in the tempo, and the circle of men reached to stroke the men to their left. None of the faces in this circle of middle-aged men was Dad. He was playing the flute.

One of the men shouted, "Aaaaaiiiiiii!" To Thea it sounded like he was in some kind of pain. She saw egg whites shoot from his dong as he pounded the last out of it and collapsed on the floor in a sigh.

Around the room, a cheer rose for the first man to go. The men stepped in closer to her, and picked up the pace. Soon two more men were moaning in the same sort of near agony. Another, weaker cheer rose from the rest of the men.

Now she didn't know if she dared scream or speak, although she didn't know if she could have done either. Not that it mattered. This could only be some horrid dream.

The men all around drew ever closer. She smelled the sweat of their naked bodies and listened to their raspy breathing surrounding her. Then they laid their big, clammy, thick hands on her, touching her from every direction. There were too many hands to count. Dream or not, those hands felt real enough. Hands on her arms and legs, hands reaching for parts still under construction, reaching eagerly for firm young flesh, groping to the tune of the lilting flute.

Every touch left a bruise. She felt, and for the first time, welcomed, the numbing effect of the drug. Still the hands probed her, prodded her, invaded her. Even numbed, her mind refused to put up with it. The hands smeared her with sandalwood oil.

Just then another of the men, this one clothed in a mostly white and gray goat, spat his best genetic stew on her thigh. He groaned in an exultation that set the rest of the manimals laughing.

Thea looked at each man palming a swollen, blunt, stupid-looking organ, pointing at her, shooting at her. All of them, all the same. Those ridiculous cyclopean organs were what a man really looked like, his one eye in monomaniacal lust to dump his seeds in something, anything.

She wished she could burn every one of the bastards, her flute-playing father included. She lashed out with both feet and partially connected with her left.

The men backed away, laughing heartily at the prey's decision to be gamey about it.

Thea continued kicking, only dimly aware she

was lying on some sort of doctor's table. She was more conscious of those brutish, ugly pricks pointed at her, and how much she despised them, how those *things* so debased the person attached to them.

The Satanic flute played on.

The walls started shifting. The floor was off level. And rolling. Thea felt the beads of sweat burst her brow. Her flailing legs were distracted long enough for someone to shove a wet thumb two inches up her vagina.

Mostly, she was startled. The physical sensation was of a huge presence punching up within her, piercing her gut, her heart, and out to her toes. Almost a pain, but not entirely. The hands were one thing. This invasion was worse. No, worse would be that hideous *thing* in her. In a moment, she knew exactly that was next.

The room was rotating. Her stomach took a ballet leap and crashed to the floor. Muscles in her back wrenched in one spasm, then another. Thea tossed a cheeseburger, fries and a shake on the goatman.

For two days after that, Thea knew only blackness and that incessant mental yowl that Elmo found deafening now. He was tired of putting up with the bombardment within this enormous mind. Probably he had stayed too long, and was accomplishing nothing for anybody.

Then Elmo bumped into something. Something soft.

The wail rose a note into a question mark and abruptly stopped. The sudden silence was almost as loud as the shriek it replaced.

Had it been a hallway, a physical place in the real world, stumbling into someone could be commonplace enough. But this place was a mind, not far from the heart of hearts. It was one place most people have a reasonable expectation of being left alone.

He had bumped into the escaped consciousness of Thea Nikolas.

CHAPTER 37

Loretta watched the elapsed time display tick off minutes and seconds. She expected him to be gone ten or fifteen minutes, but thirty minutes rolled past, and still Elmo had not returned. She tugged at her knuckles. It gave her the willies, sitting in this room with Elmo's immobile shell. She was dealing with two nearly lifeless bodies in one day, and at this moment both of their minds were shoved together in her patient down in 116.

Sending Elmo in after Thea didn't seem like such a good idea any more. If a hospital could send her into a panic, how could she possibly do anything but freak out—if she could be freaked out any further—when she found a man wandering around inside her mind? Loretta clenched her jaw. She tried not to think about whether she had destroyed 'Terry Norwood.'

Thirty-nine minutes. Forty. *He's all right. She's all right. How long can he stay in there?* Loretta tried not to look at that body, but she found no joy examining the rows of monitors, nor did she dare touch the keyboard for fear of somehow aborting his trip, or worse, preventing his return. She scratched at her orange nail polish.

* * * * *

Thea Nikolas curled into herself, tied in a mental straight jacket. But this queer presence that had bumped into her. Was this a spare self come to see

271

how long she intended to remain in hibernation? *I'm not coming out. I'm in charge here, and I'm shut down, waiting for death to come along and make it official.* She didn't expect the presence to respond.

"I'm the Sisters Psychic Search and Rescue Squad. I've come to haul you out of here." He had an advantage as long as she couldn't detect his thoughts as he could hers, but he expected it wouldn't last long. "So you've cracked up? Is that what all this is about?"

It had been hours since she had functioned with anything close to normal thought, and she had nothing to focus her. Elmo tried not to think about thinking about being male.

"Have I?"

"What else would you call comatose depression and suicidal tendencies?" the presence asked. "A healthy body and sound mind?"

"Maybe I am *crazy*. I believe I have you in my head."

"Don't give it another thought, sister." How long could he keep her off balance?

"How did you get here?"

"I don't much understand it myself. Look, can we get out of this dirty basement?"

"This isn't happening."

"Of course not," Elmo responded. "How about this doesn't happen down here with your Dad the dirty old man and a few of Mexico's worst."

"You don't know what I've been through. I'm staying here." Thea paused. "To die."

"They didn't tell me this was going to be an over-time job. What kind of Psychic Search and Rescue squad would let me let you do that?" He felt her laugh a little. He might be getting through. "And I know *exactly* what you've been through. I followed the trail

in here to find you. Now come on, you might even consider regaining consciousness."

"I'm going to die."

"Not on my shift, you're not."

"There's nothing to come back to. My life is over."

"You're all of forty-one years old. Your life's just getting halfway up to speed. You don't need to start over again. If you have the courage to open your eyes, you get to find out where life goes from here."

"Can we go up slowly?"

"Sure, I can use the overtime." But she's due to start sensing my thoughts any time, he knew. There's a lot of intuition in this mind, once she's functioning. Distract her. "That bubble on the roof. Was that the same bubble you saw on the beach?"

"I felt it was, but there's no real way to know for sure. Where is it from?"

They were moving gradually up to a sleep level, up toward a still-distant light of consciousness. "Probably thousands of light years away."

"What do they want?"

"I wish I knew," he said.

The light was drawing closer. She was growing more alert, asserting her abject curiosity. She couldn't see him. Their communication was more like a phone call. She very much felt the tone of his voice.

"Who are you?"

Her tone was warm curiosity, but he wanted to deflect the question.

"Just a sister with a job to do."

It was a small lie, but this time she sensed it.

"Wait. You're not... You're a ..."

"Someone hauling you out of consuming your-self. Now if you'll excuse me, it's way past my bed-time."

273

"You're a *man*!" She gasped, physically gasped. In a moment she would open her eyes unless this shock tumbled her back to her depths.

"Are you going up there?"

"You *are* a man! How can you..."

"Your life's waiting for you. Go."

"Yes," she said. He could feel that she would.

"Bye, baby, it's been fun. I'll leave a business card with the receptionist." He directed his thoughts out of the body and called "Out."

And they parted.

* * * * *

In Elmo's control room, the computer blorped. The elapsed time display froze at 43:11. Loretta saw Elmo's near-comatose body take a deep breath. He stirred. She popped up to her feet and put her hands on his shoulders. "Jesus, Elmo, are you all right?"

Elmo opened his eyes. His face remained expressionless, save a weary relief to be home. After a moment, he loosed a faint smile. "I thought Voojoos didn't believe in Jesus."

She looked blankly at him before she chuckled. "I was worried. "Jesus, you've been gone..."

He checked the monitor. "Forty-three minutes and eleven seconds. And there you go calling me Jesus again."

This laugh was more relief than anything else. Her voice dropped to a personal tone. "Were you . . . there? Did you . . . ?"

He nodded solemnly, opened his mouth to speak, then stopped.

Loretta waited. She thought about a cigarette.

"Her mind ..." He groped for words. "It's majestic. Like the circuits of the space station stacked up against the wiring in a radio. Gigabytes of storage,

274

finely tuned sensory input, and more on-board processing power than any damned computer."

Loretta couldn't squeeze in a word.

"Some of her data brings her to a few peculiar
conclusions. But with that data, there's logic in it. That
brain could light a small town. Not as orderly a mind
as it might be, but the perceptive power alone ..." Elmo
ran out of steam.

"You didn't freak her out?"

"She was 'freaked' when I got there. She was
bundled in a corner, getting started on dying. I told
her I had come to haul her out. She was too confused
not to come along. She looked like she might resur-
face soon. But she needs to want to take that last step
out herself." He swiveled in the chair, aiming himself
at the door.

"We have some wine left," Loretta said. "Can we
get out of this room?"

"Thea is probably waking up right now. She
needs you there."

"What did you call her? Thea?"

He nodded. "Thea Nikolas. You've heard of her."

"You mean like *the* Thea Nikolas?"

"That's her."

"Jesus."

"Loretta, you're just going to have to leave him
out of this."

"Who?"

"Jesus."

"Oh," she said. "It's an expression, you know."

"Yeah," he smirked. "Like 'you know' is an expression. You know?"

"Anything else, Elmo?"

He nodded. The light reflected off his glasses.
"Her girlfriend Andrea Norwood is here looking for her.

I checked her into 144 a few hours ago. Norwood asked if I had seen Thea."

"What did you tell her?"

He smiled. "Seen her? I hadn't then, and can't say that I have yet."

"No, you just came back from a forty-three minute stroll through her head. You think I should tell Norwood that her girlfriend is here?"

"I don't know what you should tell her. Except that I want to talk to Thea."

Loretta tossed her head. "You want to talk to Thea Nikolas?"

"If it's all right with you."

"Thea Nikolas doesn't talk to men."

"I know that better than you do. But she'll talk to this one. Just tell her that the Sisters Search and Rescue Squad wants to have a word with her."

Loretta laughed. "Sounds like you kids had fun. Now there's something I owe you." She planted a big, sloppy kiss on his mouth. "Thanks," she said. "You've been using this mind transfer thing for sex, and here your body didn't even get laid."

A wicked grin crossed Elmo's face. "How can you say that? I've been inside Thea Nikolas for forty-three minutes and eleven seconds."

She reached to his top shirt button. "Good. Now it's my turn."

Elmo winked and smiled. "Now get downstairs. Thea needs you there."

CHAPTER 38

Observation notes: Xaq Hobesian Arbidor 7906021

Less clear information is generated from this experiment. Not a transfer for the performance of sexual congress, this pass has its own distinguishing features. It involved, for the first time, a male crossing over to a female body, from which is generated much physical curiosity; neither sex has a comfortable level of understanding of what the other feels, although they discover that the expressly physiological sensations are analogous, although not identical.

More difficulty is produced by this pass because the exchange was one of personality, and there was no sexual reward for the traveler. Yet here as in no other circumstance, what appears is a need to render assistance to an individual in distress, to the point where the traveler disguised his identity in order to make his assistance more palatable. What is displayed is a selflessness especially uncommon in this human era of immediate gratification. In this particular subject, at least, is a seed of the thought that the species may have attained, if only momentarily, a degree of humanity that bodes well for subsequent generations.

* * * * *

Elephants sat on her eyelids.

Thea didn't especially want to open the damned things anyway. Too much trouble to brush them aside, too big, too gray, too heavy. She felt her breathing pick up. Oxygen, *yes*. She gulped at it. She rolled toward the elephants. They rolled out of the way for a moment, but when she exhaled they rolled right back.

The voice came again from within her: *stay down, it's all too much.*

But another voice prodded her on. A voice in a dream. A male voice? *He will betray you,* her first voice complained. *Stay down!* She rolled her lungs at the elephants again, pushing a little harder, exhaling slowly, but yes, gradually rolling back the beasts.

She opened her eyes.

Dark. At least, as much dark as was afforded by blue corridor light through a skimpy drape. But no lights in the room. That was dark and quiet. She heard cars navigating the parking lot and voices punctuated by slamming doors. It all sounded vaguely like a grumbling elephant. Same motel room.

What am I doing here? Was I just talking with someone? I'm hungry.

Somebody out in the parking lot burst into a cackling laugh. The steel pool gate rattled shut. Out in the street, a car passed by with a stereo loud enough to rattle the windows. Around the corner, a roaring engine yielded to screeching brakes.

Same old damned Lamp Post Motel.

She felt the aching reply to her attempt at swinging her feet to the floor. She pushed through the pain and fought her way to her feet. They felt like thunderbolts surging through her nervous system, rattling her brain. She focused on the pain, put all her effort into pushing it down while she managed to stand up. She wasn't sure exactly when she was standing. Every time she raised her head, the room would tilt and whirl.

Then, somehow, she was standing. She shuffled

more than walked to the back of the room, hurried along by a bladder threatening to give way. The shirt and jeans she was wearing when she lost consciousness yesterday were gone, replaced by one of Loretta's ultralight peekaboob negligees. Thea giggled, but it hurt to laugh, and it was hell on her bladder.

She dropped gratefully to the seat, half a moment before the door opened. She heard Loretta step in, and the pause before, "Are you in here someplace?"

"In the bathroom," Thea shouted above the exhaust fan.

"Are you all right?"

"Not yet. But I may be getting there." She tried to make her voice a little cheerful.

"Can I get you something?" Loretta said from just outside the door.

Thea sat back against the toilet tank. The cold porcelain was bracing. She sighed, relieved to be relieved. A whisper of a smile came to her lips. It took a deep breath to overcome the now rattling exhaust fan. "What do you say to a pizza with garlic, green chile, and onion?"

"I'd say we'll both have dragon's breath in an hour."

Thea heard the smile in Loretta's voice, and could barely detect the sound of feet walking from the bathroom door across the room to the phone. She braced herself to stand. The legs didn't ache quite as much, but they were stiff from—how long, half a day, more?—in the bed. She felt a little smile play her lips. *I can make it just fine.* Even as the thought fixed itself in her mind, she wondered about this sudden willingness to rejoin the world.

It was a strain, but she pulled herself once more to her feet. More walking, not less, is what she needed.

She thrust her chin forward and stepped out of the bathroom. Her toes moved from the cool tiles to carpet. "I'm keeping you from your work, aren't I?"

She watched Loretta rotate her athletic frame, a curl on one side of her mouth. "Yeah, of course. So what? My job is a crime. I make enough money that I could almost afford to be a junkie like the rest of the pros. What's the fun of being a professional slut if I can't find the time to help a bird with a broken wing?"

Thea walked stiffly to her and put a hand on her shoulder. "I've been a pretty sick bird. And here you've been my personal nurse for nearly a week."

"Part of the job," Loretta said with a wink. "There are lots of girls in this business who need somebody to pick them up and not ask a lot of damn questions. I just got you the best help I could."

Thea grazed Loretta's left cheek and whispered, "Can I do something for you?" She wasn't sure herself if she was talking about sex; a hooker sure didn't need any more of that.

Loretta's eyes hardened just a bit, but her lips kept their affable arc. "In fact, there is, Thea."

Thea was nodding and receptive. But the mention of her name left her mouth dangling at the end of a gaping jaw.

"I want you to talk to a couple of people for me."

Thea squinted. "What could I possibly ..."

"In the morning. I want you to talk to Andi Norwood. She's here looking for you." She pointed over the back wall of 116, up at 144. "There."

Thea spent a few seconds wetting her lips, which kept going dry. Swallowing was tough, too. "Andi ..."

"Another thing, since you're asking. Could you have a little chat with Elmo Skinner?"

She had never heard the name before, but rec-

280

ognized it as familiar in some way she didn't understand, almost as if it were her name. Though she had never met him, she saw his face in the mirror, coated with shaving cream. She had no brother, but she supposed this is how she might have felt toward him. When Thea did swallow, it was still hard going down.

"Yes, I will need to speak with him."

* * * * *

Yot looked up, hunched over the keyboard. Still. Again.

Xaq had surrendered any hope of pulling him away. Watching television was some diversion, but it did little to engender any respect for the civilization that created it. He took another crack at Yot. "Ho, when do we finally snare some xufa? I think that's where we started this trip. This was going to be big fun, remember?"

Yot made no perceptible response. He rapped at the keyboard incessantly, his eyes in a perpetual loop between keys and screen. After a minute, he leaned back, tapped out a short final instruction, and stood away from the machine. "That will take a few minutes."

"Dare I ask what you're doing locked into the machine now?" Xaq asked from the bed.

"Do you recall what you . . . came here for?"

"Big fun. Xufa. Can't say I've found much of either."

"How about . . . research?"

"Uh . . . sure. I'm studying the effects of mental migration of twenty-first century Earth."

Yot squashed his jaw into the contorted smile of the clown face, accompanied by a whining voice.

"Sounds like a pile of feco to me."

Xaq sat up on the edge of the bed. "You've got a better idea?"

Yot nodded repeatedly. "Database."

"Wha?"

"The full recorded data of . . . the Lamp Post Motel, from Skinner's rankings to every bit of video stored in his system."

Xaq's eyes opened wide. "You could . . .?"

"Not 'could,' feco face. I am. Downloading it all right now."

Xaq laughed. "You're three steps ahead of me every time. Perfect. *Now* can we go find some twenty-first century xufa?"

"Now would be good. Let me finish the download. It should be done any ..."

The computer in the corner beeped.

Yot grunted. "Got it." He turned back to the machine. He copied the data to a crystal and started buttoning up the files for an evening's escape.

Among the routines Yot ran before shutdown was a security check that reviewed his file status in the GlobEx computer.

Here the machine issued a strange little chirp. The screen told the rest of the story.

ACCOUNT CLOSED BY ORDER GLOBEX SECURITY. AUTHORIZATIONS DENIED. PICK UP CARD AT NEXT TRANSACTION. IMMEDIATE SECURITY NOTIFICATION.

"Ho, Xaq. I think we just... fell in that pile of feco. Game's over."

Xaq walked over to the computer. He read the screen, and felt the blood drain from his face. "No, that can't be."

"No? Well, there it is."

"Impossible. Rej said everything works out according to plan."

"He said that. How long you say you've... known this guy Rej?

"About two thousand years."

"In a noble line of work, is he? Never steps outside the law, I suppose."

"Are you saying we shouldn't have come?"

"No," Yot said, sitting down on the bed opposite. "I just don't believe every...word he says."

"So what do we do? Leave?" His voice was shaking. "Are we in that much trouble?"

Yot shrugged. "Maybe. And then maybe I've just got to fix it." Those were the last words Yot bothered to say for a while. He was back inside the machine, getting in the Global Express back door to the files. He traced the messages from Phoenix to New York security. The tricky part was breaking into the main computer during a high-security alert. Yot could look into the software at the other end of the line and read the anticipated responses. He dodged password barriers like befuddled tacklers before breaking through and canceling the security alert. He found the nature of the security breach and went back into the history files and "corrected" the data to include James A. Zachary's file back over two years. Then, to cover his tracks, he placed a bug in the GlobEx files that would have accounted for the security officer's missing the original data. He was reasonably satisfied that he had again beaten the system. But the fact that they had found him out was unsettling.

"That should take care of it," he said over his shoulder.

"Looked pretty easy," Xaq said.

"Shows how much you know," Yot grunted.

"Then you've taken care of the problem."

"I think. I hope. Some of these people aren't as primitive as they look." He flashed the clown face again, mostly at himself. "Did you say something before about snaring some xufa? I could use some."

"Good. I'm hungry."

CHAPTER 39

Friday morning had a few scattered puddles and forty per cent humidity—unusually high for the desert—to show for Thursday's storm. The sky was cloudless, washed clean even of the city's nearly perpetual brown haze, rendering the Catalina Mountains north of town into suddenly sharp focus. Cars surged toward Davis-Monthan Air Force base, their gaseous emissions congealing into black particles that settled on the surface of the swimming pool at the Lamp Post Motel.

The parking lot was a series of slamming car doors and gunning engines as the previous night's clientele evacuated. Up along the concrete balcony, Betsy rapped at the door to 137, and Tyrone played back a perfect reproduction of Betsy's chant: "Housekeeping."

A door slammed in 109, rattling several windows in the vicinity. A blond, muscular man in an open shirt and jeans torn at the knees stomped his boots along the pavement, muttering for the benefit of entire parking lot, "Damn bitch." For punctuation, he started his Ford pickup with a roar that shook still more glass. He did his best to deposit his tread on the Lamp Post parking lot, but his automatic transmission blunted that attempt. Instead, he roared off into traffic, shouted, "Fucking bitch!" in case anyone on the premises missed the opportunity to enjoy the perceptive acuity of his earlier remark.

Another man of about forty-five, dressed in a pink shirt and purple tie, opened the door to leave

129. A pair of arms ending in glowing green finger-nails took hold of him from behind before the door closed with a thud.

From the love room, 122, a freckled eighteen-year-old emerged buckling his belt with "Lloyd" tooled into the leather on the back. He wore a smile so broad it threatened to crack his jaw. Lloyd fired up a battered Toyota and howled with the music on the radio.

* * * * *

The lord of the Lamp Post opened his left eye. From the angle of the light through his window, he knew he had overslept nearly two hours. He didn't care. One corner of his mouth found a little smile. He shat, showered, shaved and brushed in his thirty-two minute morning routine. For no good reason, though, he applied toothpaste to brush backhanded.

The computer listed Thursday night's occupancy at fifty-eight per cent. He skipped the proverbs and dates in history. No messages waiting, not even from Arbidor. A quiet day was all he wanted. Order. Predictability. Calm. On a Friday? Hardly likely, especially during this week of weird.

Elmo came down the stairs to his office, but he pictured Thea Nikolas assessing herself in a mirror. He shook it from his mind. He looked over yesterday's cash summary, verified the linen supply and tuned in on Tyrone's audio circuit in 135.

"Tyrone, you clean the tub and scrub down the toilet."

"Yas, massuh," Tyrone responded flatly.

Elmo lifted an eyebrow. Betsy was developing a little programming skill.

He resisted the urge to tune in 116. He had

never looked in or even listened to Loretta's room. What went on there was her business. He could just find out if Thea was conscious. No, that he would see about in person.

Out at the reception desk, a man with good posture and salt-and-pepper hair turned in his room key. "This place is all right. You got any other Lamp Posts? In Phoenix or Vegas or someplace?"

Elmo smiled. "Can't say that I do. This is the one and only."

"I'll remember it next time I'm in town," he said, handing Elmo the keycard to 131.

"We always appreciate it."

He busied himself with coffee and a prune danish from the microwave. It was still too early to knock at 116, or even call. He looked over the theft rate for the month, down to a dozen towels, four pillows, seven bedspreads, a shower curtain, a toilet seat and a three nine-volt smoke alarm batteries. August was a slow month. Things disappeared at a faster clip when occupancy was up.

* * * * *

Interstate 10 begins as an on-ramp in Santa Monica, California, a few blocks from Pacific Ocean. It winds out through San Bernadino, Indio, and Blythe before crossing into Arizona through wonderful Wickenberg and on to Phoenix, Arizona's capital, principal city and self-styled Mecca of the redneck right, a lump of Texas dropped into the Sonoran Desert. From there, Interstate 10 winds a 120-mile thread southeast to Tucson, two hours of tiresome highway with mostly drab desert, a few modest mountains, past saddlehorn-shaped Picacho Peak where a meager and inconclusive battle was the only Civil War action in the state. This tenuous connection with history was a marketing device to lure motorists off the highway for a cup of coffee, a soft ice cream, or a slightly-better-than-nothing burger.

It was at historic Picacho Peak on Friday morning that Mort Phipps shook sugar into his whitened coffee. He and Tilly were going to share the moment that he would catch a credit card criminal—and the reward. After that, seeing as they were at a motel anyway...

"They need to shorten this road to Tucson," he said.

Tilly found that outrageously funny. She found everything funny today. Today she might land Mort's reticent rump in a bed.

"The heat's gonna kick in now with the sun come up," Phipps said.

Tilly wasn't sure if she was supposed to laugh, but she did, just in case. Phipps sipped at his coffee. A couple of semis roared down the highway.

"I never done no security alert before. But I told 'em I wanted to come down and make the collar. That's police talk, make the collar. It means like arrest him, you know?"

Tilly fluttered her eyelashes. "We won't be in danger?" Her tone was desperate for something even vaguely adventurous.

"Not much. Not if you know what you're doing." *I hope I know what I'm doing*, he thought.

An hour later, they were at the front desk of the Lamp Post Motel, demanding to see the manager. Chubby little Tilly stood a step behind him, wearing a glow of goofy admiration for her man. Phipps pushed out his chest as he presented his Global Express Security identification badge.

"Morton B. Phipps, Global Express security detail, Phoenix." He rattled off the words as fast as he could, exactly as he had practiced mentally half a dozen times on the highway. "I put out that there security alert on James A. Zachary. There is a serious discrepancy in our records what requires my investigation. My records show he charged three hundred dollars here. You got him registered?"

Great, Elmo thought, a *young* pompous fart. "I've seen no security alert."

"Issued at 16:31 hours yesterday. I'm here to follow up."

Elmo nodded wearily. He reached for his front desk keyboard and sent a query to Global Express on James A. Zachary. Zachary had checked in Tuesday. Just before all this started. A security alert triggers half a dozen warnings when a suspect card is authorized. The terminal flashed a message: Account 3745 458 459214 James A. Zachary located. Amount to authorize?

It didn't say 'processing, please wait' or 'system security notice,' 'request denied,' or even 'howdy.' Some emergency. Elmo rolled his eyes before looking up. "There is no security alert on this account. It's too early in the day for jokes, Mr. Phipps."

"I'll have you know I issued a security alert sixteen hours ago."

He invited Phipps behind the desk to read the computer screen. Elmo typed in $100 for credit authorization. Five seconds later, the computer responded: AUTH 005.

"That's not possible," Phipps stammered. "This is a level two alert. You should get dire warnings. You should get instructions to confiscate and destroy his card, and call us immediately." He looked at Tilly, who was clenching her teeth and motioning with her head to get a room and the hell out of this office.

Elmo sighed. "Look, why don't you call your office and straighten this out? We can talk about it later."

Tilly nodded eagerly.

"Well, yeah, okay. But he's here, right, this Zachary guy? You seen him?"

"Only when he checked in on Tuesday. But he is registered."

"What room? He could be a dangerous criminal."

Tilly stamped her foot.

Elmo kept his voice businesslike. "You clear this up with Global Express and you have them call me. Without higher authorization, I'm going to have to insist my guests maintain a certain degree of privacy."

Phipps glanced at Tilly. He walked around to the customer side of the desk. "Okay. Can I rent a room?"

"Certainly."

The procedure was automatic. For these two he didn't want or need a camera. Elmo put them in 117.

* * * * *

Andi stared out the window at the row of squat apartments out back of the Lamp Post. She had been staring out that window for an hour, observing the occasional car, a few black kids taunting each other, and an unshaven, bent-over old man in tattered pants picking through the motel dumpster for cans or bottles.

Cosgrove was sleeping. Noisily.

Andi started greasing up with sunblock and

taking up her vantage point at the pool. Yesterday the sun had disengaged her brain and sucked up her energy, so she grabbed Cosgrove's Panama hat wrapped in a purple and blue band. Lydia had warned that stakeouts were mostly boredom and usually a failure. All the movies she had seen told her the same thing, but movie stakeouts usually had a payoff. She was reading a paperback Western, plowing through pages mercilessly, stopping only at every sound, scanning for any sign of Thea in the neighborhood, perhaps returning to the Voojoo services at noon. Andi planted herself back at the pool, scanning the horizon like a radar dish behind mirrored sunglasses. It was nine-thirty in the morning, and besides engines rumbling down Craycroft, quiet. A maid and a machine were moving down a row of rooms. Andi retreated to page 673 in her old West epic. Out of the corner of her eye, she did see a little man with a mustache and boring clothes going up the stairway and rap on the door at 126, but she paid it no mind.

* * * * *

Elmo's shoulders and eyelids sagged. More than anything, he would have preferred to be back in bed. Yesterday had been the longest day he could remember. Today could be worse.

What do I say to a traveling spaceman who stops at the Lamp Post Motel? Do you ask him who recommended the place? Was there an interplanetary travel guide that singled out the Lamp Post Motel, Tucson, Arizona, USA, Earth as a best buy?

He shuffled across the concrete steps on the steel stairway, his footfalls ringing the metal. After the storm last night, today was still cool and relaxed. He breathed deeply. The air revived him a bit, but he still stood for several moments, just staring at the door to 126. Twice he lifted his hand to knock. Each time he hesitated, wondering what he was going to say.

Who are you? What are you? Where do you come from? Are there more of you here? What the hell are you doing to me? What do you want?

He really had but a single question. He was sure there was no answer he could understand: *How can you move a man's mind?*

Finally, he held his breath and rapped his knuckles against the turquoise door.

What else can you do to me?

At first there was only silence from within. It was nearly a minute before the door opened. One wary eye appeared through the crack he opened first. Zachary.

"I'm the manager. May I speak with you?" He wanted to sound firm but not threatening.

"We were just leaving."

Aren't they always? he wondered. "It's important I speak with you. May I come in, please?"

Xaq shrugged. He opened the door.

CHAPTER 40

For the hundreds of times Elmo had walked into rooms strewn with newspapers, beer cans, food bags, soda cups, and pizza boxes, it still inspired a loathing of sloppy minds. He found some comfort in this looking like a very human mess. These aliens could well *be* guys from Los Angeles.

But there in the corner was the big guy sitting at an odd-looking computer. The big one spoke. "Ho, Elmo. You're enjoying your . . . travels? Been a while since you've been laid, eh innkeeper?"

Elmo sputtered. He'd been screwing up his courage to come through that door, prepared for a confrontation where he would be firm, logical and finally force their hand to confess that they knew about and conducted his "travels." No dainty I-know-who-you-are dance, no eyeball-to-eyeball war of nerves, no accusations, no denials.

"Huh?" Xaq said.

"Arbidor," Elmo said directly at Yot.

"Actually, that's *his* name," Yot said. "But you can call him Xaq."

The big one rose to his feet. He stuck out his hand, which Elmo took unenthusiastically. "The name is Yot. Come on, Elmo, we got lots to . . . talk about. Maybe some coffee. We know how much you like the stuff. Helps get those . . . eyes open, right?"

Elmo tilted his head. *Is this too easy? Is there a trap here? What are they going to do to me? I'll pin them down where they can't do anything crazy.* He cleared his throat. "Can we talk at Mr. Stein's establishment next door?" Phil could scare up some rolls or something, and always had a coffeepot warming. There he should be relatively safe. Safe from what, he wasn't entirely sure.

Phil Stein's it was. The front door was open, as was the back door sixty feet back, letting the morning air float through the room. Elmo hesitated for a moment. He skipped his hideaway in the back, and found a corner booth clearly visible from the bar.

A waitress stepped toward them, but Phil appeared from a back room. He put an arm in front of her to hold her back, and approached them himself. When Elmo sat out in the open, Phil kept a sharp eye on the party.

Phil applied his host's smile. "Welcome back, Mr. Skinner. You have guests today."

Elmo gave a clandestine nod approving Phil's cautious tone. They ordered a round of coffee and Phil shuffled off, his eyes flicking back to the table even as he retreated.

"You came to...talk to us about something," Yot said.

Elmo didn't answer immediately, but nodded several times to himself. They seemed ready enough to cooperate. He tipped his best card. "A security man was looking for you. From Global Express. He says you have no account to back up that credit. He hasn't the faintest idea who you are."

Xaq looked nervous. Yot's face was blank.

"He says he issued an emergency alert on your card. Funny thing is, my computer verified the account is active. It seems that since yesterday morning, when he didn't exist in the computer, this nonexistent James A. Zachary developed a respectable credit history with Globex. Not a dime past due. His only charges are the current bill at the Lamp Post Motel and a few department stores, a restaurant and some bars."

Neither of the two spoke.

"Your computer can change those locked files and cancel the security alert," Elmo said. "Or am I mistaken?"

Yot's voice was a hoarse whisper. "The machine is a tool. I manipulate the files."

Elmo looked at a knot deep under a quarter-inch layer of urethane on the table top. "You're not from around here."

A glint flicked in Yot's eye. "No," he said. "Not by a long shot."

Elmo stopped. "Who—what—are you?" He held his hands open. "What are you doing here?"

Xaq drew circles on the tabletop, where his eyes focused. "It's better for all concerned if you didn't know that. It's better if you don't know anything at all."

Yot took a deep breath and released it. He looked at his friend. "How much do we put this man through without so much as an explanation?"

"Telling him skews my results," Xaq muttered through clenched teeth.

"Results?" Elmo twisted up his lips.

"I thought you'd forgotten your bluppo research," Yot said. "I've been collecting all your data. You've been moaning about something or other since we got here."

Xaq glared back but said nothing more.

"Look," Yot said to Elmo, "we're graduate . . . students from the future doing research in the . . . past. The specifics of where and when we . . . come from don't matter, and you're better off not knowing.

But we are human. In fact, we're descendants of Earth people."

Phil arrived with the tray of coffee mugs. He made eye contact with Elmo, and said with a twinkle, "Of course. I'm just back from serving as the ambassador to Uranus."

Elmo waited for Phil to withdraw with a satisfied grin. "You came here in a bubble. Sitting right up—there, I believe." He pointed through the ceiling to the spot on the roof of the motel next door. "Yes?"

"Maybe," Xaq said.

"Someone has seen it, and reported it to me."

"You're the innkeeper. Have you seen this—what did you call it—bubble?"

Elmo clenched his back teeth. "Not exactly. Not personally. But someone has seen it—and more than once."

Xaq didn't say anything. Yot sipped coffee.

"Yes," said Yot. He looked at his friend. "Enough feco, Xaq, don't you think?" He turned back to Elmo. "Yes we did. And yes, it is right about—" he pointed through Phil's ceiling—"there."

"And it's invisible?"

"For most purposes."

"So how come one person could see your so-called invisible bubble?"

Yot dropped his head and snorted. "I knew it," he said more to himself than Elmo. He looked Elmo in the eye. "The shield must be leaking infrared. Most of the time it's not much . . . of a problem. Most people can't see that low in the spectrum. I can't see the leak, so I can't always . . . tell it's there. But somebody... somebody with an extraordinary range of vision could see that infrared. Somebody like... Thea Nikolas."

Elmo's felt the memory he brought back from

Thea's recollection. His voice oozed disgust. "You watched them rape her."

Xaq tilted his head. "What is rape?"

"What do you study?" Elmo shot back.

"Sexual anthropology."

Elmo let out a cold laugh. He took a long pull on his drink, then became professorial. "Then consider this a vital piece of your research from the Nikolas Feminist Lesicon. Rape is an act of violence, degradation and contempt. It is sexual only in the sense that it is *unwanted* sex. To the victim, and especially to this victim, forced sex is the most deeply insulting act one human being can commit on another."

Xaq looked hurt. "We thought she was having big fun."

At the bar, Phil muttered, "Schmuck."

"Some advanced civilization you come from. You witnessed a crime. You had complete power to stop it."

Xaq started sounding a little angry. "We're here to observe, not interfere. I had no idea this wasn't just another part of contemporary culture. I thought xufa was xufa."

"Then you're dumber than you look. Your so-called non-interference left a brilliant, capable woman psychologically crippled."

Yot broke in. "Come on, Elmo. We didn't know. I'm sorry, but there's nothing we can do about it now."

Elmo took a long swallow of his coffee before he narrowed his eyes. His voice was barely audible. "Maybe there is. Maybe there is."

"What did you have in mind?"

Elmo scratched his chin. He felt a few rough spots his razor had missed. His other hand drummed on the tabletop. "Could you find those rapists? Could

297

you locate and identify them?"

Yot looked at his hands before he responded. "It would take some effort. Maybe quite a trick to program it. But I think I can. I stored their brain wave patterns."

Elmo's eyebrows climbed his forehead. "Can you locate them from this distance?"

"Where we come from, we measure...distances a lot longer than anything here on Earth. Yes, Elmo. I believe I can find them."

"Show me." He swallowed the rest of the coffee.

Xaq and Yot looked at each other. Yot shrugged and tossed down his drink.

CHAPTER 41

"We're never going to find any xufa," Xaq murmured as they trudged back to 126. Upstairs, Xaq flopped back down on the bed. Yot took up his nearly permanent position at the computer. Elmo pulled up a chair directly behind Yot. He noted every typed command and its syntax for parameters and options. He watched Yot retrieve the data on the attackers. He saw Yot set up the search scan, beginning at the location of the attack on the beach in Puerto Peñasco, radiating outward in a two-mile wide spiral. Thousands of brain matrices ran through the screening process. When the search pattern had reached sixty miles from the point of origin and a million minds scanned, Elmo started losing hope. They might be anywhere on Earth. "We might have lost them. What can we do now?"

"We can keep spreading out, or we can scan for a close instead of an exact match."

"What might cause that?"

"Could be any of several causes. They might be drunk, or maybe sober having been drunk that night on the beach. Maybe they're sleeping. Maybe they're on some drug now that they weren't then."

Elmo nodded. "Look for the close match. I'll bet they're there. Don't bother scanning north to Phoenix. Set the pattern for the area around Rocky Point. Can you compensate for changes like those without a string of false positives?"

Yot smiled. "You're not a bad engineer, you know that? Exactly what I had in mind. Here, I'll rescan the sorted data while the search pattern extends outward." The screen had a crisper resolution than anything he had ever seen. It opened a window to monitor the rescan while the search pattern spread.

Elmo felt weariness crawling out of his bones, slogging into his bloodstream, taking hold of his muscles. Xaq was on the bed, writing some notes with an odd-looking pen.

"There! That's them."

Elmo's head popped up. He straightened his back and refocused his eyes. "Are you sure?"

"I wasn't at first. But they match the physical pattern exactly of the men on the beach."

"What can you tell about them?"

"It does take a little time."

Xaq piped up from the bed. "What good does it do you? What can you do about it? We can't undo what's been done."

Elmo looked over his shoulder. "Not entirely." He felt a twinge in his lower back as adrenaline made for the bloodstream. But I have to do something."

"Two males, thirty-two miles from the beach, now about a mile apart. Both drunk and asleep."

"Can you pinpoint them to a street address? Get their names?"

"Estevan Martín Soto Maldonado, 372 Calle de los Brazos, twenty-six years old, single, criminal by trade, heroin addict. Wanted for questioning in three murders and half a dozen robberies."

"Perfect!" Elmo shouted. He pulled a pen and small pad out of a back pocket and wrote it all down. "How about the other one?"

Yot didn't answer, but pumped away at his keyboard. Elmo watched the screen. In a moment, it was there: Hector Angél Lopez Bracamonte, 44 Avenida Luz, twenty-seven, addicted to alcohol, cocaine, and heroin. Violent temper. Charges pending in nine murders with questions about several more, fourteen rapes including a councilman's wife, six beatings, five robbery counts, two more for fraud and an even dozen for narcotics trafficking.

"Quite a gentleman," Elmo moaned.

"Looks like he keeps busy," Yot replied.

"Now get us a line to the police down there. Transmit their names and locations."

"Easy on the orders, old boy. We don't have to do this," Xaq snarled from across the room.

Elmo stood up to answer. "You, Mr. Sexual Anthropologist, could have stopped that rape it the moment it began. You could have captured these two bastards and drowned them. It was too much trouble then, eh? Well now. Mr. Anthropologist, you will make amends. Besides, I don't see you being any particular help. Would you rather I turn you over to that asshole from Global Express?"

"That's *Doctor* Anthropology, if you don't mind, and I don't see the big deal about this rape thing. There's nothing like that where we come from."

Elmo sighed. He nodded thoughtfully. "Then maybe there is some hope for the future. But it looks like where you come from, a Ph.D. goes pretty cheap."

Yot put a hand on Elmo's arm. "It just takes a moment to execute. There's the Federales, the Judicial Police, and a few other jurisdictions. They're connected by teletype. I sent it to every one of them. Is that what you had in mind?"

Elmo smiled and sat back down. "Thank you. That is exactly what I had in mind."

"There," Xaq said, "are you satisfied?"

"Not yet," Elmo said. "Not yet."

Xaq groaned from across the room. "Now what?"

Yot interrupted him this time. "Ho, feco-breath. I've been doing all the work over here. This is supposed to be your trip, but the hardest work you've done is going to Kentucky Freud Chicken. I believe the colloquial expression is pipe down."

Xaq gazed around the room with studied indifference.

"What's next?" Yot asked Elmo.

Elmo bit his lower lip. He stretched his neck, spread his fingers and tapped his foot. He looked around the room.

"Yes?" Yot said.

"Could you...?" He stopped. It was preposterous. "Put me into them? Both of them? At the same time?"

"You haven't had your psi-fly for the day," Xaq said.

Elmo answered without turning around. "Enough for a lifetime."

"Two at once could be tricky, especially at this distance," Yot said. "The system's not as effective over distance or diluted into two minds. Some of you will still be here. You won't be able to command their bodies much. The best you can do is create a vivid dream."

Elmo stroked his mustache. "That will do nicely." Elmo watched Yot typed the command:

TRANSPORT ES /45 newmatrix ES-M /45 newmatrix HL-B /SIMUL /autoexit.

"Ready?"

Elmo had a wan smile. "Probably not. But let's go."

He took a deep breath. The vacant feeling took

hold as he disengaged from his body. It must have been the distance that made this transit time last several seconds. He felt the minds drawing near.

His first sensation was burning anger, two raging emotional fires in stereo. He was able to sort Lopez from Soto after a moment. He felt the dull half-sleep brought on by drunkenness, he felt tongues lolling around in mouths, and he anchored his sensations to the chunk of himself in room 126 of the Lamp Post Motel.

He wasn't touring these limited minds. He focused his thoughts on his/Thea's memory and feeling. Elmo dredged back in his mind for the still fresh sensations.

He focused on Thea's deep and abiding hatred for all things male: brutish, testosterone-poisoned creatures more animal than human. Unspeakable ugliness in that wretched lump between their legs that she had learned to loathe at an early age, a weapon of ultimate maleness that had the discourteous effect of pregnancy and propagating more males.

Elmo called up the picture of salt air and the befuddlement of something very unusual floating out there over the water. He pumped into their minds images of themselves through Thea's eyes. He fed them her revulsion at some particularly poor samples of the gender she despised, overridden for that moment by her dire need to have someone, even some vile male, validate the presence of that . . . thing.

Together, all three men, Lopez, Soto and Elmo, experienced Thea's rare moment of trust utterly betrayed, the half-understood Spanish taunts, her internal collapse beginning from the moment they snatched her arms. Together they felt Thea's revulsion when they had unsheathed their misshapen clubs.

They were manhandled back and forth between these despicable creatures, their clothes were torn by thick, hairy hands. They felt the sharp bite of penetration, the body alarm shrieking, the abhorrence and hatred and disgust and horror and fear and holy misery. They felt the body lost from control, marginally conscious, aware that this horror continued, that her thighs and vagina were being beaten raw. A pause. The physical pain subsided, a stab of self-blame during the pause, interrupted by a more violent jostling, an unspeakable poking that finally sent her tortured mind into total blackness.

Elmo lingered on that blackness, pushing the agonized picture into these convoluted minds, and then from deep inside Thea Nikolas, he unleashed that scream, that wailing alarm that echoed within her for three days, that signal of defeat, of mourning, of shame and humiliation all lumped in with constant physical pain. In each of them he sensed the reaction. To Lopez there came a shame that was alien to him. Soto snarled in anger through the sleep, tossing until he found himself awaken in a panic.

Elmo called "OUT" and found himself in the chair in room 126, crying uncontrollably. It took several seconds to settle back in his own mind and shut off the tears.

Both Xaq and Yot were standing directly over him. When he saw Elmo's eyes focus, Xaq spoke, with his first note of genuine concern. "What did you do?"

Elmo tried to control the sobs that seized his chest. "I showed them how it felt. When they're arrested, they'll go quietly."

He took a few breaths. The weariness had returned, with reinforcements. "If you were recording the data, you'll be able to analyze how rape is such big fun."

CHAPTER 42

Mort Phipps brushed his hand along the flattop hair. He snarled at the telephone. "I called the security alert on that guy. What the hell's going on?"

"You got off easy. New York is putting a caution on your file."

"What file? What caution?"

"In your personnel file."

"What's that mean, Hank?"

"It means they're watching your ass,"

"What about the alert?"

"They canceled your big deal alert."

"Without ever talking to me about it?"

"They could have canceled you, Mort. They said there was some sort of glitch in the system that blocked this Zachary's records, or you would have seen them. So it wasn't entirely your fault. But they'll be watching you just the same.

"That's it? It's over? Security alert fizzled?"

"That's it. Now have your ass up the freeway by tomorrow morning, and they may get a chance to forget about it."

"Shit." He hung up the phone.

Tilly draped herself over Mort's shoulder flashing her best smile. "You still got me, honey."

Mort narrowed his eyes. "Them bastards done something to me. I'm gonna get that Zachary motherfucker."

He looked at the telephone in his lap. A slightly askew black-and-white sticker read EMERGENCY 911.

So he dialed it. He brushed again at the plane of his hair while he listened to the ringing line.

"State your emergency, please."

"Give me the police. I want to report a robbery."

* * * * *

Elmo passed the door to his room and shuffled down the stairway. He was wrung out from the torment he had dredged up and projected across hundreds of miles of desert. He was been drained by the relief of having done something to the guilty bastards. Now he had to tell Thea that he had exacted retribution. He didn't stop shaking his head until he reached the bottom of the stairs and turned to 116. He raised his hand to knock, pulled it back once, then rapped quickly before he had a chance to reconsider.

After a minute, Loretta came to the door. "Yeeees," she said in a voice that sounded as sleepy as her eyelids looked, but somehow still sexy. Her eyes dredged upward a little wider. "Hi, Elmo. C'mon in." She tugged him through the doorway and shut the door behind him.

She was there, exactly as he knew she would look. He was seeing her for the first time through his own eyes.

Thea gasped. "A man..." She stood up from the bed, a little unsteady, dressed in a plaid shirt and jeans. Though she had never actually seen that face, she recognized it. Her eyes told her she had felt this face, known it, been warmed by it.

Elmo felt at a loss for where to begin, so he leaped into the middle. "Excuse me. I know this is hard for you. But you have the strength to overcome that. Don't you Thea?"

She wanted to say something. She moved her lips, but found no words. She seemed to want to nod, but stiffened instead.

"I am not all men, Thea. I'm not even very manly. I'm not loaded with muscles, I don't like guns, and haven't made love to a woman for six years. I'm not a representative of my sex, good or bad. I'm just one Elmo Skinner, alone."

Thea bit her lip. Her jaw quivered.

"You know I won't hurt you. Don't you?"

Thea looked away from his eyes and nodded. Tears gathered.

"Could we speak privately?" He looked straight at her. She looked at Loretta, who just shrugged.

"Hey, it's okay by me honey. You're going to have to speak to a man sometime," Loretta said. "This man is as good a place to start as I could think of. Besides, I thought I'd take a swim." She pulled a swim suit out of a drawer and was gone in five seconds, before Thea could object.

Thea swallowed hard, pulled back her shoulders, cleared her throat, and looked Elmo square in the eye.

"Yes. Yes, of course. I want to talk with you. I want to—thank you." There was a slight tremor in her voice, but he heard conviction in her tone. She could hold his eyes for only a moment. She could find no words, or too many words. She, too, didn't know where to begin.

She looked at the second button on his shirt. "Thank you," she said at last. "I think you saved my life."

"It's a life very much worth saving." He resisted reaching for her hand. "You are an extraordinary human being."

"I'm famous. So a lot of people know who I am
. . ."

"No. Fame is a natural result of what you are. You are a living commitment to womanhood. I have never seen such devotion. You have a mansion of a mind. You absorb information at incredible speed. The knowledge you carry with you—it's unbelievable. The way you can reach into all that data and extract the essence of a situation. You understand the forces of the universe, politics and social relationships. You have a mind of enormous scope." He paused. "I should know. I've seen a few minds lately."

Thea lowered her eyes with a shy smile.

"And for all the force of your personality, you're still humble enough to feel."

"That there's so much I don't know," she said. She was looking at his shirt button again.

He looked for her eyes. "You mean how to get past this problem you have with the male of the species?"

Her voice was strained. "I'm trying." She sat back down on the bed. "This is new to me and I'm trying hard. Right now."

Elmo sat across from her. This time he did take her hand. He knew she would at first recoil; he bet she would gradually relax. "I know you are, Thea. I've met a good number of lesbians, probably more than I ever expected. But not a one of them has the male problem you do."

"You don't understand," she protested.

Elmo sputtered. He tried to not raise his voice. "Don't understand? Who in this world but me could understand? I spent the better part of an hour dredging through your mind. I heard your father bragging about the 'special heritage' bullshit. You've let it limit the possibilities in life to half the human race. And it doesn't have to. It was demented, a perverted thing for your father to do. But you've got to lock that monster in its cage."

She tried to meet his eyes, but could only hold that gaze for a few seconds.

"I hoped I had left enough of me behind for you to put it back in perspective."

"But those men ..." The pain of her fresh wound was in her voice.

"On the beach? Oh, I've taken care of them." Elmo allowed himself a smile.

Thea looked puzzled. For the moment, the question seemed to mitigate her discomfort of being alone and talking with this man. "What do you mean? Taken care of what?"

"With you I was on a search and rescue mission. This morning—just a few minutes ago—it was search and destroy. I hunted down those creatures while they slept. I assaulted their minds with the most vivid dream they will ever experience."

To the puzzled look, Thea added a tilt of her head.

"I gave them both your memory of their raping you."

For an entire minute, she blinked at him. Several times she tilted her head, and a few times she looked ready to say something. But mostly she blinked. A smile started at the corners of her mouth. "You mindfucked them?"

Elmo smiled. He hadn't been sure himself why he had been so determined to strike back at them until he told it to Thea: "I did it for you."

She was still not meeting his eyes. "The *Federales* know where to find the bastards. They'll be in jail in a few hours."

She stood up and took a step toward him. Her body tried to pull her back. More than the physical pain, old habits seemed to hold her back. But she continued. She reached her arms around him, awkwardly as he was still sitting down.

He stood up for her. As gently as he could, he put his arms around her, feeling the strength of her will in her taut skin. He held her and closed his eyes, knowing the pain she had known, hoping his touch could take some of the sting.

Tears again welled in her eyes. Even as she was fighting off her body's habitual urge to pull back, she lay her head on his shoulder. "Wasn't that very painful for you?"

It was Elmo who pulled back now, so they faced each other. "Of course it was, for a while." He smiled. "But afterward? It felt great."

Her eyes seemed to swim, as unfocused as her question. "Why? Why did you do that for me?"

Elmo's smile faded. Her eyes were just inches from his, but now it was he who looked away. Instead, he grasped her arms and set his jaw.

She winced at the contact, but didn't pull back. Not until she heard his words.

"I walked through your mind. I came to understand you. I learned to care for you. Maybe in some strange way I even love you, Thea."

The room was silent. Noise out in the parking lot seemed a thousand miles away. Elmo hardly believed what he had just said.

"You can't. I can't." The well of tears opened again. "How can I possibly..."

"You can!"

She pulled back. Both sat on the beds, but he

kept her hands clasped in his.

"But Andi and I..."

"Are about through, from what I've seen in your mind."

She exhaled and nodded sadly. "It's still too..."

"You can beat this male thing, damnit. You're *doing it.*"

"It's still so hard."

"So you need practice."

"Elmo I ..." Her hands retreated to her lap. "It's too much. As hard as I try, this is so...alien. No, it's worse than that. It feels evil."

"It's just uncomfortable. You can get over it. Try on the idea that at least some men are okay. You have the strength. Use that powerful mind to turn off that prejudice. You know how irrational it is to exclude everything male from your life."

She stood and walked across the room. "It's not that easy. What you left behind in me—my memory of you—is the only reason I can stand to be here with you at all. But that's still a long way from..." She sighed. "I'm sorry Elmo. It's impossible."

Anger rose in Elmo's voice. "You think this is easy for *me?* I loved exactly one frail, innocent woman and one golden boy in my whole life. Some dickhead in a jet turns them into burned meat." He shook his head. The edge in his voice turned to sadness. "I never wanted that ache again. I wouldn't let myself get close to anyone."

"I know," Thea said. "You left some of your ache behind."

"We touched," he whispered. "We are both better for it. It doesn't have to stop now. Let me touch your hurt and heal it. Let me stand you in front of any man, unafraid. Thea, let me help."

"You... you've done so much for me. You pushed me back to the world when I was ready to die." She reached for his hand. "Until I felt some of you in me, I could never have done just this."

His eyes, magnified by the glasses, reached to her. "Then say it. Say you could love me."

She dropped his hand and stood. Moving her legs brought back the hurt of bruised muscles, but she walked across the room to a more comfortable ten feet away. She picked up one of Loretta's gold bracelets and ran her fingertip around the circle.

"If love is sharing each other's strength and each other's pain, then I can say I love you. If love is caring and understanding, then maybe I love you."

Standing was painful. She leaned against the desk. "But..."

Elmo was seated facing away from her, and twisting to see her was becoming uncomfortable. He shifted to the other bed, allowing the distance. "Why," he asked, "does there need to be a but?"

Thea sighed. "Because love means something else. Love means finding joy in each other's company. I can love your mind. But I can never love your body. Try as I might, your male body is repugnant."

"Am I so different?" he snapped. "Okay no knockers here, a prick with low mileage. A little more body hair, maybe. I could lose the mustache. Some different distribution of body weight. So what? We're both people."

She pulled the wooden chair from behind the desk and sat down. "I know. I've always known that. It's just that this revulsion is so . . . so visceral. It's a physical thing."

"You can get over it."

"In time, maybe. But not now, not right away.

I'm grateful for psychic search and rescue. But you're asking the impossible."

He had no fight in him. He had felt enough of her to know every word was true. Elmo walked to the door, his shoulders sagging. He looked back at her once. "Who knows what's possible?"

CHAPTER 43

Andi looked up when the iron pool gate rattled shut. She was immediately smitten with the woman she saw, athletic, with a shock of flaming red hair. The woman smiled and said good morning, but Andi was incapable of speech just then. There was something feral about her, an animal energy, even a touch of the goddess. Andi watched her dive in the pool and grind out twenty laps, Andi's own body responding with warmth and further interest. Even as she watched, the swimmer emerged from the chlorine-scented water.

Andi was a little embarrassed at how she stared, but only a little. This woman set off warnings *like prepare to shape the rest of your life around her.* By the time the swimmer reached for a towel, Andi decided this was the most overtly sexual creature she had ever seen. When she spread herself over the chaise lounge just four feet away, Andi felt her pulse quicken.

"You're quite a swimmer," Andi said as casually as she could manage.

Loretta smiled, but kept her eyes closed as she lay her head back on the lounge. "It's my exercise. It's a little tough jogging in a hundred and eight degrees. So I swim."

Andi liked her sultry voice. "You're used to this heat?"

"I don't think anybody gets used to it. We air condition every building and car and learn to live with it in between."

"Then you live around here?" Andi said.

"Right here."

"You mean Tucson?"

"I mean right here at the Lamp Post Motel."

"How..." Andi waved her hands in the air, feeling for a word. "Exotic."

Loretta laughed, and that made Andi smile. "Exotic? Sure, in a tawdry sort of way. My name's Loretta. Welcome to the Hump Host Motel."

Andi eagerly reached out a hand to touch her arm. "I'm Andi Norwood from Palo Alto."

Loretta's eyebrows shot up. "Are you indeed? Well tell me, Andi Norwood from Palo Alto, might you be here looking for somebody?"

"I..." Andi had thought she was picking this woman up, and making some progress. She curled her face in a question mark. "How on Earth would you know that?"

"There's this woman who's been telling me all week she's *Terri* Norwood. From Palo Alto, California, if you can imagine that. She didn't want to call anyone. I figured someone was bound to come looking for her. You've got a les look about you, you're both roughly the same age, she's appropriated part of your name. So I figure that must be you. And if you're looking for Thea, you've come to the right place."

* * * * *

A hand pulled back the curtain in 126. Through one eye, Xaq stole a look out the window. A white police car slowed on Craycroft and turned into the Lamp Post. "Yot, we've got company. Police. Can we please get the hell out of here before we miss our window home?"

315

Yot grabbed a cardboard box jammed with their twenty-first century booty: shirts, sunglasses, and condoms. "We're gone," he said, and moved to the door. Yot had a palm-sized controller in his left hand and infrared glasses across his face.

"Let's go!" Xaq demanded.

"Hang on while I set us up." As Yot stepped over the railing, he stepped out of view into what looked like thin air.

"That's the man, officer." Xaq saw the man with the squared-off head point up at him.

"I'll cover the other end of the stairs," one policeman said.

He saw the other officer move toward the stairs directly in front of him, reaching for his gun. The man in the tan shirt ran up the stairs in front of the city cop and the drawn weapon. "He's the sonofabitch all right."

Xaq was fascinated for a moment by the animal hatred this primitive beast could display at it charged up the stairs at him. The hesitation was long enough for the man to round the top of the stairs.

"Get *in!*" Yot pleaded from apparently empty space. "I'm right in front of you. Follow my voice."

"Who's that?" shrieked the flattop.

"Where?" Xaq demanded. He was standing at the rail facing the pool. "I can't see you."

A hand grabbed Xaq by the shirt. He placed his hands on the balcony rail and vaulted over the parking lot. He felt, but did not see, the doorway into the bubble, although from there the interior was visible. His left foot dangled behind. A second later there was a hand on his ankle. "Go!" He felt the grip tighten as the bubble pulled away, leaving Mort Phipps with a water-damaged penny loafer in his hand and a policemen with his gun in the air, trying to figure out exactly what they were seeing. They rose up through the heat, barely escaping the Lamp Post Motel.

Below they saw police officers knock on the door of the rather recently vacated room 126.

* * * * *

"Damn, there it is again." Major Putnam nearly spilled his styrofoam-clad coffee on the radar console. The blip was right where they had lost it three days ago, a mile north of the base. It was small on radar, but visible enough. Putnam estimated it was the size of a helicopter. He turned to the infrared scanner. The same hot infrared trace. A mile? Hell. He dashed out the door, tracking mentally where it should be as he moved. He ran down a corridor and burst out the door. He fixed his eyes on the space in the sky where it should be, due north and moving west, altitude maybe two hundred feet.

Nothing. Not even a glimmer.

He shuffled back inside. He stopped when he reached Colonel Dayton's door. Instead of returning to the radar room, he stepped inside.

"The colonel's on the phone," the secretary said. "If you'll have a seat I'll..."

"No," Putnam said. "This can't wait." He took long strides to the colonel's door and let himself in.

The colonel, round and bald, chomped on the cigar he never lit. He looked up with curious annoyance. "Let me call you back," he grumbled and hung up the phone.

"What the hell's bothering you?"

The words gushed as fast as he could pour them. "That bogey. We picked up from just where it left off

317

Tuesday. Same infrared scan. Seems to be retracing its steps, headed southwest toward the border."

"So?"

"It doesn't move very fast. Let me give chase."

"Putnam, I think you've had enough flying for one lifetime."

"I want to know what this damn thing is. I want to see where it goes back. I could be in the air in twenty minutes."

"You haven't flown in six years, Putnam. Now you want to go zooming off after some UFO?"

"Don't you want to know what it is, colonel? Suppose it is some alien intelligence."

"Then we'd have more explaining to do with no good answers. And suppose this so-called alien intelligence shoots your ass out of the sky?"

"Nothing that hasn't happened before."

"That was your own damn negligence, Putnam. You should have been out on your ear then."

"Yes sir, but the Air Force needed every trained pilot it had. Look, wasn't five years locked into captain enough?"

"Apparently not enough for you."

Putnam tapped his foot. "Sir, they're getting farther away."

"I shouldn't let you go."

"Thanks, colonel."

"I haven't said…"

"No, sir. But you were about to."

"I was about to tell you to watch your fool ass and don't get too cute with government aircraft."

Putnam nodded, mostly suppressed a smile, and snapped "Yes, sir!" He sprinted from the office to get into a flight suit.

* * * * *

Thea was in a video stupor. A week ago she was famous for not speaking to men. Then when she had on the beach, she was punished mercilessly. And now a man was professing some sort of love to her; a gentle man, perhaps a good man, in his sleazy way.

When she heard the door open, she expected to see Loretta and only glanced that way.

And there, tall, blonde, willowy, with that touch of sadness in her eyes and that slightly crooked smile, was Andi. Her throat was a tangle of cobwebs, allowing the word to emerge only as a hoarse whisper. "Andrea."

Andi turned slowly, then loped to the bedside. She took Thea in her arms. "Tell me you're back. Tell me you're all right."

It required some effort, but she nodded, then fell into a hug. She clung to Andi with all her might, held tight to the body of her lover, drawing strength from the contact. She felt her energy recharging, clung tighter and whispered Andi's name. Andi squeezed back a little harder, but released her grip when she felt Thea wince in pain.

"I'm still sore from the bruises." She kept a hand on Andi's arm. Any touch was energizing.

"Loretta told me how she found you. I should never have let you chase that . . . that thing down the beach."

"It's not your fault."

"Why wouldn't you call me?"

Thea's eyes fell. "I was afraid. Andi, I was ashamed."

"What for?"

"They were men. The whole world knows I speak

319

to no man. For one moment I put it aside. I *spoke* to them. And they did their very worst to me because of it."

"Because of nothing," Andi said. "Because they were the kind of scum that turns up now and then and destroys anything they touch. You just happened to be there. They would have done it to anybody. You're not to blame."

"How many men have said right to our faces that all I really need is a good rape? Those bastards on the beach were defiling a symbol."

Andi took her hand. "You're more to me than some damned symbol of les. I want to know you're going to be all right."

Thea found a wan smile. "I think so."

Andi knitted her brow. "You had us tied up in knots worrying." Andi's voice cracked. "When were you going to call?"

Thea fiddled with the sheets. "I couldn't. I don't know. Everything around me felt trashed. I felt life betrayed me, and death was all I had left."

The scold in Andi's voice was still warm. "Your life is too valuable to give up so easily."

"Men," she said. "Men defeated me," Thea whispered. "I'd had enough."

Andi's scold turned angry. "No. Not you. Not yet. You've got a life of hellraising yet, and I'm not about to stand by and let you abandon it."

"But don't you see? It makes my life a lie."

Andi was up on her feet, pacing near the bed. "You want to talk symbols? Then where is this lie? Could you have stopped them? Being raped is never your own fault. You've said it yourself. You talk about testosterone poisoning, of men's abominable treatment of woman. They just demonstrated what you've been saying for years."

"It hurts," Thea said.

"I know. I'll help you get over it."

An accusing tone seized Thea's voice. "You make it sound like a bad report card. You don't know how deep the hurt goes."

"Don't I? Do you know the torture I've endured all week? All of us have. Joanne and Donna couldn't believe I refused to call the police, or the Mexican consulate, or somebody." Her voice broke. "We thought you might have been carried away by your fucking invisible flying saucer."

"I just couldn't..." Thea stopped. "Andi, it's here. That bubble. It's outside, on the roof. It's the same one. I saw it again."

"You've been under a strain."

"Don't give me that shit." Thea struggled out of the bed. Andi reached out to help, and Thea needed a hand to walk, but she pushed her away. She hobbled to the door and pulled it open. The humid residue of the monsoon rushed in. Thea stepped outside and out from under the upstairs balcony. She looked toward the roof.

Nothing was there. She scanned the area more closely. Nothing at all. "Really, it was there. It's moved."

"I want to believe you," Andi said.

"It was there on the roof, about ten or twelve feet in diameter, and it gave off this faint red glow."

"Thea," Andi sighed, "I want to go home."

Thea didn't respond immediately. She was staring blankly toward the street. She didn't understand how she knew, but she found a remembered image of two men at the motel desk. "James A. Zachary. Room 126."

CHAPTER 44

The reservations list hopped to the screen. Those prepaid or secured by a credit card glowed yellow. Elmo paid them little mind. He was tapping a pencil on the desktop, staring past the screen at a face that was not there, looking at a woman who would have no man. He should call 126. Could they do anything to change Thea's mind? Could anyone? He knew the effort she needed for a mere conversation. How could he expect anything more?

He heard the office door swoosh open and the front desk bell ching. For the moment he was grateful having a customer occupy him. Elmo navigated around his desk to the front office, dipped into his pocket for a smile and greeted his guest.

The man was tall and stooped, wearing tattered pajamas and battered slippers. He was probably around sixty, with a brush of ginger in the otherwise gray hair that drooped across his forehead. His eyes opened only slightly, surrounded by what looked like sandbags anticipating a flood. He leaned heavily on the reception desk, breathing through his mouth. When he opened that mouth, all that dropped out were sounds bearing only a passing resemblance to human speech, floating on a carrier wave of rum.

Elmo's smile dropped to the floor. "Excuse me?"

From the subsequent jabber, Elmo discerned that the man claimed to be a colonel, and that he needed toilet paper, soap, a light bulb, a pack of cigarettes and a quart of bourbon.

"What room are you in, sir?"

"Howzaman s'posed to know the frogging room number?"

"It's on your key, sir." His plastic smile expanded slightly. "May I see your key?"

The question was more than the colonel could handle. He dabbed at where pockets might be on another garment. When he found none, his tone turned surly. "Don't got no key in this damn Lump Lost Motel."

"Where is your room, sir?"

"Over there." He made no indication of where.

"Why don't you take me there and I'll let you back in your room. The maid will be along with soap, toilet paper and even fresh towels." He came around the desk, took the man by the arm and headed toward the back of the building. The colonel wasn't upstairs, or he would long since have tumbled down, and he showed no signs of fresh bruises. They lurched back to 110, where the colonel waved an unsteady index finger.

Elmo pulled the passkey out of his pocket and popped the door open. The bedding was all on the floor. The room reeked of smoke, vomit and booze.

The colonel smiled. He said "Thank…" and left it at that. Until he remembered. "Hey, what about my Marlboros and Jim Beam?"

Elmo found a fresh smile from his pocket. "Colonel, you'll have to get your own frogging booze and cigarettes." He closed the door to the smell, grateful he wouldn't personally have to clean it up.

He walked with wider strides as he surveyed his realm, across the back row from 117 to 122. Halfway along the row, he stopped in his tracks.

He smelled something: a stink, bitter and sinister. The smell of his world in ashes. The last time he smelled this smell, Elmo tripped over Nat's tricycle.

It brought an immediate wave of nausea, but a deep breath held that back. He stood there in front of 120, considered whether to open the door. The drapes were open. It was vacant. He could see the fire along the far wall, the flame still fairly small, but the wall charred by black smoke.

To the left, 119 was vacant. At 121, the room to the right, he knocked loudly, jabbed his passkey into the lock and opened the door. A couple was dressing. "There's a fire next door. You've got to leave here now."

They stood in their underwear looking at him.

"Now, please. I'll meet you in the office in a few minutes."

"Can I get my pants on?"

"Quickly, please." Elmo picked up the phone, jabbed a key for an outside line and dialed 911. "There's a fire at the Lamp Post Motel, Craycroft at 30th. Have them come around the corner on 30th Street to the rear parking lot, room 120 in the middle of the down-stairs row."

The couple was tossing on clothes and grab-bing what they could, heaving clothing in the window of a banana-yellow Plymouth.

He darted to the fire extinguisher case on the back of the main building. The glass was already bro-ken. In place of the extinguisher was a half-empty Coors quart bottle.

There should be another extinguisher upstairs. He dashed up the concrete-on-steel stairs two at a time. Where a fire extinguisher had been, there re-mained only a few cigarette butts.

He clattered along the balcony running the long row from 132 to 123. There, finally, was the bright red extinguisher, seated comfortably behind the glass. He fumbled through his keys for a moment, found the small one that opened the glass door, and pulled it out.

A few steps down he found Betsy and Tyrone cleaning 126 after a checkout. "Fire in 120! Call the people in that wing and get them out—now!"

The extinguisher was heavy enough to slow him down. From behind came the heavy horn and slow wail of the Tucson Fire Department. They arrived at 120 simultaneously. He opened the door and was driven back by the thick, choking cloud that tasted of funerals. Extinguisher in hand, he stood transfixed by the evil.

A fireman nearly knocked him down pushing past him into the room with a massive extinguisher of his own. Now he felt curiously detached from the men in heavy yellow raincoats lumbering around in the heat, lunging to protect his motel with metal cylinders that spat a cloud of chemicals at the blaze. In a minute, it was out. The stench of smoke dissipated in the toasty morning air.

He stood there in the parking lot gawking, making no move to speak to anyone.

A fireman, the chief from his cap, shouted, "Hey, where's the manager around here?"

Elmo stepped forward slowly. "I am," he said quietly.

"Well, you ought to have a look at this."

"Yeah," Elmo said dreamily. His steps felt unreal. Only now, with the threat to his current treasure passed, did he taste the fear churning his gut. It was the fear of again losing all. It wasn't even a close call; there was plenty of time. But it was still possible for flames to consume his life. He felt gravity dragging at his bones, but he followed the chief into 120.

The most intense charring was a narrow section of wall separating the bedroom from the dressing area. The burns were shallow except directly around the thermostat, where the fire etched black inches into the lumber framing the room.

"Electrical," the chief said with a sigh that indicated he had mentally closed the case.

Elmo nodded. He looked at the soot crawling across the ceiling and up the side walls. The drapes and carpet reeked with that smoky stench. The air conditioning vent was at the edge of the damage. That thermostat. Charred as it was, the basic shape was there, and there was something queer about it. Round. With a thermometer display in a bubble at the front and center. Nothing at all like every other thermostat on the building, rectangular, flat, the thermometer along the top.

"I'd say you got the wrong thermostat for your voltage," the chief said.

"Wendell," Elmo replied.

The chief closed one eye and looked at him. "How's that?"

"My handyman," he explained. A chuckle pulsed through him, then another, then a flurry of them. "I should send him to the CIA. He'd make a hell of a saboteur."

A twisted frame of a man stepped into the doorway.

Elmo's tone dropped the polystyrene cordiality for jalapeño sarcasm. "How splendid to see you again so soon, inspector."

"Splendid yourself, Skinner. Your right-hand man been at work again?"

Elmo stiffened. Something about Haskell-

Smythe made him feel like a million ants had chosen his skin for a marching ground. "And how would you know that?"

"I have big ears," the inspector grunted. "And you got a big problem." He handed Elmo an eight by ten sheet of red cardboard with black block type:

CITY OF TUCSON
BUILDING SAFETY DIVISION
DO NOT ENTER, UNSAFE TO OCCUPY
C O N D E M N E D
   This _____ **has been Con-demned**
   by the City of Tucson
Use of the same is hereby prohibited till property released to the owner.
   BUILDING SAFETY DIVISION
   DO NOT REMOVE UNDER PENALTY OF LAW.

Haskell-Smythe used a black marking pen to write "Room #120" in the blank space and adorn the lower right corner with a series of swirls and squiggles that passed for his signature. He pulled a little hammer out of his back pocket and nailed the sign to the door. "Have a nice day, Skinner." He cackled once, then disappeared as quickly as he had come.

Elmo's shoulders sagged. For no apparent reason, he thought of Betsy making that checkout with the robot. Then he remembered what it was about that room. That checkout she was making up was 126. They were gone, and with them, his way back into Thea Nikolas' mind, where he could communicate without the body that so disgusted her.

With a quick excuse to the fire chief, he was down the row, up the stairs and across the balcony to

327

126. Betsy and Tyrone were just finishing.

"How long ago did they leave? Where did they go?"

Betsy held up her hands. "Whoa, boy. You talking about the two fruits been here all week?"

"Did you see them?"

"Nope. But they left this morning. The towels still wet. Oh and they left something. You want Tyrone to take it downstairs?"

Elmo wrinkled his nose. "Left what?"

Betsy shook with hearty chuckles. "They left your favorite toy, boss."

He cocked his head.

"A c'puter, Mr. Skinner. Least I think it is. But it ain't nothing like no c'puter I ever seen."

Elmo's mouth fell open to an "O." As in cOmputer. As in the door to Thea Nikolas' big, magnificent brain, and maybe a passage to her heart. Slowly, the corners of his mouth pulled the "O" into a great big boyish grin. He put his hands on Betsy's shoulders and gave her a kiss on the cheek, and nearly leaped into the room to the computer.

Betsy was left standing on the balcony looking at Tyrone. She put her hand to her cheek. "The boss, he been acting da-amn strange lately."

"Yas massuh," said the robot Tyrone.

CHAPTER 45

Airborne! Nose up, headed for the sky, with Davis-Monthan falling away below. It felt like yesterday, not seven years ago, when he was in the cockpit leaping from the Davis-Monthan concrete, orienting himself by the familiar peaks. The Santa Rita mountains were to his left, most of Tucson and the Catalina mountains to the right. He had already climbed well above the jagged but modest peaks of the Tucson Mountains dead ahead. Putnam hadn't forgotten the high he got from the cockpit. He reveled in surging over the desert, remaining just under Mach 1 until he left civilization behind. He adored the roaring engines slamming him through the sky. But he kept his wits and triple-checked fuel consumption rate. Radar mapped the surrounding terrain with a grid showing the probable location of the bogey based on its last known trajectory.

Out over the reservation, he kicked into Mach 1.4 and edging near the Mexican border. The Air Force disapproved of flying into Mexico. "It just pisses them off, so we don't go flying into their territory without a damn good reason," Colonel Layton had said half a dozen times.

His computer beeped. The screen blinked. He picked up his bogey easily on infrared, maybe a hundred miles away at ten o'clock crossing the line into Mexico. Seven years on the ground was enough for one man. Putnam didn't have the taste for any more. But anything short of heroic would leave him languishing in Air Force bureaucracy until he could take retirement. He brought the throttle up to a five-minute burst of shrieking power at Mach 2, closing half the distance to the bogey. It was still moving in a straight line toward the edge of the Gulf of California.

His computer beeped. The screen blinked. He picked up his bogey easily on infrared, maybe a hundred miles away at ten o'clock crossing the line into Mexico. Seven years on the ground was enough for one man. Putnam didn't have the taste for any more. But anything short of heroic would leave him languishing in Air Force bureaucracy until he could take retirement. He brought the throttle up to a five-minute burst of shrieking power at Mach 2, closing half the distance to the bogey. It was still moving in a straight line toward the edge of the Gulf of California.

Putnam cut back the engines when he crossed the Mexican border. He was within twenty miles of it, probably still too far to spot his target if it was the ten or so feet across he expected. But he was ready, and closing steadily at a now-modest 630 miles per hour.

Then something odd happened to the sky, as if the clouds out on the horizon were out of focus. No, more than that. They looked warped. He raised the infrared viewer. It still looked strange. He replaced the viewer and picked up the dot almost immediately. Gotcha, you bastard! He let his F-22 close the gap before easing back on the engines. Now the whole damn sky looked wiggly. Never mind, he could see it now, closing in on an infrared bubble, pulling up alongside. Triumph!

That was when everything went black. He felt

the molecules of his body separated for a moment, shifted out of phase. He might have lost consciousness. But the next thing he remembered was a dead silence. No engine roar or sloshing wind. Quiet. And black. A deeper black than he had ever known, but ablaze with stars that seemed inches from his fingertips.

He felt peculiar. He was still in the cockpit, but he felt . . . loose. Light.

They used some kind of weapon on me. I shouldn't have approached so suddenly. He had only begun to wonder where he might be when he saw the enormous ball beneath him, a golden swirling sphere with massive ribbons of color that were the signature of what sure as hell looked like Saturn.

In the back of his mind, Putnam knew this was appropriate cause for panic. But he was alive, and so far unhurt. He had oxygen for another hour. And beneath him, for thousands of miles, swept the mosaic of a thousand rings. He noticed a beam of light leap from the ring surface. It played past him, and then it was on him. He saw the flash, felt slightly electrocuted for a moment, and remembered nothing else.

* * * * *

It was one pain-in-the-ass computer. For its apparent resemblance to a contemporary model, it didn't accept Elmo's commands. He tried to call up a file list, but drive directories brought up nothing. He pushed stray key combinations, used all the function keys, and got gibberish. Meaningful gibberish to someone, perhaps. He typed **HELP**. The machine responded: **+ka6@**. A request for a parameter? He tried again: **HELP ME**. Nothing. He typed help with any keys his fingers touched. There was a pattern in the machine. There is a pattern in every machine. He just had to find it. He spent hours typing commands, watching the rejections. Here and there he got the hang of a command that spat out raw programs. From that he could study the language, break down the system and build it back up again to uncover the functions that moved minds around. Maybe.

Broiling noon slid past. He sat at the machine for hours, making notes on the back of a motel brochure. He needed to print out some of this stuff and see it in hard copy. Better still, if he could couple this machine with his own, he could run system queries using his machine to study the other.

He summoned a robot, stood watch as steel arms cradled this exotic machine, and inched with the robot the few feet to his command center. He caught a slight wobble halfway back to the command room. He lunged to grab the computer, but the robot recovered flawlessly. Not so Elmo, whose heart was doing a rhumba in his chest.

He spent half an hour making a cable that could connect the two machines. Another half hour went into adjusting the cables to fit. From down in his stomach came a rumbling complaint of neglect. He had no intention of slowing down now, but he did pause long enough to call the pizza joint across Craycroft to deliver a submarine sandwich.

He took a long, wary look at the connection. He reached for the power switch. For all he knew, turning on the power would blow up both computers.

Nothing blew. He moved to his gray tufted chair. First he called up his database and created a new file from the notes scratched on his brochure. Those few patterns he could discern, he laid in. The rest of the data lay at the end of that cable. Elmo directed his machine to connect with COM3.

Smooth as current through gold, his computer responded: CONNECT.He called up the file directory again, this time filtered through his familiar operating system. A list tumbled across his screen as fast as his monitor could display it, and kept rolling for half a minute. At the end of the scroll, the tally: 461 gigabytes in 8,328,180 files. Elmo gulped. That was a lot of data for anyone's computer. He copied the contents to a DVD.

The knock at the door nearly lifted him from the chair. It was the fat kid from the pizza joint with a pineapple and bacon pizza. Elmo wouldn't take the box. "Do you know this brings your delivery accuracy record down to sixty-two per cent for this year?"

The kid looked at him blankly.

"I ordered a submarine sandwich."

"Oh, no sir, that goes to room 120."

"But there's no one in room 120."

"Oh sure, man, they got this sandwich."

"I'm sure no one's there. The room has been condemned. Now do you think I could have that sub before the President orders it to active duty?" He paid with a ten dollar bill that, after tax, left a tip of twenty-six cents.

The kid swallowed. "What do I do with the pine-apple and bacon pizza?"

"Use your imagination," Elmo said, and closed the door.

He took the bag into the command room and ripped his teeth into salami and ham, lettuce, provolone, onions and bread. His computer chewed the file list, looking for a pattern that could start to decode all this. Long after he had done away with the lunch meat, the computer churned away at the data, decompiling and reorganizing, examining from a hundred angles.

Downstairs, the Friday afternoon customers were checked in by the congenial robot. The Lamp Postsign showed 106 degrees and proclaimed "Air Conditioning."

Elmo's fingers danced over the keys. There was some sense in here yet, he felt it. His eyes were locked on the screen. In a decoding box, letters fell into place. He watched them assemble, shaking his head at the foolishly simple command his machine suggested: Arbidor. He pressed 'enter' to initiate the command.

And then . . .

His screen was a splatter of green and blue, sparkling across the surface. Little bits of yellow danced, leaping from place to place, sometimes individually, sometimes in groups. They moved together toward the lower right corner and jumped to a final configuration what spelled out two words: **Ho, Elmo.**

He stared, then laughed. He typed back: HO, ARBIDOR.

The computer made a sound like a burp.

We felt it was best we leave. We never came looking for trouble, but it came after us. We cannot afford too much mucking about in the past; it has dangerous implications for the future. We thought only subtle interference, maintaining a low profile as you might say, would be harmless. We meant to cause barely a ripple. But Global Express was not unaffected. From there could have come police, and from there real problems. So before our difficulties could grow irremedial, we have returned to our own time and place.

For all Xaq will know, we left this computer

behind accidentally in our haste to leave. Consider it my compensation for your being his test subject. I hope we have not damaged you, nor caused you much inconvenience.

I have provided a training program on use of the transfer system and the rest of this machine's capabilities. To call it up, simply type ELMO.

Goodbye Elmo Skinner. May your future shine like your formidable sun.

CHAPTER 46

Something shot past them, something silver and thin.

"What the hell was that?" Yot shouted.

"Too damn close is what it was. Just our luck we come through into traffic," Xaq moaned. "Can we go home now?"

Yot spread his hands across the controls. He was looking out over the planet for Saturnopolis. "Almost there, ace."

"We never did snag any twenty-first century xufa."

"No," Yot said. "Such are the hazards of time travel."

Xaq dropped his chin on his hand. The swirling methane clouds were the sight that had all his life meant home. "Did we get out of there clean?"

Yot found the city without instruments where the city domes broke the gaseous surface and towers guided navigation. "I think."

"You *think*?"

"Well, I think Global Express is convinced they...made an internal error. I gave them all the evidence they...need to believe it. So yes, I think we're out of there clean."

"With the two thousand year account intact?"

"Mmmmm," Yot said. "I think."

Xaq watched the city draw near. A navigation beam guided them through the three chambers in the gate. From there they shuttled directly to Rej's basement.

When they opened the door, Xaq hopped out with a radiant grin. Rej was dressed in underwear, sitting at a table hunched over a stack of blue and yellow paper. "Made it back all in one piece, old buddy."

The small, thick man put his hand to his beard. He looked at both of them carefully before he spoke. "And just who might you be?"

"Rej, old man," Xaq said, "don't tell me you forgot..."

"What hasn't happened yet," Yot reminded him. "Look, Rej, in a few days we'll meet in a bar a few blocks from here, past the Saturnopolis School of Cosmetology and Concubinity. You'll send us to 2008 Earth."

"Why should I believe you?" he said from under heavy eyelids.

"Because we just got back. We set up a bank account for the three of us that should be ripe right about now."

"Hmmmm, good idea," Rej mused.

"It was *your* idea," Xaq said.

"I guess it is now." He leaned his head to the right. "Everything went well, then?"

"Great," Xaq said a little too enthusiastically. "I spent four days—I mean real Earth days—in a microcosm of primitive sexuality. I've got a pile of data the size of Mt. Lemmon."

"What's a Mount Lemon?" Rej asked.

"An Earth fruit with a . . . healthy libido," Yot said. "Don't worry about it. Now if I've got this right, we'll get...together with you after we leave on this trip we just came back from, and ...then we'll harvest the money. Two weeks okay with you, Rej?"

"Sure, two weeks." His face looked like he was working out a puzzle. "What bar?"

"The Snarling Beja."

Rej nodded. "I know the place. I'll be there." He wagged his head. "How much money did you put away for us? What's it worth now?"

Yot took three steps to the stack of blue and yellow paper. "Why don't we calculate it exactly right now?"

Rej nodded and peered at them. A little smile started at the corners of his mouth. "Yes, let's do that."

"Thirty thousand dollars, at a quite modest rate of ten per cent, over 2042 years . . ."

"Is quite a sum," Rej croaked approvingly.

"Lovely," Xaq said.

* * * * *

One chronic problem of the Lamp Post Motel was no restaurant within a mile for a good breakfast. Max Zorn once tried to interest Denny's in the old bowling alley across the street. The Voojoos bought it instead, and they didn't serve breakfast. Chinese, and pretty good Chinese at that, was a half mile down Craycroft. Italian food was just down the block. A fast food spot up the street served an almost edible creation of bacon and eggs in a pita bread. But a sit-down breakfast, eggs any way you like them, fruit and yogurt, pancakes with half a dozen syrups, whole-grain bread and nuclear coffee—that took some driving.

In the booth behind the plate glass, Andi was next to Thea. Her eyes, her body, and her attention pointed to Loretta. She still couldn't resist the absolute sexiness of this redheaded creature, and her mothering Thea though the week.

Besides, she was tired of trying to communicate with Thea. Whether it was Thea's trauma of the rape and the aftermath, or continuing resentment for Andi's allowing her to wander off after that damned bubble, she felt a wall between them, a wall that had never been there before. Andi didn't know if she was supposed to breach the wall and break through, how long that might take, or if she was just supposed to accept it and walk away. Why the hell hadn't she called? It was a lousy way to say goodbye.

Loretta was before her, ripe and radiantly feminine. Andi found it more comfortable to ask, "If you ever went into another line of work, what would you do?"

Loretta tilted her head back and lolled her tongue around her mouth. "Oh, that's hard to say. I like this work, at least a lot of it. It's psychology, and I can get a hell of a lot more honesty out of a man under the covers than any shrink with a couch in a glass office. Besides, there's something about being in the business of sex that's satisfying. No wonder they can't stamp out my business. People want sex. An awful lot of men who come to me want more than the wife can provide. Guys get laid, guys feel better. The wife doesn't have to put out when she doesn't want to. So where's the harm?"

Andi held up her big hands. "Oh, I wouldn't begin to attack your profession. The only real harm is that it's against the law. And that it attracts a pretty sleazy clientele."

Loretta nodded. "I can deal with the working people with rough hands and coarse manners. I can handle the mean-tempered ones. The really scummy ones are the power freaks. Like the inspector."

"You can't stay in that line of work forever," Andi said. She glanced over at Thea, who was studying the pattern in the Formica tabletop.

"I think I'd stay in the 'service' industry. It serves a real need. Demand is steady, and growing." Loretta smiled up at the waitress who was arriving with the food. A plate of *huevos rancheros* and refried beans saddled up in front of her.

"Gracias."

Thea got a jalapeño omelet with a slice of cantaloupe and tomato juice. She attacked the plate mercilessly.

Andi got no conversation from Thea, so she concentrated on her wheat pancakes, boysenberry syrup, and Loretta. "Maybe move up into administration, madam?"

"Probably not," Loretta said after a forkful of egg and salsa. "I'm not like most of the girls on the street. I don't think I could find any girls to suit me."

"Could you just move up to a more exclusive clientele? You'd live better."

"I've thought about it," Loretta said, reaching for the refried beans. "But what would Elmo do without me?"

Thea looked up from her plate for the first time. She didn't speak, but she mouthed the word: Elmo.

They drove back to the motel in silence. Loretta made some calls. At noon she left Thea and Andi so she could make it to the Voojoo service.

Thea wanted to walk around the parking lot, trying to return some strength to her legs. The heat softened her skin some, making it a little easier to walk.

Andi was glad to have a request she could fulfill. She was ready to support some of Thea's weight, but Thea held her back.

"Okay." She hesitated, then blurted, "Can we think about going home?"

Thea didn't respond immediately. She walked gingerly to the front of the parking lot, Andi at her side. She glanced up. "The bubble is gone."

"Damn the bubble, Thea, I want to go home. I want to get out of this godawful heat and get back to my store. I want to take you home."

Thea whispered. "I don't think I want to go home. Damnit Andrea, the boys in the bubble were the ones I saw on the beach, and they came here. They're the ones who put Elmo's mind into mine."

"They did what?" Andi's crooked smile wilted.

"It's kind of hard to explain," Thea ventured.

"Try it."

"Things have been happening that aren't real life," Thea said. "I would have killed myself, eventually, when this . . . this, well presence steps into my mind, somebody placed there by the bubble guys."

"You need more rest," Andi said.

"But they're gone." Thea furrowed her brow. "You still think I'm crazy. If aliens sound crazy, how do you explain how somebody else's mind appearing in my brain?"

"I don't need to be Freud to explain it. Maybe it's nervous exhaustion." She softened her tone. "Come home, Thea."

"In the same breath you call me a loony and tell me to come home. No. No, Andi, I don't want to go home. I don't know where home is."

"Classes start next week at Stanford."

"Maybe I'll take a sabbatical."

"Come on, Thea you can't . . . "

"Don't tell me can't. I can. If I'm not there, they cancel a few classes.

"You're not serious."

"Look, right now I don't know what I'm going to

341

do." She walked slowly, treading softly, trying not to limp, back to 116.

* * * * *

Thea spent the afternoon in brooding silence. The three of them went to the pool. The water took the weight off her legs. The cool felt good. She relaxed, but her silence remained. She resented how chatty Andi and Loretta were getting. Maybe she should just drown here. At least then she wouldn't have to decide anything. She spent half an hour seated on a step, in the water from her waist down. The sun blasted at her skin, burning away some of the aches.

She was just standing to dry herself when she felt something. A presence, thoughts. Her mind detected a flashing busy signal. She heard her name in an unfamiliar, no, it was a familiar voice, almost like her own. This had happened before, but she was conscious now and the intrusion was noticeable.

She lost her balance in her confusion and fell back in the water. "Elmo!" she cried.

The splash caught Loretta and Andi, who had been looking at each other in meaningful ways. They looked up simultaneously. Andi saw Thea splashing in the water, said something that sounded like ammo or emma. Andi saw a serenity-etched smile on Thea's face beneath the water.

"Oh Goddess, she's drowning herself."

CHAPTER 47

Elmo noticed right away that she, and therefore he, was wet. In his pool, of all places. For the five years I've owned the Lamp Post Motel, I think this is the first time I've been in the pool. How's your day been so far? Before he had the thought completed, he saw her trying to figure out how to relate to Andi. He was touched by the sadness she felt once she knew the bubble was gone.

"But if they're gone, how did you . . .?" she thought. And by thinking the question, she knew. She saw Elmo at the computer for most of the day, she sensed his urgency until he broke through seconds ago.

"I had to come. You couldn't talk to me while I was wearing that body."

This was new to Elmo. Each time he been in someone else's mind he had slipped quietly into the background and gone along for the ride or planted a dream. When he rummaged though Thea's mind, she was mostly unconscious. But now, sharing full consciousness in her body, being connected to her thoughts, he felt the power of her immense will. This mind in motion was an irresistible force carrying him.

Likewise, having been unconscious at the time, Thea hadn't developed much of a sense of Elmo on his first visit, even if he had left behind some memories. Now she found Elmo's parts unknown, the boy whose reprieve from loneliness burned up by a blundering pilot. She felt the cavern it left within him, how he spent five years in hiding behind circuits, software, and a motel desk.These thoughts had taken but a second, after which time both of them realized they were in waterover their heads and hadn't given any thoughtto breathing. Elmo would have gasped, but Thea closed her mouth and exhaled slowly through her nose. As much as they might be sharing them, they were her mouth and nose. He relaxed and let her take control.

They felt a rush of water and strong arms taking hold of them. As they broke the surface, Thea realized Loretta was hauling her out of the water, laying her down on a towel at poolside. The two of them were getting confused in there, but both of them were surprised when Loretta started mouth-to-mouth. Both of them had the same response, returning a long, warm kiss.

Loretta pulled back in surprise.

Thea was giddy with laughter. She brought Loretta's face down to hers and kissed her again, a long, moist, loving kiss. There was something in this kiss that wasn't quite Thea, somehow familiar. "That's thank you," Thea said. "For both of us."

Andi shook her head. "Could somebody tell me what's going on here?"

Thea looked her straight in the eye. "Elmo's with me." She pointed to her head. "Here."

"I thought you said they left," Andi said.

It was Elmo's slower speech that came from Thea's lips, explaining the computer left behind. And asking if they could get out of the heat.

They retreated to 116. Elmo felt the still-aching legs and thighs. He helped Thea push her body across the parking lot. Loretta was hardly in the door before she was peeling off her green tan-thru bikini. Loretta stood full before her, feet apart, hands on

344

her hips <u>a la</u> Wonder Woman. If she thought she might embarrass Elmo, she was wrong. Elmo reinforced by Thea was stronger and smarter.

"I'm better here," the part of Thea that was Elmo said.

Loretta raised an eyebrow. "Hadn't the two of you better sort your selves out first?".

"We're doing just fine," Thea said. He nodded agreement as she spoke. "I've been hoping to share a bed with you all week." Her tone shifted to his. "I'm picking up where I left off last night, making up for lost time, and checking out the new equipment." Thea walked to Andi and took her hand. "Andrea. We want you to join us."

Andi's eyes glistened. She took Thea in her arms.

Elmo found Thea's memories of the three years they had spent together in Berkeley. Thea had been autographing Sisters at Womonbooks when Andi arrived, uncharacteristically late. They had spoken over the phone to arrange the autograph party, but not met face to face. When their eyes connected, both of them lost their balance. When the party was over, they were off on a torrid affair that lasted somewhere around two years. If the ardor had cooled, they settled into a comfortable life together. Every love affair has its cycles, and at the low points, the flame could be rekindled or left to die. Lately the two women had been spending more time on their own, which was mostly Thea's doing. A camping trip with Andi's Tucson friends was supposed to be a rekindling. Instead it had been the break.

Thank you, Thea's fingers said on Andi's lower back, *for all you cared when I started not caring. Thank you for the nights in front of the fire, biking on Trea*sure

Island and hiking Mt. Tamalpais, for the coffee shop nights and the political intrigues, thank you.

Andi's eyes were large and sad as she reached around Loretta for Thea. The two of them fell together as they had a thousand times before, arms sliding into the accustomed contours, legs comfortably intertwining. Their cozy familiarity gave Elmo a stab of jealousy and a sense that he was trespassing.

"My guest is a little uncomfortable, Andi."

Andi smiled just a bit. "Why any friend in Thea Nikolas..." She laughed easily and laid a big wet kiss on Thea. "This is for you, Elmo."

A satisfied smile spread across Thea's face. It was too many years since Elmo had satisfied a lover, a gratification he had quite forgotten. It was a long time since he had felt the comfortable familiarity of established live being rekindled once again. Only by feeling it now did he realize that this was what he longed for once again. *I know what you're thinking, and I damn well am going to give her up.* Elmo didn't need to argue. There was no point in arguing. She felt his thoughts even as he shaped them, and she could sense how he treasured this intimacy with her lover. He replied with a mental grunt. *Can't get any damned privacy around here.*

"Elmo, are you still in there?" It was Loretta. They nodded slightly.

"How does it feel to be les for a day?"

"Les for a day?" asked Thea's voice in a tone that added a sprinkle of Elmo's mild drawl to Thea's bulldog inflection. "I guess we hadn't mentioned it. The conversations in here go by pretty fast. I want to say something, and the other knows and feels exactly what I mean. So we've had plenty of time to decide."

346

Andi realized she had been wearing that question mark on her face all day. "Decide?"

"That the two of us are better than either one of us. That Thea Nikolas can use Elmo's sense of order, and Elmo is ready to live life on a grander scale than can any to be had at the Lamp Post Motel."

Andi craned her neck forward. "You're...?"

Thea smiled, not unlike the proud smile of a woman telling her husband she's pregnant. It washer inflection, what there was of it.

"Elmo stays. Permanently."

* * * * *

No thought went undetected, no emotion passed without both of them thinking or feeling it. She remembered when he was nine and how some big kid with a crewcut beat him up every week. He agonized with her manuscripts. Elmo wanted to plan to gradually introduce her to the male of the species, but she thought it as he did. He felt her reluctance, but with it a willingness to expand, to borrow his strength. *Look at the control room, then. Let me shut it down.* She learned his attachment to that equipment, his love of the circuits and their magic feats.

As Thea walked across the parking lot, they felt the softness of the hot asphalt, something Elmo had never noticed in his body. Thea took inventory of the computers, video and all the rest of Elmo's electronic smorgasbord as they walked through the office. She laughed that they didn't have Elmo's keys, but they knew exactly where to get the spares from the back of the lower left-hand desk drawer. Beneath the bruised muscles, Elmo felt this body's firmer muscle tone as

347

they climbed the stairs. She had a big smile on her face when she pulled open the door. Neither of them had given a thought to the one other thing they would find among the metal, plastic and silicon:

Elmo Skinner's unconscious body.Thea felt the wave of me-ness that rippled through Elmo, the shock of seeing himself from outside himself. The face he had seen only in a mirror or on the video screen, his stupefied face. He saw his body limp in the gray-tufted chair.

His body was slowly but definitely dying.

Maybe you should go back. This is like suicide. She knew he could have commanded "out" at any point. Until that moment, nothing had shaken his resolve to stay. But seeing his clothes twisted along his slumped body, the spittle dripping from the corner of his mouth, he had to wonder if this was really such a good idea. Thea was far too caught up in Elmo's feelings to be afraid of this male body. Besides, she now knew this body. She took his pulse. Slow but steady. *Can I let me die? Thea, I want to stay, but . . .* She listened to his breathing. *I know, I feel it. Maybe you should go back and prepare to come back later. Maybe we can reach an accommodation from separate bodies*. But she knew as he knew: *If I go back I won't come back, and you won't have me.* She felt his determination as he reached for a screwdriver, opening Arbidor's computer, pulling out the main circuit boards, and rushing out of the room before he might change his mind. She wanted to give him more time to consider, but this didn't stay his moving her hands to pop the circuit boards in the microwave oven. *Metal shouldn't go in the microwave. It all shorts out. And Let him die, we're better off together.* They set the oven for forty seconds and pressed start.

Thea Nikolas stood back. Sparks showered inside the microwave, sparks that fused and melted sensitive circuits into the smoldering ruin of Elmo's last door home.

Thea stood there staring through the glass. The oven beeped angrily at them every five seconds. It's for the best. She opened the oven door, found an insulated glove to grab the smoldering circuit boards, and pulled them out, unable to take her eyes from them. It was Elmo who comfortably reached for a waste basket and dropped them in. I had to destroy it. *It was something from hell.* She protested. *It was from the future.* He rejected that argument. *Same thing.*

CHAPTER 48

Xaq presented himself at Dendiger's door as ordered. His shoulders sagged. His eyes looked mostly down. He still wasn't much in a mood to talk.

Dendiger was in a common tunic when he opened the door. But he wore something else that Xaq had never seen on Dendiger before: a big, hearty smile.

"Ho, Arbidor, come in, please, make yourself comfortable. Always a pleasure to see a former student."

What fecing insanity was this? He didn't see the joke.

"Relax, boy. Sit down. Join me in a drink of jandow, perhaps?"

The professor seemed to have drunk a good bit of jandow already. Xaq stood in the middle of the room. Dendiger poured a drink of the thick orange stuff and shoved it in Xaq's hand, then knocked a shot back himself and refilled his glass. Seeing Xaq still standing, he guided the young man to a couch and sat them both down.

Xaq sipped his drink. He saw his hand shaking, but the jandow braced him. "I don't understand, professor. Yesterday, feco, every day I've seen you, you've maintained a formal distance, shown no sign of a warm side. Here I show up to be sentenced, the worst day of my life, and here's this complete transformation. I don't get it."

Now that he had found a smile, Dendiger couldn't get rid of it, so it remained splayed across his face. He even maintained the grin sipping his drink without spilling a drop. It faded somewhat when he spoke.

"A department chair is no small burden, Arbidor. I have a duty to the university to educate people in anthropology. My profession obliges me to see that these products are of consistently high caliber. But the nature of sexual anthropology is extremely sensitive. It attracts the perverse, who, like you, sniggers his way through school. I am required to maintain the quality of my academic stock. I either fail them or give them mediocre grades and lack of incentives to proceed. Most of them drop away.

"But you have been persistent, Arbidor. You're a passably good student. Your dissertation on the exodus was a fine piece of work. What you have is an attitude problem."

Xaq sneered. "You mean I don't look down my nose at sex as something base and animal, or consider it the lowest point of human nature."

"Exactly. An attitude problem. So you see, it is nothing personal. I needed to remove you from the program. And now that my department is back in balance, I feel like celebrating."

"At my wake. Forgive me if I'm not so cheerful about it." Xaq took a long swallow of jandow.

"You are free of the program. Can you not celebrate that?"

"Not until I know what you're going to do with me. Back in the twenty-first century they would have called it probation or a suspended sentence. Released on my own recognizance. Is that all there is to it? I'm out, and you're satisfied?"

"Not quite." Dendiger's damnable grin remained. He swirled the fluid in his glass. "You were less than forthcoming with me yesterday."

"I was scared."

"I wanted you scared."

"Congratulations."

"There's a recording I want you to see from the vidchron, Arbidor. Something about the Lamp Post Motel even Elmo Skinner didn't know."

"You knew about it. All about it."

Dendiger nodded as he reached for a control button. A screen emerged from a blank wall. The scene was a bar, definitely the same time period, but Xaq recognized neither the humpbacked bureaucrat or the cowboy handyman. What he did recognize was the currency, ten one hundred dollar bills.

"Who are they?" Xaq asked.

"I thought you might recognize them. The older, deformed man is the city inspector who turned off the gas and later condemned a room at the Lamp Post Motel. The one getting the money is Wendell. He had been employed as a handyman at the Lamp Post. Wendell broke things so the inspector knew just where to look for the break. He did chores like leaving gas lines open, installing thermostats that start fires and jumbling Elmo's orders at the pizza place. You see, Wendell is a mole. Hidden underground to do someone's bidding"

The picture faded.

"I have a mole, Arbidor. He does errands for me from time to time. But of course you've already met."

On the screen was another bar, this one contemporary. Xaq felt the jandow churn in his stomach. It was the Snarling Beja planetside in Saturnopolis, and the figures on the screen were himself, Yot and Rej.

"You planned..."

"Everything," Dendiger said with a renewed smile. "Right down to setting the Air Force and Global Express on your tail."

"What will you do to Yot?"

Dendiger broadly waved his arm. "I will pay him what we agreed."

Xaq's face was blank and uncomprehending.

"I sent him with you to look after you, to keep you from getting lost in the past, or destroying the present somehow."

"Then what will you do to me?"

Dendiger came back to the couch, the jandow bottle in his hand and the insufferable grin across his face. "You left a mess behind you, Arbidor. When you returned, you brought one of them with you."

"That's not possible. It was just us."

"No, you brought along a Putnam, the Air Force pilot who followed you. He was just catching up when you crossed through. You pulled him along through the warp. He was a bit surprised to find himself over Saturn."

"There was nobody..."

"He is here, Arbidor, at the University Hospital, maintained unconscious until we can arrange to return him to the twenty-first century."

CHAPTER 4

Elmo had one task to perform with his unconscious body. Thea of course "heard" him hatch his plan, but was willing to go along. She returned to the control room and Elmo's body. He let her hold back, getting used to the idea of this man thing in front of her. But it was her very revulsion he needed to break, so he stepped them forward, unfastened his belt and pants—from outside, a strange experience in itself. Go on, touch it, he urged, knowing those were the same words her father had used. *It really can't hurt you now.*

She unsteadily reached into the pants, exposing Elmo's modest member. He felt some of her disgust. He knew what the physical response would be to her touch. He watched his dong load up on blood, in slow motion because the body was unconscious. He felt her fear and her determination to push past, he felt the voice that called from within to withdraw, and he pushed from his end until she took his cock firmly in hand, gave it a couple of jolts, felt it stiffen up in an old, familiar way. *Is it necrophilia when you whack off your own dead body?* Together, they burst out laughing.

Elmo/Thea looked at Loretta. "You're ready for a job change. Take over the motel. Rent the camera rooms at a higher rate and let the couples come in here to videotape themselves in the act. You've always had the best business mind in the place, especially when it comes to marketing sex."

Thea Nikolas and the original consciousness of Elmo Skinner turned her back on the electronic eavesdropper's paradise.

Now about Andrea, I was thinking . . .
I really did intend to leave her.
No, if she can stand the two of us together, I'd like her to stay with us, at least on a trial basis.
Elmo, let's go visit Molly and Nat's graves.

They walked gingerly down the stairs and out of the Lamp Post Motel forever.

* * * * *

Captain Melvin Putnam opened his eyes in the cockpit of the F-22. Had he blacked out? These strange swirling images. Over Mexico? And Saturn? No that couldn't be. He was so thoroughly disoriented, he couldn't tell how old he was, or exactly what day it was, or just what he was doing in the cockpit. Almost by itself, his right hand continued the motion it had begun, pushing the eject button before the F-22 crashed on the edge of the park. He felt the explosive bolts break, and the force of being catapulted into the screaming wind outside, tumbling out over the park. The parachute popped out and he found himself gliding down toward fences and trees. He heard the sickening, rumbling thud of his aircraft making its final landing in a little house off the park.

His watch said Tuesday, August 20, 2002. Somehow, he knew there was a rhinoceros in the cage where he tumbled down. As he scrambled safely over the fence, he had an overpowering sense of dejá vu.

About the Author

Joe Gold is a freelance writer and marketing consultant in San Francisco. Raised in Woodbine, New Jersey and Philadelphia, he spent 29 years in Tucson, where he was a newspaper reporter nominated twice for the Pulitzer Prize; an advertising agency owner, creative director and writer-producer-director; and a manager of the Lamp Post Motel that his father built. He is active in the National Writers Union, currently working on his next novel.

Also available from Dailey Swan Publishing, Inc.

Confessions of a Virgin Sacrifice
By Adrianne Ambrose

$12.95

Beyond the Fears of Tomorrow
By Casey Swanson

$ 9.95

Apers
**By Mark Jansen
and Barbara Day Zinicola**

$12.95

The Pub at the Center of the Universe
By Dale Mettam   **$12.95**

Revenge
By JH Hardy

$12.95

The Bones of the Homeless
By Judy Jones   **$15.95**

Coming this winter 2006

The Freddie Anderson Chronicles
By J. Ben Ricks